Praise for
How to Dazzle a Duke

"Funny, superbly sensual, and filled with sassy wit and appealing characters, this rewarding story will be in demand." —*Library Journal*

"A delightful work full of bantering conversation, clever transitions from scene to scene." —*Romance Reviews Today*

"I have loved Claudia Dain's courtesan series from the very first book . . . Sophia is such a vivacious and scandalously rich character that one would have to be simply mad to miss her adventures! Miss Dain is deucedly clever, witty, and the fabulous cast of characters she has created are a delight to revisit and learn more about each time. Don't miss this fun romp through the ton . . . You are going to love this series!" —*Sapphire Romance Realm*

The Courtesan's Wager

"Outrageous, offbeat, hilarious, and sinfully sensual, this romance employs lively, sassy dialogue, rare wit, and an effervescent sense of fun . . . Another winner."
—*Library Journal*

"Dain concocts another wonderfully witty story, complete with unforgettable characters, sparkling dialogue, a clever plot, and amusing situations." —*Booklist* (starred review)

"Dain is a master of the Regency romp, and this one has witty repartee and an authentic setting. The characters are engaging, unpredictable, and outrageously funny."
—*Romantic Times*

contin

"A clever story and highly entertaining." —*Fresh Fiction*

"Told in a delightfully dry, tongue-in-cheek voice, this romance chronicles verbal skirmishes and even a physical brawl or two as part of an ongoing battle in the war of love." —*BookPage*

The Courtesan's Secret

"Clever, smart, fresh, and passionate . . . [A] lively romp . . . Delightfully entertaining." —*Library Journal*

"Highly amusing repartee and some wickedly attractive open ends round things out." —*Publishers Weekly*

The Courtesan's Daughter

"This cleverly orchestrated, unconventional romp through the glittering world of the Regency elite [is] graced with intriguing characters, laced with humor, and plotted with Machiavellian flair." —*Library Journal*

"[The author adds] a feel for the ton . . . Well written." —*Midwest Book Review*

"Wonderful . . . Great dialogue . . . Sophia the seasoned courtesan [is] so feisty and fun . . . Don't miss this fresh and extremely fun romp through romantic London. It is, as Sophia would say, 'Simply too delicious to miss!'" —*Night Owl Romance*

Daring a Duke

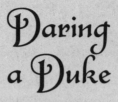

Claudia Dain

BERKLEY SENSATION, NEW YORK

THE BERKLEY PUBLISHING GROUP
Published by the Penguin Group
Penguin Group (USA) Inc.
375 Hudson Street, New York, New York 10014, USA
Penguin Group (Canada), 90 Eglinton Avenue East, Suite 700, Toronto, Ontario M4P 2Y3, Canada
(a division of Pearson Penguin Canada Inc.)
Penguin Books Ltd., 80 Strand, London WC2R 0RL, England
Penguin Group Ireland, 25 St. Stephen's Green, Dublin 2, Ireland (a division of Penguin Books Ltd.)
Penguin Group (Australia), 250 Camberwell Road, Camberwell, Victoria 3124, Australia
(a division of Pearson Australia Group Pty. Ltd.)
Penguin Books India Pvt. Ltd., 11 Community Centre, Panchsheel Park, New Delhi—110 017, India
Penguin Group (NZ), 67 Apollo Drive, Rosedale, North Shore 0632, New Zealand
(a division of Pearson New Zealand Ltd.)
Penguin Books (South Africa) (Pty.) Ltd., 24 Sturdee Avenue, Rosebank, Johannesburg 2196,
South Africa

Penguin Books Ltd., Registered Offices: 80 Strand, London WC2R 0RL, England

This is a work of fiction. Names, characters, places, and incidents either are the product of the author's imagination or are used fictitiously, and any resemblance to actual persons, living or dead, business establishments, events, or locales is entirely coincidental. The publisher does not have any control over and does not assume any responsibility for author or third-party websites or their content.

DARING A DUKE

A Berkley Sensation Book / published by arrangement with the author

PRINTING HISTORY
Berkley Sensation mass-market edition / July 2010

Copyright © 2010 by Claudia Welch.
Cover art by Jim Griffin.
Cover design by George Long.
Cover hand lettering by Ron Zinn.

ISBN: 978-0-425-23546-1

BERKLEY® SENSATION
Berkley Sensation Books are published by The Berkley Publishing Group,
a division of Penguin Group (USA) Inc.,
375 Hudson Street, New York, New York 10014.
BERKLEY® SENSATION and the "B" design are trademarks of Penguin Group (USA) Inc.

PRINTED IN THE UNITED STATES OF AMERICA

10 9 8 7 6 5 4 3 2 1

To my three chicklets—
you are the heartbeat of my joy.

One

London 1802

Miss Jane Elliot of New York had traveled to London to have an adventure. She was, as yet, not having one. She had been in Town for a single day and a morning, which was perhaps too soon to have arranged for anything in the way of excitement; however, she knew it was not the fault of a disadvantage of time, but purely a disadvantage of company. She would never be able to arrange any sort of meaningful adventure with all the obstacles, and by obstacles she meant *men*, in her path.

She had her two brothers with her, ships' captains both, who were, it was perfectly obvious, not the sort of men to allow a woman to wander freely about the Town. She had thought that, once ferried to their aunt and uncle at Hyde House, things would loosen a bit, enough for her to find her feet and get her bearings. She'd also thought, hoped really, that English men, her cousins namely, would be different from her very American brothers.

They were not. Her cousins, beginning with Lord Iveston, who was soon to be married, down to Josiah, who was not, barely allowed her into the large back garden to get a breath of air. What they imagined could possibly happen to her in a back garden she couldn't begin to guess.

She'd finally been allowed to leave America and see something of the world and all she was seeing was a back garden. There were more back gardens in New York to have satisfied every urge for back garden exploration by now. She was twenty-one and ready for an adventure.

It was very difficult to have any sort of adventure with two older brothers at her heels.

Too many men, that was the trouble. Entirely too many male relatives. Why, including her cousins, who did seem very eager to take on the job of watchdog, that made seven fully grown men who had obviously made it their chief ambition to keep her from adventures of any sort whatsoever. So typical of men, really. They did seem so selfish about keeping all of life's adventures entirely in male hands.

The one pleasant surprise she'd found within the walls of Hyde House were the new wives dwelling there. They were very British, of course, which created its own challenge, but they were female, and that was very welcome indeed. She was prepared to tolerate their bone-bred British delusions of superiority for the implied comfort of their common sex.

"I should have known that it would be Penelope Prestwick," Louisa said, shaking her red head almost playfully. "If any woman was capable of snatching Iveston up, I knew it would be she. I've always thought her to be the most clever of women."

"Is that the word you used?" Amelia asked. "I must be remembering it differently."

"Yes. You certainly must," Louisa answered, giving Amelia a rather arch look.

Louisa and Amelia were cousins. They had married brothers, just this Season, in fact. They were quite close and therefore quite often sharp with each other, and it was plain that neither minded being sharp in the slightest. Jane was not quite certain if it was a British trait or merely a trait within their family. Either way, she was making it a point to tread as carefully as she could with them, at least for the present. How she decided to treat them later, as they all became more familiar with each other, would rest entirely upon how they treated her now while they were still comparative strangers.

Men were a challenge, of course, but women were equally so. It was never sound policy to put too much trust in anything a woman might say. Or a man. And most especially a British woman or man.

She was from New York, after all. Was she to be expected to think otherwise?

"That's not at all what you said, Louisa," Eleanor said. "Why pretend otherwise? It's only us. We're all family."

Eleanor, Louisa's younger and only sister, had quite a habit of making the most forthright remarks. Jane had warmed to her nearly instantly.

But, of course, upon that remark, Louisa looked askance at Jane with a swift movement of her eyes, and then looked at Amelia. Amelia smiled and looked at Jane without any hesitation whatsoever. Or rather, without any noticeable hesitation.

Family? Yes, they were all family, after a fashion.

It was all rather complicated, as families usually were.

Jane's mother was sister to Molly, the Duchess of Hyde. Amelia and Louisa, cousins through their mothers, who had been sisters, were married to brothers, who were the sons of Molly.

So.

Were they family? Yes. By marriage, which was not as firm a thing as blood, but nearly so. Were they bound by the usual bonds of family devotion and loyalty? It didn't seem likely.

They were British, and of the aristocracy at that.

She was American, and certainly no one she knew had forgotten the war for independence, and the British navy did have the most unattractive habit of snatching men off American ships whenever the mood struck. As her father was in shipping and as he had been quite involved during the recent revolution, it was not something she was inclined to ignore.

How her mother and Aunt Molly had ever kept alive the bonds of familial devotion was a bit of a mystery, unless one believed that the bonds of family were unbreakable, that is. Her mother devotedly believed so. Her brothers and her father were leaning firmly against the notion. Jane was nominally undecided, mostly for her mother's benefit. Being in England, with her British relatives, was supposed to encourage her to fall in with her mother's conclusions about the matter.

It was perfectly obvious that her mother had sanctioned this voyage to England in the hope that Jane would become entranced by the British side of her family, a highly unlikely outcome.

Jane had come because it was an adventure. Or it should have been an adventure, if she could only find a way to see beyond the walls of Hyde House and the back garden. Would the women of the family help her? More importantly, *could* they help her? One did hear the most amazingly unlikely things about the women of the ton, and of the many things they were and were not permitted to do.

"You did not approve of Penelope?" Jane asked Louisa. As Jane had been introduced to Miss Penelope Prestwick only last night and had found her to be quite pleasant, she was curious as to what possible objections Louisa could have had to her.

"Approve?" Louisa said, setting down her cup on a nearby table. They were in the music room of Hyde House, a truly impressive room of huge proportions and a fortune in fine furniture and musical instruments on display. Jane, whose own lovely home in New York could not begin to compare, had spent most of her first day in Hyde House trying not to gawk. She was confident that she had mastered the response as today was midmorning of her second day. "It was nothing so tawdry as approval, Jane."

As a setdown, it served quite well. Jane, however, merely smiled and raised an eyebrow. Louisa, Henry's wife, was somewhat sharp as a rule. Henry, her cousin, seemed to find that endlessly amusing. It was unfathomable, really.

"Not disapproval?" Jane replied. "Then I suppose it was simply that you didn't like her."

Eleanor burst out laughing. Jane quirked a smile at Eleanor and then turned back to face Louisa. Jane had learned after only an hour of knowing her that one did not turn one's back on Louisa Blakesley. She was not vicious precisely, but she was volatile.

"Of course she did not like her," Eleanor said, tucking her feet up underneath her, her slender body curved into a ball on the end of the small settee placed near the window facing Piccadilly. "Louisa did not like anyone who might have taken Lord Dutton from her."

"Penelope Prestwick was never going to waste an ounce of interest on Lord Dutton," Amelia said, shaking her blond head slowly. "It was a duke or nothing for her and Dutton is nothing of the sort."

"And now she's got Iveston," Eleanor said, squirming slightly, her knees moving under her muslin skirt.

"And in only a day," Amelia said, smiling. "An impressive bit of work, that."

"You hardly seem bothered by it," Jane said.

"Bothered? Why should we be bothered?" Louisa asked, eyeing Jane with a tad too much scrutiny than was polite. Jane had quickly become inured to it.

"Is it not a bit forward?" Jane asked softly.

"But of course it is," Louisa said, leaning back upon her

chair. "How else is a woman to get the man she wants if not by being forward? Men are so very backward about everything, aren't they, and a woman is simply forced to bring them to heel. I can't think but that American men must be the same. Aren't they?"

"I'm afraid I lack the experience to know," Jane said, setting down her cup on a highly polished table to her right.

"Truly?" Louisa said with a definite sparkle of mischief in her vivid blue eyes. "There is no special gentleman in New York who has captured your heart?"

"Certainly not my heart. Not even my attention," Jane responded instantly, her mouth quirking into a half smile.

"Truly?" Eleanor asked, sitting up pertly on the sofa, her feet upon the floor once again. Eleanor had very little capacity for stillness, which sometimes reminded Jane of a bird in a cage, fluttering and hopping about, inquisitive energy and warbling joy battling within her narrow frame. "You are not betrothed, or even spoken for?"

"Not even whispered for," Jane said.

"But, your family," Amelia said, putting down her cup and leaning forward, every movement expressing concern, "they are not eager for you to make a good match?"

"I think they expect that I will, but they are not anything so energetic as eager," Jane said. "I am far too young for marriage to be the business of the day."

"But aren't you one and twenty?" Eleanor asked.

"Yes," Jane said, smiling fully. "Is that old by English standards?"

"Not old," Louisa said, "but old enough. Are you not eager to be wed?"

"Since no man has been able to capture my attention, let alone my regard, I should say that I am far from being eager. That's logical, isn't it? Or isn't it?"

"Are all American women like you, Jane?" Eleanor asked, her dark blue eyes glittering with curiosity. Eleanor was curious about a great many things. It was entirely likely that she was kept sequestered and allowed only back garden adventures as well.

"I have no idea," Jane answered dryly, "since I rarely leave New York and there are, I'm told, women in other areas of the country. I take it that not being eager for marriage has made me entirely contrary, then? Am I now determined to be unnatural in my interests?"

"But you are interested in men, aren't you?" Louisa asked.

"Tolerably," Jane responded with the barest hint of sarcasm. "When I happen to find one who will sit still long enough for me to study him. I can't begin to contemplate marriage without a thorough study of the man I might deign to consider. I've yet to find a man who will sit quietly long enough for me to perform a proper examination."

"There is that," Amelia said with a soft sigh. "They can be very difficult to pin down. Something in their diet, no doubt."

"Or their education," Eleanor said, nodding, her eyes bright.

"Or the general arrangement of their," Louisa said baldly, "manly bits."

Jane laughed. Louisa laughed with her. It may have been the first unguarded moment between them.

"Louisa, you are grown coarse," Amelia said, though she was grinning.

"Oh, no," Eleanor said, "she's always been coarse."

"Thank you, Eleanor," Louisa said, reaching over to pull her sister's dark red hair.

Eleanor swatted Louisa's hand away and tucked her body into a ball again, her gaze returning to Jane.

"But Jane," Eleanor said, leaning forward, "it is all of love matches in America, is it not? You are free to marry where you will?"

"Within reason, certainly," Jane answered. "Is that not true here? You may not marry where you will?"

"As long as everyone agrees," Amelia said, "and by *everyone* I mean fathers, naturally."

"And fathers can be difficult," Eleanor said.

"Some make quite a study of it," Louisa said. "Melverley is an absolute genius at being difficult. One can't but wonder if he was born that way or acquired his genius through years of effort."

"Effort, I should say," Eleanor said with a half smile.

Jane had not yet met Lord Melverley, Louisa and Eleanor's father, but every indication was that he fulfilled every notion Jane had of the typical behavior of an English lord, her uncle excluded, she tentatively assumed, based solely upon her study of him last night at dinner. Though as Uncle Hyde had married a Boston woman, it seemed likely that Molly had exerted a most welcome influence upon him. Who knows what sort of man he might have been without her? Entirely like the monstrous Melverley, almost certainly.

"Would your father be difficult, Jane, if you decide to fall in love with someone here?" Eleanor asked.

The question caught her completely wrong-footed. Fall in love with an Englishman? The idea was laughable.

"Eleanor, you are too bookish by half," Louisa said, twirling one of her red curls around her finger. "One doesn't decide to fall in love. One simply falls."

"And gets caught by some likely man," Amelia said, smiling.

"If it's as haphazard as all that, then one is left to hope that the man *is* likely," Eleanor said, "which requires far more trust in chance than I am comfortable with."

"If one requires comfort, one should not fall in love," Amelia said.

"As I also require comfort, I do think that love may elude me," Jane said, believing that closed the subject nicely.

Eleanor was not at all astute at determining closed doors.

"But Jane, you can't mean that you'll marry without love, not when it is so simple to marry for love in your country," Eleanor said, her dark blue eyes bright with alarm.

"Eleanor, no, I only mean that I may not marry at all. It is possible."

"But not likely," Louisa said.

"Why not?" Jane asked.

"Surely your father would never allow that," Amelia said.

"He certainly wouldn't force me to marry," Jane said. What a perfectly odd conversation.

"Yet would he force you not to marry?" Louisa asked.

"I beg your pardon?" Jane said. The conversation had gone completely beyond her. She had never spent so much time discussing marriage in her life, to so little purpose. This is what happened to women who were restricted to back gardens.

"You may marry where you will, love where you will?" Louisa asked. At Jane's nod, Louisa said, "Then you are in the perfect situation to find love and a husband, Jane, here and now, at the height of the London Season. We shall see you married before you know it."

"I don't want to be married before I know it," Jane said, resisting the urge to rise to her feet and pace the room, which she was certain would be seen as impossibly rude and fulfilling every expectation these British relatives of hers had of rough American manners. What the English thought of Americans was obvious and without question. Rusticated bumpkins, every one of them. Rough and unruly, untutored and unfashionable, ungrateful and fractious. *Fractious*, perhaps she might concede, but only when properly provoked. England had most properly provoked them and likely always would.

"But Jane," Eleanor said, reaching over to take her hand. Far from being comforted, Jane found the action appalling. Was she in need of comfort? She was not. "Did you not come to London to find a suitable husband?"

"No, I did not," Jane said. "Whyever would you think that?"

"Because that's why every unmarried woman comes to London for the Season," Amelia said. "To catch a husband."

Jane felt herself blanch. Had her mother known of this? She could not. She absolutely could not. It was one thing to form a possible bond of warm feeling with her English relations, but it was not to be anticipated that she could ever be tempted to go so far as to marry one of them. Her mother could not be such a hopeless romantic as all that.

"I can assure you that I had no such notion. I came to have an adventure, and to become better acquainted with my cousins . . . and their wives," Jane said stiffly.

"An adventure?" Eleanor asked, her eyes gleaming as the words left her lips. "What a wonderful idea."

"If you're looking for an adventure, the London Season is the place to find one," Amelia said, studying Jane. As Amelia was not in the habit of studying her, Jane found it disconcerting. "You may even find that you fall in love."

"I think that highly unlikely," Jane said. It was flatly impossible, but she saw no need to be pointlessly rude.

There were a few moments of strained silence, which Eleanor spent looking at her curiously. Louisa and Amelia looked less curious than mildly amused. What there was to be amused about Jane couldn't possibly guess.

"Have you ever met an English gentleman, Jane?" Louisa asked.

"A few," Jane answered. "My cousin, Cranleigh, most obviously."

"And what do you think of Cranleigh?" Louisa asked, not at all kindly it seemed to Jane.

Jane cast a look at Amelia, who was smiling and staring at Louisa. Amelia then looked at Jane and winked. "Yes, Jane, do tell us what you think of Cranleigh," Amelia said. "I do wonder if you think him as big a brute as I have always found him to be. Or is he better behaved in New York than in London? I do suppose that's possible, though I must confess to thinking it unlikely."

"And I must confess," Jane said with a grin, "that, being ignorant of London standards on this sort of thing, I cannot make any sort of comparison. In New York, Cranleigh, as a guest in my parent's home, was hardly brutish enough to have made any impression of brutishness upon either my family or our acquaintances. Or at least they made no comment upon it."

"*No comment*, but that is an entirely different matter, Jane," Amelia said, cutting off Louisa, which was most pleasant of her. "That may only prove that you Americans are more forbearing than we are here."

"Oh, I hardly think that," Jane said. "As our revolution must attest, we are not forbearing when other avenues are open to us."

"The avenue of taking up arms against your lawful king?" Louisa said.

Jane snapped her gaze to Louisa and said, "I believe it was his lawfulness which was in question, Louisa. And I further believe that the question was firmly answered."

A stilted silence, which was surely not unexpected, settled over the room. Eleanor, as was also not unexpected, broke it.

"I should like to visit New York," Eleanor said. "What must it be like if Cranleigh fit in so well there?"

Amelia laughed. Even Louisa chuckled. Jane smiled and nodded at Eleanor. It was such that the moment passed and they settled, slowly, into the outward semblance of female sociability.

"What sort of adventure did you think to have, Jane, if not love?" Louisa asked.

"The adventure of travel," Jane said, "for one."

"And for another?" Louisa prompted.

Jane was not going to reveal her mother's hopes for her,

no, nor her brothers' buried animosity toward the British government. This was neither the place nor the company for confessions of that sort.

"An adventure of any sort, but of what particular sort, I have no idea. As I am to leave promptly after the wedding upon the first tide, I can't think any further adventure is open to me," she said.

"Are you open to suggestions?" Louisa asked.

It sounded amiable enough, but as Louisa was not an amiable sort, Jane was properly suspicious.

"Do you have one?" Jane countered. "Something lawful?" she added as Louisa was opening her mouth. Eleanor barked out a laugh.

"You could arrange it, you know," Louisa said, staring at Jane with a very nearly challenging look. "If you truly want to stay, to have your adventure, I know the perfect person to make it happen."

"Sophia Dalby," Eleanor said, leaning forward, her eyes alight with excitement and mischief. Jane was certain it was mischief. Whyever should Eleanor, who had seemed a most pleasant girl until this instant, want her to fall into mischief? "Tell her you want to stay and she'll arrange it handily, Jane. Of course, when one deals with Lady Dalby, one must expect a few surprises."

"Quite a few, I should say," Louisa said crisply.

"And yet quite pleasant, when taken as a whole," Amelia said, smiling at Jane.

"Very true," Louisa said. "It is when one breaks it down into bits that one feels the swell of panic. Best to just ignore the particulars and enjoy the results, Jane. One must show no fear when one treats with Sophia Dalby. I do wonder if you're up to it. She can be quite formidable."

"Don't lie to her, Louisa," Eleanor chided. "She's always formidable, Jane, but she does get the job done."

"There is no job of mine that requires doing," Jane said, sounding a bit prim, truth be told, and which she was certain cast her in an unfavorable light. The British were always going on about how rudely mannered the Americans were; she was determined to be judged better.

"Oh, well, if you're going to be missish about it, then you should avoid Lady Dalby completely. She'd eat you whole," Louisa said, picking up her cup to take a sip of her tea.

"I'm hardly afraid of her," Jane said, sitting up very straight, her neck tense. This town house brawl was just the sort of adventure she had imagined happening whilst in an English salon in London. Women never quite said what they meant. It was quite exhausting trying to keep pace with their pointless manipulations. "I simply have no need of her."

"No need for an adventure?" Eleanor said, looking quite forlorn, clearly on Jane's behalf. "When she could, and would, I am certain, so easily arrange for you to have one? You can't go back to New York so soon, Jane. We've just met you. Don't you want to stay?"

Stay? Not particularly. But she did want an adventure, even an English one. If Sophia Dalby, whom she knew by reputation if not experience, could arrange for her to stay and thereby have an adventure, and if she could tweak Louisa's nose in the bargain, well then. What was there to consider?

"I should very much enjoy talking to Lady Dalby," Jane said, staring at Louisa, smiling at her in a very firm manner. "How soon can you arrange it, Louisa? Or can't you?"

"Tomorrow at the wedding, I should think, Jane," Louisa said, smiling very much like a cat over a twitching mouse.

Mouse? Jane was no mouse. But if Louisa didn't yet realize that, so much the better.

Two

THE marriage of the Marquis of Iveston to Miss Penelope Prestwick was a quiet, joyous affair. The couple was quite clearly in love, their families delighted by the match, and the wedding breakfast, reflecting that delight, was very nearly the biggest social event of the Season.

Or so Jane had been told. She was inclined to believe it. Hyde House was filled nearly to bursting, or should have been had it been a normal-sized house. As it was, Hyde House, the blue reception room in particular, was comfortably full of guests who gave every impression of enjoying themselves as two more of their number found themselves successfully wed.

Jedidiah and Joel, her two older brothers, were stuck to her side like burrs, looking quite solemn in their black coats and breeches. Jed was wearing a light blue China silk waistcoat, which did relieve the somberness of his aspect somewhat. Joel was wearing a silver gray waistcoat, which should have looked stark, but which looked rather elegant instead. As Joel was not normally given to looking elegant, she found she was quite entertained by it now. Joel and Jed did not look entertained, at least not overmuch. They looked about the expansive room with expressions of stoic observation. There were very many Englishmen about, which was always slightly off-putting, but having a sister amongst the suspect throng was something they would enjoy even less.

It was perfectly plain why having an adventure was so very difficult. And it was equally plain that she was going to follow Louisa's suggestion, however spitefully made, and do something to achieve her own ends.

What else could she do? Return to New York after only days in England, and those days confined to a house? An extremely large house, but still, only a house. She had not traveled the Atlantic, a truly spectacular experience during which she had not experienced the slightest discomfort, to see a house. She was going to make something of this trip, something memorable, and then she would return home like the good daughter she had always been and would continue to be. Once she was back in New York. What happened in England, once her brothers were gone, would serve as her adventure.

She was determined to enjoy every moment of it. The only obstacle left to her was to begin it somehow. Jane had no idea what *it* would be, but she was certain that Louisa had something slightly malicious in mind and Jane intended to face *it* squarely, coming out of *it* the clear victor.

She did hope Louisa was around to see it.

"What are you smiling about?" Joel asked.

She turned her head slightly to look at him. "It's a wedding. I'm happy."

"That's not your happy look," Joel said. "That's your *planning something disastrous* look."

"*Disastrous* by whose definition?" Jane rejoined, grinning.

"Father's," Jed said, looking down at her with stern fondness from his extreme height.

Jane was not a small woman, but her brothers were both so tall and so firmly built that they were quite able to intimidate nearly anyone with the smallest effort. But Jane was not nearly anyone; she was more than accustomed to dealing with her slightly overbearing brothers.

"Father is not here," Jane said. "I am. I shall smile in whatever fashion suits me as often as I wish to."

"But not at whomever you wish to," Jed said, giving a look bled of some of its fondness and reinforced with stern disapproval.

As she had been seeing such looks from him for the past ten years, since Jed had turned fifteen and become suddenly and so seriously aware that he had a sister whom some man might find appealing, she found she could ignore him nearly effortlessly.

"And whomever should I wish to smile at here, Jed?" she said softly, casting her gaze about the room. "They're all British, aren't they? Whatever could an Englishman do that should cause me to smile?"

"I'm not going to answer that," Jed said.

"I'm just glad that you're going home on the first tide," Joel said on the heels of Jed's comment.

"And I'm glad that I won't have much longer to try to manage the both of you at once. You've such skill at forcing me into a foul temper. I shouldn't like my English cousins to see me as anything less than remarkable in every way."

"As most of our English cousins are freshly married, I can't believe that they'll think of you much at all, Jane," Jed said.

"Then I'm safe from scrutiny, which is such a relief. Now I may behave in whatever manner I please," Jane said with a completely wicked grin.

Jed scowled at her. She was quite immune to his scowls; he ought to know that by now.

"Never that, Jane," Joel said, "and never here."

"Do not think that I would ever do anything to cause

Aunt Molly any dismay," Jane said. "I wouldn't think of it, as you should well realize."

"Because you care so deeply for Molly?" Joel asked.

"Because I don't dare provoke Mother, and you know she would hear every word of whatever romp I might find myself in."

"You are not going to find yourself in anything resembling a romp," Jed said, looking quite alarmed.

"But of course not, Jed, haven't I just explained that? No, I shall put on my best behavior and no one shall find any need to tell Mother anything at all about anything. As to that, I can't think what you're both so bothered about. I shall be back on a ship to New York practically before the sun has set tonight. Not at all what I was expecting of this trip, but what choice do I have?"

"None," Jed said, though he was looking at her skeptically.

Yes, well, she might have played her hand a bit too boldly. She was not at all known for such quick and easy acquiescence. Still, she had to quell her brothers' anxiety about her if she had any hope at all of trouncing Louisa and her inane challenge. Inane it certainly was, but she was going to win it all the same.

Joel was opening his mouth to say something dire, she was entirely certain, when Penelope, Iveston's bride, was before them, a spectacular-looking woman at her side. Jane was almost certain she knew who the woman was; she had a very particular air about her, a nearly shimmering veil of allure resting easily upon her beauty. Jed and Joel reacted as men always did when faced with a beautiful woman, which is to say, they stood straighter, smiled brighter, and forgot everything they had been about to say or do.

It was most convenient.

"And may I present Sophia, Lady—" Penelope was saying before Jed jumped in and cut her off, in exactly the manner a man used when he was faced with a beautiful and available woman, which is to say, with far more direct-ness and urgency than was called for.

"Lady Dalby," Jed said, nearly jumping out of his shoes. "Sophia. It is good to see you again."

An understatement, if ever there was one.

Sophia Dalby. Of course it was. It could have been no one else. She fit every description Jane had ever heard of her, and she'd heard at least two dozen during her lifetime.

"You know each other?" Penelope said, Iveston coming up behind her in the same instant and putting his hand upon her waist. Truly, she would not have thought it possible that Iveston, an Englishman and, what's more, a marquis, would have so much overt affection in him. Particularly as the rumor of him, gleaned without any effort at all from Eleanor, was that Iveston had been considered by one and all to be a most peculiar fellow, the sort who rarely spoke and even more rarely left his house.

Penelope had, it was concluded by one and all, worked nothing short of a miracle upon him. Penelope, from Jane's brief interaction with her, seemed just the sort to achieve one. She was a most direct, forthright sort of girl, just the sort that Jane had always preferred. Of course, it could be argued that Louisa was equally direct, but it wasn't at all an attractive quality in her. She misused it somehow, of that Jane was instinctively certain.

"I've heard stories about Sophia, Lady Dalby, all my life," Jed replied.

"Darling," Sophia said with a languid and inviting smile, "I can't possibly be that old." Casting her gaze to Penelope, Sophia said, "We met briefly two years ago, when Captain Elliot was on his return from his first trip to China. But I have not had the pleasure of meeting the other Elliots. Mr. Joel Elliot, is it?" Sophia turned her dark-eyed gaze upon Joel with the grace and scrutiny of a hawk. Joel reacted appropriately.

"It is, ma'am," Joel said, bowing with all the crispness of

a boy just put to sea, his smile taking over his whole face. Sophia was exactly as described, *exactly*. Which did put Jane in mind of just what Sophia might be able to accomplish on her behalf. "Though it's captain as well. My first ship, my first time in a London port, my first meeting of the famous Sophia Dalby."

Joel's mouth was clearly running away with him. The next thing would be for him to start peeling off his coat. *Men.* As if Sophia Dalby would want anything to do with a boy like Joel, or even Jed. Oh, they were men by every acceptable standard, but Jane was more than certain that Sophia Dalby had more exacting standards regarding men than most. Quite right of her, too.

Jane moved fractionally and stepped on Joel's foot nearly as hard as she could.

"My sister, Miss Jane Elliot," Joel said, cocking his head sharply, in response to her foot, likely. She could step quite firmly, as the occasion called for it. It called for it quite often, as it happened. "She insisted that as I was coming to London she be allowed to grab a ride across. I'm going to leave her here while I go on to China."

Still blathering, but as Sophia was looking her over quite carefully and seemed to be listening very closely to what Joel was saying, Jane let him blather on. One of the many things her mother said about Sophia was that she had an unparalleled ability to make things happen and to make them happen to her advantage. If Jane could manage for Sophia to want something for *her*, such as a prolonged adventure in England, then there was hardly any doubt at all that Sophia would see it done.

"She was going to spend a few months with Aunt Molly," Joel said, still blathering, poor dear, "perhaps see a bit of England, and then return to New York on the first Elliot ship. Now that Jed's here, she'll be going back sooner than any of us thought."

"And I'm to suffer for it," Jane said, cutting Joel off out

of pure necessity. The way he was going on, he'd still be talking an hour from now, and still saying very little. "I thought I might be here for at least part of the Season, but we had a leak belowdecks on the larboard and had to stop at Nantucket for repairs."

As Sophia was looking at her with blatant encouragement and not a little interest, Jane continued. She *was* going to win Sophia to her cause. She simply had to. How else to get what she wanted and to thumb her nose at Louisa in the bargain?

"Then we spent two weeks in the Azores, and now I've come to find the Season is nearly over and Jed ready to ferry me off. Arriving for Iveston and Penelope's wedding has been a wonderful thrill, but it seems that it's all that's allowed me."

A blatant bid for pity and aid, but she was that determined to stay.

"How absurd," Sophia said. Jane felt a thrill that reached her toes. She was going to stay. She was going to have her adventure and Louisa was going to choke on it. "I know Molly would love to have you for a year. There is no need to rush off simply because your brothers must."

"We promised our father," Jed said, which was so typical of him. Jane could almost recite his lines for him, like something out of a play.

"And your mother, too, I should expect," Sophia countered, "but they could hardly have known that Miss Elliot would not have any time at all to experience the joys and intrigues of London Society."

Penelope made some noise, drawing Jane's attention, which had to have been intentional, and made some movement of her eyes and mouth that indicated . . . what? Concern? Alarm? Excitement? Perhaps all three, and perhaps nothing at all. Jane glanced at Penelope, raised her brows slightly, and returned her gaze to Sophia.

"Intrigues?" Jane asked.

"Joys?" Joel said.

"Father?" Jed reminded them all. As if anyone could ever forget Father. But he was in New York. What could he do about anything in London?

"There isn't much use in mentioning fathers to Lady Dalby," Iveston said, his brilliant blue eyes shining in mirth. "She simply ignores their existence when there is an intrigue at her fingertips."

An intrigue? Was there an intrigue? Sophia cast another glance at Jane, drawing her in, her black eyes abounding in humor. Oh, yes, there was an intrigue, and Jane was hip deep in it with Sophia Dalby. She couldn't have been happier.

"Lord Iveston, you are utterly wrong," Sophia said, smiling. Her smile was for Jane, of that she was certain. "I never ignore fathers. I give them the most careful and most studious attention," she said. After a moment's pause, she continued, "And then I do what I want with their tacit approval, even if their knowledge of what they are approving is a bit faulty."

And upon those words, Penelope coughed lightly and looked at the floor. Jane was instantly even more intrigued than she had been a moment before.

Intrigued . . .

Did intriguing with Sophia lead to marriage? That was not at all to be desired. She wanted to stay and she wanted to test the boundaries of her freedom, but to somehow find herself married, and to an Englishman, for what else was there in London, that was not at all what she wanted. Marriage would end what little freedom she currently enjoyed. Would a husband allow her to make a spontaneous trip across the Atlantic? Hardly likely. Brothers were trouble enough to manage. A husband gave every indication of being far worse.

"I could never achieve Father's approval," Jane said. "He's not here and Jed won't move from his promise. I've tried."

"I haven't tried," Sophia said softly, smiling up at Jed.

Jed shook his head again and again, but he was smiling even as he shook.

Jane knew what that meant. Indeed, it was hardly possible that anyone could miss it. She was going to stay in England. She was nearly completely certain. She was, in the blink of an eye, involved in a minor intrigue with Sophia Dalby.

Perfectly well and good. But she was not going to marry an Englishman, if that's what Sophia had in mind. Jane was quite firm about that, and would bring it up to Sophia directly, if the occasion ever called for it.

"And on that promising note, I do believe there is a cousin of mine you must meet," Iveston said, his hand firmly on Penelope's arm.

"Who?" Penelope said, staring hard at first Sophia and then Jane and then at Jed and then back to Jane. She was trying to communicate something, but Jane couldn't determine what. Likely that she should be wary of conspiring an intrigue with Sophia, but Jane already knew that. She'd heard more than one story about Sophia over the years; she wasn't a complete dolt.

"Quite distant," Iveston said, his hand tightening as his grin widened. "Can't quite recall the name. Do come, Pen. We mustn't linger where we aren't wanted."

"Aren't wanted? Are you mad, Iveston? 'Tis our own wedding! Of course we're wanted."

But she said the last as Iveston was dragging her off, Penelope's brother, George Prestwick, shaking his head at them from across the wide room. George, whom she'd shared a single meal with and nothing more, seemed a most genial sort, which was not precisely how she would have described Penelope. No, not at all.

"She can't stay," Jed said, which pulled her gaze from George Prestwick, a most handsome man of black hair and black eyes who looked very much like his sister, back onto her brother, who did not look good to her at all at the moment. Jed was such a stubborn sort. She couldn't think where he'd got it from. "Not without someone to watch over her."

Yes, well, that was the entire problem. Too much watching. She was a grown woman, not a dribbling infant.

"She's not without family in Town," Sophia said.

"All men," Jed said.

"Yes, darling. All men," Sophia said with a soft smile aimed directly at Jed. He seemed to wilt a bit and then flush about the throat. "Men are so very careful, so very attentive to a beautiful woman, but not quite so attentive when that woman is their sister. Now, while these men, these close cousins of yours, are men, they also have wives. I don't suppose you'd trust them?"

"New wives," Jed said stiffly, his flush fading somewhat.

Sophia laughed softly and tapped Jed's folded arms with her fan. He flushed again. *Merciful heavens*, everything she'd ever heard, and a good deal that had merely been implied, was being proved true in less than ten minutes in Sophia's presence. She was the most artful manager of men that Jane had ever seen, not that she had seen much of that sort of thing in her life. New York was a bustling city, but did not boast many women of Sophia Dalby's range. As to that, Jane doubted there were any. Surely she would have heard something by now.

"Darling," Sophia breathed, taking in both Jed and Joel with her gaze, "trust an experienced man of the sea to see things so clearly, and to be so unafraid to state the situation so boldly. I am quite breathless. One does grow accustomed to the British way of doing things, but you have reminded me, most powerfully, how compelling American men can be. How long did you say you were staying?"

Jed looked nearly tongue-tied, and Joel completely so. Jane was nearly quivering with delight. Never in her memory had anyone so effortlessly rendered her brothers impotent, even for a moment. Certainly Mother and Father had tried, but they had only achieved their brief successes after repeated and energetic endeavor. This, *this* was superbly astounding. Jane wanted to learn how to do it immediately. She was certain it would make life much more pleasant, with husband or without one. After all, one had to deal with men regularly in this life. Better to do it with an arsenal of weapons than without. Sophia clearly had a full arsenal and used her weapons with both skill and grace, as well as without hesitation, which is precisely how any sort of weapon should be used.

Jane, far from wanting to inject herself into this duel, kept her mouth closed and her eyes open.

It was while her eyes were thus open that two gentlemen were added to their number. Jane's eyes opened even wider as they were introduced.

The Duke of Edenham walked into their circle of conversation as if he had every right to enter where and when he chose. Dukes were like that, according to every rumor of them. This duke was quite tall, quite handsome, and quite elegant looking, if one liked the type. Having never been exposed to his type before she was withholding judgment. He *was* very handsome. He also did not seem at all overawed by her brothers, which was refreshing. In New York, there were very few men who would risk anything at all with her for fear of her brothers' comeuppance. Such a nuisance, really. Her brothers were always at sea. What sort of squeamish man lived in fear of what would happen six months in the future? Life in New York was far more dull than it should have been. She blamed her brothers entirely.

The second gentleman was the Marquis of Ruan, a most dangerous and rugged-looking man, not nearly as elegantly arranged as the Duke of Edenham, but handsome nonetheless, though in a more ruthless fashion entirely.

It was perfectly obvious that Sophia was well acquainted

with both men. Jane would hardly have expected anything less.

The introductions having been made, the immediate result being that Jed had escaped from Sophia's highly focused attention, Jed then gave every indication that he was going to leave this newly arranged circle of conversation and drag her with him. She was not ready to leave. Sophia hadn't got her way yet, had she? Which meant that Jane hadn't got *her* way. She was going to stay, and she wasn't going to leave Sophia's side until it was formally decided that she was to remain in London.

Jane put the most innocent look upon her face, for her brothers' benefit, obviously, and ignored both the duke and the marquis. But the duke was staring at her with the most peculiar expression on his face. His odd behavior was not helping her at all.

She ignored him more pointedly.

He continued to stare.

Joel shifted his weight and rolled his shoulders a bit.

Oh, mercy.

Looking innocent and disinterested was not putting the duke off one bit. How very like a duke to behave as he pleased and attempt to ruin her plans in such thoughtless fashion. Could he not go off and bother some other poor girl? Some girl who did not have two brothers at her elbows?

"Edenham," Sophia said, "I'm so delighted to see you here. And your enchanting sister, she is with you?"

"Yes," the Duke of Edenham replied, turning his gaze from Jane just long enough to make eye contact with Sophia, cast a quick glance over Jed and Joel, and then look into her eyes. He had lovely eyes, a warm shade of brown, and quite a nice brow. She averted her gaze after noting only the most obvious details of his appearance, which she would argue quite forcefully if Jed said one word about it, and then turned to stare with bland attention at Joel. Joel rolled his shoulders again and kept his gaze on Edenham. Edenham kept his gaze upon her. The stupidity of dukes was thus proved. "A cause for celebration. We wish Hyde nothing but joy."

Sophia smiled and said, "With three sons married within a single Season, I can assure you that they feel nothing but joy. And with the happy addition of the Elliots to share in their joy, why, what can they do but smile away their days? Which brings me back round to you, darling," Sophia said to Jed, laying her gloved hand upon his arm in a light caress. "Surely you must allow Miss Elliot to stay and partake of the general joy to be found within Hyde House. I assure you that she will be well cared for."

It was perhaps not the ideal thing to say to sway Jed to release them all from their father's instructions. Only a little over a day in London, within the very walls of Hyde House, and the Elliots had heard word of how three of Hyde's sons had come to be married in a single Season.

The word was *ruin*.

No one seemed especially bothered by it, certainly not the sons, yet neither were their wives, which was most strange, wasn't it? Of all the things she had been told about the British, their odd habits and proclivities, a facility and easiness about being ruined was not among them.

"Not as well cared for as upon an Elliot ship," Jed said, which was likely very true.

"Truly?" Sophia said brightly, her gaze almost resolutely removed from the Marquis of Ruan. Jane began to wonder if Sophia was not on the most cordial of terms with the man, which would not surprise her in the least as some of what her mother had told her about Sophia left no doubt that Sophia could and did make a very firm enemy and that her enemies were entirely deserving of the position. Jane gave Lord Ruan a cold look of bland curiosity at the thought. "No storms?" Sophia continued. "No violent waves? No enemy ships? No contrary currents? No pirates?

What has quiet and serene Hyde House to offer by way of excitement that an Elliot ship cannot merely match but overmatch?"

"Men?" Joel said. Jed gave him an approving look, annoyed but approving.

"British men, most assuredly," Sophia said, casting a casual glance in the general direction of both Edenham and Ruan. Edenham blinked and continued to stare at her. Ruan's mouth tightened, against a smile or a grimace Jane could not determine. "But what is that? Certainly they are not to be feared. Or do you think otherwise, Captain?"

Well, then, there was a pretty insult, and delivered so sweetly, too. Jed looked properly angered. Joel did not appear angry so much as bewildered by the sudden turn the conversation had taken. As to that, Jane felt much the same. Is this how Sophia got what she wanted? By insults? She had not heard *that* about her. Not at all.

"In the proper circumstances, it is wise to consider any man with due caution," Jed said stiffly, eyeing both Edenham and Ruan. Edenham ignored him. Ruan returned the look and nodded sharply.

"And what of improper circumstances?" Sophia said. "I do confess to having more experience of men in improper circumstances."

"If we are speaking of English men, then I must confess the same," Jed said, smiling slightly.

"Captain Elliot, you shock me. I am intrigued," Sophia said, smiling, and raising her fan to obscure her face, which naturally resulted in all the men, Edenham excluded, staring with increased intensity at her. Jane needed a better fan, if only to shield herself from Edenham's obsessive gaze. It was becoming something of an embarrassment to her, and was not at all helpful with her brothers standing at her elbow and witnessing his complete break from polite behavior. Or what she assumed was polite behavior. The two countries could not be *that* different, could they? "Please, tell me all," Sophia urged. "Is it improper circumstances to which you refer, or improper men? Or is it the extreme Englishness of both which results in the impropriety?"

"Lady Dalby, you have left me," Jed said, his eyes twinkling. "I fear the conversation has twisted out of my hands. I am a simple man. I beg you to show me mercy."

"Lady Dalby is not known for showing mercy," Lord Ruan said abruptly, "though she may be partial to men who beg, Captain Elliot. You would do well to show her the same caution you practice when facing an unidentified ship."

"But Lord Ruan, how absurd," Sophia said, her voice soft and her gaze sharp. "I am flying my colors boldly, as is my practice. There is no mystery attached to me."

"Lady Dalby, you are a woman," Ruan responded, his green eyes searching Sophia's face. "You are as mysterious as the sea. As turbulent. As unfathomable. As compelling. And as dangerous."

Sophia said nothing for a moment, but there was something that passed between them, something sparkling and hot, something buried and smoldering. It was gone almost before it had begun. Jane was left with the shimmer of it before her gaze, and then it vanished.

"Which is why Jane will come home with me," Jed said. "I would see her stay a calm pond of decorum and not become a turbulent sea of mystery."

"Lovely," Jane muttered. "I suppose that was intended as a compliment?"

"Of course," Jed said, looking both annoyed and befuddled. *Typical.*

Sophia laughed. "But, darling, she is your sister and, like any brother, you do not see her clearly at all. Miss Elliot is already a sea of mystery to any man who is not related to her."

And, naturally, both Jane and Sophia could not resist the impulse to glance at Edenham, who was still staring.

"The sea can be calm at times, usually the most inconvenient times, is that not so?" Edenham said, sparing a glance for Jed. "There is no cause to anticipate any trouble for Miss Elliot. I cannot think but that Hyde would care for her as a beloved daughter."

"Now I am a calm, *inconvenient* sea?" Jane said. "Can not a new metaphor be framed? I grow weary of this one as it does nothing at all to flatter me."

Sophia laughed, as did Jed and Joel, which was something of a relief. Edenham smiled. Ruan did not; he studied her, which she did not enjoy at all. Lord Ruan was capable of a very focused gaze. She was not certain that was destined to be flattering to her either.

"You must forgive the Duke of Edenham, Miss Elliot. He is confounded, I do believe, by your beauty and your originality, a product of your American education, I should guess," Sophia said.

"Ah, something acquired then," Jane said, smiling. "Not something I possess innately."

"You possess your beauty innately, Miss Elliot," Ruan said softly. "Only your education, your way of thinking and expressing yourself, could have been acquired."

"I see you know very little of women, Lord Ruan," Jane said, upon which Sophia chuckled without apology. "I acquired what beauty I display by the same method I acquired an educated mind: by exhaustive effort."

"I don't believe a word of it," the Duke of Edenham said quietly, his gaze riveted to her face. The man was as subtle as a thunderclap and her brothers were far from being witless.

"Believe it, sir," Joel said. "I've been witness to the transformation myself. It has been a wonder to behold."

"Oh, shut up, Joel," Jane snapped good-naturedly.

"There's no need to make a complete pudding of me. I was a gangly child," she said, risking a sliding glance at Edenham. He stared. Tedious, to be sure. "I was all teeth and eyes and knobby limbs."

"Very true," Jed said, nodding. "'Tis why I christened the third Elliot ship the *Plain Jane*. For my sister, and rightly so."

"You see what toil I have struggled against," Jane said, elbowing Jed in the ribs. He grinned and grabbed her hand and held it against his waistcoat.

"And by toil you grew into your eyes, your mouth, your form," Ruan said, looking at her with such a look, with such a soft look filled with appreciation, that she was in danger of blushing like a girl with plaited hair and mud-splattered stockings.

"Exactly so, Lord Ruan," she said, lifting her chin. "Let no one convince you otherwise. Certainly no woman would ever do so."

"How utterly true," Sophia said. "Every woman knows that beauty requires payment, and not every woman is prepared to pay its price."

"Payment?" Jed said. "You have lost me again, Lady Dalby. I fear ever to be outdistanced by you."

"Oh, don't worry, Captain Elliot," Sophia said lightly. "I shall allow you to catch me if, or when, I decide to be caught."

"Much like a ship under sail, coming about to level her guns a broadside," Ruan said, breaking the seductive spell Sophia was weaving.

"How nautically put, Lord Ruan. That's it precisely," Sophia said, her dark eyes glittering.

"The *Plain Jane*," Edenham said. "You were not insulted?"

"Of course I was, your grace, but what does a brother care for that when he is doing the insulting? It is only when others insult me that their blood boils hot."

"And are you insulted often, Miss Elliot?" Ruan asked.

"Unfortunately, no," she said.

"Why unfortunately, Miss Elliot?" Edenham asked.

"Because I should like to see what happens, your grace. My brothers have promised hideous things to befall the man who does so. I have yet to see a single thing. It's most disappointing, I assure you. It's all talk, as far as I can tell."

"Which is exactly as it should be, Jane," Jed said. "It's hardly proper for a gently reared girl to be privy to such things."

Gently reared, indeed. With their home on the East River, the ships docked right outside the house? Did Jed think she did not have eyes and ears? What did he think she did whilst he was at sea? Embroider by the fire? Hardly.

"Is that a confession, Jed? Have you trounced some fellow behind my back? I require names and dates, if so. A woman must have a record of such things. It adds mightily to her appeal, which is certainly obvious, even to a man who happens to also be a brother," Jane said.

"I confess nothing," Jed said, trying for a stern look and failing, at least with her. He might have much skill at subduing a fractious seaman with a mere scowl, but she was his sister, which was a very distinct advantage to possess.

"Nothing to confess," she said. "I thought as much. It is a sad thing when a woman cannot tempt a man to even the small danger a brother offers. Plain Jane, indeed. Most apt."

"A most clumsy attempt at garnering a compliment, Jane," Joel said. "Shameful."

"To arrange for a compliment?" Sophia asked. "How completely absurd. If a woman cannot ask for what she wants, and certainly deserves, why, what sort of woman is she? And indeed, what is she fit for? Does the shame, if we must deal in shame, not belong to the man who stubbornly and willfully refuses to give a woman what she wants and, without any question at all, deserves?"

The men, by which she meant her brothers, looked

abashed in the extreme. It was quite comical. The other men, by which she meant the English ones, looked mildly amused. That was also quite comical. Sophia did have such a way about her, such a wonderful way of putting men both at ease and at a disadvantage. It seemed quite a tricky thing to learn, but so useful on so many occasions. Jane was determined to try and develop a talent for it.

"And upon such counsel I become more determined than ever to see Jane safely upon the deck of my ship," Jed said.

"But darling," Sophia said softly, "I can make you less determined easily enough; it is only that I perceived you to be the sort of man who would prefer not to be managed by a woman. Was I wrong in that?"

Jed chuckled, his dark blond brows pulled low and his mouth surrendering to a grin. "Lady Dalby, you are managing me even now."

"Am I? I do apologize if I am. Some would say that it is a most appalling habit of mine, and though I can't agree that any sort of skill at managing anything could possibly be appalling, still, I can't think how I might have acquired such a useful habit. Can you?" Sophia smiled at both Jed and Joel without a particle of shame. Indeed, she was obviously delighted.

"Lady Dalby," Jed said, dipping his head in salute, still grinning, "I don't believe it is possible for you to have any appalling habits. On the contrary. Most definitely on the contrary."

"Naturally, I find myself quite fully in agreement with you, Captain Elliot. And as we both agree," Sophia said, smiling at each of the Elliots in turn, "I shall be delighted to take Miss Elliot under my wing, as it were, and, together with your Aunt Molly, make certain that darling Jane has the most splendid visit in London that any American woman has ever enjoyed. As my habits are flawless, and as your aunt is devoted, and as Miss Elliot is clearly eager, the matter appears to be quite completely settled. Wouldn't you say?"

Jed and Joel had been rendered speechless, that much was obvious. Jane smiled and held her tongue, knowing that it was entirely possible to break the spell Sophia had woven about them. Before anyone could think to argue, and only Jed might have done so, stubborn as he always was, Cranleigh arrived and, murmuring something about someone they must meet, bustled them away from Sophia and across the room.

Sophia had neither been denied nor decried.

And that was when Jane knew for absolute certain that she was going to remain in London after all.

Three

"What a remarkably attractive family," Sophia said as the Elliots were escorted off by Lord Cranleigh. "How fortunate that they were here to witness the marriage of Lord Iveston to Miss Prestwick. And how delicious that darling Miss Elliot shall remain in London for a time. I do think she'll enjoy herself to the full, don't you, Edenham?"

She did not include Lord Ruan in her remarks. She was slightly irritated with the Marquis of Ruan. She had thought that, after his weeks of devoted attention, he would continue on as he had done and that their flirtation would culminate in an entertaining affaire that would last for as long as she liked, and then he would disappear back into whatever shire had consumed him until this current Season. For she had never met him until now, and the more she pondered that, the more the fact intrigued her. Where had he been? What had he been about for all the long twenty years she had dwelt on English soil? It was not possible that she had been out in Society and not caught a glimpse or a word of the tantalizing Lord Ruan.

Or, he had been tantalizing until he had stopped his

pursuit of her. A man who did not ardently pursue was a complete bore and not worth a single thought. And so she had refused to think of him. She was very adept at controlling where her thoughts roamed and so she had neither sought out nor seen Lord Ruan for a full three weeks, if not more. Seeing him now aroused nothing in her.

Nothing at all.

Sophia glanced at Edenham and he looked only slightly less besotted than he had when facing Miss Elliot. She swallowed every inclination to smile and waited serenely for his answer. She even allowed her gaze to shift over Ruan for a moment or two. He was looking at her with all the intensity of a wolf, which was perfectly fine, but just a few weeks late, wasn't it?

"I can only hope so," Edenham said, his eyes still upon the spot where Miss Elliot and her brothers had disappeared from sight. The blue reception room at Hyde House was quite large and quite well appointed, but it was also quite filled with the very cream of London Society. The marriage of the Duke of Hyde's heir was not a celebration to be missed, Molly Hyde had made certain of that. "You are convinced Miss Elliot will be staying?"

"You are not?" Sophia said, the barest of smiles teasing her lips.

"I'm convinced," Ruan said, "though I was not asked, was I?"

"No, Lord Ruan, you were not," Sophia said, staring fully into his eyes. Remarkable eyes, like green blades. She looked again at Edenham. "A shameful oversight. I do hope you will forgive me."

"Yes, your shame is quite apparent, Lady Dalby," Ruan said, his voice calm and controlled.

Yes, well, they were both calmly in control, weren't they? Perhaps that was the problem. Neither one of them was the sort to give in or give over, not for anyone and not for any reason. That was never going to change.

"Darling Lord Ruan," she said pleasantly, looking at him again, "shame should never be apparent. That is in such poor taste, is it not? To feel shame is quite sufficient. One need never trot about in gauche displays of shame."

"'Tis a private thing," Ruan said, staring at her in much the same fashion that Edenham had been staring at Miss Elliot. She was nearly moved by it. But she was not. "You are adept at keeping private things private, are you not, Lady Dalby?"

"I am, Lord Ruan," she said. "I do believe the same *should* be said of everyone. If it is not, it is to their . . . shame." She could have smiled, had she chosen to, but she did not choose to.

"As to private," Edenham said, "I had not heard of Hyde's American relations. There is no disaffection between Hyde and the Elliots, no shame at the connection?"

"Not at all, Edenham," Sophia said, turning her attention fully upon Edenham. "I surely would have heard of it. It is merely that oceans and governments stand between them."

"And wars," Ruan interjected, just to be troublesome, she was certain.

"Long over now," Sophia said. "Yet even then, Molly and Sally remained as close as it was possible to remain under the circumstances."

"And the circumstances are?" Edenham asked, lifting a brow in a truly ducal display.

"Quite as simple now as they were complicated then," Sophia said, waving her fan in the region of her bodice. Ruan's eyes stayed fixed upon her face. How very like him. "Molly and Sally, as I'm certain you must have surmised, are sisters who were reared in Boston within a shipping family. Molly met and married Hyde, and when things in Boston became difficult for Loyalists, moved to England with all the lovely heirs she had provided for Hyde. Sally married Timothy Elliot whilst in New York visiting a cousin, I do believe, and as Captain Elliot was and is a determined Patriot, the sisters were thus divided. And yet did they not remain sisters? Of course they did. They waited out the war, held their families together, and insisted upon maintaining a familial connection between them. They did so with rare skill and their children should, and I'm certain do, thank them for their foresight and loyalty to this day."

"Loyalty?" Ruan said softly. "Yet not to country."

"I was speaking of family loyalty, Lord Ruan, though they were certainly not disloyal to country, were they? Would any dare question Hyde's loyalty? He fought determinedly for his king whilst in the American colonies, did he not? His record is well-known. But, were you not aware of it, Lord Ruan? How can that be? Where have you been that you are not in full possession of those particular facts?"

Ruan smiled, his eyes sparkling devilishly. "I know the facts, Lady Dalby. It is the peculiar arrangement of the facts and the shadows they create upon a life that I find intriguing."

"Yes, you would," she said. And meant it. That was the entire problem with Lord Ruan, he seemed far too interested in mining the depth of facts concerning people. It was most inconvenient of him. What *had* he been doing this past month? Mining, most like. A most disagreeable practice for a man to devote himself to. She wanted no one mining the facts of her life, looking for shadows.

"So they are close, then," Edenham said. "Harmonious."

"I should say they are," Sophia said, "which is so pleasant to observe within families, and yet so rarely seen. I do wonder why that is? Lord Ruan, you have never mentioned your family. Is there no harmony between you? Do confess, what is the source of your family discord?"

Ruan smiled fractionally, his gaze shuttered. "I make no confessions, Lady Dalby, to either harmony or discord."

"A private shame, then?" she said crisply. "How noble of you. It is most agreeable of you not to parade your shame publicly. I do hope you haven't suffered too egregiously. Have you? Will you confess that much?"

"Not *too* egregiously, no," he said. "Though as to suffering, I make no claim to surpass others of my acquaintance in that. We all suffer, do we not, Lady Dalby? It is how we bear up beneath the weight of it that is the measure of us. I take your measure, and you take mine, and by so doing, we learn the mettle and the merit of each other. It is what we do, isn't it? It is how we know and understand each other."

Ruan's gaze had grown quite serious, and she did not care at all for his line of thought. Far too solemn and far too philosophical; of what use was any of it? One lived as best one could. *Suffering? Merit?* They were words nailed to ideas. They had no meaning. They served no purpose.

"I have always found, Lord Ruan, that I prefer a more physical understanding, a more animal knowing. I had hoped you shared my inclination. As you do not . . . " she said softly, and then she shrugged delicately and turned, dismissing Ruan, to face Edenham. "But darling Edenham, I have been remiss. How are your precious children? Thriving still?"

"I would not bore Lord Ruan with observations about my children that would surely fall upon disinterested ears," Edenham said.

"Oh, but perhaps Lord Ruan has children of his own," Sophia said, turning her eyes upon Ruan again. "Do you?"

Ruan smiled and bowed curtly. "I do not, though not for lack of trying, Lady Dalby. It is my most endearing flaw, I can assure you. But if you will excuse me?"

He made his way through the throng with the grace of a snake. Sophia watched him until he was lost in the crowd.

"Perhaps we could find a more sequestered spot, Sophia?" Edenham said, looking over her head to survey the room. "It is rather close in here, is it not?"

"A fine assembly," she said. "Everyone in Town is here

to honor Hyde, and to be seen honoring him. Caro and Ashdon are on their way, I believe, and did hope to arrive in time. I am so sorry they seem to have been delayed."

As she spoke, she and Edenham wound their way to a corner of the blue reception room, quite near the door to the stair hall. Hyde House, quite a large home on Piccadilly, was an utterly perfect place in which to hold large and impressive entertainments. The rooms were arranged in something like a square circle, the stair hall comprising the large middle square with two reception rooms, a music room, a drawing room, a dressing room, a bedchamber, and an antechamber comprising the outer parts of the square. It was entirely possible, and indeed it was encouraged, that when large parties were hosted that the guests move about the circuit of rooms at their inclination. It was the only way to keep things from stagnating, much like swiftly moving water circulating through a pond. One did not want pockets of still water, not unless one enjoyed what resulted from men and women finding themselves in secluded and undisturbed corners. Which, of course, many did.

"I want your help, Sophia," Edenham said abruptly.

"Of course," she said brightly. "Anything at all, Edenham."

The Duke of Edenham, looking quite somber, stared at her quite determinedly. "I want to marry again," he said.

"But how lovely!" she said. "And of course you should. Do you know whom yet?"

Why had Ruan never married? He hadn't, she knew that. As a marquis, he should have been determined to assure his legacy, finding a wife and getting heirs upon her as soon as he had reached his majority and abused the privilege of title and wealth for as long as he could. That was the tradition among the English, wasn't it? How was it that Ruan, far past his majority now and, one assumed, all flagrant abuses of privilege behind him, had not married some proper girl and produced one or two proper children by her?

"Miss Jane Elliot," Edenham said, breaking into her pointless speculations about Ruan. "I will marry Miss Elliot."

He looked quite serious about it, poor darling. Jane Elliot? He had clearly been fascinated by her, to be sure, but marriage? Quite precipitous.

Sophia nodded and said, "But darling, haven't you only just met her?"

Edenham looked just slightly embarrassed by the question, which was completely amusing, but then he quickly gathered his composure. In point of fact, he looked utterly ducal and proud, if not to say arrogant. He clearly meant to have the girl, and could see no difficulty in snatching her up.

How very British of him. She could read his reasoning quite easily. He was a duke. She was a simple American girl, with a family connection to the Duke of Hyde, never a hindrance in matters of this sort. He was titled, wealthy, handsome, eligible. She was beautiful, young, well connected, and, he had to assume, properly impressed by his grandeur.

She cared for Edenham, she truly did, but he did not understand Americans at all.

"I have," Edenham said, his arrogance sitting quite comfortably upon his features. "And I have decided. She would make me an ideal wife, I believe. I am, you will be forced to admit, a good judge of women. Haven't my three previous wives been exemplary?"

"They have," Sophia agreed calmly. "Yet I must point out that you were not married for any great length of time to any of them. Through no fault of your own, naturally."

That the delicious Duke of Edenham had married a perfectly lovely and acceptable woman once, got her with child, and then watched her die upon her birthing bed had been a tragedy. A not uncommon one, but still, a tragedy. That it had happened again to his second wife upon the

birth of his second child was the subject of much specu-
lation, not very much of it flattering to Edenham. That it
had happened to his third wife, and that his son had been
stillborn, was the sort of horrific concurrence of events that
Society loved to get its teeth into.

Edenham, thrice married and thrice widowed, was the
subject of lurid legend, the seed of his legend resting firmly
on his . . . seed.

Ridiculous bit of nonsense, but when did that ever matter when the life of a salacious rumor was at stake? The
rumor and the ensuing whispers about the man were simply
too fantastic to discard. Edenham was such a lovely man,
truly what any woman, any English woman, would want in
a husband. Unfortunately, the younger women in Society
were afraid of him. The older, more experienced women in
Society didn't need him, not as a husband at any rate. Only
Penelope Prestwick, who only this morning had become
the wife of the Marquis of Iveston, had been of enough
resolve of character and determination of purpose to actually want to marry the Duke of Edenham. Of course, once
she had got a closer look at Iveston, all resolve and determination for Edenham had flown north with the geese.

Edenham had not had a good time of it, truly. He
deserved better, but did he deserve Jane Elliot?

He would certainly believe so, though what Jane Elliot
believed was an entirely different matter, not that Edenham
understood that. Yet. Still, he would have such fun running
after her. And darling Edenham could do with a good bit
of fun.

"Thank you," Edenham said to her remark, his gaze
riveted upon Miss Elliot, who stood completely across the
room from them. She was an amazing beauty, her hair the
glossy dark brown of mink, her large and expressive eyes of
shimmering hazel, her features elegantly arranged. Small
wonder that Edenham was completely taken in. "Since you

agree with me, and since it is clear to me that you have some warmth of acquaintance with the Elliot family, I would ask you to help me present my suit to her."

Sophia nodded slowly and kept her gaze slightly averted. Her warmth of acquaintance with the Elliot family was not, perhaps, quite as intimate as Edenham hoped. The connection was tenuous and irregular, though not unpleasant. Still, Jane Elliot most obviously wanted to remain in England for a time, and she was not shy about asking for help in managing her brothers. That showed both wisdom and cleverness, which truly did not conjoin as often as they should. It also displayed a certain boldness that Sophia found irresistible.

The question then became: Would Miss Jane Elliot of New York enjoy being pursued by the Duke of Edenham?

The answer was obvious: Whyever not?

It then became a question of strategy, the most intriguing question of all. Playing at strategy was such fun. She couldn't think why more people did not engage in the practice, but even a casual survey amply proved they did not. How else to explain the general muddle?

"That may prove difficult," she said to Edenham, looking up at him. He truly was an utterly spectacular-looking man. Jane would have such a marvelous time with him.

"Why, if I may ask?" Edenham said, looking properly outraged. "I am in the pink of health and possessed of every attribute a woman seeks in a husband. I am a duke, after all."

He may have puffed out his chest a bit as he said it. She was nearly certain he did so. He most definitely lifted his chin and looked down at her from his impressive height.

Sophia nodded and let a smile escape her lips. "Yes, darling, and this is precisely the problem. What does an American girl want with a duke? They have no use for them, you see, not you personally, you understand, but as a concept, as an ideal." Sophia paused for a moment before applying the spur. "To her, you are simply a man far older than she, living in a country that is foreign to her, with three dead wives and two small children to his credit. Why, my darling Edenham, would Miss Elliot want to marry you?"

Edenham, to his immense credit, did not turn and bolt for the nearest exit.

It was one of the finest reasons to like a man, one who did not run at the first hint of resistance.

Sophia's thoughts strayed to Lord Ruan for a fraction of a moment, but she regained control quickly enough, as was her practice.

Four

LADY Louisa had seen it all, indeed she could not but believe that everyone had seen it, yet she could not make herself accept it. It was inconceivable.

Lady Amelia believed it, found it completely remarkable, and was trying to put a good face on it. It was very like her.

Penelope, Lady Iveston, who should have been blissfully enjoying her wedding breakfast with all the joy reserved for brides, was so stunned that she could barely find words to express it.

Barely. She did find the words. Penelope had never been totally without words, at least not unless Iveston was somehow involved. As Iveston was not involved in this turn of events in any manner, she found she had much to say, once the initial shock had worn down.

"I tried forever to get Edenham to notice me," Penelope said hotly, "and he was never more than passing civil, and barely that. Why, I could hardly arrange for him to look fully at me for even a minute."

"Not quite the thing to discuss on the day of your wedding, is it, Penelope?" Amelia said softly.

"I should think I can safely discuss a man who paid me not one whit of attention, particularly on the day I married the man who can't keep his hands off me even in a crowded room," Penelope said. It was just the sort of rational, slightly rude thing that Penelope made a habit of saying. Amelia hadn't yet grown accustomed to it. Louisa had no intention of trying.

"What can he see in her?" Louisa said, looking across the room to where Edenham stood talking to Sophia Dalby in a secluded corner. Not precisely *secluded*, if one insisted upon absolute accuracy, but certainly out of the main throng. There was no need to be ridiculous about accuracy *now*, was there? It was enough that the Duke of Edenham, whom nobody wanted to marry unless they were desperate to marry a handsome duke, which, in fact, did include very many women, was clearly captivated by Jane Elliot, American.

Oh, yes, Jane was beautiful. Louisa knew she was beautiful, could plainly see that she was beautiful, but Jane was far from being the only beautiful woman in the room. This was London, after all. Edenham had certainly seen a beautiful woman before now.

He'd been married to three beautiful women, and shouldn't that have taught a man that there was more to a woman than beauty?

No, probably not. They did get so distracted by things of that nature. If she weren't quite beautiful enough in her own right she might find it excessively annoying.

"She's quite supremely beautiful, for one," Penelope answered, looking at Louisa as if she were an imbecile. "Added to that, she's a very pleasant sort of girl. I like her."

Penelope gave Louisa a very searching and slightly accusatory look, as if they all didn't like Jane. Of course Louisa liked Jane, it was only that Jane was so very different. An acquired taste, surely. But why then had Edenham not required the necessary time to acquire a taste for Jane? It was beyond comprehension.

"I like her, too," Amelia said, looking at Louisa with a slightly warning aspect.

"I like her!" Louisa said, which, as she had spoken a bit abruptly and not at all quietly, had caused Lord Raithby to start and stare in her direction. She nodded at Lord Raithby, who was quite handsome, and smiled slightly. Raithby simply looked, and then looked away. Raithby, it was quite well known, was completely horse-mad. Of course he wouldn't know what to do when a beautiful woman smiled at him, a married woman at that. She was firmly married to Blakes, and couldn't be happier about it, which should have proved to Raithby most fully that he was in no danger from her.

Men really were so slow on most days. One was kept in constant turmoil in trying to bring them round to anything resembling good sense.

Which put her right back round to Edenham and his utterly obvious fascination for Jane. One would think that, being a duke of mature years and with three wives to his credit, or debit, depending on one's perspective, Edenham would have learnt some sort of rudimentary composure around women. He gave every appearance of being entirely lacking in composure regarding Jane. With any other woman in Town, and for as many years as anyone could remember, he was completely composed. As to that, he was not at all affected by Sophia Dalby and *every* man was affected by her, Blakes excluded, naturally.

Most definitely excluded, if he had any sense at all.

What was it about Jane Elliot that had captivated the Duke of Edenham?

And what could be done about it?

"She is Blakes's cousin, after all," Louisa said, trying to see Jane in the crowd and failing. The room was an absolute crush. "Family bonds, and all that."

"And all that," Amelia repeated, smiling devilishly.

Amelia, who had always been so generally quiet and well mannered, had got quite sparkish upon marrying Cranleigh. What to think but that Cranleigh was a horrid influence on her? There were rumors that Amelia and Cranleigh had been slightly involved in something torrid for years, but Louisa discounted that entirely. It was not at all possible to be *slightly* involved in anything torrid with a man. Was not Blakes the most solid proof of that? Anything torrid with a man was a full-blown event, no half measures about it.

"The point I'm trying to make," Louisa said, tossing a red curl over her shoulder, "is that since Jane has snared the Duke of Edenham without any effort at all—"

"Without any *obvious* effort," Penelope cut in. Penelope made a habit of being unaccountably precise. It was extremely trying. "She may just do it very well. Who knows what techniques they practice in New York? They might know things about snaring men that we know nothing of. *Yet.* I shall ask her. I'm certain she'd be happy to educate us about it."

"Educate other women in how to effortlessly snag a handsome man's undivided attention?" Louisa asked, her brows raised. "That's quite naïve, isn't it?"

"Not if Jane is as pleasant and as charming as you believe her to be," Amelia said, smiling fully, not even trying to hide it behind her fan, the bold thing. Louisa couldn't think what Cranleigh had done to Amelia, but she didn't care for it in the least. Between Amelia's new bold ways and Penelope's frank ones, Louisa was quite put out fully half the time.

"Are you suggesting that you *need* to find new ways to attract a man?" Louisa asked. "I had expected Lord Cranleigh to have persuaded you that he is quite all you should want. Or are you still pining for some duke or other?"

Amelia, far from blushing and stammering, which she

might have done a six month ago, laughed and said, "Louisa, if you believe that, you are the last person in Town to do so. Certainly Cranleigh thinks nothing of the sort. I did think you had a more finely developed sense of humor. Perhaps Blakes is responsible for your bleak temper?"

"You have been very churlish of late, Louisa," Penelope said, her black eyes studying Louisa's face. "Not feeling quite the thing, or is it simply a row with your husband? I can't think it's a good sign to be in conflict so quickly and so heatedly after only having been married a few weeks. It does point to a habit of contention, which I believe should be avoided, unless absolutely necessary. Was it necessary?"

"I did not have a row with Blakes!" Louisa snapped. "Yet if I did, I should certainly have won it, and I would not be in anything like a bleak temper after having made my point with him."

"And what was the point you made?" Penelope asked, tilting her head quizzically at Louisa before turning to face Amelia, and winking.

Louisa, beyond all control of herself, burst out laughing. Amelia and Penelope joined her, naturally. She had been made a proper fool, and it had been done very handily. She did like Penelope, especially now that she was safely married.

"Now, what is it you have in mind for dear Jane?" Amelia asked when they had resumed the carefully composed aspects one put on for public display. "She is family, and she is an American, and I don't know but that we should be very careful of her for those two reasons alone. I know I should very much dislike being made uncomfortable if I ever should visit New York, which I hope most heartily to do."

"I can't think how gaining a duke's attention should make any woman uncomfortable," Penelope said. As Penelope had been doggedly determined to marry a duke and nothing less, and as it was her wedding day to the Duke of

Hyde's heir apparent, her opinion was just slightly shaded. "What she does with it is entirely up to her. Shouldn't that be a highly pleasant circumstance? I would have found it so."

"Did she look to you to be pleased by Edenham's attention?" Louisa asked Penelope.

Penelope looked down at the floor, pondered, and then looked up again. "No, she did not. In fact, if I had to hazard a guess, she looked a bit displeased, which I cannot comprehend in the slightest. What is there to be displeased about?"

"Let's ask her," Louisa said. And, with that, they tried to move through the crowd as gracefully as possible.

❧

LORD Raithby watched the three Blakesley brides of the current Season make their most determined way through the throng that had turned the spacious grace of the blue reception room at Hyde House into something not unlike a tavern brawl in both noise and excitement.

He had heard enough of their conversation to be slightly alarmed. Just slightly. He was not married to any one of them, he had no sister to fall prey to their plots, and he did not know Jane Elliot. No, he had nothing to be alarmed about.

But there was just something tickling at the back of his thoughts, some small remembered bit of a conversation he had dabbled in with George Prestwick, Penelope's brother, a month or so ago. On the night that wagers were flying left and right about whom Penelope would marry. He had won twenty pounds based solely on the condition of Iveston's cravat, courtesy of Miss Prestwick. George Prestwick had been quite alarmed by the wagers flying about about his sister, causing Raithby to be more than glad he did not have a sister of his own to worry over. Still, it had caused him to think of other things besides horses and wagers, and he had not quite shaken himself free of it yet.

It must be a horrid thing to be required to fuss over a sister, seeing that her good name remained good, that she married a proper gentleman, and that she didn't shame her family in any way remotely obvious. Terrible burden. He was quite relieved not to have to bear it.

Still, as a man, he supposed he ought to feel some sense of responsibility. Not to the women, naturally, but to the men. That was logical. Completely.

He really should tell someone, someone who would care, who did have the unwelcome responsibility of maintaining and enforcing a sister's good name.

Raithby, nodding absently, listening to only every fourth word or so of what the Marquis of Penrith was saying, which as Penrith was talking about how worried he was concerning the safety of his sister and mother, who were traveling in Italy, was quite effortless to ignore as well as being quite ironic, looked about the room for a man he might confide in.

He spotted George Prestwick near the doorway to the red reception room. George Prestwick, the man who had got the idea of sisters in his head in the first place.

Again, ironic.

∞

THE Duke of Edenham wanted to marry again. He had suspected he wanted to marry again before seeing Miss Jane Elliot. Seeing Miss Elliot had forced the conclusion and provided him with the focus for his quest. She was beautiful. A mild description for what she was. She was the most beautiful woman he had ever seen. There was something about her beauty, some noble quality to it, some classical aspect to the arrangement of her features that called to him as a Greek siren of old.

He would marry her.

She was an American, true, but her uncle was a duke

and her upbringing gave no hint of having been shoddy. There was the fact that she had not reacted in any way to him. He was not accustomed to that. Women either reacted to him a bit nervously, the tragedy of having buried three wives clouding their judgment, or they fawned over him. He enjoyed neither response, yet, as it was the norm, he had become acclimated to it.

Miss Jane Elliot had not seemed impressed by him in the slightest, though as she was an American, he had wondered at the accuracy of his observations. Sophia Dalby put a nail in his uncertainty. According to Sophia, Jane did not find him appealing. No, nor intriguing, and definitely not desirable. In fact, upon silently reviewing Sophia's list of his attributes, as well as reviewing the manner in which she listed them, he found he could not think of any reason for Jane Elliot to want to marry him that did not involve his being a duke of England.

Which was flatly preposterous.

"I am not old," Edenham said a bit stiffly.

"Darling," Sophia said with a smile, "hardly that. I did not say you were old, only that you are far older than Miss Elliot. She is, I would guess, not much above twenty. And you are, what? Forty?"

"Don't be absurd. I'm just thirty-eight. Not even two months ago. I'm hardly doddering."

He said it grimly. He could hear it in his voice. Sophia would shred him to bits if he did not pull his composure about him and display a more vigorous resolve.

Thirty-eight was *not* old. He was in his utter and complete prime.

"And naturally, you look marvelous," she said. "It is only that, to be precise, my observation was that you are quite a bit older than she, not that you were in any way not absolute perfection as a man. Which you are. And which you know perfectly well, Edenham. I can't think but that it's an abysmal habit to fall into, that of arranging for people to compliment you at every turn."

Edenham barked out a laugh. "You, of all people, say that to me?"

It was a well-known fact, indeed nearly a legend, that Sophia Dalby arranged for compliments, and gifts, nearly upon the hour. Not that anyone faulted her for it. She was very good at it and quite deserving of whatever she received. She made certain everyone knew that as well.

"I'm the ideal person to say, darling. I understand the urge so completely." Sophia smiled unrepentantly at him, which resulted in his smiling at her in return. She was very like that, the sort of woman one simply had to laugh with. It was why he enjoyed her friendship so fully. Most people, and nearly all women, found him somewhat distant, or at least he was treated distantly, if not fearfully. Sophia did not fear him, far from it. She tweaked his beard mercilessly.

Which, now that he put it to mind, might be exactly what she was doing now regarding his intention to marry Jane Elliot.

Of course. That was it. That made more sense than a lovely girl from a slightly backward nation not being perfectly and immediately available to him, especially as he *was* a duke, not in spite of it.

Damn Sophia for having a bit of fun when he was at his most earnest.

"Sophia, I will compliment you upon the hour for the remainder of the Season if you can aid me in arranging things with Miss Elliot."

"Darling, I do think you do me an injustice. I'm quite certain I could induce you to compliment me upon the hour without the addition of Miss Elliot to the mix. But, seriously, Edenham, you are jesting, certainly. Why should you want to marry Miss Elliot?"

She was forcing him to put it into words. It would sound ludicrous when spoken, he knew that. Yet, if that was the price for her aid, and he knew without hesitation that if Sophia lent her weight to the issue all would fall in his favor, he would pay it promptly. She was, after all, on quite intimate terms with Molly Hyde and clearly had a warm connection with the Elliots of America. Who else was there to consider when arranging a marriage? He'd done it three times. He knew how the game played out, the important players in the arrangement and how a competent marriage contract was constructed. If anyone in Society knew how to make a marriage, it was he. He had more than enough experience at it, hadn't he?

"She's exquisitely beautiful," he said simply.

"She is that," Sophia said, smiling pleasantly. "You have noticed, I must assume, that there are other beautiful women in Town?"

"Not as beautiful as she," he said. It was nothing but the truth. He had seen her, had felt the bolt of love pierce his heart, and determined to marry her within the instant. One look at her remarkable face, and he had known it.

"She is exquisite," Sophia agreed. "You find it no hindrance that she is an American?"

"As the Duke of Hyde is her uncle, I do not," Edenham said, which was nothing but the truth and perfectly reasonable. "She is well connected to a fine family. I should think that Hyde would be most pleased by a connection to my house."

"Oh, certainly," Sophia said, nodding, waving her fan over the lower portion of her face. Hiding a smile? There was certainly nothing amusing about their exchange. One was never quite certain of such things when dealing with Sophia; she had a most exaggerated sense of the humorous. Usually, he found that a delightful quality. It was most displaced now, however. "Yet what of her brothers, whom you've just met, and her parents, whom you have not? Do you think they will be equally as desirous of a connection to a duke of the realm?"

"I should think so. They appeared to be reasonable, capable men, if a bit churlish on occasion."

"And what would that occasion have been, Edenham?" Sophia prompted, her fan moving more vigorously. Damned annoying bit of female nonsense. Women and their blasted fans. Attempt a serious discussion with one and their fans positively leapt about their persons. "Darling?" Sophia prompted.

Edenham thought back to his first sight of Jane Elliot, to his fall into bottomless love, to his determination to marry her, and then to his actual meeting of her. And her brothers. He had not been paying much attention to the conversation, truth be told, his heart and mind settling so quickly upon Jane that he could not hold to the conversation for more than the few bits and pieces that wormed their way past the chorus in his head that sang of his love for her and his urgent need to marry her.

There had, he was entirely certain, been a great deal of controversy over whether Jane should either stay or go. That was one of the points he wanted Sophia to manage, though it looked nearly managed now. There had also been, he was somewhat certain, a slight discomfort, perhaps even something so strong as distrust, emanating from the Elliot men and aimed fairly precisely at . . . at . . . why, at Edenham and Ruan, now that he puzzled it out.

"I shan't believe it," Edenham said abruptly, the penny having dropped. "They are firmly and not unhappily related to Hyde!"

"Are they? You assume very much, I think," Sophia said, finally moving that damned fan away from her face. "They are American, darling. Very firmly and not unhappily American."

"When she marries me, she shall be as British as I am. As British as you are, Sophia. You were from America once. You are British now."

Sophia looked up at him, her dark eyes sparkling

speculatively. "That is likely your greatest problem, Edenham. Have you not considered that the Elliots may not want their sister to become an English duchess? As to that, why do you believe Miss Elliot would?"

"Because," he sputtered, "she, that is, a woman, all women want to be . . ."

"A duchess?" Sophia finished for him. "I think you might find that Miss Elliot views such matters through a different lens. In your pursuit of her, I do encourage you to try and remember that. This will likely not be a courtship that resembles the pattern of your previous wives. It will call for some creativity and flexibility on your part. Are you up to it, Edenham? Can you adapt your skills enough to catch what I am certain will be a very elusive Miss Jane Elliot?"

"Most assuredly," he said. Was there any doubt of it? None. He was a duke of England. He could manage an inexperienced miss from the former colony of New York. And her surly brothers, as well. Though perhaps not all three at once. Not without Sophia to aid him. "You will aid me?"

"Darling Edenham, I will do everything in my power to see that you achieve everything you deserve."

He was immediately comforted. And then, upon turning the words over again in his mind, was slightly more suspicious than comforted. Still, Sophia was his best avenue to marriage with Jane Elliot, and if the avenue was dark and bumpy, he was prepared for a few jolts. He was a duke. What was the worst that could happen?

Five

GEORGE Prestwick, as had very many people in the room, witnessed the Duke of Edenham fall into a near stupor upon meeting Miss Elliot. As she was a remarkably beautiful woman, it was no mystery as to why Edenham had plunged. The question was, what was Edenham going to do about it?

That question had been answered almost before being fully born. Edenham had nearly dragged Sophia Dalby into a corner and engaged her in a most earnest conversation for nearly a quarter hour.

The current question, and one did have to keep one's wits fully about one as things were progressing at a furious rate, so furious in fact that no one had found the opportunity to place a single wager yet, was whether Edenham would marry Jane Elliot or simply seduce her. As her brothers were very much present, and not the sort of brothers one discounted in questions of this sort, the situation became very much more complicated.

It was as George was considering with whom to place

his wager and what precisely his wager should be, marriage or seduction, that the Lords Raithby and Penrith joined him.

Raithby, whom George knew only very slightly, was the Earl of Quinton's heir, and one of those horse-mad gentlemen who rarely left the paddocks for the reception rooms of Mayfair. That he was in attendance at the wedding feast of Hyde's heir was likely due entirely to the fact that the Earl of Quinton was in attendance today as well. Quinton, quite a quiet man, though of a forceful nature, was not likely to have looked kindly on his son missing something as important as that.

Raithby was lean, tallish, possessed of blue eyes and dark hair, and sported a scar upon his left cheekbone that was reputedly the mark of a quirt delivered by some fellow in a horse race. Raithby had been riding a bay mare. Raithby had won. This anecdote, illustrating both Raithby's prowess and devotion to the race, as well as the origin of the scar, was well known and oft repeated in White's coffee room. George had heard it three times in a single month, in fact.

The Marquis of Penrith, slightly older than Raithby, was often to be found in the reception rooms of Mayfair, and in their ballrooms and dining rooms and stair halls as well. Penrith was golden-haired and green-eyed and quite a convivial fellow. He was so convivial, in fact, that most of the mamas of the ton would not allow their daughters anywhere near him. It was something about his voice, apparently, some husky vibration that very nearly sent proper young girls running into his arms, where they were quickly removed of their propriety. Or that was the rumor. George was not so well connected that he had witnessed anything of that sort for himself. But he shouldn't mind to, as long as the girl wasn't his sister. As Penelope had been married just this morning, he found he could relax in ways he hadn't done for a full year, if not more. Penelope, as much as he loved her, was . . . challenging.

"Prestwick," Raithby said by way of greeting.

"Raithby. Penrith," George responded.

Penrith looked at him curiously. Raithby looked around the room for a bit, cleared his throat, looked him in the eye, and then dropped his gaze in the vicinity of his second waistcoat button. Most unusual.

"About your sister," Raithby said softly, "good bit of work today, isn't it?"

"It is," George said, though he did wonder at the phrasing of Raithby's congratulatory message.

Raithby nodded, still staring at George's waistcoat button.

"Hyde must be delighted," Penrith said. "Though I have not seen him. Have you, Prestwick?"

"At the ceremony, but not since," George said. "I do think him a most private man, rather like Iveston in that, I daresay."

"Yes, one seldom sees Hyde out beyond his responsibilities in the Lords and the occasional evening spent at White's," Penrith said, "and even then, one seldom hears him speak much. Lord Iveston appears very like him."

Raithby simply nodded at all of this, his gaze having moved up a single button. George supposed that, eventually, Raithby might work his way up to staring him in the eyes.

"According to Pen," George said, "Lord Iveston has very much to say, if he is interested enough in the conversation. I must say that I've found him to be a very agreeable sort."

"And speaking of sisters," Raithby said, which was not precisely what they had been speaking of, but as George and Penrith were also agreeable, they waited politely for Raithby to drag the conversation onto the topic of sisters, "I . . . you may remember that I do not have one."

"I'm so sorry," George said, grinning. "Is it that you want one? I suppose the earl may still have it in him to provide you with one, Raithby. Buck up. Hope springs eternal and all that."

Penrith chuckled and ducked his head, his green eyes studying Raithby's face. "A bit late in the game to start wishing for a sister now, isn't it? I should think that, if you want a woman about, there are more pleasant ways to see it done."

Raithby did not look at all pleased, but neither did he look offended. He simply took an audible breath and said, "Yes, mock me if it pleases you, but I'm about trying to do something damned near noble and I should like at least a bit of tolerance shown me. I have no sister. I have none of the worries that go with having one, which, if you will remember our conversation that singular evening at Lady Lanreath's soiree, you impressed upon me with scalding morbidity."

"Oh, not that," George said. "Please tell me I was not morbid. I do think I must have managed it better than that."

"You did not," Penrith said airily, "though no one blames you in the slightest, Prestwick, as it was your sister and Iveston's cravat was a scandal."

"And again we are back to sisters, of which I have none, yet I find that I have acquired a certain sensitivity that is not at all welcome, let me assure you, and feel I must take the part of a brother, or at least a man, in the current situation," Raithby said in a rush of pent-up emotion.

"The current situation?" George prodded.

"That of Edenham and Miss Elliot, I should think," Penrith offered.

Raithby nodded, his blue eyes gleaming. "I think there must be something afoot and while it does not affect me in the slightest degree, I do think that, well, perhaps we men ought to hold together and blunt things if at all possible. She is a sister, after all."

"Miss Elliot," George prompted.

"Precisely," Raithby said.

"And you propose . . . ?" George inquired, his eyebrows raised.

"That we inform her brothers of what's happening. Or going to happen," Raithby said.

"Or might not happen at all," George said.

"Don't be absurd, Prestwick," Penrith said on a snort of derision. "Edenham has been chatting up Sophia Dalby for nearly half an hour. They're practically at the baptism of their first child."

"Not Sophia and Edenham's," George said.

"I know you're not blind, Prestwick," Penrith said. "'Tis Miss Elliot who has Edenham jumping out of his cravat."

"Not cravats again," George moaned softly.

"You would prefer boots?" Penrith said, laughing.

"Ridiculous," Raithby muttered. "It is not at all necessary to remove one's boots. Do be serious, I beg you. This is awkward enough. I feel very much like a boy telling tales to the headmaster."

"And what tale are you telling?" George asked.

Raithby sighed slightly and nodded, as if giving himself permission to speak. "I don't know what, if anything, is afoot regarding Edenham and Miss Elliot."

"Oh, there is something," Penrith cut in.

"Be that as it may," Raithby continued, "I happened to overhear a conversation between Lady Louisa, Lady Amelia, and Lady Iveston." George groaned. Raithby did not allow it to deter him. "They also noticed a certain interest upon Edenham's part and are even now discussing it with Miss Elliot." And at this, the three men craned their necks this way and that, searching the room for the four women in question. They found them near the far doorway leading from the blue reception room to the stair hall, heads huddled together like cats over a squirming mouse. "Given that they are all recently married, and that they all, according to Penrith, sought out aid in acquiring husbands from Sophia Dalby"—and here Penrith shrugged and nodded, not one whit apologetically—"I did think that it might be something of a service to Miss Elliot's brothers to inform them of the situation."

The three men stood silently, staring at each other at that. They then looked in unison at the women, still chewing on the proverbial mouse, then stared at each other again, then turned to look at the Elliot men, who stood talking pleasantly, if a bit reservedly, with Lord Cranleigh and Lord George, his younger brother.

"And what shall we tell them?" George Prestwick asked, not precisely eager to beard those two American lions in their den. He had met them over dinner and found them to be . . . *guarded*, would be the innocuous word for it. Penelope, not known for choosing innocuous words when plain ones would serve better, had pronounced them politely hostile, as if there could be such a thing. And yet, it was apt. "That the Duke of Edenham is talking to Lady Dalby? To arms! To arms!" George said, only half in sarcasm.

"You know them," Raithby said. "You are related by marriage now. I should think that, given what you said about sisters and the worry they cause a man, something should be said."

"But what is there to say?" George said. Truly, what? Miss Elliot was leaving on the earliest tide, and leaving on the arm of one of her brothers, as well. What harm could befall her in a day or two?

"The women seem to have more than enough to say," Penrith said. "That indicates something, doesn't it?"

It did. And not a bit of it anything good.

❧

"BUT of course I noticed him," Jane said. "How could I not? He was staring at me without any subtlety whatsoever. It can't have done me a bit of good, I assure you. My brothers still have their heels dug in about my staying on. Lady Dalby has done her part, and she will win out in the end, I am certain, but the duke did not help matters in the slightest."

Penelope stood with her head cocked and was staring at Jane as if she were an oddity. Amelia had her mouth agape, her blue eyes wide in disbelief, before snapping her mouth shut with a sharp click. Louisa looked at her with one red eyebrow raised in near derision, or perhaps full derision, it was so difficult to tell with Louisa, and her arms crossed over her chest.

"But, you can't tell me you don't know what it means, Jane," Penelope said. "The Duke of Edenham, the most handsome and enticing Duke of Edenham, has been captivated by you! Are you not intrigued?"

"No," Jane said, crossing her own arms over her chest.

"Flattered?" Amelia asked.

"Hardly," Jane answered.

"Bewildered?" Louisa asked with a tight smile.

Jane tilted her head at the implied insult and smiled sweetly at Louisa. "Not at all. This isn't the first time I've endured this response in a man, though perhaps you cannot say the same, Louisa?"

Amelia chuckled and then, looking at Louisa innocently, pressed her lips together against a smile. "I do think you may be missing the point, Jane," Amelia said.

"Have I? I thought the point was that I remain in London so that I may enjoy a proper adventure."

"You could have a proper adventure, I'm sure," Louisa said slowly, "or you could, if you dared, enjoy an adventure properly."

"What a clever twisting of words," Jane answered. "I do wonder if they mean anything."

"Jane," Penelope said, stepping forward, her dark eyes earnestly beseeching, "do ignore Louisa if you can. She simply hasn't been herself since first Amelia and now I have married into the Blakesley family. She did think, I presume, to have complete freedom to dominate the men as the only young wife amongst them."

"No, Penelope, I'm afraid that's not quite it," Amelia said, lifting a hand to check the condition of her blond hair. It was perfection, as usual. "Louisa has always been this way, this *is* herself, you see. It is only that she hates to see a good man squandered, as do I. You could make good use of Edenham, Jane. He's quite good friends with Sophia, he knows all about women—"

"After three wives, he should," Louisa cut in.

"And," Amelia said briskly, "he could, with very little effort, make your stay in Town deliciously memorable."

"Deliciously?" Penelope asked. "But that's what Sophia always says. I shouldn't think that Jane would want anything *delicious* to occur with Edenham, do you?"

"I don't know," Amelia said, looking at Jane. "Do you?"

"What would be the point?" Jane said, not at all sure she understood the ramifications of the word *delicious*, but entirely suspicious since Sophia was somehow involved, and everyone on two continents, perhaps three if one included France, knew what *that* meant. "Sophia has already arranged with Jed and Joel for me to stay. Nearly. What do I need with the Duke of Edenham?"

Penelope actually gasped at that and looked a bit flushed about the throat.

Well, but really, what did she want with an Englishman, and a duke at that? That made it all inexpressibly worse. But they wouldn't see it that way, not these English girls, and there was no point in trying to explain it to them as they wouldn't understand it anyway. Particularly Louisa. Jane was developing the firm impression that Louisa, if not actually stupid, was perilously close.

Louisa, proving Jane's point neatly, said, "Jane, you are missing the point entirely. I'm beginning to think you are doing it to annoy us all. The *point* is that the Duke of Edenham is, for the *moment*"—which was said was such malicious pleasure that Jane squared her shoulders and faced Louisa with a degree of determination that was just shy of a dockyard brawl—"and surely it *must* pass, intrigued by you. A clever girl would make use of his temporary interest to her advantage. You want to stay in London. You want, you claim, to have an adventure of the sort you cannot have in New York. Who better to open every door for you than a duke? Molly will be so eager to aid this struggling infatuation of his that she will allow you nearly boundless freedom. Hyde will comply, as is his habit when dealing with his wife. Sophia, who is set to aid you and who is on warm terms with Edenham, will surely do all in her power to see that you get exactly what you want. How can your brothers stand against such an onslaught? Now, do you want your adventure or don't you? If using Edenham and his fleeting curiosity about you, which likely springs from your . . . interesting manner, which I am certain is quite ordinary in New York, but not at *all* the thing here, can gain you exactly what you *say* you want, why not use him? The man is a duke. He can withstand a bit of rough handling, though I can't see it coming to that, can you? How *do* you manage men in New York, Jane? But perhaps you lack the experience to manage Edenham whilst you use him to good effect. Is that the source of your refusal? A simple case of . . . cowardice?"

Amelia gasped under her breath. Penelope simply stared in openmouthed shock at Louisa. Jane, however, did none of that. Jane smiled, a full, bright smile, and said, "Afraid of an English duke? Louisa, you are a wit. I had no idea. And here I thought you somewhat dull, but that is only when compared to the women of New York. How you fare here I have no idea. Differing standards and all that."

And now Penelope turned to gape at Jane, her dark eyes going quite wide. Not quite what she had in mind for her wedding breakfast, Jane was quite certain.

"But of course I shall use the Duke of Edenham as best I may. He has delivered himself up to me so tidily, hasn't he?" Jane continued. "I should have thought a duke, especially one with three previous wives to his credit, would have more subtlety, but then, I am discovering that what the British say about themselves and what is actually true can be violently different. Having never been out of England, I fully comprehend that you would not be able to see the distinction. You shall simply have to take my word for it, won't you?"

Louisa smiled crookedly, one eyebrow cocked quite high upon her snowy complexion. "Indeed, I shall, Jane. But, how do you plan to use Edenham to your advantage? Perhaps we could help you with that."

"I don't need help when dealing with a man, Louisa. I know precisely what I'm doing," Jane said, lifting her chin and looking at each of her cousins' wives in turn, beginning and ending with Louisa. It seemed appropriate, and necessary. "I shall make good use of Edenham. Watch and see."

"Oh, I shall, Jane," Louisa said. "I can't wait. When do you plan to begin it?"

"Now ought to do nicely," Jane said, and without another word she strode through the crowd and away from them.

The three women remained silent for a few moments, staring after Jane.

"She's going to find herself married to him, if she's not careful," Penelope said, shaking her dark head ruefully.

"Of course she is," Amelia said, looking at Louisa with a very saucy expression. "I don't think being careful is going to make one bit of difference."

"Of course it shan't," Louisa said, smiling brightly. "I wonder how long it will take her to realize that?"

"But," Penelope said, moving so that she faced Louisa fully, "you mean to say that you *want* Jane to marry Edenham? Why? And why did you provoke her so? You insulted her at every turn, Louisa."

"But of course I did," Louisa answered. "How else was I to get her moving in the right direction?"

"Edenham's direction," Penelope clarified.

"Naturally," Louisa said. "Do you think it wise to waste a perfectly lovely duke?"

"Of course not!" Penelope said.

"Here he was, practically begging to be snatched up by Jane and what was she going to do? Just leave him there, that's what," Louisa said. "Horrible misuse of a duke. I can't imagine what Jane was thinking, to disregard him so."

"Perhaps she was thinking that she didn't want to marry a duke?" Amelia said, starting to laugh.

Penelope pondered that for a moment and then said solemnly, "No, that can't be it. That's not possible, is it? I shouldn't think so."

"Even if she was thinking that," Louisa said, sharing a look with Amelia, "Edenham will convince her otherwise very shortly, I am fully convinced. Poor Jane really does not know a thing about Englishmen, does she?" And here Louisa began to laugh along with Amelia. Penelope did not laugh.

"But why, Louisa? Why should you want to see Jane married to Edenham?" Penelope asked.

"Let that charming girl leave England? I should say not," Louisa answered. "I simply adore her. She's the first woman I've yet to meet who can give as good as she gets. Do you know how rare that is? Why, besides Eleanor, I can't think of a one. No, let Edenham do all the work of convincing her. We shall have the pleasure of her company for years and years."

"Molly would certainly love that," Amelia said.

"She certainly will," Louisa said. "And I shall be the one credited for arranging it. Don't think I haven't thought of that."

And this time, even Penelope laughed.

Six

But of course, Jane had no idea what she was going to do with the Duke of Edenham. Whatever did one do with a duke? And it wasn't as if she were all *that* experienced at managing men. She had enjoyed some minor victories in New York, the sort of victories her brothers would never hear of, which would be very minor indeed.

Still, there had been Reliance Jones, a most handsome blue-eyed man of nineteen to her sixteen. He had walked with her along Wall Street twice, once at sunset, which did nearly shout *romance*, didn't it? He'd climbed abroad a sloop bound for Madras and she'd not seen him since. But he had taken her hand in his as he said good-bye.

So, one touch of the hand.

Then there had been Nathaniel Talbott, sawyer's apprentice. He'd been twenty-two and possessed of dimples. She'd been seventeen and possessed of curiosity. Nathaniel had kissed her, once and most chastely, near a pile of wood shavings. She still thought of him every time she saw kindling. Or at least more often than not.

One kiss to her credit.

And she'd never forget Ezekiel Biddle. He'd kindly volunteered to help with the haying on their Harlem Lane farm and, being a kindly, eager man, had also volunteered, without being asked, to spend the next two days following her around the farm and sitting at their table, eating cake. It was on dusk of the second day that he put his arm around her shoulder, letting his hand slip to the top swell of her left breast. She'd let it linger there for a full three seconds before doing the right thing, namely, removing his hand and telling him that he should not expect any more cake.

One brief caress of the breast.

Not a bad list for a girl of good family, was it? She had nothing of which to be ashamed, certainly not a lack of experience. She knew what men and women did together, and she knew what they did not do, until they were properly married, that is. She would certainly be able to hold her own with Edenham. He was a duke, widowed, with children. And he was old. He probably wasn't even interested in the coils of the flesh any longer.

However, he had looked at her long and hard, and most inappropriately. That should be enough of a start to get what she wanted of him. Though what she wanted was still a bit of a mystery to her. She was certain of only one thing: proving to Louisa that she was just as proficient at men as any British girl. She anticipated no difficulty at all, even if she was unclear about how one went about proving that to a woman who had been ruined.

Oh, no, she had not forgotten that bit about Louisa's history. Not very honorable of her, was it? But then Louisa did not strike Jane as being much concerned with what was honorable. Still, it seemed entirely logical to her, given her initial meeting with Edenham, that he would do what he seemed unable to stop doing, namely, staring at her as if she were the moon and he were a wolf, and that just a bit more of that would convince Louisa of whatever it was that Louisa wanted convincing of.

Simple.

As to the wolf and the moon metaphor, Jane found it entirely comforting. While normally thinking of a man as a wolf was not at all comforting, being the moon was highly so. The wolf could never reach the moon, could he? And so it would be between Jane and Edenham. She had not a moment's doubt of it. All she had to do now was find him and allow him the opportunity to proceed. Oh, and it would help if Jed and Joel weren't around to muddy things up. Nothing new there. Still, it was a large gathering and they likely wouldn't see a thing.

All she had to do was find Edenham.

❦

"ALL we have to do is find Edenham," Penrith said to Raithby and George Prestwick. "If you're uncertain of your welcome with the Elliots, what more is needed than to warn Edenham of the plot?"

"Warn him of the plot?" George said. "He's the *author* of the plot. You're the one who pointed out that he was talking to Sophia Dalby. You're the one who foretold disaster as the result of that."

"It depends upon how one defines *disaster*, I should think," Raithby said.

"I should say *marriage* would sum it up nicely," Penrith said, nodding like a sage.

"And I'm not afraid of the Elliots," George continued, ignoring their asides. "It is only that I do not know them well and also that I am still unconvinced that anything dire is afoot. People are talking to each other. What is that? People are *always* talking to each other."

"Your perspective has changed, hasn't it?" Raithby said. "It's not your sister on the block now, is it? I thought you had more chivalry in you, Prestwick, I truly did."

George stared hard at Raithby, who merely stared back at him. He then stared at Penrith, who was not looking at him at all, but gazing about the room.

"Bad news," Penrith said softly, looking across the blue-walled room. "Miss Elliot has left the Blakesley wives and is going it alone. She appears to be looking for someone. You don't suppose it might be . . . no, things can't be galloping along at that alarming rate, can they?"

"Of course they can," George said, and a bit morosely, too.

Penelope had found herself betrothed to Iveston hardly more than twenty-four hours after meeting the man. Or that's what they both swore to. There were some who argued that they must have been meeting quietly for weeks before that, but George knew that wasn't true. Practically. One did want to believe one's sister, after all. Which did force his thoughts upon the Elliots with depressing precision. Which did, sad to say, nearly compel him to do what service he could for Jedidiah and Joel Elliot, the same service he wished someone had done for him.

"I think she's found him," Penrith said. "I can't see Sophia, but Edenham is just to the left of the secretaire, talking to . . . talking to . . ." Penrith lifted his chin and angled his shoulders against the crowd, bumping just slightly into the Duke of Calbourne. Penrith grew still and then turned to face them.

"Talking to whom?" Raithby asked.

"Lady Paignton," Penrith answered.

"Ah," George said on a sigh of relief. "Well then, that's solved."

Lady Paignton was a widow. But that was not the best or truest description of her. Bernadette, the dowager Countess Paignton, was the most ruthlessly seductive woman of her generation. She could, and did, snatch up and enjoy any man she wanted, drinking of him until sated and then dropping him as quickly as she had picked him up. Strange to say, but the men never complained of being dropped. The rumor was that she simply exhausted them, wrung them dry, as the saying went.

If Lady Paignton snatched up Edenham, what could poor, innocent Miss Elliot do about it?

Nothing, that's what.

"Whatever Edenham had expected of Jane Elliot, with Sophia Dalby's aid, is now dealt a mortal blow by Bernadette Paignton," Raithby said. "A simple, effortless solution."

"The best sort of solution to any dilemma," George said.

Penrith looked at both of them as if they were raving, his cat-green eyes narrowed in disbelief. "I can see that neither one of you knows Sophia Dalby at all. I did not mean to imply that Lady Paignton has solved the issue, merely that she has complicated it. Do you know nothing of Bernadette's involvement with Edenham's sister? Or her dead husband, as to that."

George, as was to be expected, felt a flush of shame for not knowing the gossip regarding Lady Paignton and Lady Richard, Edenham's sister. One was expected, when one went out in Society, to know all the pertinent details. And they were all pertinent details. He really should not have spent so much time up at school; all that learning was doing nothing to help him now. Casting a glance at Raithby, he saw the same look of bafflement.

"You really should leave the paddock and come to Town more, Raithby," Penrith said. Quite true, and took the searchlight most effectively off his own ignorance. "Bernadette tangled with Lord Richard, quite under Lady Richard's nose, setting it quite completely out of joint, dropped him cold, and not a six month later the man was dead."

"The connection being that she tangled with him and killed him, or that she dropped him and killed him?"

Raithby said with a wry smile, looking not one bit abashed.

"How do you know this, Penrith?" George asked on the heels of Raithby's remark. "You weren't in Town then, were you?" As Penrith was most assuredly younger than George, and as it could not have happened all that recently, he was most eager to find a reason for his ignorance. Call it an excuse, if necessary.

"Lady Penrith told me," Penrith said simply.

"Your mother told you?" George asked.

"A most reliable source, you will admit," Penrith said.

"Most assuredly," George replied. And he meant it. It was a profound advantage to have a well-informed mother. Damned inconvenient that his had died before she could be made proper use of. He was certain she hadn't meant to die inconveniently, but that didn't take the inconvenience out of it, did it?

"But why then should Lady Paignton so boldly approach Edenham? Surely she can't expect . . . well, I don't know what she expects," Raithby said, staring across the room at her, and at Edenham, who was looking down at her with chilly civility.

"I do," Penrith said, his eyes glittering.

"I thought you were involved with Lady Paignton," Raithby said. "Someone mentioned something of the sort."

"Not involved, merely dallied with," Penrith replied. "And I'm more than convinced that Bernadette was dallying with me in one or two salons in Town to some purpose."

"Of course to some purpose," George said. "The purpose is obvious."

"Please allow that I might have some experience and know of what I speak," Penrith said somewhat sarcastically. "Lady Paignton is not above making good use of a man"—and here Raithby burst forth with an abrupt laugh—"to achieve her own ends"—which resulted in a chuckle from George. Penrith soldiered on. "I was dallied with, I tell you, and not in any way pleasurable to me. Oh, very well," Penrith said with a crooked smile, "perhaps slightly pleasurable. But she had something else in mind entirely, I promise you."

"What does it matter what's in a woman's mind as long as her body is well occupied?" Raithby asked, rhetorically, clearly.

"It depends very much upon the woman," the Duke of Calbourne said, inserting himself into what was a private conversation without a hint of shame. Calbourne was not known for showing shame, or that was the rumor of him.

Calbourne, always the tallest man in any crowd, was extremely jovial and widowed. The rumor was that he was jovial *because* he was widowed. His marriage had not been a love match, but then no one had expected it to be. His wife had produced an heir and then died after a respectable period, certainly nothing like Edenham's three wives, who had died abruptly upon giving birth. No, Calbourne's wife had died in a quite ordinary way and no one had thought a thing about it, again, nothing remotely like Edenham.

It was one of the reasons that George felt a faint twinge of guilt about Miss Elliot possibly getting involved, even slightly, with the Duke of Edenham. He did have the most lurid reputation where women were concerned. Miss Elliot was now family and George truly did feel she ought to be protected somehow. Though he supposed her brothers could do that better than he could, and would likely enjoy it more, but, being American, they might not fully understand how a duke must be treated. In all, it was not impossible that they might do more harm than good.

This protecting women business was deucedly complicated.

"Calbourne," Penrith said, clearly not a bit disturbed that their privacy had been breached. Again, dukes did expect, and get, special consideration.

Poor Miss Elliot.

"Penrith," Calbourne said with a slightly mocking smile.

"You heard," Penrith said.

"And saw," Calbourne answered.

"You are acquainted with Lady Paignton?" Penrith asked, his green eyes sharp. Penrith clearly had some plan and was not above involving the Duke of Calbourne in it.

Calbourne smiled, without a trace of mockery this time. "Not as well as I'd like."

"Tonight might be the ideal opportunity for you," Penrith said, smiling in return.

"And *immediately* might be even more ideal?" Calbourne asked.

"Isn't *immediately* always to be preferred when deepening a friendship with a beautiful, available woman?" Penrith countered.

"I am to snatch up Lady Paignton, in a manner of speaking, so that Edenham may, without distraction, indulge in his fascination for Miss Elliot?"

"Well put," Raithby said.

"Yet not entirely accurate," George said. He had never before spoken more than a greeting to Calbourne; this conversation was probably not the best way to strengthen their acquaintance. Ah, well, perhaps Miss Elliot was worth the effort. "We are endeavoring to save Miss Elliot from Edenham."

"Save Miss Elliot from Edenham doing what?" Calbourne asked.

"We aren't entirely certain," George said.

"It's only that she appears in need of saving. Somehow," Raithby said, mumbling the last bit and staring at the floor beneath his feet, looking utterly befuddled.

A woman could do that to a man, and usually did. They seemed to enjoy it, too.

"Women specialize in that look. It's seldom true," Calbourne said.

He was likely correct. As Calbourne was approximately ten years older than they, he did have experience on his side.

"Then do it for Edenham," Penrith said. "He can't want Bernadette at his elbow, ever, but most especially when he's all eyes for Miss Elliot."

Calbourne looked across the room, quite easily done as he was so very tall, and studied Lady Paignton. Or at least George presumed he was studying Lady Paignton. Why study anyone else?

"And what would I get out of it?" Calbourne asked softly.

"Lady Paignton?" Penrith answered.

Calbourne smirked and, with a nod, walked across the room. The crowd parted for him.

Dukes.

∞

DUKES.

Jane had all she could do to keep from shaking her head and clucking her tongue. She had found Edenham easily enough. Edenham had been standing alone against the center window of the blue reception room, Sophia Dalby smiling brightly at her as they passed each other in the crowd. It was very difficult not to form the conclusion that Sophia was encouraging her to simply approach Edenham and do whatever she wanted with him. What, she couldn't imagine.

That was the problem. She truly couldn't imagine what it would take to convince Louisa that she had Edenham in the palm of her hand. She really should have got that all straightened out before charging over here. This was no way to conduct a challenge of the power of her allure.

And then, which was most annoying, before she could reach Edenham, another woman had very nearly snuggled up next to him. She was a most beautiful woman in a completely rampantly sexual way.

Oh, yes. Jane understood rampant sexuality when she saw it. New York was quite a busy port city, after all.

Undeterred, Jane did not even slow her steps. She was going to continue to weave her spell all over Edenham, somehow, and Louisa was going to see it, and then she was going to go about her business. How long could it take? Ten minutes? Hardly more. She wasn't going to allow another woman being present to interfere with her objective.

Edenham, fulfilling every expectation of him, lit up like a bonfire upon seeing her. Jane did everything in her power not to smirk. He made the introductions. Lady Rampant's name was actually Lady Paignton.

She *was* beautiful. Dark-haired and green-eyed, lushly formed, her features exotically arranged, Bernadette, Lady Paignton, was the sort of woman men simply fawned over. Yet, the Duke of Edenham was not fawning. It was mildly gratifying. Actually, it was very gratifying. Perhaps that would be enough to satisfy Louisa?

Jane risked a glance to where she had left Louisa, Amelia, and Penelope.

Louisa was not there. Neither was Penelope. Amelia was, but she was not alone. No, Amelia was with Cranleigh, Lord Ruan, Jed, and Joel.

Of course. It just couldn't be simple, could it?

Amelia caught her eye and cast a look at her of equal parts helplessness and frustration. Jane was equally frustrated, but helpless? Not even slightly. Jed and Joel gave every appearance of being completely engaged by something Lord Ruan was saying. Jane made her move in that sliver of unpredictable opportunity.

"And is your husband here with you, Lady Paignton?" Jane asked just as Lady Rampant leaned close enough to

Edenham to brush her ample breast against his sleeve. A woman that generously proportioned ought to wear a more closely fitted bodice. One would think her modiste would have more skill.

"My husband isn't anywhere, Miss Elliot," Lady Paignton answered. "Unless being in the graveyard is somewhere."

Ah, a widow. That explained the loose bodice. Whatever did her husband die of? Excess?

"My condolences, Lady Paignton," Jane replied. "But of course your husband is most definitely somewhere. In heaven, I should think. Wouldn't you?"

Lady Paignton smiled at Jane in a completely unfriendly manner and said, "I should be very much surprised, Miss Elliot, and he, I am quite certain, would be more surprised still."

Edenham, staring at her as was his most peculiar habit, said softly, "Lord Paignton was a man given to excess, Miss Elliot."

Excess? Jane believed it readily.

"I was not aware that the Lord God was intimidated by a little excess," Jane said. "If that is so, what hope for we New Yorkers?"

"Can there be such a thing as a *little* excess?" Lady Paignton asked, one sable eyebrow raised provocatively.

"It depends upon where you live," Jane briskly replied. "Anyone living above Canal Street is quite adept at measured excess. Anyone living below Canal Street is flagrantly excessive nearly as a birthright."

Edenham chuckled, his brown eyes shining. He was charmed by her; she could read it clearly in him. Could Louisa? Where *was* Louisa? Smiling, Edenham asked, "But of course, now it must be revealed, Miss Elliot. Do you live above or below Canal Street?"

"It is as clear as the full moon," Lady Paignton cut in, moving her breasts about once again. It was most crass of her, not that she seemed to care about being crass, not with that bodice. "Miss Elliot most assuredly lives above the line. There is nothing remotely flagrant about her."

Jane chuckled, eyeing Edenham appreciatively, sharing the joke with him alone, and said, "Then London standards are clearly less particular than New York's, Lady Paignton, for I most assuredly live below Canal Street. Indeed, far below. I am most reliably excessive, which I am certain the duke must remember."

"In what way?" Lady Paignton asked, her tone a bit more contained this time. She would not want to appear strident in front of a duke, would she? Of course not.

"In being," Edenham answered, still smiling, "excessively plain, Lady Paignton. Or so Miss Elliot reports. For myself, I cannot see it. Not at all."

Edenham's gaze grew so focused and so solemn that Jane wanted to squirm. She did not squirm, but that was only because she was certain Lady Paignton would notice.

"But, your grace," Jane said, "have you not considered that I may be an excessive liar? Perhaps I do not live below Canal Street. How would you ever know?"

"A liar? I won't believe it," Edenham answered.

"Men never want to believe a woman is a liar," Lady Paignton said. "It is so civilized of them, and so convenient."

Jane felt a flush of camaraderie with Lady Paignton, which she quickly suppressed. She was not in this part of the room to impress Lady Paignton. As to that, there was little point in impressing Edenham if Louisa were not available to witness it.

Little point? What absurdity. There was *no* point. She certainly did not care if she impressed Edenham or not.

He was rather simple to impress though, wasn't he? Why, Reliance Jones had required more effort. She had expected, if she had thought to expect anything, which she most definitely had not, something different of a duke. What, she couldn't have said, but something, certainly. What was a duke, after all? A man of excessive privilege and unnatural arrogance and an absurd degree of power.

And in Edenham's case, a duke also happened to be excessively, unnaturally, and absurdly handsome.

He was remarkably attractive; she was honest enough to admit that much. He was tall, lean, broad across the shoulders, and quite, quite fit looking in general. Didn't dukes sit upon their large, pampered arses all day barking orders at their lessers? And didn't they consider everyone to be lesser?

Of course they did, but perhaps more so when they grew older, growing into it, as it were.

Edenham was not young, but neither was he old. At least not horribly old. But it was likely to occur at any moment, his tumble into decrepitude. Though, looking at him again, struck unwillingly by the look of stark appreciation in his eyes, perhaps not at *any* moment. Not in the next day or two, which was all that could possibly matter to her.

Day or two? What was she thinking? The next *hour* or two would be much more than sufficient to prove whatever it was she had to prove to Louisa, and Jane was only allowing for that much time because Louisa was so strangely absent. It was not unlikely that she had made herself scarce on purpose, just to hamper Jane's efforts with Edenham. That seemed entirely like her.

As to that, as Louisa was not in the room to witness Edenham's fall into . . . whatever he was supposed to fall into, and as Jane was not at all certain what he had to do to prove to Louisa that Jane was fully as capable as any English girl at . . . doing whatever it was that English girls did to Englishmen . . .

Jane snorted under her breath in derision. At herself.

She'd been neatly tricked into making a fool of herself to satisfy some base urge in Louisa. And to answer to her own pride as an American. As a proud American, she did not need to answer to anyone, and she had nothing to prove, and certainly not to Louisa, whom she did not even like, even though she barely knew her. Some people were very simple to evaluate and Louisa was one of them.

"I think you have misjudged me, Lady Paignton," Edenham said, breaking into Jane's thoughts. "I am well disposed to believe that some women would lie, about anything and for the most base of purposes. It is only that I do not believe Miss Elliot capable of that. You, however, are clearly capable of anything."

Jane very nearly gasped. How inexpressibly rude! How completely *ducal* of him!

Lady Paignton looked properly stricken, which was precisely how he had intended her to feel. Yes, she was a questionable woman with questionable taste in fashion, but no one deserved such a setdown, particularly in public.

"And you, sir," Jane said stiffly, eyeing Edenham like the rabid wolf he clearly was, "have proven equally so. You have fulfilled every expectation I had regarding a duke of England, which is surely no compliment to you. Lady Paignton, I should very much like to introduce you to my brothers. May I?" And before Lady Paignton could say a word, for indeed she looked quite without words, Jane linked her arm in hers and pulled her across the room to where she had last seen Jed and Joel. Louisa and her pointless challenges be damned.

Seven

"I'LL be damned," Calbourne said softly.

Edenham turned slightly to look at Calbourne over his shoulder. Calbourne was taller, but not by much. Calbourne was younger, but not by much. Calbourne was a duke without a wife, but with an heir. In that, they were much alike.

"I'm in no position to argue it," Edenham replied, turning his gaze back to Miss Elliot, who was now lost in the crowd of Hyde House. With a sigh, he turned to face Calbourne.

"I thought to save the situation for you," Calbourne said, a very amused smile on his face, which was not at all complimentary to Edenham, Edenham was entirely certain, "and instead I find that the little American has taken things into her own charming hands and saved Lady Paignton, from you, I suppose. She has no idea who Lady Paignton is to you, that's obvious."

"The little American's name is Miss Jane Elliot," Edenham said without too much chilliness. It was never good policy to display any sort of upset in front of the Duke of Calbourne. He was precisely the sort of man to make endless sport of such a situation, not that Edenham held that against any man. A man found his pleasures where he could, after all. "As to what she knows, as she's just arrived in London—I should say she knows nothing whatsoever."

"Which could play entirely to your advantage, Edenham, if you have any inclination to engage in a mild form of entertainment with her."

"I intend nothing of the sort," Edenham said, beckoning a servant with look, taking a glass of champagne from the proffered silver tray and taking a casual sip.

"She's related to Hyde, is she not?" Calbourne asked, looking about the room, possibly for Miss Elliot. "Of course she is. She'd hardly be invited if not. Some connection through Molly, I should think."

"Molly's niece, though there is also some connection to Lady Dalby, though of what sort I am not yet certain."

Upon the words, Calbourne turned rather desperate around the eyes. "Lady Dalby? Run, Edenham. Do not dally with this slip of a girl. If Sophia Dalby is backing her, you'll be married by tomorrow noon."

There was a thought. He'd asked Sophia's aid in helping him, but perhaps her efforts would bear richer fruit if she offered to help Miss Elliot. Of course, given Miss Elliot's current state of mind, what would Jane want but to be helped onto the first ship for America?

How had it gone so wrong, so quickly? He was not an immodest man, and certainly having three dead wives to his credit did put some women off, the younger, less experienced ones mainly. Of experienced women, he nearly had his pick. Jane Elliot was not experienced, at least not discernibly. Jane Elliot was also not afraid of him; that much was more than obvious.

"Do you think so?" Edenham asked softly, casting a gaze at Calbourne. "I think Miss Elliot would be very much surprised by that turn of events. She doesn't appear to hold me in high regard."

"True," Calbourne agreed with entirely too much enthusiasm. "Still, I've seen what Sophia can do. It's chilling. Are you certain she's not tangled up with Miss Elliot somehow?"

"Completely," Edenham said briskly. He could speak with complete authority on that subject, after all.

"What is it that set her off? Miss Elliot, I mean?"

"Something to do with Lady Paignton, I should think," Edenham said.

He had been brusque with Bernadette, not undeservedly, yet Miss Elliot had reacted violently. Perhaps something to do with her American upbringing? And there had been that odd remark she'd made about him behaving very much like a duke, which had sounded fully like an insult when it was no such thing, and worse, which did lend a great deal of weight to Sophia's opinion of the situation.

This might be more difficult than he had initially thought. Americans did have that habit, didn't they, of being unaccountably difficult. Pity he had fallen in love with her at first sight. She did seem a rare bit of trouble, even for a woman. Still, he was decided. He was going to marry her. How to get her to agree to it became the question.

"She'll feel a proper fool when she learns the true situation there," Calbourne said, looking blasted pleased about Jane, the future Duchess of Edenham, looking a fool, proper or otherwise. "I wonder if I should tell her? Of course, as Lady Paignton is at her side, that might prove awkward."

"I should think so," Edenham said. It was quite obvious where this was going. One needed only to wait for all the appropriate words to have been uttered and then each of them could get on about their business. The business in this situation being women, clearly.

"Perhaps the thing to do is for me to somehow remove Lady Paignton from her side, then you may explain, in however much detail you choose, the particulars to Miss Elliot. That should take care of that, don't you think?"

"And all for me?" Edenham deadpanned.

Calbourne grinned. "Not at all, Edenham. *One* for you, and one for me."

❧

STRANGELY, Lady Paignton did not seem at all grateful at having been rescued from the Duke of Edenham's arrogant cruelty. These English were a strange race. Jane had very nearly dragged her away from him, which defied logic, didn't it? Certainly no woman should endure being spoken to in those terms and in that particular tone. Perhaps she was simply too stupid to know any better.

Jane looked at her, taking in the lustrous hair and exotic green eyes. The heavy bosom. The fat circlet of rubies around her throat, which wasn't in the peak of taste for a wedding breakfast, was it? More theater than wedding, at least by New York standards, and as New York standards had served thousands of people quite adequately so far, she saw no reason to adjust her perspective. Particularly with Edenham's cold words still ringing in her ears, and with Lady Paignton's sultry and nearly sullen expression staring her down.

Some people simply refused to be helped.

Jane did what any charitable woman would do; she helped anyway.

Lady Paignton did brighten when they joined Jed and Joel, who were talking with Cranleigh and Amelia. Upon the conclusion of the introductions, indeed, during them, Jed and Joel brightened considerably themselves.

Lady Paignton seemed to thrive on the response. But who wouldn't?

"We were just discussing the situation along the Barbary Coast, Lady Paignton," Cranleigh said. "American ships suffer greatly there."

"Have you suffered, Captain Elliot?" Lady Paignton asked Jed, her green eyes smoldering with an emotion that was not compassion.

Jed was a stern sort of man, which was hardly surprising as he'd been a solemn sort of child. Dutiful, serious, observant, contemplative: all in all, a rather perfect son and older brother. He'd never bullied, rarely lost his temper, and, in fact, rarely put a foot wrong. He was not going to do so now, with Lady Paignton, no matter how rampant her seductive allure. Jane had no doubt of that whatsoever.

"When one American crew suffers, we all suffer," Jed replied, his blue eyes slightly glacial as he stared down at her. The American situation in the Barbary states was not something Jed was prepared to be teased about. Whatever chance of a flirtation with Jed that Lady Paignton might have had, she had just lost it.

Lady Paignton seemed just a bit startled by his response, or perhaps his lack of one. What sort of woman needed to seduce every man she met? The poor woman must have some wound she was desperate to hide. That, or she was simply a tart with the moral fiber of a cat.

"Every nation requires a navy," Cranleigh said, ignoring Lady Paignton almost completely. It was obvious that Amelia expected nothing less of him. Good man. "You have yet to manage one."

"A navy requires money, Cranleigh," Jed said. "America has very little of that."

"And without open shipping lanes, we'll never acquire any," Joel said.

Joel was a completely different sort of brother. He was and always had been the brother she laughed with, played with, shared secrets with. But when she was in trouble, when she was confused and needed guidance, she poured out her heart to Jed.

She was very blessed in her brothers, and when the occasion arose, she even confided that to them. Being who they were, they never even teased her about being overly sentimental.

"I can't imagine how a country may be run without a navy," Amelia remarked.

"For good reason, Lady Amelia," Jed said.

"But however did you win your war against us without a navy?" Lady Paignton asked, which was not very diplomatic of her at all. Jane was certain Lady Paignton was known for other things entirely.

"With some difficulty, by all reports," Jane said, hoping to end the conversation. Talking of wars, and of being such recent enemies, could not possibly be a good topic of conversation. "Lady Amelia, is it true that you should like to visit New York, or is that simply a malicious rumor started by my brother?"

Amelia smiled and said, "It is most assuredly true. I should very much like to see New York."

"And Paris," Cranleigh said, his light blue eyes glinting with humor. "And Alexandria, and Athens, and Cadiz, and Nantucket. My wife, you see, wishes to see the world."

"And having married into a family with a shipping connection," Amelia said on the heels of Cranleigh's remark, "I see no reason why my wishes should not be indulged."

"Perhaps because of the very many wars going on?" Lady Paignton asked.

"As there is no war now, I think we must jump whilst we can," Amelia said, her blue eyes slightly cool as she faced Lady Paignton.

It was becoming perfectly clear to Jane that Lady Paignton had some sort of reputation that was not truly to her credit. Perhaps the Duke of Edenham might have had some small reason for his rebuke of her. Still, he had been entirely too sharp, no matter the offense. Dukes, she did not suppose, were noted for displaying restraint. Why should they bother?

"Lady Amelia is possessed of a great supply of daring,

as you can plainly see," Cranleigh said, his pride in her evident.

Having met Cranleigh when he came to New York years ago, Jane would not have thought it in him to put even an emotion such as pride on display. Amelia had worked some great change in him, or else Jane had been wrong about Cranleigh from the start. No, that was hardly likely. She was hardly ever wrong; in fact, she couldn't remember a time when she had been wrong, but one did like to err on the side of caution and humility.

"It certainly is plain to see," Lady Paignton said slowly, her eyes glittering speculatively. "Any woman who would compile a list and interview potential husbands is most assuredly daring. Though, I did think that Sophia Dalby was the inspiration behind that bold plan. Was I wrong?"

A list of husbands? Jane hadn't heard a word about that. It was impossible not to be intrigued by the notion. Once one got over the shock, it seemed quite a logical way of going about it, and clearly bore such rich fruit. Amelia had got Cranleigh, hadn't she? And, knowing Cranleigh, that had not been a simple task.

Jane looked at Amelia with new eyes. Blond, blue-eyed, and very pretty, the daughter of the Duke of Aldreth, whom Jane had met but briefly, Amelia had looked and certainly behaved with soft-spoken civility. In no fashion did she look or behave like a woman who would compile a list and interview men as possible husbands.

Just what sort of questions would comprise that type of interview anyway?

That Sophia Dalby was intimately involved in the venture was the least shocking aspect of it. It sounded just like her. Perhaps Lady Paignton was involved in some intrigue with Sophia? That might explain her odd behavior tonight. Certainly *some* explanation must be found to explain it.

"Lady Dalby," Amelia said, laying a hand on Cranleigh's

arm, calming him, one assumed, "has quite a remarkable way of arranging things, especially for her friends."

Given the way Amelia delivered the statement, Jane was left to conclude that Lady Paignton was no friend of Sophia's. Which, of course, resulted in her wondering why. She was not so naïve as to believe that all the lords and ladies of the realm were intimates and confidantes; there were two opposing political parties in England, sometimes violently opposing. America was just the same, perhaps a legacy of her nation's time as a colony, and certainly the two sides did not often mingle socially, at least not unless there was something to be gained. She didn't suppose that changed no matter which continent one lived upon.

"She certainly does," Lady Paignton said, turning her gaze upon Jane. Jane stiffened slightly in preparation for an assault of the social sort. "And are you a friend of Lady Dalby's, Miss Elliot? I do think you must be."

"Must I be? Why?" Jane said, lifting her chin.

"Why, because of the Duke of Edenham, certainly," Lady Paignton said, smiling. "He gives every appearance of having been influenced by her, wouldn't you say?"

"Not knowing the duke, I would *not* say," Jane said firmly. Joel smiled and ducked his head, his lips compressed. Jed simply stared at Lady Paignton, his look not at all friendly.

"Well, I know the duke," said a very tall man, joining them, inserting himself between Jane and Lady Paignton. Jane did not at all enjoy having an obstacle between herself and her opponent, for that is what Lady Paignton certainly was. Why, she could not have guessed, but whys hardly mattered in a fight. "I can say without hesitation that there is no conspiracy between Edenham and Sophia. What nonsense. What could Sophia arrange that Edenham could not quite simply arrange for himself?"

The men would not meet her gaze. The women stared

at her pointedly, especially Amelia. Jane found it all very confusing, all except the bit about Lady Paignton attacking her. There was nothing confusing about that. If she didn't find Edenham so irritating, she'd regret helping Lady Paignton at all. Which did make it seem as if she'd snapped at Edenham for his own sake and had not been trying to help Lady Rampant at all, which was something she was not prepared to consider. Though there might have been some truth to it. Some.

"May I present the Duke of Calbourne?" Cranleigh said with a very peculiar smile upon his face.

Jane was becoming more aware by the minute that there were very many currents running through this throng and that she was in danger of being swept along with them to smash against a hidden shoal if she weren't careful. It was to her credit that she was always careful, or at least when it was convenient. As she was being introduced to *another* duke, she was fairly confident that it wasn't currently convenient. How many dukes did England boast? She had been under the impression that they were somewhat rare. As rare as pigeons, by her reckoning.

The introductions were made, Lady Paignton reacted predictably, Calbourne reacted to her reaction predictably, and Jane was suddenly certain that this was going to be the longest day of her life. Did the English aristocracy do nothing but eat rich food, drink costly wine, and practice seduction upon each other?

Of course they did. They made war upon the world. A respite from their bedroom battles, certainly. One did enjoy some variety in life, after all.

Jane could not repress the sardonic smile that tugged at her mouth as a result of her thoughts. Indeed, why should she? If they could spend their lives upon one seduction after another, could she not spend a few hours mocking them? Not at all what her mother had hoped for this visit, but there was nothing Jane could do about that. She saw what she saw. She was not going to lie to herself about it. No, nor to her mother either. She could hardly wait to tell her, in fact.

"You are amused, Miss Elliot?" Calbourne asked her, his own grin pleasant enough. Calbourne was a very attractive man. He was quite tall, which was the first and firmest impression of him, but he had pleasant features which were nicely arranged, dark brown hair cut short, and hazel eyes.

"I am merely entertained, your grace," she answered with a mild smile. "I think that must be the point of such an affair as this, to entertain one's guests, to enjoy the companionship of one's equals, and are we not all equal in the eyes of God? Or is that strictly an American concept? Perhaps the English are of the belief that they have no equals?"

Cranleigh stared at her perhaps more seriously than he had yet done, his ice blue eyes glacially still. Jed's expression also altered, his gray blue eyes warning her, but warning her of what? Caution pulled at her hem, but she was tired of caution. She was tired of being on her best, most guarded behavior while those surrounding her reveled in their misbehavior, their arrogance, their silent scream of superiority.

"I had never before considered that celebrations could be divided along the lines of nation and race, Miss Elliot," Calbourne replied, looking not the least bit offended. He did give every appearance of being good-natured, but of course, she'd only just met him. "Have you noted differences between the English and the American? Could you list them?"

"Ah, and yet another list," Lady Paignton murmured, looking at Jane, her exotic eyes stripped of all seduction for once. "Beware of list-making, Miss Elliot. Such a practice can lead you into places and situations which are not at all entertaining."

"I've never found the making of lists to be entertaining

in the slightest degree," Amelia said, smiling gently at Jane. "As I have become somewhat infamous for my one attempt at lists, I must encourage you to resist the questionable temptation of compiling one. Tedious business, I assure you."

"As I was on your list, Lady Amelia," Calbourne said lightly, breaking the tension fully, "I can attest that being on a list can be a tedious business as well. The competition nearly broke me."

"And being off the list nearly broke me," Cranleigh said, smiling fractionally at Calbourne, but casting one more speculative glance at Jane while he did so.

"A man who can sail around the Horn and not be broken by it, broken by a list?" Joel said. "That's quite a list."

"Dangerous things, lists," Amelia said lightly, looking again at Jane.

"I am convinced," Jane said. "No lists. I must admit that I never before felt any urge at all to make one, yet with all these warnings, I find I am intrigued. I should not have thought there could be so much danger, so much power in such a simple thing as a list. Yet I shall not make one for the very simple reason that I can think of nothing to list."

"Perhaps you could list the dukes you've met," Eleanor said, sliding into their number like a ferret, positioning herself between Cranleigh and Amelia, which caused Cranleigh to look down at her and grin abruptly. Cranleigh had gone quite soft since marrying, that much was obvious. He hadn't been at all softhearted when he'd visited them in New York. "You've met two now, haven't you, Jane? That's quite a lot, you know."

"Is it?" Jane responded. "What will you think then when I report that I have now met three? I do think that England has many more dukes than is reported. Perhaps in an effort to increase their value, the total number has been underestimated?"

Eleanor grinned, her dark blue eyes shining. She was

a pretty girl, quite slender, not at all grown into herself, but blessed with dark red hair and dark blue eyes and a riot of freckles. She seemed quite like a sprite, all joy and curiosity and frank good humor. She might have been the nicest person Jane had yet to meet in London, excluding Aunt Molly, naturally, but including the rest of the family, Louisa most specifically. Louisa and Eleanor might be sisters, but the only thing they had in common as far as Jane could see was their general coloring. Their natures could not have been more disparate, which was such a fortunate thing for Eleanor.

"But who? Your uncle, Hyde, of course, and now the Duke of Calbourne, but don't tell me," Eleanor said in a rush, reaching out to clasp Jane by the arm, "not the Duke of Edenham. Oh, Jane," she said, clearly coming to the correct conclusion without any help from Jane, "you are fortunate. He hardly goes out, quite a recluse on most days, I'm told."

"You're told?" Cranleigh said in mock severity. "Who told you that? What part of your education does that cover, I wonder?"

"Social congress, Lord Cranleigh," Eleanor replied promptly, not at all diminished by his censorship. "I can't think why anyone should need protection from knowing what everyone else knows. I shouldn't like to be thought ignorant, would you?"

"I shouldn't mind being found ignorant about anything concerning Edenham. His business is surely his own, Lady Eleanor," Cranleigh said. Amelia was Eleanor's cousin and therefore Eleanor became Cranleigh's responsibility by marriage; he looked on in some amusement. It was rather strange to see Cranleigh being so protective. He hadn't displayed that trait at all while in New York, but of course, what was there to protect against in New York? They didn't have dukes popping up around every corner.

"I certainly don't care about his business in the slightest;

it is his personal life which captures the imagination, doesn't it?" Eleanor said, staring boldly into Cranleigh's eyes.

"She's grown up quite a bit this Season, hasn't she?" Cranleigh said to Amelia.

"It's all the marriages," Amelia answered. "Quite hard to keep the lid on after that flurry of activity."

"I'm most observant," Eleanor said. "And curious."

Joel chuckled and shook his head ruefully. He had done that quite a lot with Jane when she was of the same age as Eleanor was now. Men clearly had an innate distaste for curious, observant women. If a man had something to conceal, it made perfect sense. But if he did not, why be upset about it? Certainly men valued a keen and discerning eye in other men. Jane had always found the disparity mildly irritating. Seeing it displayed now, aimed at Eleanor, she found it fully equally so. Of all the viewpoints that British and American men could have shared, *this* was the one they agreed upon?

"I find I must admit to sharing the same traits, Lady Eleanor," Lady Paignton said, looking politely at Eleanor before turning her gaze toward Calbourne, whereupon she did not look nearly as polite. Calbourne didn't seem to mind in the slightest. "Curiosity and then observation. And then satisfaction, I should think."

"And if not satisfaction?" Calbourne asked.

"Then more curiosity, a bit of careful observation, perhaps experimentation," Lady Paignton said in a low voice. She might have been said to purr. Certainly Jane was inclined to say it, though she did hope Eleanor would not. Eleanor was still a girl. Did the English think nothing of exposing their children to a blatant seduction? "As satisfaction is the goal, I do think all attempts should be made to achieve it. I can't think I'm alone in that. Would you agree, Lady Eleanor?"

The absolute gall to drag an innocent girl into such a thinly veiled and highly debauched discussion!

"Lady Paignton," Eleanor said, her dark red brows quirked at an angle, giving her quite a piquant expression, "you are precisely as described. I am so pleased to have finally met you, matching rumor to fact. Having said that, I must agree with you. Curiosity, observation, satisfaction. Yes, fully. You have satisfied me completely. I do thank you."

"So you do have something in common," Jane said quickly. She had no confidence that Lady Paignton would not react poorly to being prodded by a young woman just sixteen. "How nice for you, Lady Paignton. I really don't know you, of course, but I must think that you are a unique woman. It must be so comforting to find another woman with whom you can share the most tender bond of affiliation, even if she is far younger than you."

Lady Paignton smiled, looking almost as if she meant it, and said, "I have three sisters, Miss Elliot, two of them younger. I am not as unique as you may think."

"Not unique?" Calbourne said. "But of course you are."

"As we are slightly less than mere acquaintances," Lady Paignton answered, looking at him provocatively, "I think you might need to observe me carefully before making such an important decision."

Calbourne grinned and, a pronounced gleam in his eyes, said, "I make all my most important decisions as quickly as possible. I avoid tedium by doing so. I highly recommend the practice, Lady Paignton."

"I find myself wondering," Jane said, "how was it that the Duke of Calbourne found his way upon your list, Amelia, particularly as the Earl of Cranleigh did not? What qualifications were required?"

Amelia did not look at all disposed to answer her, having gone quite pink in the cheeks. Eleanor, however, was more than happy to supply the answer.

"It was a list of dukes and heirs apparent, Jane," Eleanor said, looking at Calbourne with a mostly innocent expression. "So, naturally, poor Cranleigh didn't have a chance. Or that's what everyone thought."

"Not everyone," Amelia said with what was nearly a wicked gleam in her blue eyes. Amelia? Wicked? It wasn't possible, was it?

"A list of dukes," Jane said. "Unmarried, I assume?"

Silence met her question and tried to bury it. She would not allow it. Jed and Joel were watching her with looks of both amusement and wariness. As well they should. She was in a temper, a mild one, a controllable one, but a temper nonetheless.

After two hours in the company of the elite of English society, she knew without question that they were, nearly to a man, utterly worthless and without a single redeeming impulse. And they thought to look down upon her? A preposterous bit of arrogance that she would battle in any way she could, without getting thrown out of the country, that is. She truly did not want to cause her mother or her aunt any actual discomfort, but a mild contretemps at, what must be admitted was a family gathering, how much trouble would that cause?

"And you were . . . rejected somehow, your grace?" Jane continued. "For what cause? I find I am most curious. Of course, I have made my own observations, but, barring experimentation, I should like satisfaction as much as the next man."

Into *that* shocked silence, Jane was forced to ask again, "Amelia? What was your objection to the Duke of Calbourne?"

Amelia, to Jane's surprise, looked at Calbourne, shrugged mildly, smiled, and said, "I found him to be entirely too tall, Jane. Easily observable. It took only a moment to remove him from consideration, though I am certain that any other woman, indeed most women, would likely find him perfectly ideal."

"How terribly gracious of you, Lady Amelia," Calbourne

responded, bowing slightly in her direction. Cranleigh did not look especially amused by the conversation, but he held his tongue.

Jane was not about to be diverted. She had dispatched Calbourne, in the mildest manner imaginable, and now she was going to see what she could do regarding Edenham. The Duke of Edenham had surely been on Amelia's list. He was a duke and he was available, wasn't he? It was the perfect opportunity to discover what Amelia had found wrong with him, and to have it out right in front of Lady Paignton added a certain mild justice to it all. It had not escaped Jane's notice that Lady Paignton did not seem at all upset by anything Edenham had said or done to her, but that hardly seemed the point. Jane had formed her own list of offenses and merely wanted confirmation of her astuteness.

A list! She *had* formed one, though quite by accident and without any effort at all. Some things just presented themselves, complete, and one took it as one found it. *It* being Edenham and his general offensiveness.

"Was the Duke of Edenham on your list, Amelia?" Jane asked with as much sweetness of tone as she could manage. Apparently it was not much, since both Jed and Joel swung their heads sharply to look at her, their eyes showing mild alarm. How two ships' captains could be so skittish in a drawing room skirmish, she had no idea. 'Twas a wonder they didn't heave to at the first sign of an unidentified ship. "I should think he must have been. Whatever did you find wrong with him?"

"You find him a pleasing man, Miss Elliot?" Calbourne said with the barest trace of a smirk.

"Not at all," Jane replied, smiling pleasantly. "I only thought to compare Amelia's list of deficiencies with my own. An American perspective versus an English one, much as you suggested earlier, your grace. A comparison study. Educational, don't you think?"

"Jane, I—" Amelia began, looking quite discomfited. Jane was sorry for that, truly, but she hadn't compiled the list of dukes to begin with, had she? She was merely discussing it. Surely there was hardly any fault in that.

"I was discounted, Miss Elliot," said the Duke of Edenham from directly behind her, "for the usual reason, plus a few more."

Jane sighed under her breath, closed her eyes briefly in resolve, and turned to face Edenham. He stood, tall and imposing, looking quite as handsome as he had before, and stared down into her eyes. He did not look angry. Not precisely. He looked . . . intense. Focused. A bit solemn. Understandable, certainly.

"And the usual reason is, your grace?" she asked, matching his solemnity, or trying to.

Really, these sorts of situations always happened to her. She always seemed to be the one caught out for doing far less than everyone else did in complete anonymity. She obviously was in dire need of practice at skirting the edge of propriety. Ezekiel Biddle had even implied as much when he'd brushed his hand along the edge of her breast. Of course, she'd known even then his hadn't been an impartial observation; still, she had considered it and decided there might be something to that.

"You haven't heard, Miss Elliot?" Edenham asked softly in reply, stepping slightly closer to her. Jane was, in the next moment, very glad to have her two strapping brothers to hand.

"Obviously not," she answered, staring directly into his eyes, though she did have to crane her neck a bit to do so. He was very tall, perhaps even taller than Jed.

"The rigors of sharing my bed, Miss Elliot," Edenham said in a low tone, his voice edged with either humor or malice, she could not be at all certain at that moment. "There are some women who do not think they can possibly survive it."

Brown? Had she thought his eyes were brown? They were not. They were hazel green, and just now, quite fully green.

Important? It must be, mustn't it? It seemed dreadfully important. So important, in fact, that she was certain she would never forget it, or him, or how he was looking at her just now.

She wasn't going to put his bewitching eyes on the list, however.

Eight

"But nothing so formal as a list, I hope," Sophia Dalby said to Molly, the Duchess of Hyde.

"Nearly so," Molly answered.

They stood in the wide doorway between the blue reception room and the stair hall, each quite large and beautifully appointed, as befitted a duke's residence in Town. As Molly enjoyed entertaining and as Hyde did not, the house was equally large enough for both their preferences; Molly gave large parties whenever she could find sufficient cause, and Hyde had more than enough space in which to sequester himself. It was upon such practical solutions that the best marriages endured.

"A woman of determination, which is precisely as I remember her," Sophia said softly, watching the interplay between Jane Elliot, her brothers, and Edenham. Of course, the others played their part, Calbourne and Eleanor, Amelia, and even Bernadette Paignton, but it was Jane who stood at the heart of it all, even without the beacon fire of her beauty. "You showed her sons the letter, I assume."

Molly snorted, and not delicately. "I had to. They would never have believed it otherwise. Sally wants Jane to have her chance, without brotherly interference, and she wants her to have it here. I should so love to have Jane near me. The only daughter between the two of us, Sophia. All those boys. Mine and hers, and this one girl. I wanted to give her a proper Season; Sally wanted her to have a proper chance at a courtship, something which has been nearly impossible for her in New York. Jedidiah and Joel have wrought terror in any man over sixteen and under sixty."

"Sally would be content to have her only daughter find a husband in England?"

Molly chuckled and surveyed the room, her steely blue eyes noting who had come to honor Iveston's marriage and who had not. "Of course not. She only wants Jane to have her chance. A London Season, simply that. The attention of lively men. The chance to experience a flirtation with someone she will never see again." Molly looked up at Sophia and smiled. "Sally has forgotten, if she ever knew, how devastating English men can be."

"She did marry an American, after all," Sophia said. "I suppose each woman must be allowed her preference, as well as her prejudice, regarding men. But what precisely did Sally instruct in this not-quite-list?"

"The boys, mine included, are to leave her alone," Molly said. "You should have seen Cranleigh's face. I thought he would pop a button on his waistcoat."

"I can well imagine," Sophia said, moving her ivory-bladed fan near her throat.

It did not escape her notice that Lord Ruan was watching her from the far corner of the blue reception room. His gaze was both solemn and intimate, a most engaging combination. It was such a shame that he had dallied and delayed, missing his opportunity with her. She was not the sort of woman who waited about for a man. Hardly that. Yet the look on his face spoke nothing of lethargy or disinterest.

On the contrary. What had he been about then, when he should have been calling on her? Something of which she would heartily disapprove, she was certain of that.

"What may she be allowed, if I may ask?" Sophia said.

Molly grinned, and it lit up her heart-shaped face like a dozen candles. "Anything that will result in a proper English husband, Sophia. That's my interpretation of the letter."

Sophia smiled and said, "Yes, a generous interpretation, I would hazard. You have someone in mind?"

Molly looked at Sophia, her blue eyes glittering in suppressed humor. "It would hardly matter if I did, Sophia, for you would pair her with whomever you thought best. Now, whom do you think best for my cherished niece? If I'm going to betray my sister in this smallest of things, I do think it should be for a worthwhile man. It will make it all much easier to smooth over, I'm quite certain."

"But, darling, I've only just met her," Sophia said.

"And when has that ever stopped you? I have only respect for you, Sophia. You've got three of my sons married in a single Season. How much easier to manage an inexperienced girl from the colonies?"

"The *former* colonies, darling," Sophia said softly, looking at Jane and Edenham, and at the two American men who were struggling to give their mother what she'd asked of them. They stood rigidly, lips compressed, chins tucked down into their cravats, a bit like turtles just before they snapped. An apt comparison, surely. "They are a nation now, and New York is no backwater. I do think Jane must know her own mind."

"And when, I repeat, has that ever stopped you? Come now, Sophia, you know perfectly well that if you set your mind to it, couples fall together like dice. Won't you push Jane in the right direction, as you've done for my three sons and, indeed, your own daughter? You can't claim you haven't got a bit of experience at it. And they're all so blissful about it, aren't they? Surely Jane will be as well. 'Tis only a question of pairing her off with the right man.''

Sophia smiled and said pleasantly, "If you insist, Molly, though I can't think what you'll tell Sally.''

"I think telling her she's to be a grandmother should settle it all nicely," Molly said, running a fingertip over her lapis cameo necklace, looking well pleased with herself.

"Yes, that should certainly settle things," Sophia said, looking across the room at Edenham staring down at Jane.

∽≈∾

JED and Joel must have settled well and truly into English ways for they said nothing to the Duke of Edenham's entirely ribald remark. Jane couldn't begin to think why. Edenham had said *bed* and *rigors* and of course the implications were obvious. Still, no one said a word, or leapt to her aid, or even indulged in so simple a thing as shoving Edenham a foot or two out of the way.

It was up to her then, clearly. She'd managed Ezekiel Biddle; she'd manage Edenham. And in doing so, she'd probably edge dangerously close to impropriety. She did hope so. It couldn't hurt her here. No one *knew* her here.

"I can't think what you must mean, your grace," she said pleasantly. "Why don't you explain it to me?"

Upon which Cranleigh took both Amelia and Eleanor firmly by the elbow and led them halfway across the room with barely a mumbled excuse to soothe the way; the Duke of Calbourne effortlessly escorted Lady Paignton out of the room altogether, Lady Paignton wearing a very amused look upon her face; Jed and Joel, acting like she knew not what, stood by grimly and said not a word. But they did not look at all pleased, which of course they shouldn't.

Edenham smiled, not at all warmly or even cordially, and, ignoring her brothers completely, which did charm her just the slightest bit, said, "I have no wish to offend you by being indelicate, but I feel someone must tell you what everyone in Town says about me. It is awkward that I must be the one to tell it, but I would not have you wander about in ignorance."

"I should hate that," she said. "I do not enjoy being ignorant. About anything. Please, teach me everything you think I should know, your grace."

She risked a glance at her brothers. They were not rushing her out of the room nor were they shoving Edenham out into the street. Well then. Not as tough as they talked, clearly. She could have had such fun, for years now, if she'd only known. Stupid of her not to have tested the waters before now. That's what came of caution: nothing. A carefully lived life with nothing beyond a touch, a kiss, and a slight caress to show for it.

As to that, Edenham was a handsome man, he gave every appearance of being smitten by her, she was far from home, and her brothers were being very cooperative for once. Either that or slipshod. It all depended upon one's perspective. She was more than inclined to think that things were lining up quite nicely, almost a perfect list of ideal ingredients.

Why not?

Why not have a little fun with the Duke of Edenham? It wouldn't hurt him to be toyed with a bit, to be baited just a little. He was a duke. He ought to be able to take it soundly, no whimpering, no pleas for mercy. At least that's what he would think, arrogant old thing. And it wouldn't harm her in the least. She'd dabble and be gone. Though she would feel better about it all if Jed and Joel disappeared somewhere for the rest of the afternoon. The look on their faces was not at all comforting. Jane had no qualms about baiting Edenham, who was he but an Englishman, but she did have serious qualms about pushing her brothers beyond that which they could bear. She was nearly positive she was a half inch over the line even now.

"Darling Miss Elliot," Sophia Dalby said, approaching

them gracefully. The woman moved like a swan. At best, Jane thought she might move as well as a duck, which was not at all the same. "I did think to introduce you to Lady Richard, the duke's sister, but as you are so deeply engaged in conversation, allow me to present the Captains Elliot to her, stealing them away for just a few moments. She's a lovely woman, but rather reserved," Sophia said to the boys, tucking her hands through their arms, leading them effortlessly away, instructing them as she did so. "You will be gentle with her? But of course you will." And with that, Jed and Joel were removed. They did not look happy about it, but they were removed.

Remarkable woman. Her timing was breathtakingly flawless. One could but wonder what she'd accomplish with a cannon and a full load of shot.

"That was well timed," Edenham said pleasantly. It was slightly disconcerting to have him echoing her own thoughts in nearly the same instant. She did not like to think that they could possibly share something so intimate as a thought. "Now, as you are so eager for instruction, what may I teach you, Miss Elliot, which you don't already know?"

Was there an insult in there? She suspected there might be. It was a slightly different proposition, baiting Edenham with no witnesses to hand, but she was not going to let caution hobble her now. What could happen? They were in a crowded room, and certainly he must have some sort of reputation to maintain, even if she did not.

And she did not. She was free, at least free enough for a minor scuffle. Taking a breath, her resolve renewed, Jane plunged. It really was shocking how she'd come to rely on Jed and Joel to keep everything in check. What sort of girl had she become? Not the sort of girl she wanted to be.

"I believe you were eager to describe the rigors of your bed, your grace," she said, which was so daring of her, wasn't it? "Is it very tall or very narrow or very lumpy? Are you plagued with bedbugs? I can't think why a duke should choose to endure such rigors in his own bed. Perhaps you are of a monastic bent? I should not have guessed it by the cut of your coat."

Edenham held himself very still, and then he smiled a bit coolly. Oh, had she yanked his tail? Poor duke.

"I see that the Puritan strain of Massachusetts has bled into New York," he said. "I should not have thought it, not from every report I hear of New York. Perhaps you are the exception? A bit lacking in sophistication and education, Miss Elliot? I suppose that may be forgiven you as sophistication and education may be acquired if some effort is applied in their pursuit."

He paused to smile coldly. She did not smile in return, yet neither did she flinch.

He continued, "But, no, I was not speaking of the physical dimensions or condition of my bed. I was referring to *myself*, Miss Elliot. I have had three wives share my bed and as a direct result of our coupling, they have each died in the full flush of their youth and beauty. It is this to which the gossipmongers hiss, certain that no woman can survive *the rigors of my bed*."

Oh, he was enjoying this far too much. Not an hour ago he'd been nearly drooling with limpid fascination over her and now he'd flip-flopped to this, this insult of her town, her character, her intelligence, and then culminating in this blatantly inappropriate comment about his sexual . . . what? He killed women with his cock?

Hardly.

She *was* from New York; she knew what a man could and could not do with his cock. She'd even heard the word *cock* used for the first time at the precocious age of four and repeated it endlessly until her mother had rinsed out her mouth with apple vinegar. But Father had laughed. She remembered very well that he had laughed. No, she was not afraid of either the word or the thing, and wasn't that a handy bit of ammunition now?

Jane did not lower her gaze in maidenly confusion, a response he surely wanted, nor did she blush, nor did she stammer. He looked a bit confused by *that*. Perfect.

"I fear I have offended you," he said.

"Fear not," she said dismissively.

"You are grown quiet."

"I'm . . . observing."

Jane ran her gaze down Edenham's body, over his snowy cravat, his pale green waistcoat, his tightly fitted breeches. Her gaze lingered there. She knew what that could do to a man, if he found the woman appealing. Joel had told her once when he was in his cups, just back from his maiden voyage as captain of an Elliot ship. A quick trip up the coast, he had not been gone much longer than a month, but still, his maiden voyage. He'd drunk to his own success, and then drunk again. And he burbled out that charming bit about the male anatomy.

Did Edenham find her appealing?

Jane held her gaze down low.

Why, he certainly did.

Smiling and lifting her eyes to his, she said, "If I understand you correctly, your grace, you have somehow gained the reputation of killing your wives by, as you so charmingly put it, the rigors of your bed. Let us speak yet more plainly. What you mean is by the vigor of your cock. I see nothing to cause alarm. I don't know what the standards are in London, but in New York you would not cause a ripple of concern. Perhaps you should move."

Nine

"I'VE never seen him so moved," Katherine, Lady Richard, said, "and I've seen him bury three wives and both our parents." She did not mention the burial of her husband, the profligate Lord Richard. What would have been the point?

"Miss Elliot seems to have quite a strong effect upon him," Sophia said. "A good thing, surely. Your brother, such a lovely man, can turn to melancholy quite without effort, wouldn't you agree? I do think Miss Elliot is bringing him out. They do seem to have very much to say to one another. How delightful for both of them."

"She does appear to be enjoying herself," Joel Elliot said, sliding a glance to Jedidiah. Jedidiah Elliot, however, was looking at her and not at Jane. Katherine, though a bit surprised, was not at all displeased. How long had it been since a man had looked at her in anything approaching interest? Not since her courtship, and even then, Lord Richard had not looked at her like *this*.

He was a remarkable-looking man, Captain Jedidiah

Elliot. Tall, excessively broad shoulders, a slightly narrow, well-sculpted face, dark blond hair, and blue eyes of a particularly compelling hue, ocean blue perhaps, which was apt, but it was the earnestness and the intense energy of his gaze which delighted her.

Yes, *delighted*. She hadn't experienced delight in any degree since her courtship. Certainly Lord Richard had known how to make himself agreeable during a courtship. She had believed he loved her devotedly, energetically, and earnestly.

He had not.

He had been that quite ordinary thing, a husband who had an affaire. In truth, he'd likely had more than one, but she was only aware of the one. The one with Bernadette, Lady Paignton.

Lady Paignton had many affaires, both while her husband lived and now when he did not. Lady Paignton seemed to have one purpose in life: to seduce as many men as she could. But Katherine did not blame Bernadette for Richard's vault into her bed. No, he had found his way there all on his own. A woman could tempt, but she could not compel.

The wound which haunted? Why had Richard not been tempted by *her*? Was she not beautiful enough? Not sensual enough? Not interesting enough? Not . . . enough?

Bernadette was here today, now. There had been no avoiding her, though she did make it a policy to do so. It was not possible to avoid Hyde House on this day of days; it would have been a blow to Hyde joy that Katherine was not willing to deliver. And so, here she was, witnessing Bernadette seducing yet another man, at the moment, the Duke of Calbourne. Calbourne seemed to be enjoying it. Though, unable to keep from watching Bernadette whenever she was in the vicinity, Katherine couldn't help but note that the Elliots hadn't seemed at all susceptible to her flagrant charms.

Yet Jedidiah Elliot gave every appearance of being very receptive to hers.

It was, to put it mildly, quite wonderful.

"That's all that matters, then," Jedidiah said, barely sparing a glance for his sister. "Your brother is an honorable man, Lady Richard?"

"Without question, Captain Elliot," Katherine replied.

"*Without question,*" Sophia repeated. "How often can that be said, I wonder?"

"It should be said of every man," Joel said, smiling.

Joel Elliot had the most delightful dimples on each side of his mouth. Long and deep, they bracketed his mouth like comical exclamation points. Dark, curling hair framed his face and accentuated his deep brown eyes. He was slightly shorter than his brother, but still a tall, well-formed man. Joel was fully as handsome as Jedidiah, though of a different sort entirely. More playful, perhaps, a bit lighter in spirit. Jedidiah was as intensely focused as a burning candle.

What would that intensity be like in bed?

She shocked herself by thinking it. When the shock passed, which of course it always must, she let the image simmer in her thoughts.

Take a lover?

Why shouldn't she?

Take *this* man for a lover? He was a safe choice. He wasn't anyone she knew, and he was leaving soon. He couldn't harm her, couldn't intrude upon her life, couldn't besmirch her reputation. He *was* leaving soon, wasn't he? Best to check on that. She wouldn't want to take a lover if he were going to loiter about Town. That would certainly prove awkward.

"Oh, but if we deal in what *should* be said of every man," Sophia said, looking up at Joel fondly, waving her fan languidly, "then the point is entirely lost, Captain Elliot. Of course men like to think that they are ruled by honor, incorruptible, unyielding, but I have found men to yield most regularly."

"And on being incorruptible?" Katherine asked with a smile.

"They are most willingly corruptible," Sophia said, "though perhaps that says more about me than it does about them. I do hope so."

"I don't believe a word of it," Lord Ruan said, having come up behind Sophia. Sophia's fan did not so much as falter, though her eyes did narrow slightly.

"I must say," Sophia said, "that sounds very like you, Lord Ruan. You have the dismal tendency of disbelieving a direct statement so that you may waste your time in scurrying about after phantom mice in fairy-tale haystacks."

"Lady Dalby," Ruan said, his voice quite low and his green eyes quite intense, putting Jedidiah's intensity to shame by comparison, which was something Katherine did not enjoy admitting, "only I may decide whether my time is wasted or not. I have yet to waste a single moment since meeting you."

Silence followed that remark. Sophia looked as cool as water, only the slight increase in the movement of her fan betraying any emotion whatsoever. Ruan, whom Katherine knew only slightly, looked at Sophia with all the sharp intent of a blade.

There was some history between them, that much was obvious. Had Sophia taken Ruan as a lover? Had she rejected him as a lover? Whatever had happened, Katherine was certain it involved being someone's lover. *Everyone* took lovers. And now she would, too. Jedidiah Elliot was still looking at her. If she could get him alone to arrange things, he would do very well as her first.

"As much as I would like to see a compliment in that statement, Lord Ruan," Sophia said, her black eyes as cold as diamonds, "I find I cannot, which does aggrieve me. I do so enjoy a heartfelt, or even an insincere, compliment.

I have found my time to have been wasted, you see, something I do not enjoy."

"I wonder when breakfast will be announced," Joel Elliot said into the cutting silence that followed Sophia's remark.

Yes, well, Katherine had to remove herself and Jedidiah from the battle going on between Ruan and Sophia. Sophia could handle herself, and him, without any aid from her. If she were going to entice Jedidiah into a liaison, she'd need the ideal surroundings and this wasn't it. She had no experience and little confidence for this sort of thing. She simply couldn't manage it with any distractions at all.

"I was wondering the same thing," Katherine said. "Would you mind terribly asking your aunt?"

"Not at all," Joel Elliot said, excusing himself and making his way through the crowd.

It did not escape Katherine's notice that Joel winked at Jedidiah as he passed him. Discretion was clearly going to be a problem for her, which only proved the point that she had chosen the right man for the job. A quick seduction and then off he went, over the seas, a clean exit, quick and tidy.

There was little better that a man could offer a woman.

❧

"HE's still just talking to her? Blakes would have dragged me into a closet by now," Louisa said.

Amelia gave Louisa a rather arch look. "She's only just met him, Louisa. Give her a chance. One look at his face and you can see that he wants to do just that."

"Yes, but does he want to seduce her or slap her? That's my question," Louisa answered. "He looks enraged, but that may be the fault of distance. I do wish we could work our way closer."

As they were stuck behind a table and hemmed in by no less than six groups of chattering people, one of them containing the Duchess of Hyde, who was looking at them suspiciously, there was little to be done about their position at the moment.

"Where were you, anyway? Jane seemed very displeased to be doing her best with Edenham and you not about to witness it. I think she believes she's won the wager already. You didn't disappear on purpose, did you? To force her to spend more time with Edenham?"

"I most certainly did not," Louisa flared, her eyebrows soaring into arches of outrage. "If you must know, Blakes dragged me off—"

"And had his wicked way with you?" Amelia cut in.

"Hardly," Louisa snorted indelicately, causing Lady Lanreath to turn and glance at her inquisitively. Louisa arched an eyebrow and waited for her to mind her own business. She did. Eventually. "That would have been lovely, and was what I was expecting, but what I got instead was a very stern lecture on how I must not interfere with Jane's first day in London Society and how I should, if I had a feeling bone in my body, which he doubted strongly, wish her well and do all in my power to aid her. Stupid, bloody sot," she grumbled. "And here I'm doing exactly that and he's too blind to see it. Typical."

Amelia laughed lightly. "Did you tell him all that? Explain how truly virtuous you are?"

Louisa smiled smugly and said, "Of course not. When Edenham asks Jane to marry him, Blakes will find out soon enough. I shall take all the credit for it, Amelia, and I want you to back me up on that. Knowing Blakes, he'll give Sophia Dalby credit for the entire marriage of his cousin to a duke. He thinks she can do anything, and will do anything. Well, I can make a match as surely as she can."

"Can you?" Amelia said sarcastically. It wasn't at all attractive. "Isn't this your first match? And, by your own words, they're still only talking."

"I have complete confidence in Jane," Louisa said stoutly, wrapping one of her red curls around her finger.

"Edenham may be a bit of a slow start, but Jane will bring him round."

"She doesn't want him, Louisa. She's made that perfectly clear. This is all a challenge for her, and she dislikes you enough to be determined to win it."

"And you think I didn't do that on purpose?" Louisa said with a lopsided grin. "As to the rest, it's up to Edenham to arouse some feeling in her. He should be capable of it, don't you think? He's had three wives. Certainly he must know what he's about by now."

"And he is very handsome," Amelia added. "I always maintained that he was the prettiest duke, if one likes the tall, dark, and dashing type."

As they had both married blue-eyed blonds, they were being entirely loyal to their husbands by remarking as such. Of course anyone with eyes could see that Edenham was exceptionally handsome, but that didn't mean they didn't find their own husbands even more so. So they would maintain if the issue ever came under question.

"You don't think she's heard the rumors of him and is afraid of him, do you?" Louisa asked.

"You really should scold Blakes for dragging you off and not having his way with you. That would be the only reasonable excuse for missing the most sensually heated exchange I've heard this week," Amelia said, leaning in closer to Louisa, who bent her head down to hear every word. Lady Lanreath had moved a step closer as well, and had an ear turned to catch what she could of the conversation. Amelia ignored her. Louisa had forgotten all about her. "Not only does Jane know the rumors of Edenham regarding his, um, prowess, but Edenham told her himself!"

"No! What did he say?"

"Something about the rigors of his bed."

"And what did she say?"

"I have no idea. Cranleigh dragged me off before Jane had a chance to answer."

"Men," Louisa snapped. "You'd think a man would know better than to drag his wife off without the benefit of a good reason. Don't they understand the dashed hopes? The ennui that ensues? The next time Blakes drags me out of a room, he'd better have his hand up my skirts within the next minute or I shall . . ."

"You shall what?" Amelia asked. "Do say you have something wonderful in mind for I shall do the same thing myself. Married less than a month and we're reduced to *talking* in quiet corners. I can tell you that, before we were married, Cranleigh didn't waste time in talking if he got me to himself."

"Staid and respectable, the both of them," Louisa murmured, shaking her head. "I think we must do something daring and unrespectable, just to keep things lively. This being married, it does require almost as much effort as getting married. I had no idea, had you?"

"No, but I can't say I mind," Amelia said, smiling like a cat. "But do you know that the last three times have been in our own bed? At night? I can't think what's got into Cranleigh; he's become nearly conventional. What shall we do to them? How to spur them to action?"

"I'm ashamed to confess it, but I'm not certain. Perhaps we should ask Jane. She seems a lively, daring sort, with unbridled American ideas. She did go right after Edenham, which did take a good deal of courage."

"Why, Louisa, I believe you truly do like her."

"Of course I do, Amelia," Louisa sputtered. "Why else would I put so much effort and thought into managing her into the proper marriage? She's not going to find herself married all on her own, not to a duke. We both know how skittish they are."

"Louisa, don't turn around just now," Amelia said, her blue eyes going quite wide as she stared at something over Louisa's right shoulder, "but the Duke of Edenham isn't behaving at all skittishly at the moment."

Well, with prompting like that, what was Louisa to do? *Not* look?

❧

GEORGE Prestwick, stung by indecision, had done nothing but look, and look again. Raithby and Penrith, who, now that the whole thing had been shucked onto his shoulders, were still arguing about what Sophia Dalby could or could not do if she had a mind to. The problem as George saw it was that while Sophia Dalby might be able to do whatever she wanted, the same could be said of the Duke of Edenham. Colluding together, what could stop them? Two Americans? Hardly. The son of a newly made viscount, which is all he was, after all, would accomplish even less.

No matter how he cut it apart, he couldn't see that anything could actually be *done* about it. The more he watched Miss Elliot interact with Edenham, the more he thought that she might be able to manage everything herself. She did look a plucky little thing, undaunted by the company she found herself in, unimpressed by Edenham, unhampered by the rules of deference. In some ways, she reminded him of Penelope, and look how well Penelope had done.

And so he watched, and pondered, disgusted with himself for his indecision while being unable to force himself off the mark. It did help that the Americans were watching Jane as well, clearly keeping a sharp eye on her. What more was there to do?

Tell them about Sophia, Edenham, and the wagers that seemed to spring from the very ground Sophia walked upon, of course.

George sighed. There was no help for it. He simply must get involved. And he'd been so certain that when Pen got herself married to her heir apparent that all this sort of thing would stop. It was women; they never knew when to stop. They didn't know how, clearly. Well then, it was just as clearly up to men to stop them. For their own good, naturally, not that they'd ever see it that way.

It was such a burden at times, being a man.

George excused himself from Raithby and Penrith, who stopped arguing and watched him make his way to where he'd last seen the Elliot brothers. It was a circuitous route he was forced to take as the blue reception room was simply clogged with people, very many of them whispering about Jane Elliot and the likely topic of her conversation with Edenham. That didn't bode well, did it? George was too far from where he'd last seen them to know what was happening now, and since he was having a bit of a time finding the Elliots among the throng, was not in any position to work himself closer to look.

Squeezing around behind Lord Dutton, who certainly smelled as if he were completely foxed, George finally spotted the Elliots near the door, Joel Elliot bowing and removing himself from their number as he watched. Well, that had been for nothing. Who was Jedidiah Elliot conversing with but Sophia Dalby and Lady Richard? What could he possibly say in front of those two particular witnesses?

But, truthfully, wasn't it simply his duty as a man to say *something*? That's what this was ultimately about, wasn't it? An exercise in doing the right thing. Because one *should*. Because one was expected to perform up to certain standards, male standards. Woman in distress and all that.

It was not beyond possible that the women, both Sophia and Katherine, would see it the same way, perhaps think him a dear lad, a latter-day Galahad, and not an interfering, naïve fool. It was possible.

That slim possibility sustaining him the final few feet, George entered their circle as pleasantly as he knew how. If there was one talent George had, it was in being pleasant.

"Mr. Prestwick, have you been introduced to Lady Richard?" Sophia asked, turning in ruthless precision away from the Marquis of Ruan, who did not look at all surprised by the action. He'd wandered into a worse coil than he'd first thought, that much was obvious. Damnation, but it was a trial being noble.

"I have not," he said, bowing to her.

Lady Richard was exquisitely beautiful. Delicately framed, her features classically refined with light hazel eyes and rich brown hair shot with gold and amber lights. She looked in many ways like her brother, the Duke of Edenham, though he was more sturdily formed. Lady Richard, as stunningly formed as she was, did not outshine Lady Dalby with her black hair and eyes and creamy skin. Where Lady Richard caught the eye with beauty, Sophia Dalby caught the cock with pulsating sensuality. What's more, Lady Richard did not seem to want to have caught the eye, while Sophia most assuredly wanted to catch a man by the cock.

It was impossible not to like Sophia for that alone. George had never met a woman who so effortlessly, so charmingly, and so thoroughly enjoyed seducing a man, even if all she ever did to him was speak his name. 'Twas small wonder the woman was a legend.

"The brother of the bride," Lady Richard said. "How happy your family must be."

"We are," he said. "Not only for Penelope but because of Penelope. She will tolerate nothing less than our supreme happiness at her marital victory. I half expect cannons to be fired at midnight. If anyone can arrange it, it would be Penelope."

Captain Elliot frowned in apparent confusion. "Marital victory? Cannon blast? Is marriage so martial here?"

"When a woman snares a duke, it is almost entirely martial, Captain," Sophia said. "Dukes are rare things, and the woman who can snare one upon the altar must be cunning and very accomplished. Not just any girl can manage it. Penelope is that rare one who did."

"My cousin does not act like a man ensnared," Jedidiah said, casting a quick glance at Lady Richard. Quick, but clearly interested. Things grew more complicated by the second.

"But of course he doesn't," Sophia said on a trill of laughter. "That is due entirely to the hunter's art. Iveston knows he's caught, but he likes it. Indeed, his only demand is that he not be set free. Is there any better footing on which a marriage may begin?"

"No, there wouldn't be," Jedidiah said, glancing again at Lady Richard. "To be caught in love would be the ultimate freedom," he added in a husky undertone.

Lady Richard cast a glance up to Jedidiah's face, and then quickly turned her eyes to the floor. Sophia caught George's eye, smiling devilishly. Lord Ruan, oddly, said nothing. George was not overly familiar with Lord Ruan, but he had thought of him as a more talkative fellow than he was proving now.

"You are not married, are you, Captain Elliot?" George asked.

"No, not yet," Jedidiah answered.

"And Miss Elliot," George continued, determined to fulfill his purpose as quickly and as delicately as he could before escaping to the far corners of the room, "clearly not married, but not spoken for?"

Jedidiah scowled a bit, his blue eyes turning a bit gray. "No, most definitely not. Why?"

The look in Jedidiah's eyes . . . the phrase *cannon blast* came instantly to mind.

Sophia laughed lightly before George could think of a thing to say, pleasant or otherwise. "Why, darling, is this gallantry I see?" she said. "I hardly know what to think. Can you, can you truly be attempting to protect lovely Miss Elliot? But how charming. I knew I liked you, Mr. Prestwick. Your family is so deliciously unusual. I am so happy that we have become so well acquainted."

George hadn't been aware that Sophia was well acquainted with his family, but that didn't seem pertinent at the moment. Jedidiah's foggy blue eyes were as cold as the North Sea, staring at him unblinkingly.

"Protect Jane from what?" Jedidiah asked George, ignoring Sophia completely.

Sophia did not behave like a woman who was being ignored. Indeed, when did she ever?

"From *whom*, Captain," she said lightly, her dark eyes sparkling happily. "From the Duke of Edenham, I should think, though that can hardly surprise you. He's been utterly captivated by her since the moment he saw her, which is not at all shocking. I'm quite certain you understand completely, don't you, Captain Elliot?"

Sophia looked at Jedidiah nearly tauntingly. George ground his back teeth together, giving himself an instant headache.

Sophia continued, her tone excessively playful, "A single look and all is lost? Or is that all is found? I'm never sure. Perhaps you should ask Edenham. I'm certain he must know. He's such an experienced man at love, three wives and all that. Looking for a fourth, you know," she said, lowering her voice. "I have it on good authority, from Edenham himself. By the look of it, he's making stellar progress, wouldn't you say, Captain Elliot?"

Ten

EDENHAM felt fury rise up in his blood to crash against his skull.

Nothing to cause a ripple of alarm?

Perhaps he should move?

This young woman of no title and no position looked him up and down like a stallion she was considering, and then rejected him as being not fit to put out to stud? She didn't even have the illogical, though understandable, reason of fear. He was feared. He was not ridiculed.

She stood facing him, this Miss Jane Elliot of New York, her chin lifted and her silvery hazel eyes alight with the dual fires of arrogance and dismissal. What in hell did she have to be arrogant about? As to being dismissive, *no one* dismissed a duke of England. Was she such a lack-wit that she didn't know that? She should never have come here if she didn't understand the guiding principles of a nation. He was a duke, by damn, and she'd treat him as such.

"Is that it?" she said, tilting her head and continuing to

stare at him. She didn't even have the wherewithal to blush. "You've nothing to say? I did think it was a good shot, but I'd no idea that a single broadside could sink a duke so thoroughly. Rather pampered, are you? Cosseted?" She shook her head in apparent disappointment. "I'll admit, I did think you would be. One hears so many things about dukes, very few of them flattering. Actually, I can't think of a single flattering remark. Have you heard any? To your face, I mean? Does anyone think well of dukes, your grace? Or are the people you surround yourself with simply too beholden to you to utter a solitary contrary word?"

Words escaped him. She was . . . impossible. Horrible. He'd fallen in love with a face, a body, not a mind, not a heart. She was as cold as January, as unfeeling as a knife.

"I suppose that's it, then," she continued in a surprisingly cheerful voice. "You've got over it now? No more calf-eyed looks? No more mute adoration while the world tumbles on all around you?"

What?

Had she meant to put him off? It made at least some sense. Why else would a lovely young woman, presumably well brought up, speak to him in such a manner, and for no earthly cause?

"I can't think how my brothers endured it for as long as they did," she said, smoothing the front of her white muslin skirt. "It should not have lasted much longer, their tolerance, I can assure you. You should count yourself fortunate, your grace."

So she had been trying to protect him from her rather ordinary brothers? That was rather kind, *misguided*, but kind of her. He could feel his heart, and other parts, warming again.

"I do wish Louisa had seen it, though. I should have liked that very much," she said a bit wistfully.

"Seen what, Miss Elliot?" he asked softly, his outrage evaporating like a mist.

Jane looked at him a bit sheepishly, her eyes shining in what he thought was embarrassment, her perfect smile sliding crookedly over her charming face. "I trust you have a sense of humor?"

"A well-developed one," he answered.

She looked at him a bit skeptically, but continued, "It's only that Louisa wasn't at all convinced that you . . ." She paused, looked at the floor between his feet, took an audible breath, and said in a rush, "I might be from New York, but that doesn't mean that I, and it certainly doesn't mean that I won't, or couldn't, but naturally that's what she implied, and so what could I do? I had to prove myself, didn't I? And you seemed quite willing. And certainly there's no harm in it. And that's an end to it. It was all for nothing anyway. She wasn't there to see it. But it doesn't matter to me and I trust, your sense of humor intact, it doesn't matter to you. There now. It's all perfectly fine, isn't it? Nothing to be alarmed about. Nothing to tell my brothers, most certainly. I trust we can agree on that."

The strange thing was, he understood her. The gist of it, anyway.

"Some sort of wager, was there?" he said. "Instigated by Lady Louisa, involving me, and you felt honor bound to defend yourself and . . . your nation?"

"Precisely," she said, staring him boldly in the eye, not a bit ashamed or remorseful or any other fool female emotion that women loved to roll about in to the exhaustion of any man nearby. "Though of course no money was involved. Hardly that. I only wanted to show her, but she wasn't here to be shown anyway, which I think must have been part of her plan."

"She had a plan, did she?" he asked, smiling. He couldn't remember when he'd felt so lighthearted.

"As I don't think she's very bright, it can't have been much of a plan"—Jane leaned toward him to whisper— "but I do think she had something in mind. Something dreadful to catch me up in, the poor American relation, the unsophisticated rustic." She shrugged elaborately and suddenly he could see her as the rough-and-tumble girl she must have been, running to keep pace with her older brothers. He fell in love with her a bit more just then.

"And what was the wager, Jane?" he asked, taking a step nearer to her, drawn in, and not against his will. No, every part of his will screamed to be nearer, to take her and make her his. Socially, legally, physically his. "Were you to insult me? Something to prove yourself a brave American? Go insult the duke and we'll think you worthy? And what was my reaction to be? How can I aid you in winning this wager you have with Lady Louisa?"

Jane's face, indeed her entire body, went stunningly still. Her luminous eyes looked up at him in shock. Yes, it was shock. What an absurd reaction. He had guessed it and he was willing to help her in her little skirmish with Louisa Blakesley. He looked around the room, eager to give her what she wanted.

"She's here, Jane. Here now. Louisa, Amelia, standing together. If we move just a bit to the right, they'll be able to see whatever you are to do," he said.

God, she was beautiful. Like a statue come to life, all perfect curves and flawless hair, skin, eyes, teeth. Her smile made his blood race.

"Can you see my brothers as well?" she asked slowly, the shock fading from her eyes. Now they were lit with that spark of wit and sweetness he had seen in them when he'd first set eyes upon her. He could hardly make himself tear his gaze away and look around the room for her brothers.

"Yes, I see them," he said. The elder brother was standing with Katherine, which he supposed must be acceptable as Sophia and Ruan were with them. Otherwise, he would not have been at all sanguine about having an American captain anywhere near his fragile sister.

"Good," she said, nodding, the barest trace of a smile

teasing her mouth. "Now, what you must do, your grace, for me to win my wager is to . . . kiss me."

His eyes snapped back from studying his sister to Jane's face. She gave every appearance of being serious. He could hardly credit it.

"The wager was for me to kiss you?"

"No," she said crisply, "not at all, but as it would take too long for me to explain all the details of the wager to you, and as I do not trust Louisa not to run from the room again, I have decided that the quickest way to accomplish the essence of the wager is for you to . . . kiss me. On the mouth."

She stared at him, waiting, he supposed.

Edenham felt the nudge of warning along the length of his spine. There was no wager, on any continent, that two women would make that would involve a public kiss between an unmarried man and an unmarried woman, not if there was any intention of them staying unmarried. It was a trap. A marriage trap.

On the other hand, since he had determined to marry Jane Elliot upon first laying eyes upon her, it wasn't much of a trap, not when he was skipping to it like a schoolboy on holiday.

And what woman would set such a trap? A woman who wanted to marry him as desperately as he wanted to marry her. Edenham felt joy run along his spine, making mock of warning. He had no need for Sophia. Jane was his. All for the price of a single kiss.

As to why Jane would endure such public humiliation by being publicly kissed, he had the answer to that as well. She would because she was as in love with him as he was with her. She wanted to marry him, and once kissed, ruined before this vast crowd of witnesses, her troublesome brothers would be powerless to cause any trouble at all.

She was asking him to ruin her, and by doing so, to secure her future as his wife.

What a clever, resourceful girl. Small wonder he loved her.

The room seemed to still for him. The noise of conversation faded into the soft yellow glow of afternoon sunlight. Jane, her pale hazel eyes shining up at him, her lovely mouth tilted in the gentlest of smiles, awaited his kiss. She glowed. Her white muslin gown, done in a striking Grecian style, her arms exposed, made her look all the more like a statue come to life. She was the most beautiful woman he had ever seen.

She was going to be his wife. All he had to do was kiss her and she would be his.

He arched his head forward, putting one finger beneath her chin, lifting her mouth to his. She didn't resist in the slightest, though her eyes widened, in alarm he supposed. It was a bold thing they were doing, highly scandalous. Such a brave, daring girl, he couldn't let her lose heart now. In just moments it would all be settled.

"Jane," he breathed, laying his hand along her jaw, lifting her head up, the white arch of her slender neck as long as a swan's. "I knew the moment our eyes met that I loved you, would love you, for as long as I live."

The final words of his declaration blended into his kiss, a gentle brush of his lips that should have been the most decorous way to ruin a woman that had ever been seen before. But something happened. At that first touch of his lips against hers, as the warmth and sweet softness of her mouth moved against his own, he fell into a well of desire of which there was no way out. He rushed down, light dimming, noise muffled, falling into her, losing every sensation, every thought except the word *Jane*, and the sensation of Jane in his arms.

In his arms . . . entirely without thought, his arms wrapped themselves around her waist, lifting her slender form clear off the floor. Her hands rested on his shoulders in delicate submission. But her mouth. Her mouth kissed him back.

She wanted him. He could feel it in her kiss.

What glorious children they would have.

A slight disturbance in the air tugged at the spell they had created between them. He fully intended to lift his mouth from hers, was halfway to doing so, when the slight disturbance boiled up into something entirely more distracting.

Jane was pulled from his arms, which he was certain would not have happened if he hadn't been so distracted by kissing her, and his eyes opened just in time to see Jedidiah Elliot throw a solid blow to his midsection.

Not the way these things usually went, but as they were Americans, he supposed they were ignorant of that.

Edenham buckled over, took a few steps backward, and raised his hands, palms open. Not in surrender, mind you, merely in a gesture of peace and goodwill. They were going to be family, after all, and he did believe in harmony within families, even if they were American. He was quite forward-thinking that way. He'd chosen Jane, hadn't he?

Jedidiah ignored his peaceful posture, came in close, and hit him again, or tried to. As Edenham's arms were raised, he used them to block the punch. That seemed to enrage Jedidiah further, though it hardly seemed possible that anything could, and Edenham found himself kicked on the thigh, just above his knee; *kicked*! If the man had managed to connect with his knee he'd have been hobbled for life.

Edenham fell arse first on the floor before jumping back up to his feet. His thigh pounded like the devil's hammer and he couldn't take a full breath since the punch to the gut.

No matter. Jane was worth it, though it was to their mutual benefit that her brothers were so often on long sea voyages. He was beginning to think that they wouldn't enjoy the close family harmony he'd hoped for.

"I'm going to marry her!" he snapped out, hoping to

break through the haze of fury that clouded Jedidiah's storm blue eyes.

"The hell you are," Jedidiah grunted, throwing another punch.

Edenham, having a far better understanding of whom he was dealing with now, dodged it.

"What's in the wind?" Joel yelled, running, *running!*, across the Hyde's reception room, the crowd clearing for him as quickly as they could. With such an inducement, they were very quick indeed.

"This English ass kissed Jane," Jedidiah gritted out, his hands still fisted, his neck thick and distended. He threw another punch to Edenham's gut, which Edenham blunted with his crooked arm, but as he followed it with a direct hit to the face, Edenham didn't do as well as he'd hoped.

The blow caught him on the side of his jaw and his teeth grated against each other just before his mouth filled with blood.

Edenham spit the blood onto the floor, which he was certain Hyde would forgive, given the circumstances.

"I intend to marry your sister!" Edenham shouted out, which wasn't very discreet, but nothing had been since first seeing Jane. Love did that to a man. Normally, he didn't find it so uncomfortable.

"Nobody cares what you intend," Joel said, standing before Edenham with his fists raised.

They both came at him then, which wasn't at all a fair fight, but when a man was fighting for his sister, he didn't care about being fair. It was over very quickly, he supposed, though it had felt an age at the time. Jedidiah and Joel Elliot, once he was down on the ground, had stopped all aggression and stood over him, breathing hard through their mouths and looking at him with all the cold hatred one reserves for a rabid wolf.

"Stay away from Jane," Jedidiah said in a hoarse voice. Given that the entire population at Hyde House was holding its collective breath, Edenham was certain that everyone had heard the warning. Hearing it was one thing, but understanding it was quite another.

Telling them again that he wanted to marry her seemed unwise. They hadn't responded well to that at all. Telling them that he had only done what Jane had asked him to do seemed equally unwise as it might put Jane in an unflattering light. Telling them that they should try and keep Jane away from *him* sounded like a petulant insult.

In the end, he decided that there was no requirement that he respond at all to a warning. He could adhere to it or ignore it at his discretion.

The only thing he was unsure of, besides the sanity of the Elliots, was what effect this beating would have on Jane. She was likely crying her eyes red, horrified by her brothers' behavior, frightened that he would beg off and refuse to marry her.

Poor Jane.

She must have run from the room, unable to bear the sight of violence against him; he was nearly certain that he had not heard any sounds of protest from her.

The Elliots watched him gain his feet and then turned and walked across the room, shoulder to shoulder. All let them pass, silence still blanketing the room. A hand was laid upon his shoulder, gripping it firmly, and Edenham turned to see Cranleigh standing at his back, his icy blue eyes looking both sympathetic and apologetic. As well he should. Such a display, in his own house and at the hands of his own relatives.

"Where's Jane?" Edenham asked, moving his shoulder out from under Cranleigh's grasp. "Is she all right?"

An expression passed over Cranleigh's face that Edenham couldn't identify and, truthfully, had no interest in. Cranleigh moved his head, a quick tilt of his chin, and Edenham followed the direction of the gesture to a spot just over his left shoulder.

Jane stood not ten feet from him. Her eyes were not red. She did not look frightened in the slightest. She stood with her arms crossed over her chest, a most calculating look in her eyes as she studied him.

A cold weight settled over him. She was not frightened. She was not even concerned. She had done nothing to stop the fight. Indeed, she might even have enjoyed it to judge by the slight smile teasing the corners of her mouth. She looked, why she looked amused!

What sort of love was this?

"Even Ezekiel Biddle would have asked," she said. "No man should be that certain of a woman's answer." And with that, she turned and walked away.

Edenham watched her go, and when the crowd swirled in upon itself, the swell of voices rising from a hum to a roar in mere seconds, he asked Cranleigh, "Who's Ezekiel Biddle?"

Cranleigh shrugged and shook his head.

Eleven

JANE found Louisa and Amelia without any trouble at all. She was having a bit of trouble walking steadily and keeping her breath from going ragged, but she managed. She was confident that no one could tell that the entire episode of the past five minutes had left her feeling distinctly jagged around the edges.

Naturally, she'd planned the entire thing. Not from the very start, of course, but from the moment that he, the mighty Duke of Edenham, had blurted out his ridiculous assumptions about her actions. And how absurd was it that the man declared himself in love with her and planned to marry her and she didn't even know his full name? Was she supposed to have been so overjoyed that the amazing Duke of Edenham had found her interesting and desirable and *worthy* that learning his name could wait until she'd produced his fifth child for him? Utter absurdity. So typical of his type, really. Of course she'd wanted to see him brought low, what else? He'd assumed that her very astute observations about his character and his actions were false, merely the foundations of a wager.

Pompous ass.

She'd won her wager, hadn't she?

It had been too completely perfect not to take advantage of. She'd win her paltry bet with Louisa and Edenham would get a proper drubbing.

He'd kissed her, for certainly even wily Louisa could not equivocate that a kiss was a kiss. There wasn't anything shaded about a man's interest if he kissed you, even in London.

But therein lay the jagged edge. He'd kissed her. He'd made some perfectly ridiculous, wildly romantic declaration that had softened the edges of her heart, and then he'd finished the deed by kissing her, turning her into soft pudding.

She hadn't expected that at all. Thank goodness that Jed had pulled her off of him for she surely could not have done so herself. Most embarrassing. She did hope no one realized that she'd actually been enjoying his kiss, his hands around her, lifting her up like an empty jug.

Jane let out a harsh breath.

Jagged.

Jed and Joel had done precisely what she expected them to do; they'd made no secret over the years of how they would behave in such a situation, that's certain. Edenham, taking hit after hit, shouting to the world that he meant to marry her . . . it had been rather sweet. Pointless, but sweet.

She wasn't entirely certain if Edenham hadn't fought back because he was incapable of it or because he'd been trying to make peace with her brothers. That seemed important to know. It would not do at all to become involved even casually with a man who could not handle himself with her brothers. No point to it, really. They'd kill him within a month, or so they'd always claimed. She believed it now.

Still, Edenham was entirely too full of himself, of his own vast self-deluded importance, to be anything more than highly aggravating. It would not do at all. A man should not go about kissing girls and then declaring them nearly wedded. Lazy bit of business, obviously. A man should work for a woman, desperately, ardently, and then she would decide if he'd succeed or not. Not him.

And while she was certain, though surprised, that his kiss had been quite wonderful, that did not at all mean that she was going to marry him. Not even close. He was duke. He was British. He was . . . the enemy.

Speaking of enemies, Louisa stood staring at her, her very pretty mouth agape. Amelia stood at her side. Amelia seemed to have forgotten how to breathe.

"I win," Jane said, narrowing her eyes at Louisa. "I'm not at all sure what I have won, but it had better be remarkable. You will make it remarkable, won't you, Louisa?"

Whatever timidity, whatever hesitation, whatever desire she'd felt to make a good impression upon her English relatives had been obliterated by Edenham's kiss. She'd made a good impression upon a very handsome, very eligible duke; that was good enough for her.

"He wants to marry you," Amelia said in a hushed voice, still staring at Jane, her crystalline blue eyes wide with shock. How insulting. How very typically insulting. "The Duke of Edenham wants to marry you!"

"I heard," Jane said flatly. "As he's been married five or six times already, it hardly seems to be an accomplishment."

"Three times," Louisa said, "two children. Three wives. And he wanted you to be the fourth."

Louisa couldn't seem to comprehend it; she really didn't seem especially bright.

"I shouldn't care to be anyone's fourth anything," Jane said. It seemed such a hard, sharp, confident thing to say.

She was quite pleased with herself. "I should like to know what I've won. You did have something in mind for this silly wager of ours?"

If Louisa had been prepared to say anything, highly doubtful, she was interrupted by the panting arrival of Penelope. Penelope, who always looked so perfectly composed, looked nearly wild-eyed.

"I've never seen anything like it!" she burst out. "This puts my rose conservatory completely out of the running! Well done, Jane! Now that you've got him, what do you plan to do with him?"

"Nothing," Jane said blandly.

"Nothing?" Penelope said, her black brows rising to her hairline. "But you have a duke, Jane. He must be used. One doesn't toss the Duke of Edenham aside. He's so . . . why, he's just . . ."

"He's the catch of this Season or any other," Amelia said softly, "as long as you aren't afraid of his . . . you know. *That*."

Jane snorted and checked the condition of her hair. "Hardly."

"Quite right, Jane," Penelope said, looking at Amelia as if she were an imbecile. "Superstitious nonsense."

"Tell that to his three previous wives," Louisa said. She did so love to throw rocks at things, likely small children.

"English wives, I assume," Jane said, staring down Louisa. "He might have better fortune with a robust American woman. One not so given to the faints."

"I don't think it was the faints that did them in," Penelope said musingly, "though I agree with you, they couldn't have been at all sturdy."

"It's probably a good thing that you don't want to be his fourth, Jane," Louisa said, a slightly calculating look shimmering in the depths of her bright blue eyes. "Now that your brothers have beaten him, and in front of everyone in Society, he can't want anything to do with you. Oh, a pleasant afternoon's flirtation is one thing, but now that your family has been shown to be so violent, everything will return to its proper course."

"A flirtation?" Jane said. "He literally shouted that he intended to marry me."

Louisa shrugged and said, "To avoid a beating, obviously. And since your brothers have refused his suit, well then, he's free and clear, isn't he? As are you, which does seem to be exactly what you want. How well it's all turned out."

It was, of course, the perfect excuse. She wasn't certain what she intended for the Duke of Edenham, though she most definitely wanted to find out his true name; she was no plodding Englishman to be content with calling a person by his title. Such an inflated bit of empty tradition, to be sure. Now that she'd rejected him and her brothers had trounced him, he *might* be a bit skittish about approaching her again. It wasn't that she wanted to marry the man, but she did enjoy kissing him. As far as adventures went, the Duke of Edenham was surprisingly fertile ground.

"It has, hasn't it?" Jane countered. "Though I'm still waiting to hear what I've won. Silly of me not to have heard the terms of your challenge before I went off and won it within minutes of its being issued, but then violent, quick action is most decidedly an Elliot trait. I trust you'll never forget that, Louisa."

Louisa, far from looking startled, or frightened, which would have been ideal, looked pleased in some strange fashion. What an odd girl.

"I'm completely confident that no one will ever forget this day," Louisa said. "Edenham's beating—"

"And my marriage," Penelope interrupted grimly. "Why does all the violence happen at my affairs? I'm such a calm, reasonable sort. It doesn't seem at all logical."

"The fault must lie with your guest list," Louisa said breezily.

"Oh, come now," Amelia said lightly, "to have your affair be remembered for years? Why is that black news? I'd be flattered. Just as I'd have been flattered if the Duke of Edenham had even bothered to remember my name. And he hadn't, not until the creation of the duke list, which was Sophia's idea completely."

"He'd barely even speak to me, even with Sophia's help," Penelope said, looking at Jane in admiration. "How did you manage it, Jane? You brought him to his knees without any effort at all that I could see." She leaned in close, her black hair brushing against Jane's shoulder. "Or is it something unseen? Some trick of conversation? Tell me, what did you discuss?"

"I have no idea," Jane said, completely distracted about the terms of the wager. Again. "About Sophia, you used her? She helped you get married?"

The three women looked at each other briefly, and then, by some unspoken agreement, looked at Jane squarely. They smiled. Even Louisa, which was flatly alarming.

"Yes," Penelope said. "She's very good at it, you know."

"That became perfectly obvious with her daughter, Caroline," Louisa said on the heels of Penelope's remark. "It was all accomplished in a matter of hours, and if she could do that for her daughter . . ." Louisa let her voice trail off. It was a slightly damning silence regarding Caroline. Having never met her, Jane could not decide if that remark were more reflective of Caroline or Louisa. She was leaning toward Louisa.

"It was simply a matter of one thing leading to another," Amelia said, looking deeply into Jane's eyes.

"But it didn't turn out at all as I expected," Penelope said, "but I am delighted that it didn't because I have Iveston, you see. Without Sophia, I'm certain I wouldn't have got him."

"Got him? You would never even have noticed him if not for her," Louisa said.

"You didn't want to marry Iveston?" Jane asked. "Then why did you go to her?"

"To get Edenham, of course," Penelope said, without any shame whatsoever. As it was the very day of her wedding to Iveston, Jane found that highly peculiar. The other women didn't, however.

"Edenham was on your list, wasn't he, Amelia?" Jane asked, her thoughts swirling. These women were raving. Small wonder that English society was in the tattered shape it was in.

"Certainly," Amelia said, nodding. "All the dukes and heirs apparent were. That was the whole point, wasn't it?"

"Was it?" Jane asked. "But you married Cranleigh. He's not a duke or an heir apparent."

"But how was I to spur him to action without the dukes, Jane?" Amelia countered, looking at Jane as if she were a complete imbecile. "It was all Sophia's idea and it was brilliant, worked beautifully and so very quickly."

Jane felt herself blinking, which was odd in and of itself. Her eyes blinked, her brain slogged along, trying to make sense of it all.

No, it didn't make sense.

"Did you want to marry Edenham as well?" she asked Louisa.

"Of course not, Jane," Louisa bit out, a bit annoyed.

"Then you wanted to marry Henry," Jane said, feeling the world right just the slightest bit.

"Oh, certainly not," Louisa said. "I was all for the Marquis of Dutton. Absolutely mad for him, for year upon year. What to do but go to Sophia for help in bringing him to heel?"

"But you *married* Henry!" Jane said.

"Of course I married Henry, Jane," Louisa snapped, scowling at her. "I'd loved him for simply ages, just never got round to realizing it, that's all, not until I'd aligned myself with Sophia Dalby."

"Can't you see how simple it is, Jane?" Amelia said. "Sophia does make it all turn right in the end. Happily ever after and all that."

"Simple? It's absurd," Jane said.

"I do agree with you, Jane," Penelope said, looping her arm through hers. "It's not at all logical, unless one measures logic by results. Then, naturally, it becomes entirely logical. You can see that, can't you?"

No, she couldn't see it, but she could see that they were all looking at her with something approaching sympathy in their eyes. Sympathy and perhaps hope. Hope for what?

"What's happened?" she asked, panic rising like a flood in her veins.

It was Penelope who answered her. Trust Penelope to say what needed to be said without hesitation.

"Now, Jane, it's nothing at all alarming. You must know that. Edenham is simply wonderful."

"He truly is, Jane," Amelia interrupted. "He was a tremendous help to me in bringing Cranleigh up to snuff. Knew exactly what he was doing and did it brilliantly."

Jane could feel her breath tightening in her chest, a vise around her lungs.

"The thing is, Jane," Penelope said, shooting a frustrated glance at Amelia for being interrupted, "Edenham is quite obviously taken with you. I was standing right there when you met and it was like watching a house on fire."

"And I'm the house?" Jane whispered.

"No, no, you're the fire," Penelope said. "I think. Anyway, he saw you, he fell instantly and deeply in love with you, which is so convenient, don't you agree? But then, to make it all perfect, to set the seal into the wax, he immediately sought a private word with Sophia, and there you are."

"And there I am where?" Jane asked, starting to actually feel the fires of anger nudging her ribs, which was lovely as it loosed the tightness of panic in her chest instantly.

"Married," Louisa said with a cunning smirk. "To the Duke of Edenham. Congratulations, Jane. You've got him."

"I don't want him!" Jane snapped, causing three or four people to turn and stare at her. She ignored them fully.

"But he's already talked to Sophia," Penelope said. "What's to be done? Besides, won't it be lovely to be the Duchess of Edenham?"

"No, it will not be lovely!" Jane said sharply. Eight people jumped and turned to stare at her. She stared back with such a hot look in her eyes that they each jumped again and turned hurriedly away from her. Quite rightly. "I am not going to be a duchess. Ever."

"But he's already spoken to Sophia," Amelia said, "and once that happens . . ."

"If talking to Sophia is all that's required," Jane said stiffly, "then I shall just have to have my own little talk with her."

Penelope and Amelia stared at her in wide-eyed silence. Louisa, however, smiled and said, "Do that, Jane. Good plan."

It was suspicious, to be sure, but what did it matter? If Edenham had asked Sophia to arrange for Jane to somehow marry him, then all Jane had to do was ask her to kindly desist. She didn't put any serious consideration into what Sophia could or could not do in getting two unlikely people married who'd had no notion to marry before her involvement, that was too absurd, but it didn't hurt to be cautious.

Besides, let Edenham wonder what she was talking to Sophia about. If that beating hadn't loosened his brains, he might even figure it out. What a delightful insult to deliver to a duke.

Arranging to marry her, indeed. He didn't even know her!

Pompous ass.

Twelve

"WHY do all my entertainments have these problems?" Molly, the Duchess of Hyde asked no one in particular. It was good that she asked no one in particular for what was there to be said? "I invite the very best people, or at least those whom are considered to be the very best, which means nothing, I'll allow, and some perfectly horrid display of bad manners and complete loss of self-control erupts in the middle of my very expensive and very well-planned event. And it always seems to directly involve someone in my family! What can that mean but that I've failed?"

As she was speaking to members of her family, there didn't seem to be any right answer to that question. They all stood in the wide stair hall, one floor above the blue reception room, light spilling down from windows on the uppermost floors, the white marble of the floor gleaming like the floor of heaven. It felt, however, nothing like heaven, not this setdown.

"It can simply mean that *they've* failed, Molly," Hyde

said, patting her on the shoulder. "Don't take so much on yourself. The boys can shoulder their own failings without any aid from you."

And he said that with a very forbidding look in his pale blue eyes, the sort of look that had controlled armies. His sons dropped their heads and stood contritely, looking at the floor. All except Cranleigh, who had escorted Edenham out of the blue reception room into a less public room of the house, which everyone considered a duty well performed, most particularly Edenham.

"That's very thoughtful, Hyde," Molly said, her steely blue eyes regaining some of their sparkle. "Very insightful, as well. I can't think what Edenham was doing, grabbing poor Jane that way. My own niece, in my own home! Of course, Jed and Joel, you might have behaved with some hint of restraint, but I shan't fault you for defending your sister. No, you had the right, but you might have chosen a more appropriate *place*. It did not have to be in the middle of my home, did it?"

Molly's voice rose stridently as she voiced the last sentence or two. Jed and Joel, standing with their hands clasped in front of them, their heads bowed slightly, gave every indication that they were remorseful. Or in prayer. The fact was, they had hurried to tell Hyde what they had done to Edenham the moment they were finished doing it. They hadn't apologized, but they had informed. It did count for something.

"I lost my head, Molly," Jed said. "It was unexpected, and I reacted."

"Yes, reacted," she said, shaking her head. "You know I can't throw Edenham from the house. He's a duke! One does not toss dukes out upon the street. It's not done."

Jed said nothing, but his face gave every indication he thought it a shame that England had such strange standards.

"Perhaps he'll leave on his own," Joel offered with a

smile. Of course he could smile; he didn't have a bleeding duke in *his* home.

"Would you like us to leave?" Jed offered in his deep-voiced, *master of the ship* manner. "I'm sure Jane wouldn't mind, not after what she's been put through."

Molly had always suspected that Sally's children were clever. Now she knew it for a fact. Take Jane from the house, when she had the Duke of Edenham in the palm of her hand? That would hardly do. Jane must stay, and the boys must stay out of her way. She was managing Edenham quite well on her own, even with her brothers in the room. Just imagine what she could do without their hovering.

It gave her chill bumps. Her niece, the Duchess of Edenham. They'd have the most glorious children between them, and Jane would live through it, too. None of this fading away, childbed fever nonsense. She was a good American girl from a strong American family; she'd produce the most lovely English children.

"Leave? My own family shunted off on Iveston's great day? I should say not," Molly said.

"It is touching how you think of me, Mother," Iveston said with the barest of smiles.

Molly gave him a hard look, this eldest son of hers, to which he merely smiled more fully. Molly sighed inwardly. Penelope had changed him. It was what women did to their husbands, the mothers watching on in bemusement.

Yes, well, she would indulge in being bemused another day. Today, she had to get Jane a duke for a husband. Edenham was just the thing.

∽

JANE finally located Sophia after a much longer search than she'd anticipated. Did the English have to live in monuments? Couldn't they enjoy life in more reasonably sized housing? Sophia was finally found in the yellow drawing room, a very large and luxurious room, as indeed they all were, talking with a very elegant woman with warm brown hair and stunning features. Probably trying to arrange a marriage for her, if everything she'd heard about Sophia held true, and Jane had no reason to believe it wouldn't.

Normally, she'd never think of interrupting what was clearly a private and perhaps emotional conversation. However, as her marital status was apparently about to change, she barged right in. It was a day for barging.

The yellow drawing room was far from empty. There were clusters of people talking in quiet tones. A very disreputable- and rakish-looking man, his dark hair falling forward over his brow, sat in the middle of one of the sofas, clearly deeply in his cups, mumbling something about ginger-haired widows and intemperate wagers. Everyone kept well away from him and Jane was more than willing to follow that lead. The last thing she needed was another Edenham situation, and who knew what that mumbling fellow might do? He could well decide he wanted to marry the next brown-haired girl who walked by him and then where would she be?

Not married, that was certain.

"Lady Dalby," Jane said as delicately as she could. "I am sorry to intrude, but if I could have a word?"

"Miss Elliot," Sophia said, turning to face her fully, laying a hand upon her arm, "how perfectly timed. We were just speaking of you."

Of course they were. She'd just kissed a duke in the middle of her uncle's home and then seen him beaten bloody by her brothers. What else was anyone going to talk about for the next decade? She only hoped Aunt Molly wasn't sobbing in her bedchamber, writing an angry, detail-ridden letter to her mother.

Actually, Aunt Molly wasn't the sobbing sort, not if she was anything like her sister.

"I find I am not surprised by that, Lady Dalby," Jane

said with a wry smile. "If you would give me just a few moments? I do apologize," she said to the beautiful woman studying her.

Jane took the occasion to study her in return. She was stunning. Warm brown hair glimmering with golden strands, light brown eyes shot with green, the most delicate features imaginable . . . and no jewels. That was odd, wasn't it? Jane wasn't given to wearing jewelry on most days, but for a wedding breakfast of this grand scale and formality, she'd worn a pair of long red jade earrings that Jed had brought back for her after his first voyage to China. This woman wore only her hair as an adornment. It was nearly biblical.

"Miss Elliot," Sophia said, "I don't believe you've met Lady Richard. The Duke of Edenham's sister."

"Oh," Jane said.

That was all she could think to say. She wasn't going to apologize. She simply wasn't. What had she done, after all? He'd kissed her. She'd asked him to, of course, but he could have refused, and should have refused, if he had any sense at all. What sort of man went about kissing a woman he'd just met? Pompous, conceited, overbearing ones, and those were just the first three traits that sprang into her mind. Give her an hour and she'd have a list that would choke Louisa. If only.

"Miss Elliot," Lady Richard said, "I am most pleased to meet you."

She said it softly and calmly, but what was that? Jane braced herself for a slap that she was half convinced was coming.

"As you may imagine, Miss Elliot," Sophia said, looping her arm though Jane's, the image of girlish confidences— Jane was instantly more alarmed than she had been just the moment before—"Lady Richard is determined to know how you accomplished it."

"*It*?" Jane asked, wondering if Sophia were holding her arm to keep her from defending herself.

"What other *it* can there be?" Sophia said on a chuckle. "The taming of Edenham."

Jane shook her head, watching Lady Richard, who did not look angry, only curious. "He looked tame to you? You must have been standing very far off."

Sophia laughed and even Lady Richard smiled. "Miss Elliot, may I call you Jane? My name is Katherine." Jane was dumbfounded yet again, but she managed to nod. "My brother knew his first wife socially for three years before he made the first step toward reaching an agreement with her father. They were married a year after that. He is not a man given to . . . impulse."

That was one word for it. Jane would have chosen another, but she considered that Katherine was more than slightly biased.

"Darling," Sophia said, smiling at her, "as you must be aware, Edenham is behaving like a man very much in love. He's thrown aside all his training and his dignity to toss his heart into your hands. I believe you could ask anything of him and he would do it without hesitation and certainly with no regret."

Jane felt a sliver of guilt slide down her spine. She *had* asked him to kiss her, and he had done it quickly enough, thinking he was doing it for her. And he had been, but not in the way he supposed. Did he regret it now? He should. She was beginning to.

"What Katherine wants to know is, how have you accomplished it?" Sophia asked.

"I don't want you to worry, Lady Richard," Jane said. "Katherine," she amended, feeling very much the roughly tutored American she'd been afraid to be called, "I don't want your brother. I don't . . . want him," she finished, feeling that it was an entirely inadequate explanation, but unable to furnish a more eloquent one.

"You do know that he wants you?" Sophia said, smiling.

"Doesn't everyone know that now?" Jane said, looking at Sophia accusingly. Sophia didn't seem at all intimidated. Jane hadn't really expected her to be. "It's precisely what I'd like to talk to you about, Sophia."

"I'm certain you do," Sophia said softly, and then she turned to Katherine and said, "Isn't it as I told you?"

Katherine shook her head, a bemused look on her face. "You will forgive us, Jane, if I may be allowed to address you so intimately, but as I have never seen my brother behave in any manner or degree to which he has behaved now upon meeting you, I did wonder how you'd accomplished it. Is it by being beautiful? Of course," she said, answering her own question, which was a blessing for how to respond to that, "being beautiful can be a woman's greatest—"

"Weapon," Sophia cut in, smiling not at all amiably.

"I was going to say *asset*," Katherine said. "Perhaps your word explains your success, Sophia. I fear I am too mild, you see," she said, looking again at Jane. "Why should I confess all this to you, you must be asking yourself, this strange English woman who unburdens her secret heart upon a stranger. I think it must be because of what you have wrought upon Edenham. He trusts you somehow, and he did it instantly. And of course Sophia thinks so well of you . . ." Katherine shrugged delicately, her eyes turned down in what Jane assumed was embarrassment. Jane was certainly embarrassed. Edenham trusted her? *Why?* He most assuredly didn't trust her now. She didn't blame him in the least.

"I can't think why she would," Jane said, feeling very guilty and very confused and not finding this adventure enjoyable at all.

"Jane," Sophia said, "you are utterly remarkable, which I think has just been proved to this entire company. The duke saw you, wanted you upon the instant, fell in love with you, and determined to marry you. If all that took even a minute, I should be very much surprised. I know all this, aside from the delicious fact that I could read every thought on his very pretty face as it was happening, because he pled with me to arrange it all somehow. I am to deliver you, darling, into his very eager hands."

"Which is exactly why I've come to speak with you, Lady Dalby," Jane said, a bit stunned to hear in words what she had only suspected. Oh, not the bit about the request, but the bit about the instantaneous quality of his commitment. A lifelong commitment? In an instant? Hardly possible. It was more likely that Edenham had seen something sparkly in the window, pointed, and expected it to be delivered within the hour. And he'd assigned someone else to arrange for delivery, in the person of Sophia Dalby. Jane felt herself get angry all over again. What sort of man courted and seduced by proxy? "I will not be delivered into anyone's hands. I am not interested in the duke's infatuation or delirium or whatever it is he is suffering from. I am not in love with him. I am not even mildly interested in him. I will not marry him. Now, I am come to you to ask you, can you make certain that I will get what *I* want? I have been informed that you are very clever at helping people get what they want. And I am most determined that you not help Edenham get what he wants. Do we have an agreement, Sophia? My mother trusts you. My aunt trusts. Now I am trusting you with my . . ." It sounded entirely too melodramatic, but she could think of no other word.

"Life?" Sophia asked.

"Yes. Life," Jane said. "I mean no disrespect to your family, Katherine, but I simply don't want him."

"Have you considered, Jane," Sophia said, "that he might not want you anymore? He's kissed you, at your instigation I'd wager." Jane bit her lower lip, but did not confess. "He has been beaten quite thoroughly by your brothers. You mocked him in some way, I should think, after the beating."

"Why should you think that?" Jane blurted.

"Because it's what I would have done," Sophia said, her dark eyes shining in humor and approval. *Approval?* Jane suddenly felt immeasurably less guilty. "What better way to add scent to the trail? American girls know this instinctively. I can't think what's wrong with the air in England that English girls can't seem to master this most simple of methods to attaining their ends."

"What ends?" Jane said.

"Darling, do you truly think that Edenham will want you less now?" Jane hadn't given it a bit of thought, truthfully. She'd only been acting on . . . instinct. "Why else would you have come to me, to ask for my assurances that I will divert him from your lovely trail?"

How did one create a lovely trail? And had she done so on purpose, or by instinct? *Oh, no.*

"You don't think he's lost interest?" Jane said.

Katherine laughed. Sophia merely smiled. "If you believed that, you wouldn't be here now."

"But why shouldn't he? As to that, why did he, to use your metaphor, pick up my trail in the first place?" Jane asked.

"Which is precisely what Katherine and I were discussing," Sophia said. "Because, darling Jane, aside from being an utter beauty, you are almost certainly the one woman in the room who should be the most dazzled by Edenham, yet who doesn't want him at all. You don't fear him. You are not in awe of him. You are not impressed by him. Naturally, he finds this illogical, unnatural, and irresistible. Men find that sort of challenge impossible to ignore. You, Jane, have captured his interest."

"Hardly a reason to marry," Jane mumbled. "He doesn't know me. He can't even *pretend* that he knows me. I don't even know his name, merely his title!"

"*Merely his title,*" Sophia mused softly. "And you wonder at his fascination for you?"

"His name is Hugh Austen, Jane," Katherine said.

"Lovely," Jane said crisply. "Hugh Austen. At least now I have a name. Should he ask for mine, it's Jane Liberty Elliot. I do so hope he asks."

Sophia smiled. "Why hope when you can act? I think you are perfectly correct. He won't be put off by mockery, I can assure you of that. And he won't be put off by the minor rough-up he endured at the hands of your brothers. The thing to do is to give him what he has *not* asked for. He has not asked to know you, Jane Liberty Elliot. Go and give him a good dose. I'll warrant that will cure him right enough."

It sounded a bit insulting, there was no getting around that, but it did make a good bit of sense. They had nothing in common and nothing to bind them. Let him see that, if he could. It would be difficult as he was fairly blinded by her, but given the chance she was confident she could make him see how absurd his behavior toward her had been. Sophia or no Sophia, list or no list, Jane was not going to marry Edenham. The thing to do was to give him a strong enough dose of her that he would see that for himself.

An hour ought to do it. She'd give it two, just for good measure.

"You won't help him, will you, Sophia?" Jane asked. "I've been told that, if you promise to help someone to marry, they'll find themselves married before they know what day it is."

Sophia smiled, a full bright smile that lit up her face. "Darling Jane, I would never think to manage any Elliot into an alliance that would be as awkward a fit as this one would be. You are of a fine Patriot family. The Duke of Edenham is as English as it is possible to be. It's perfectly obvious that you would never suit. Indeed, anyone not blinded by the tremors of romantic love can see it plainly, just by looking at you."

Perfectly obvious, it certainly was. Yet it felt just the slightest bit insulting. She agreed, most definitely she agreed. But why was it so *perfectly* obvious?

Just by looking? What did that mean? Hadn't everyone agreed that there was nothing at all wrong with the way she looked?

"Yet he is very determined to marry me," Jane said. "You can understand the source of my concern."

"Completely," Sophia said soothingly. "But not to worry. Edenham, as Katherine will confirm, is possibly the most romantic man of anyone's acquaintance. There is a reason why he keeps marrying, despite his heartbreak upon the untimely death of each of his lovely wives. He loves to love, you see. He relishes being in love. A more devoted father and ardent husband cannot be found. Edenham *will* marry. You can rest easily in knowing that he will not marry you. I shall make it my personal mission, if it comes to that, though I hardly think it will. Just let him find out who you truly are. That will settle things as quickly as even you could want."

Yes, definitely insulted. There was no way to interpret the words otherwise. Edenham was not in love with her, he was in love with love and with the condition of being married, no matter to whom. Although once he spoke to her, truly delved into her heart and mind and thoughts and character, he would be revolted and run into anyone's arms but hers.

Yes, that was the gist of it.

At the moment, Jane couldn't think why her mother liked Sophia at all. Perhaps she'd changed over the years, England and its aristocrats, of which she was a member, hardening her. It made perfect sense.

"He is the most lovely of men," Katherine said, "though I know I see him with a sister's heart. He has been through much disappointment, and while he suffers in the midst of it, he does always find his way through. A most resilient man, my brother. You need not worry on his behalf, though it is kind of you to do so."

Right then. So whatever Edenham suffered by way of pangs of regret that Jane had somehow eluded him would be swiftly tucked up and forgotten, his life unmarred by his brush with unrequited love.

Jane looked at each woman, first Katherine and then Sophia. They smiled politely in return. She smiled politely, if a bit frostily, in response.

"What thoughtful, kind counsel," Jane said. "It is so generous of you to take the time to assure me that Edenham will survive so robustly from his little misadventure in romantic discernment. I can't tell you how free I feel now. I can do whatever I must, knowing that he shall never suffer more than a moment's discomfort. I am so comforted, you simply can't know. Thank you so much."

Jane left them with barely a nod of her head. She was going to find Edenham, otherwise known as Hugh Austen to his rare and exalted intimates, and she was going to make such an impression on him that, though his love, or whatever he called it, *was* unrequited, he would burn candles to her name at her parting, if anyone did that sort of thing anymore. If anyone could bring back the fashion for it, a duke certainly should be able to.

❧

KATHERINE and Sophia watched her go, twin smiles on their faces.

"She's going to be lovely for him," Katherine said. "I can't wait for his children to meet her."

"I do feel a bit sorry for her," Sophia said. "I don't think she quite understands what she's got ahold of. Oh, well. Edenham will demonstrate that to her soon enough. Now, Katherine, what are you going to do about the volatile Captain Jedidiah Elliot?"

Katherine smiled, a crooked half smile of embarrassment and determination. "I'm going to do my utmost to set him on fire. What are my odds of success, do you think?"

"Never play to the odds, Katherine," Sophia said silkily. "Only you know what you can do. Everyone else is left with guessing."

Thirteen

"I'M not leaving," Edenham said, wiping his mouth with the back of his hand. His hand came away bloody.

"I'm not throwing you out," Cranleigh said, walking at Edenham's side until they reached the stair hall. He then escorted Edenham up the stairs to the second floor where a washstand awaited in Cranleigh's bedchamber.

Hyde House was large, quite large; some might even call it excessively large. Edenham had heard a rumor that Molly, the American-born Duchess of Hyde, had done just that upon first walking through the front door. He'd always discounted it, until now. Having met Jane Elliot, he was prepared to believe it.

Fractious, ill-tempered people, the Americans. Or it might have been simply a family trait, one which Jane shared with her maternal aunt. As Cranleigh was also somewhat fractious and ill-tempered, perhaps it was not an American trait. At the moment, his lip bleeding and his ribs aching, a blinding headache circling around the top of his head like a crown, a gift from the fractious and ill-tempered Elliots, he was undecided. It seemed important, though why it should be he had no idea.

American or not, shared bloodlines or not, Jane was who she was. He wanted her despite it.

Because of it.

One or the other. His pounding head would not allow him a moment of quiet to decide.

Cranleigh motioned him toward the washstand, a white porcelain ewer on a dark-stained walnut chest set between two long windows draped with dark blue linen damask, and sank silently into an armchair upholstered in the same blue damask.

Edenham washed his face in silence, checking for loose teeth: none.

When Edenham was finished, he turned to look at Cranleigh and they stared at each other in silence for a few long moments.

"As a guess," Cranleigh said, "I'd say that you hoped that by ruining her, she'd be forced into marrying you. Hurrying it all along at a full run, no detours, no delays, no denials."

"I've seen it work before," Edenham said, shrugging as he walked across the pale gold carpet to slowly ease himself into a matching chair.

His spine hurt, likely from falling to the floor. Damned tricky business, this courting an American. He'd never had so much trouble arranging a marriage before. Of course, it was his first attempt at ruination as the path to marriage. Likely there was some sort of mysterious finesse required in those situations, though he couldn't think what. Wasn't ruination the most blunt of marital weapons? It was simply applied clumsiness in seduction that resulted in ruin and then marriage.

A bit of trickery there, clearly. He had found nothing simple about ruining a woman into marriage.

Cranleigh snorted in what Edenham assumed was laughter. "The tongue of a diplomat, Edenham. Of course you've seen it work before; first Blakes, then me, then Iveston. The three of us, all in a single Season. A country gig with Sophia Dalby, ruination not twenty-four hours later, and married before the wind changed. The thing you miscalculated was the woman herself."

"You don't mean Sophia," Edenham said. It wasn't really a question.

"No, though I don't say that's not possible," Cranleigh said, his light blue eyes narrowed in thought. "Jane. She's not going to be pushed into marriage to anyone, nor will her brothers allow it. It's the American strain. They don't like to be forced into anything, and will fight like the devil to do what they please."

"You like them," Edenham said, looking over at Cranleigh without moving his head. He had his head braced against the back cushion and it soothed the pounding.

Cranleigh smiled slightly. "I do. I didn't think to at first, but I do."

"Tell me about them," Edenham said, meaning Jane, naturally.

Cranleigh chuckled, eyeing Edenham with a knowing eye. Edenham shrugged, unapologetic.

"I sailed to New York during the XYZ dustup, when America hated France more than Britain. A rare moment in history, you will agree. Timothy Elliot, my uncle," Cranleigh said softly, pausing to pick his words with evident care, "sailed a privateer during their war for independence, and is what you'd expect of such a man. He's no fool. He's got courage, conviction. A cool head in the most heated of circumstances. He barely tolerated me at first, then did tolerate me. Eventually." Cranleigh chuckled under his breath. "He's an American Patriot, everything that implies. It's only because Sally, my aunt, won't give up Molly that we all find ourselves tangled together. The war should have ripped us apart for good. It may yet." Cranleigh shrugged.

"You sailed with the elder brother, Jedidiah?" Edenham asked.

"To China," Cranleigh said, nodding slightly. "His second voyage, my first. And only. I should like to go back. Fascinating place. Jedidiah is much like his father, though perhaps a bit quicker to act."

"I could have made the same observation," Edenham said, rubbing his jaw. The man's fists were as solid as a mule's kick.

"They are a seafaring family," Cranleigh said after a few moments of silence. "Salt water in their blood, is the way they tell it. Even Jane."

Edenham said nothing at that. He let her name, the word that conjured images of her silver-eyed beauty, settle into the shadowed corners of the room as quietly and as thoroughly as gray mist. When all was still again, he spoke.

"Tell me about her life."

Cranleigh sighed, leaning his head back against his chair. "Her middle name is Liberty," he said softly. "Think on that, Edenham. She was born in 1781."

"Yorktown," Edenham said. The year of Washington's defeat of Cornwallis.

"Yes, but it was not for that she was named," Cranleigh said. "Salt water in their blood, remember? Do you remember the battle of the American frigate *Alliance* against our sixteen-gun sloop-of-war *Atalanta* and the fourteen-gun brig *Trepassy*? 'Twas off the coast of Newfoundland."

At Edenham's silence, Cranleigh continued, "Our ships had every advantage. We had sweeps; the *Alliance* did not. She sat like a felled log in a dead calm sea. Barry, the captain of the *Alliance*, could make no steerage and could do nothing while our ships stationed themselves off his quarter and used their guns to good advantage."

"Every advantage," Edenham said, studying Cranleigh's rugged face in the quiet light. "Yet . . ."

Cranleigh smirked ruefully and shook his head. "Four hours later, four hours of being a nearly helpless target, and then a small breeze arose. A single small breeze. The *Alliance* poured a broadside into the *Atalanta* first, and then she turned on the *Trepassy*. Captain Edwards, of the *Atalanta*, lowered his colors. The captain of *Trepassy* was dead."

"Liberty," Edenham said softly.

"You have your title, your heritage, your lineage. *Liberty* is the title they bestowed upon her. She will not give it up. Not any more than you would give up your dukedom."

"You think I have no chance."

"Having got Amelia, I will not say that any man may not have his chance. It is only, what shape does his chance bear? Will he know it when he sees it?"

"I will know it," Edenham said softly.

"But will she?"

Edenham straightened abruptly in his chair, scowling at Cranleigh sitting in the fading afternoon light. "She is more than her nation. She is a woman."

"Convince her of it, not I," Cranleigh said, staring solemnly into his eyes.

"I shall," Edenham said, leaning back against the chair, his eyes staring into the shadows.

❧

KATHERINE found Jedidiah Elliot at one of the windows in the yellow drawing room, staring into the quiet order of the Hyde's back garden. He was alone, his brother having gone off she knew not where. It was her chance, perhaps her only chance, and she was determined to take it. That Bernadette, Lady Paignton, was nearly nuzzling the Duke of Calbourne in the blue reception room had been the final spur, not that she enjoyed admitting that, even to herself.

She was going to beguile a man, tempt him to her with only the promise of herself to propel him. Not her name, not her title, not her money, not her lineage. Just her. Only her.

Could she do it?

A better question, would *he* do it?

Having watched him beat her brother to the floor, he didn't seem the most romantic of men, though was it romance that drove men and women together, dark couplings in dark corners? There was something violent about that, wasn't there? Violent and dangerous; Jedidiah Elliot seemed entirely suited to that.

How to approach him, that was what she couldn't decide. Directly? She didn't know how to do that. She also didn't know how to indirectly encourage him to make the suggestion that they become lovers. Although even that was likely too intimate a word for what she wanted for them. Just . . . coupling. Quickly. Passionately. A fleeting meeting of bodies in the dark. Most assuredly in the dark. She would never manage it in the light of even a single candle.

Her husband hadn't wanted her in the light of a single candle. Always in the dark. She had thought herself beautiful, been told so from the cradle, but he hadn't treated her as if she were beautiful. She didn't know what to think anymore, except that beauty did not mean what she had thought it was supposed to mean, a binding charm of sorts, the kind of thing one found in fairy tales of tall towers and deep moats and dragon's breath.

Her gaze strayed to Jedidiah's back again. If anyone would fight the dragon, he would. If he wanted to. If he were inspired enough.

How did a woman go about inspiring a man to face dragon's breath for her? To take her in the light of a thousand candles?

Richard had taken Bernadette in a maze at the Earl of Quinton's at half past eleven in the morning. There had been three witnesses, one of them Edenham. That might have been the worst part of it, that her brother had seen it, seen that she could not hold her husband, the man she had married for love.

Love. It existed, she knew. It was only that she could not seem to inspire it in a man.

Desire, then. She would inspire desire. It was a start. Perhaps she could move from there to love, tutoring herself in the amorous arts in the school of romance.

Katherine laughed silently, mocking herself. Love and romance. She was a fool, hopelessly inept at the very thing all other women knew instinctively. Just look at Jane. She had inspired Edenham's desire, love, and devotion upon a single look. Even a beating had not dimmed his resolve, she knew that without question. He was even now working out how to attain her, in spite of Jedidiah's rejection of his suit.

"He's my brother, you know," she said to Jedidiah's back, all hope of a plan tossed beneath her feet. She had no plan. She could execute no plan. Perhaps the tie that bound their siblings would serve to tie them, however briefly.

Jedidiah turned, his cool blue eyes showing slight surprise, and regret? She did not know him well enough to read him. Could a man be seduced upon the wings of regret? Probably not, though Sophia would certainly know how to manage it.

"I didn't know," he said. His voice was low and solid, like ships' timbers. She was being romantic again. He had a low voice, pleasant and resonant, that was all. "I would do it again, even knowing. She's my sister."

Katherine took a step nearer, looking out the window at his side. There was nothing to see. It was only a garden. She pretended to study the gravel walks, the trees blowing in the afternoon breeze, the call of birds, ignoring the pale and distorted reflection of herself in the glass. Distorted, most assuredly. What was she doing? This was not at all like her.

Which was precisely why she was doing it.

"Of course you would," she said. "I am a sister. I know very well what a brother will do. He will not blame you in the slightest."

Jedidiah looked down at her, a tilting of his head that bespoke annoyance. She simply could not manage to seduce a man. It was flatly humiliating. "I suppose I should be relieved by that? He deserved it. He knows he deserved it. Frankly, he deserved more, but it's my uncle's house and I'm a guest in it. I would do nothing to abuse his hospitality. Which is what your brother did in attacking my sister."

"He loves her," she said.

"He desires her," he countered swiftly, still staring at her. She kept her gaze on the subtle patterns in the glimmering glass, afraid to look into his eyes. She was the worst seductress of her generation and had no place in any fairy tale, unless it was as the toadstool. "There's a difference."

"Doesn't the one lead to the other?" she said.

"Which one, to which other?" Jedidiah said on a huff of breath, turning away from her to face the window again.

"I was hoping you would tell me," she said softly, turning her head slightly to study his profile. He had a sharp, clean profile. Richard's profile had been softer, his chin less defined. She had found him handsome when she'd married him. Thinking of his face now, she saw him as boyishly attractive. There was nothing boyish about Jedidiah Elliot.

"Lady Richard," he said, his face completely composed, indeed, shuttered against her, "I can't think this is a proper conversation for us to be having."

"I suppose it isn't, though I am surprised that a man of your background is so very concerned about what is proper and what is not."

"You mean because I am an American?"

It was said with a certain bite. Now she'd offended him. She really should have asked advice of someone with more flair for this before she started, someone such as the very sheltered and very virginal Miss Elliot.

"Actually, I was referring to your experience upon the world as the captain of a merchant ship. Does your being American play any part in that? I must rely upon you to tell me. I have enjoyed limited exposure to Americans."

A short bark of laughter escaped him. "I'm sure that's true."

"Everything I've said is true, Captain Elliot."

"And all the things you haven't said, Lady Richard?" he said, turning from the window completely to give her his full attention. His face was very fine, even discounting profile.

"True as well," she said, staring up into his eyes. He revealed nothing. His face could have been carved from stone, his eyes blue marbles, and he did not blink or fidget or waver in his attention. That was the only way she had of knowing that he did, or might, feel something. A man that intent, it had to mean something, didn't it? Something she could build upon, something to hang her heart upon. "Can you hear my thoughts, Jedidiah? Can you hear all I have not had the courage to speak?"

"I think I can . . . Katherine," he answered.

Hope flared in her heart, or was that desire? A low pulse just below her ribs, a skittering flash just under her skin, the temptation to become lost in the power of his gaze: desire, most assuredly desire. And she could not feel desire alone. That was not possible. Not when he devoured her with his eyes, his presence blocking out everyone else in the room, though the yellow drawing room was far from crowded.

"You want me to," Jedidiah said in a hushed voice, and she found herself lifting her weight to the balls of her feet, "allow your brother to court my sister."

Her heels hit the floor with an audible bump.

"No," she said serenely, covering it all with the mask she'd worn since leaving the nursery and which she had perfected since becoming Lady Richard, "that isn't what I was thinking. But would you?"

Fourteen

Now that Jane was looking for Edenham, she couldn't find him anywhere. She hadn't actually looked everywhere, but she'd looked in all the normal places; the music room, the blue reception room, and the red reception room, where they were to have dined, and would still dine, if Molly would just call for breakfast to be served. Jane supposed they were all waiting for Edenham to pull himself together, straighten his cravat, brush his hair, and wash away the worst of the bloodstains. That would take some time. Either that, or he'd left Hyde House in either a fury or a sulk and she would never see him again.

No, that wasn't it. He was still here. No man of any salt would leave after a well-deserved setdown. And no matter what else she thought of the arrogant Duke of Edenham, she did think he had salt. Quite a lot of it. There were not many men who, having met her brothers, would kiss her upon her wish, and then, almost without complaint, endure a beating.

In fact, she could think of no one else who had done half

so much. Certainly Ezekiel Biddle, while very desirous of cake . . . and other things, had not risked even a tenth as much. Why, Ezekiel had made his move whilst both her brothers were at sea. That didn't give any appearance of effort, did it?

"Tell me the truth about that kiss."

Jane sighed, looking over her shoulder at Joel, who'd almost magically appeared behind her. As she was in the music room, again, her second search of that particular room, and it was a very lovely room with its aqua wallpaper and display of beautifully crafted musical instruments, and as Joel didn't have any interest in the difference between a pianoforte and a brass horn, she knew he'd been searching her out to ask her just this question.

Joel knew her too well. It was that fact which was the source of most of their disagreements. The other source was Aunt Molly, what Joel called The English Wrinkle, which had nothing to do with Molly's appearance and everything to do with her choice of a husband. A nice girl from Boston and what had she done? Married an English duke, that's what.

"What truth do you think there is?" she countered.

Joel gave her his *don't be ridiculous* look and waited.

"You saw everything just as it happened, or nearly so," she said. "I can't think what you want me to say beyond the obvious. He kissed me. He paid for it."

"*Why* did he kiss you?"

"Lovely," she huffed, walking out of the music room, ignoring the stares of the other guests, and stepping through the wide doorway into the blue reception room. "Because he *wanted* to? Because he found me irresistible?"

"No, that's not why," Joel said, dogging her steps, grinning slightly.

"Why do *you* kiss a woman, assuming you have?" Jane said with a sharp smile.

"Because she wants me to," Joel countered without pause.

Oh, this wasn't going well at all.

"I should have thought that any man would believe any woman wanted to be kissed, if he wanted to kiss her," Jane said.

"Then you'd be wrong," Joel said. "What did you do to make Edenham kiss you? I know you must have done something. He's no green fool, to fall into a woman's net."

"I hardly *made* him! As to what I did, I don't think I did anything at all. The man saw me and has been acting like a green fool, as you so sweetly put it, ever since. I certainly didn't ask to be the object of his obsession."

"But," Joel said, his dark eyes alight, "you did ask for something. Did you *ask* him to kiss you?"

She might have blushed. She did seem to feel a certain warmth on her neck, just above her collarbone.

"Jane," Joel said, shaking his head at her. "Why? You knew what would happen."

"It's a complicated story," she said, refusing to look at him. As she looked across the room, she couldn't help noticing the Duke of Calbourne and Lady Paignton. They seemed to be giggling. Or at least the duke was giggling. Lady Paignton was smirking. "It involves Louisa." That explained most of it, excluding the part about Edenham's arrogance. The man had already been thrashed once; if she told Joel about what Edenham had assumed, he would almost certainly be due for another go.

"You should ignore her," Joel said.

"Ha," Jane deadpanned. "You should ignore Edenham. Now we're even."

"Jane?" Joel said, his voice gone quite deep.

"Yes?" she said, still watching Calbourne and Lady Paignton. What were they giggling about? And why would a duke giggle? She never would have imagined it was possible. He didn't look at all ashamed of himself either.

"I shan't be ignoring him and neither shall you," Joel said. "Edenham's here."

Jane snapped her gaze away from one duke and onto another. She saw Edenham instantly. He was striding across the blue reception room from the doorway to the red reception room. He did not look pleased, yet neither did he look angry. He looked . . . bloody marvelous, as she'd once heard her cousin George say under his breath.

His cravat had blood on it, a bright red smear lining the top of one fold. His waistcoat was wrinkled and missing two buttons. His lower lip was split and swollen and he had a purple and black bruise coming up on the left side of his jaw.

He looked not at all like a duke, but very much like a man.

He was so very, very handsome, wasn't he, when he wasn't looking so proud and untouchable? He looked very touchable now. Very determined and resolute and all those other words that meant a man who would not be stopped and who would not behave in any way like a man who could be stopped by civilized rules and common courtesy.

In other words, not at all like Ezekiel Biddle and those other two, whatever their names had been. She couldn't recall a single thing about any of them, except that they had circled once, too far away from her to make any impression at all, and disappeared from her life. All that remained was this man. Edenham. Hugh.

Oh, my.

He walked straight up to her, which did strange things to her stomach, squeezing it, causing it to flop about a bit, nodded once to Joel, and then, looking deeply into her eyes, she was sure it was deeply because she found she couldn't look away even slightly, said, "I want you to meet my children."

"Now?" she squeaked. She cleared her throat. No more squeaking! She was an accomplished American girl, not given to squeaking at handsome men, especially not dangerously rumpled handsome men with greenish eyes and straight perfect noses and the most cleverly shaped ears she'd ever seen.

Ears. She had noticed the beauty of his ears. This was bad, wasn't it?

He smiled briefly. "No, not now. But tomorrow? Can I expect you? Bring your brothers as well." He glanced briefly at Joel. She didn't know what Joel did. She couldn't stop looking at Edenham and his bruised lip. "Bring anyone you want," he said. "Will you come?"

She stared up at him, unable to form a word.

"Will you?" he breathed.

"Yes," she said, though she didn't actually *say* it. She giggled it.

That was bad.

❧

"IT's looking bad for poor Edenham," Calbourne said. "I shouldn't wonder but that he's married by Friday."

"This Friday or next?" Bernadette asked.

"Does it matter?" Calbourne said, looking down at her, grinning. "He'll be married. Poor fellow. Though I can't think he minds it, he marries so often." Calbourne shook his head; it was inconceivable to him.

"You'll never marry again?" Bernadette asked, her green eyes pensive.

"I've got my heir. Alston's thriving. I'm thriving. I have no more need for a wife, which is not to say I don't need a beautiful, enticing woman in my life," he said, grinning.

"For as long as she can entice you, I assume," Bernadette said. "How long is that, usually?"

"I haven't given it any thought."

"Likely because you can't remember?"

Cal lost his grin. This was becoming more serious than he liked. Women, particularly women like Bernadette, who had married, been widowed, and now could do as she pleased, which is to say, she could please any man she chose, were the sort of women he enjoyed best. He was not interested in women who were interested in marriage. Not unless there was a wager involved, that is. He'd endure most anything to not be found on the losing end of a wager.

"Do you want to marry again, Lady Paignton?" he asked, taking a step back. They had done nothing, engaged in nothing remotely scandalous. Yet. Which was all to the good if she were marriage-minded.

"I?" she scoffed. "No, not at all. If you will excuse me, I see my sister and have yet to greet her."

With a smile, she wound her way through the throng to her sister, Lady Lanreath, another dark haired, green-eyed widow. The women in that family had bad luck keeping their husbands alive. Cal spared a second look for Antoinette, Lady Lanreath. She was a beauty. She wasn't the sultry seductress that Bernadette was, but almost the exact opposite, elegant and ethereal, slightly untouchable, very nearly chilly.

He turned away from them both with very little difficulty. He was done with marriage. As long as he kept his distance from Sophia Dalby, he was confident he would stay unmarried.

Fifteen

"SOPHIA, you're punishing me for having kept my distance," Lord Ruan said.

"Punishing you, Lord Ruan? I am hardly that energetic," she replied.

He'd found her in the stair hall, alone, and there'd been no simple way to avoid him. If she could have, she would have. She wasn't afraid of Ruan. Hardly. It was only that she had no interest in him any longer. She might have had, a month ago, but now . . . she indulged in a mental shrug. He had kept his distance when he should have been in ardent pursuit. She demanded that and much more from a man.

"I have been most energetic," he said. "And with your goodwill in mind. I hardly expected a reward, but this refusal to speak with me isn't like you."

"Lord Ruan, you don't know me well enough to know what is like me or not."

"I think I might. Now."

The stair hall was quite large, as was everything in

Hyde House, but Ruan, his green eyes glittering in the soft sunlight that illuminated the hall in a warm glow, seemed to fill it up. He was a man who pulsed energy, quietly and steadily. His hair was black, his eyes were green, and his face bore the traces of a life lived dangerously. He was a marquis. There should not have been any trace of danger in his well-constructed life.

"Now?" she prompted, her brows raised in question.

"I had a bit of business to settle with Lord Westlin," he said.

Sophia smiled and lifted her chin. The Earl of Westlin was one of her oldest enemies, and had been her first protector of note when she'd first come to London. He was also the father of Caro's new husband. Her daughter would be the next Countess of Westlin. Wasn't life delicious that way?

"How unpleasant for you. I do hope you managed to get everything you deserved," she said.

"Thank you," Ruan said, his small mouth quirked in a half smile. "It was the final scratch of the pen, the conclusion of a service I did for him in exchange for a bit of land that my father always wanted. My absence from Town is explained by that errand. I wanted to inspect the land before signing the papers, making certain that I was getting what I had been promised."

"A wise course when dealing with Lord Westlin," she said.

Ruan shrugged slightly. "It was the least I could do for my father. I did so little for him while he was alive."

"Yes, it is easier to serve the needs of the dead," Sophia said. "They aren't nearly as demanding as the living. One has to truly strive to hear their complaints from beyond the grave."

Ruan smiled slightly and dipped his head down, looking at her from beneath his black brows.

"I wanted to do you a service as well, Sophia. I told you before, I wanted to play the hero for you, kill the beast—"

"But darling," she interrupted, "are you saying you've killed Westlin? Did he die screaming or merely whimpering? Don't leave out a single delicious detail."

Ruan did not smile, which had been her intent. No, he frowned. Entirely too serious and not at all what she wanted of any man. "He deserves to die for what he did to you."

Not that again. How very tedious. Of all things, she would never have guessed that Lord Ruan would turn tedious.

"As he will die one day," Sophia said, moving past Ruan, "you can take whatever pleasure you will from that inescapable fact. All that is required of you is patience, Lord Ruan."

Ruan did not allow her to pass. He grabbed her wrist and turned her to face him. It was their first touch, the first contact of his hand on her body. She could feel the hard sculpting of his palm on the inside of her wrist, his strong fingers leashing her to him. She allowed it, testing the feel of his hand, twisting her wrist slightly, measuring how firmly he held her. No man touched her unless she allowed it. If they believed she wanted it, so much the better.

"Sophia, I know," he said in a hoarse undertone, his green eyes slicing into hers with all the subtlety of a saber. Sophia stiffened and held his gaze, her black eyes as hard as granite. "He drank deeply, with my encouragement, drank and sank into memory. I was there as the memories bubbled up."

"That sounds most unpleasant," she said, twisting her wrist within his hand, pulling free. He did not stop her. He could have, if he'd wanted to. She would have stopped him if he had. Perhaps they understood that much about each other. She hoped so.

"I want to help you," he said.

Sophia laughed abruptly. "You want to help yourself. Let's be honest about that, at least. Play the hero? Over something that happened decades ago? No, Ruan, you were curious, that is all. Knowledge is power—there is nothing truer. You wanted a form of power over me. You don't have it. No one does. If not Westlin, then certainly not you."

He did not pull away from her. Perhaps he should have. Perhaps he truly thought that he held some sort of power over her, though what kind she would not contemplate.

"All right," he said, facing her, not touching her, though she could see that he wanted to. "I was curious. You arranged for your daughter to marry Westlin's heir, for her to be ruined by Westlin's heir—"

"Ruined?" she said, cutting him off. "He kissed her, touched her breast a time or two. It takes more than that to ruin a woman, or it should. She wanted him and she got him, that's all that matters. As for arranging her marriage, that is my duty to my daughter. She loves him. I did my duty well. There is no stain upon that marriage, no revenge beyond the great knife it was to Westlin's cock. As you must have heard from Westlin's drunken babblings, I think I deserved at least that much from him."

"Sophia," he said, taking a step closer to her, trying to tower over her, no doubt. A foolish ploy. Did he not know that he took a step closer to her blade? Having heard Westlin's tale, did Ruan not know that she was now always armed? No man touched her without her consent. Never again. "I am not his ally. I hate what he did to you, what they all did to you. I only wanted to find out why these men are your enemies, why you seek to destroy the third Marquis of Dutton."

"Ruan, you see dragons where there are none," she said. "I told you that. Why couldn't you believe it?" She chuckled. It was not a pleasant sound. "Oh, yes, because

I am a woman. I don't know what's best for me. Only you can know that, the man who has been caught by the flickering light of my infamous allure. What gives you the right to meddle in the shadows of my life? Even Dalby, who made me his countess, knew to let that part of me remain in shadow."

"If a man loves you, no part of you should remain in shadow," he said solemnly.

"Loves me?" she said lightly, smiling at him coldly. "Do you dare to claim that you love me? How could you possibly, Lord Ruan? You only know the barest trace of me."

"I know that is so," he said. "I suspected it, and now I know it. You keep yourself well hid, Sophia, still that girl hiding in the wood of Westlin's estate, still hiding from the men who hunted you down like a wild animal before they raped you."

Such a tame telling of what happened that long ago season. Such a quick and bloodless declaration of what the girl she had been had survived. He thought he knew, thought he understood what had happened to her, but he understood her less now than he had before he had mined these bare facts of a distant past.

Pity. It was pity she saw in his eyes. Pity? When she'd survived all her trials, and defeated all who had arrayed against her? What fools these English were, to read the story of her life so wrong.

Sophia laid her hand upon Ruan's chest and smiled up at him. He looked mildly alarmed, as well he should.

"What did Westlin tell you, Ruan? Did he tell you that I shamed him in front of his friends? Did he tell of my base trickery and how he paid me for it? Did he tell you that I never once cried for mercy?" She withdrew her hand from his chest, showing him the blade she had pressed to his thigh. A thin, sharp blade, hidden within the spines of her fan. She was never without a weapon, and Westlin and the wild hunt of her on his estate was why. "I won, Ruan. I won then, and I'm still winning. Anyone who cannot see that is a fool."

"Yes, you have defeated them, in your way. Their daughters ruined, their sons . . . what have you planned for Dutton? He drinks himself stupid, out of fear of you, I think."

"You English," she said, shaking her head at him, "you think all paths are straight, from one firm point to another, seen clearly on the sun-washed horizon. My path is not straight. You cannot see where it started or where it will end." All playfulness dropped from her like a mask. "You think I would harm innocents? I was innocent once, Lord Ruan, long ago. I have done nothing to the current Lord Dutton. Everything he is, he has done to himself."

"*You* are English, Sophia," he said.

She smiled. "I thought so once," she said, walking away from him.

The stair hall was quiet, deserted, which it should not have been. The house was full of guests and the meal was overdue. The stair hall should have been a wild riot of activity. It was not. Perhaps it was the cold chain of destiny, tying her to this moment and this man. It was possible. She carried a blade; she could cut herself free of even destiny, if she were strong enough.

She was at the door to the blue reception room when he called out, "Tell me what happened, Sophia. Tell me, if only to wash Westlin's drunken ramblings from my head."

"Still curious, Lord Ruan?" she asked, facing the door.

"Only about you," he said softly.

He had not moved toward her; she could hear his careful distance. He did not fear her blade, that she knew. She had seen that much in his eyes. Ruan had lived with danger, that much was clear.

Still not facing him, her eyes on the heavy door before

her, she said, "Flattery? Sophia Dalby cannot resist it, can she? Very well, Lord Ruan. This small portion of my path I will reveal to you."

She turned to face him, her eyes not sparkling with the sheen of Lady Dalby's seductive gleam, but with the dark and unreadable gaze of an Iroquois of the deep woods.

"Westlin was my protector. He took me up and paid quite nicely for me. I was a virgin, you see. Always such a good price for young, pretty virgins. He was quite happy with me, as well he should have been. But then he was told that I hadn't been a virgin after all, that he hadn't been the one to pluck the rose." Sophia laughed under her breath. "But darling, you can only be a virgin once and it pays so well to be one. Would you like a virgin, Ruan? I can be one easily enough, if that is what you prefer. Some men do, you know. Virgin upon virgin. With the supply so scarce, what's a girl to do but try to meet the demand?"

Ruan's eyes looked at her darkly across the marble floor of the stair hall. Not a conversation, then? A soliloquy? She could play it that way.

"The second Marquis of Dutton, I think, was the one who divulged it. Such an uproar. They were visiting Westlin at Idmiston, his estate in Wiltshire. Melverley, Dutton, Aldreth, Cumberland. Westlin. My protector."

Sophia quieted, remembering, her gaze dropping to the hard marble floor.

"Aldreth wanted no part of it, but he did not attempt to stop it, and that kind of cowardice bears its own scars. The others stripped me bare and set me out upon a meadow bordering a wood. A hunt, you see. Hunt the Iroquois. Hunt the Indian girl. I was just fourteen."

She looked up at Ruan and said, "Did you know that among the Iroquois the children are fully their mothers? They are of her tribe, her people. I *was* English, you see. I was always English because she was. But not here. Not then. Not anymore."

"I'm sorry, Sophia," Ruan said, his voice hoarse and low.

She smiled, a full smile that showed her teeth. "They thought it would take minutes. I eluded them for two days and a night. Naked, barefooted, no weapon, and on unfamiliar ground. Two days, Ruan. I was defeating them, which Englishmen do not endure well, especially at the hands of savages."

Her smile faded as her thoughts drifted back, the memory of that long hunt, the bleeding of her feet, the wild, pounding fear. She would have run home if she could have, but of course, she couldn't. She was trapped on an island and her home had been lost to her long before Westlin had entered her life.

She pulled her thoughts back and chained them to this story, this one story that Ruan was so eager to hear. Let him hear it, then. It could no longer touch her, chained as it was in the deepest part of memory.

"They caught me, and they did what men do when they catch naked girls running from them. Men do love chasing things and catching them, don't they? But you see, Ruan, even in that moment I had my victory. No tears fell from my eyes. No pleas for mercy from my lips. No hesitation. Dutton was so cup-shot by then that he could not rouse himself to play the man. He fell against a tree, vomiting. I can still recall that smell even now, the scent of damp oak leaves and whisky vomit. I took them in, one after another. I took them in, again and again. They thought to break me, to punish me, but I did not act like a woman being punished."

"Did that not make it worse?" Ruan asked.

Sophia's head snapped up, her eyes sharp. "Not for me. I *am* an Iroquois. I will *not* break. They wanted to destroy me. I proved that it was not in their power to do so."

Ruan nodded, his eyes hooded, shielded.

"I left Westlin after that, after I'd got what I wanted

from him," she said matter-of-factly. "I went to Dutton and then to Melverley, seducing each of them into very profitable liaisons. Each in their turn gave me what I asked for: money, property, jewels. As was my due. I proved to them that they had not frightened me, nor punished me, nor harmed me in any way. I sliced deeply into their pride, and then they paid me handsomely. I defeated them in every way open to me. Do you think to pity me, Ruan? Why?"

"For the woman you might have been, Sophia. For the life they stole from you."

But it was not they who stole it. It was someone else entirely. Someone she still hunted for, though not in the way Westlin had hunted her in his wood. No, not quite so loudly, but just as relentlessly.

Of course, Ruan had his story, the one he wanted from her. He did not need to hear another. Her paths had been many, and had many twistings and dark turnings. Ruan wanted a straight path, full of light so that he could understand her. What folly. But then, he was English, wasn't he? They were rather known for folly.

Sophia smiled, her dark eyes sparkling as Lady Dalby's always did. "Everyone loves the woman I am, Lord Ruan. I am quite famous for it. You should know that as well as anyone. Wasn't it for love of Sophia Dalby that you sought out Lord Westlin and got him drunk enough to talk about that which he is determined not to remember? Tell me, Lord Ruan," she said seductively, "are you more fascinated now, or less? More, I should say. You are a man who likes mysteries and layers and intrigues with his women. Have I intrigued you, darling Lord Ruan?"

He stared at her, his green eyes smoldering, likely in frustrated anger. She did hope so.

"I have, haven't I?" she said silkily. "Now you must decide, is everything I told you true, or did I just weave this tale to give you what you wanted? I am very good at giving men what they want, which I'm certain can be no surprise to you. Good afternoon, Lord Ruan."

Lady Dalby left him standing alone in the stair hall, making her way out into the light and noise of another London party of yet another London Season.

Sixteen

"NEITHER one of them is going to give you what you want," Bernadette, Lady Paignton, said.

Antoinette, Lady Lanreath, looked at her sister in mild horror and asked, "And what is it that I want?"

"To marry again, of course," Bernie said on a pout. "You were very clear about it and I haven't forgotten a word. You were inspired by Penelope and what she'd managed for herself and you said you wanted a bit of it yourself. I've done all I can, Toni, at least with the available dukes, and I do think that if you want to marry again you might as well be a duchess, but neither Edenham nor Calbourne seemed interested."

"Oh, Bernie . . ." Antoinette said on a lingering sigh. "What have you done?"

Bernadette slanted a gaze at her older sister. "I only talked to them, Toni, just to get an inkling of how they felt about the subject of marriage. Calbourne isn't the least interested in marriage, and Edenham is probably interested in marriage, but not interested in marrying you. He seems completely taken by that American niece of Hyde's."

Antoinette worked her fan around her throat, doing a stellar job of covering her agitation. "How did you ever have the cheek to talk to Edenham after everything that . . . happened? Did he actually speak to you in return or did you do all the talking?"

"It was a bit awkward at first," Bernadette said, "but the one thing you can always count on with Edenham is that he'll do the polite thing. Cut me direct? He'd rather cut off his arm. Of course, Lady Richard wasn't anywhere near him, and I do think that helped."

"It must have," Antoinette said, scanning the room. Were they ever going to eat?

"Has Edenham left? I do think he must have after that setdown he took at the hands of those Americans. They're awfully attractive, aren't they, Toni? I get shivers of—"

"Yes, I don't need to hear about your shivers. And, no, he hasn't left. He's talking with Miss Elliot, and as her brother is at her side I don't think any more blood will be spilt. At least not today."

"Rotten bit of luck," Bernie said, looking through the crowd until she saw Edenham standing with Miss Elliot and the younger of her two brothers. Utterly handsome man, truly, and so unpredictable. There was much that could be said for unpredictability, within strict parameters, naturally. "You're not upset about the dukes? I did so hope you'd be a duchess this time round."

"No, I'm not upset," Antoinette answered. "It might surprise you to know that I have my own plans."

"Are you trying to say you have a man in mind?" Bernadette asked.

As subtlety regarding men was not Bernadette's strongest point, Antoinette might have been expected to give her sister a tepid and entirely vague reply. As it happened,

Antoinette was not in the mood to be tepid, not after watching the Duke of Edenham make a complete fool of himself over a woman, and clearly not care that he might look a complete fool. Naturally, the result was that he didn't look foolish in the slightest, merely determined and unafraid.

"That's it precisely, Bernie. Now, if you'll excuse me?" she said, and Antoinette glided across the room toward the man in question.

Bernadette lost sight of Antoinette almost immediately as she made her way into the red reception room. As Joel Elliot was in the blue reception room, Bernadette made her way to him. Why not? She'd done her good turn for Toni; now it was time for her to enjoy herself.

It was rather difficult to make her way to the knot that was Edenham, Joel, and Jane Elliot. Everyone, for obvious reasons, wanted to be near to them in the hope that something exciting would again occur. As she wormed her way through the crowd, she even heard more than one person suggest that inviting Americans to formal affairs would be an excellent way of livening things up. How did one get them to agree to it, was what the Earl of Quinton was overheard to say, once they found out how deadly dull they always were?

Bernadette took exception to that. They weren't *all* deadly dull, and as Lord Quinton rarely left his estate he was hardly in a position to make sweeping pronouncements. Now there was a man she had no interest in pursuing. Quinton, Raithby's father, was entirely too serious for her. Being serious about anything but making a name for yourself for having a rousing good time entirely missed the point, the point being . . . she hadn't worked that bit out yet, but she was close. She could feel it. There had to be a point, didn't there? There must be.

Finally! She'd made it to Joel Elliot, and didn't he look as charming as he did an hour ago. Apparently getting into fistfights agreed with him completely. His cravat looked as fresh as when she'd first met him.

Edenham, strangely and for the first time since she'd had that rather indiscreet affair with Katherine's husband, seemed pleased to see her. Bernadette, quite experienced at these sorts of things, understood immediately and without complicated explanations that Edenham would be quite content to have her take Joel Elliot off to some distant spot, leaving Jane to him.

She didn't anticipate any sort of problem accomplishing *that*.

And she did want to make amends in some way, however small, for the disaster that had been Richard. She'd found him barely tolerable, and she'd had no notion that Katherine believed him faithful, which he most assuredly had not been, and she'd not intended any hurt to befall his wife. Far from it. Her own husband having been a complete rogue, she understood that particular situation too well.

"Captain Elliot," she said, leaning close to him and giving him a nice view down her bodice, "you're looking quite refreshed. How is that possible? I feel positively wilted in this crush. Do I look it?"

"Not at all, Lady Paignton," he said, his dark eyes twinkling.

"What a charming liar you are," she breathed, brushing her breast against his arm as she looped her arm through his. "Might I ask you to escort me out into the twilight air? I believe Hyde has a spacious garden. Do you know it?"

"I do," Joel said, looking a bit discomfited, staring at his sister and then back down to her. "Though I do hope you are not disappointed to find it is not twilight yet."

"Not at all. Perhaps we should linger until twilight finds us? You don't mind if I borrow your brother for just a few moments, Miss Elliot?" Bernadette said. "I promise to return him in the same condition I found him. Or nearly so." She laughed softly.

"Not at all," Jane Elliot said, her pale hazel eyes gleaming. "Enjoy yourself, Joel. I shall be perfectly safe right here."

"Perfectly," Edenham echoed, his eyes very carefully not gleaming.

One had to be so careful around brothers. Bernadette was so relieved she had nothing but three sisters to bother about, and they were truly no bother at all.

And with that thought, she gently led Joel Elliot through the room, giving him every impression that he was leading her.

This was going to be such fun.

❦

JANE watched Joel being led like a calf to the butcher by Lady Rampant and suppressed a sigh. She did hope Joel could handle himself. Lady Rampant . . . Paignton looked up to the task of eating him alive.

"He'll be fine," Edenham said, his warm voice cutting into her thoughts with alarming precision. Did she wear every thought on her face? She decided to experiment, thinking something very personal, and looking into his hazel green eyes as she did so.

Edenham's eyes widened and then he grinned. "But Miss Elliot, I don't think the Hyde garden is large enough for *all* of us."

Jane, to her absolute horror, found her breath caught in her throat, which made her cough in a very indelicate manner.

"You are very forward, your grace," she said, when she'd got her breath back.

"You have more than enough evidence to support that observation, Miss Elliot," he said, lifting his gaze from hers to look at the crowd around them. She did not look about. It might have been because she could not stop herself from staring at his face. "I must ask, does it offend you?"

"And if it did, you would change your manner?" she asked.

"Either that or convince you to be forward with me," he said, taking her by the arm and leading her through the room to the doorway to the music room. The crowd parted for him serenely. Because he was a duke or because he was bleeding? Or because they wondered what he'd do with her next?

What he'd do with her . . . there was a phrase to send shivers along her scalp. And elsewhere.

The music room was not especially crowded. Edenham even managed to find them a pair of seats near the pianoforte, but that may have had less to do with luck than with the fact that he was a duke. Would an earl or viscount or a mere mister be able to deny a duke a chair if he wished one? She had no idea. It didn't seem so, but she truly didn't understand the whys and wherefores of a society built so firmly upon rank and the resulting precedence.

The chairs were small, but upholstered and comfortable, at least for her. Edenham, with his long legs, looked a bit like a grasshopper perched upon a thimble.

"Now, Jane," he said once they were seated, "I do think we should take this quiet moment"—which was absurd as there were easily a dozen people in the music room, all strangers to her and yet certainly familiar to him—"to discuss why I want to marry you."

Naturally, she was rendered speechless by that statement. And then she rallied. Was there ever a proposal made so dispassionately?

"Certainly," she said, sitting forward upon her chair. "And then we might discuss all the reasons why I don't want to marry you." She smiled brightly as she said it, not at all caring who heard her. She didn't know anyone in this room, after all. "The fact that I don't know you at all must rank near the top of my *list*." *Ha.* This list idea was working out brilliantly. She'd have to thank Amelia, or whoever had first mentioned it, later. "But then there is the fact that you are English and I am not. That certainly must appear in the top three."

"And where would my being a duke rank, Jane? I should be most disappointed if that fact did not rank at least in the top two," Edenham said, looking not the least bit insulted.

Bother. She'd had no idea it was so difficult to insult a duke. One would have thought they took insult at nearly everything.

"I should say that I hate to disappoint you," she said, "but since I don't, I won't, but I am not going to allow you to determine either the content or the ranking of my list of objections, *Hugh*," she snapped.

Edenham smiled. And she did not like it in the slightest. It should have enraged her. It did not. It most definitely did not. It did very strange things just under her heart. In fact, she found it difficult to take a full breath.

"You've taken the trouble to find out my name," he said softly.

"It was no trouble," she said stiffly, and then winced. That hadn't come out right at all.

"I'm so glad," he said. "It does show we have so much in common, our minds working along the same course. I, too, have learned your name and it was no trouble at all. *Libby*."

Libby? An abbreviation of Liberty? Who had told him that? And who had given him leave to assign her a pet name?

He'd given himself leave, of course. He was a duke.

"Whom have you been talking to?" she asked. "Not my brothers."

"Whom have you?" he said, trying for an innocent look and missing it by miles. "My sister?" She must have made a face for he smiled and said, "Libby, you do warm my heart. Already meeting the family, finding out all the little details that are sure to charm me."

"That is not what I was doing!" she said, rather sharply as someone across the room twanged a string on the harp.

"No? And yet the result is the same."

"It is not," she said, aware she was sounding more and more like a pouty three-year-old child. "I did not know she was your sister, and I should think you'd be ashamed to make a spectacle of yourself with her in the room. I am quite certain my brothers are much more careful of me than you are of her."

"By *spectacle*," he said, leaning closer to her, lowering his voice, "I presume you mean the moment when I kissed you?"

Another shiver moved across her skin, lower than her scalp this time. Much lower.

She blinked and had to remind herself to breathe, her eyes going to the bruise on his jaw. It was bigger now, more purple. She tried to think if she'd always had a preference for men with . . . physical disturbances. They *had* all been laborers of a sort, the kind of men with rough hands, always sporting a few minor bruises and cuts.

Mercy. What sort of woman was she?

Not a very nice sort, clearly. She only hoped her mother never found out.

"Or was it the moment Jedidiah threw the first punch?" he said, watching her face very carefully. Too carefully. Edenham rubbed his bruised jaw lightly, her eyes trapped by the gesture. "He had the right. You wanted him to, didn't you?"

"You deserved it," she said.

"True," he said softly. "I kissed you, at your request, a detail I can't think you want your brothers to know." She could feel herself flushing. She stopped looking at his face and felt her skin almost instantly cool. "I paid the price for that kiss," he continued. "I think that squares everything, don't you? Now we may begin again, on far more intimate footing."

"I hardly think so," she said, looking into his eyes again.

"Would you care to make a wager on that?" he breathed, a slow smile taking over his face.

As it happened, she did not. A loosely worded wager with Louisa had started all this. She was not going to jump into the same pit twice.

"You don't make wagers?" he asked, studying her face.

"I certainly don't make a habit of it, no," she said, averting her gaze to look around the room. Six people were staring at her, five of them women. She didn't know a single one of them. It was something of a relief that Louisa wasn't in the room; Louisa would very likely do something awkward, like come over and blurt out that Jane had won the wager concerning Edenham. Yes, that was exactly the sort of thing Louisa would do. "I suppose you make wagers all the time," she said primly.

"Because I am a useless, brainless, spineless duke of England?" he said.

Her eyes jerked back to his. "If that's how you define yourself, I'd hardly think to argue with you."

"No, not about that, you wouldn't," he said, not precisely smiling, but doing something pleasant with his mouth. His bruised mouth.

She looked away abruptly.

Edenham narrowed his eyes, a slight furrow between his brows. "I gather that your brothers have trounced many a man, any man they feel has . . . sailed too close to your anchor line?" She turned just as abruptly back to him. "Trying for the nautical metaphors, as you can see. I thought you'd like that."

"I don't," she said, shaking her head. "What I mean to say is, I don't care how you choose to express yourself. And there haven't been that many men."

"How many?"

"Really, this is absurd," she said, starting to smile.

"I already know about Ezekiel Biddle," he said. "That's one. Did he endure a trouncing, too?"

"Of course not," she said, her nose in the air.

"I suppose that means he didn't kiss you."

Absurd conversation. She was going to say nothing more to encourage him in it.

"Perhaps they simply didn't catch him at it," Edenham said. He had the most wickedly playful look on his face. She couldn't seem to look away from it. "I know someone has kissed you before I did. You kiss like a woman who's been kissed before."

"There's no need to shout it!" she hissed, looking over her shoulder. Her brothers weren't in the room. Neither was Louisa. Cranleigh was. She wished he weren't. Cranleigh had met Ezekiel Biddle once; she had to assume he'd forgotten all about it. It wasn't at all likely that Ezekiel could have left a lasting impression upon him. They'd only met briefly, and Ezekiel wasn't the sort who left a lasting impression upon a person even after extended exposure.

"Ah, so they don't know, these watchdogs of yours," Edenham said, grinning in a perfectly wicked way. He was going to use that bit of knowledge against her, she was certain of it. Dukes, and all that. "So, Ezekiel Biddle, that's one. Were there more? Of course there were. You're a beautiful woman. A man can overlook two raging brothers for a woman who looks the way you do."

"I do believe you think you've just flattered me, but I am not the sort of woman who runs around New York kissing men, and I'm also not the sort of woman who falls into a dead faint because some man thinks I'm beautiful. But I can see that you're the sort of man who thinks that I am that sort of woman, which is the very finest reason I can think of to not want to marry you!"

And with those words, she rose to her feet and walked out of the music room. Edenham sat with his mouth open and his shoddy attempts at charm crushed. It was a stunning look on him. She did hope he made a habit of displaying it more often.

❧

"YOU'RE making a habit of saying the wrong thing to her," Cranleigh said, taking Jane's chair. "Are you certain you want to marry her? You don't seem to get on very well together."

"Bugger off," Edenham said, staring at the floor between his feet.

It had been a good start. He could see that, feel it in the air that shimmered around her, like . . . like . . . oh, he couldn't think of a nautical reference and so let the thought drift.

Cranleigh, like the thoughtful, sensitive man he was, laughed under his breath.

"She's not from here, you do realize that?" Cranleigh said when he'd stopped laughing. "America? Life, liberty, and the pursuit of happiness? An entirely different way of looking at things, Edenham. Entirely different. She might make you the most miserable wife, if you can get her to agree to marry you in the first place."

"I told her she was beautiful," Edenham said. "There's no place in the world where that is the wrong thing to say to a woman. No place, not even sodding New York."

Cranleigh raised his eyebrows and held his tongue.

Edenham gave in.

"All right. Tell me," he said, still staring at the floor. A small black ant crawled next to his shoe. He watched its progress and had no urge to step on it. There was a metaphor.

"The *Plain Jane*," Cranleigh said softly, looking at Edenham. Edenham stopped looking at the ant to lift his face to him; it was the least he could do as the man was trying to help him. "She was, you know. She wasn't a beauty, not even pretty. *Plain* was putting it nicely. A girl gets treated a certain way when she's not a beauty. Then she gets treated another way when she becomes one. Jane noticed the difference, understood the reason behind it, and didn't like it."

Edenham stared at Cranleigh, his brow furrowed. What woman didn't enjoy being beautiful? New York women? He didn't believe it.

"You *saw* all this?" Edenham asked.

Cranleigh snorted. "'Course not. Her mother told me. I think she was trying to build family feeling or some such. Anyway, I'm certain she likes being a beauty, 'tis only that she doesn't like men who like that she's a beauty, if you catch the difference."

"Bloody hell I don't," Edenham said.

But he did. Katherine fought against something very like it, though not exactly like it. It should be enough that a woman was beautiful, more than enough to make her happy; it was damned complicated when it wasn't.

"That's it, then," Edenham said, his gaze going back to the floor. The ant was gone.

"No, there's more," Cranleigh said. Edenham lifted his head again. "This bit gets very tricky. I'm not sure I can explain it. I'm not actually sure there is a way to explain it. She's kissed someone, more than one you said. Now, it might be fine enough for a girl to kiss a man, even more than one, but it's not fine to talk about it. It's as if you're saying she's loose in her ways."

Edenham let out a heavy sigh and dropped his head back down. The ant was back. Sturdy, relentless ant. It was nearly inspiring.

"You still want to marry her?" Cranleigh asked.

"I do," Edenham said softly.

"I don't mean to pry, but why?"

Edenham lifted his head and looked into Cranleigh's

light blue eyes, the eyes of a man who'd just married a woman he'd been hopelessly in love with for more than two long years.

"Damned if I know."

Cranleigh nodded and dropped his gaze, presumably looking at the ant. "I understand completely."

Seventeen

JANE didn't know where to go. Joel was with Lady Paignton in the back garden, doing something she was sure her mother would disapprove of. Jed was talking to Edenham's sister in the yellow salon and from the look in his eyes, she did not want to interrupt them. Her cousin Iveston was talking to Penelope's father, Penelope standing at his side. That looked very personal. Her cousin Cranleigh was in the music room with Edenham and she wasn't going back in *there*. Obviously, she didn't care in the least where Louisa was. She was afraid to look for Sophia, afraid of what she'd say and of what Jane would find herself saying to her; she was determined not to look the fool, and she was starting to suspect that was very difficult to avoid when talking with Sophia.

Jane sighed and looked around the blue reception room again, half afraid, half hoping that Edenham would come out of the music room and do something scandalous, like kiss her again. But he wouldn't. She'd had to ask him to the first time, and the last time. Certainly the last time. She didn't go about kissing men just because they wanted to kiss her. She had to want to kiss them, too. And she didn't. Hardly ever. Why, she hadn't even kissed Ezekiel Biddle, which was part of the problem with Ezekiel Biddle. Certainly if a man was going to . . . reach for cake, he should do some preliminary work at the start. A girl didn't enjoy being *grabbed*. Or fondled. Or brushed against with nothing having been done to set the mood in advance.

Laziness, pure laziness. What else?

The very least a man could do was to put some honest effort into it.

The guests around her, while not staring at her too overtly, were starting to grumble a bit loudly about the delay regarding breakfast. When one was invited to a duke's residence to dine, one did expect to actually dine. As the kiss, the fight, and the cleanup were long over, she didn't feel one bit responsible for the delay and so could look the grumblers directly in the eye, smiling in placid innocence.

"Jane!"

Jane jerked and turned, Aunt Molly staring her down with her gunmetal blue eyes. Jane felt instantly less innocent.

"Yes?"

"What are you doing?" Molly said in a rigid undertone, her lips smiling and nearly immobile while she talked behind her teeth.

"Doing?"

"Where is Edenham? You haven't lost him, have you?"

She had no response to that. When had she become responsible for the Duke of Edenham? *Hugh.* Her stomach flipped just a bit around one edge, just one.

"Jane," Molly gritted out, still smiling at the guests surrounding them, the room, the house, the world in general, "you are not seated anywhere near Edenham at table. I can't allow breakfast to be served until you've . . . made a firmer impression upon him. Now, go find him and *do it*!"

A *firmer* impression? He'd kissed her, been bludgeoned

for it, declared his wish to marry her in front of one and all, and gave every appearance of being taken with her charms, as defined by her beauty. Still. Jane huffed. Could any London girl do better? She thought not.

"I think I've impressed him more than sufficiently," she said stiffly, adopting Molly's technique of smiling frozenly whilst talking behind her teeth. It was actually not that difficult. "He did ask to marry me, if you hadn't heard."

Molly nodded to a cluster of older gentlemen on her right, smiling enthusiastically. "And was beaten for it. Has he asked you since?"

Jane's smile drooped a bit. Molly shot her a warning glance, and Jane's false smile returned to its former false brightness.

"I don't want to marry him!"

"Whyever not, you silly girl?" Molly said. "I married a duke. It's been nothing but a pleasure. Smile and nod at the Marquis of Penrith, quickly now, or you'll end up on White's book. That man has a wager going on every *on dit* in Town. If he wagers you won't marry Edenham, the odds are, you won't."

Jane followed Molly's gaze; it settled upon a very handsome man of dark blond hair and nearly feline features. He was watching her avidly. She nodded. He nodded.

"I am not going to marry Edenham," Jane gritted out behind her smile.

"Whyever not? He's a fine-looking man, rich as Midas, has an impressive estate, and he's a duke," Molly said as they moved through the crowd.

"He's English," Jane said tightly.

Molly huffed. "I'm English."

"You're American. You married an Englishman," Jane said.

"And have I suffered? I have not. Hyde adores me, as well he should," Molly said. "You know your mother hoped you would find someone interesting whilst you visited me.

You do realize that your mother knows the London Season nearly as well as I do; I write her everything about it and have for years. You can't think the timing of your visit has to do with the *tides*, can you?"

Jane stopped and stared down at Molly; Molly was quite petite, her own mother was taller by at least two inches, though they did resemble each other strongly. Perhaps that is what made it difficult to make light of Molly's words. In so many ways, subtle or not, it was very much like talking to her mother.

"She can't have expected me to marry someone from *here*!" Jane said, her false smile forgotten.

They were very near the door to the stair hall. Jane had been trying, and succeeding, in leading Molly away from the doorway to the music room. She didn't think she wanted to attempt managing both Edenham and Molly at the same time, especially on an empty stomach.

"I shan't talk about what she expects," Molly said, looking at Jane almost critically. Critically? What had she done? "I'll only say that she wants you to enjoy experiences and people outside of what you would normally find in New York or Boston or Philadelphia."

"Which I am," Jane said.

"And which you should continue to do," Molly said, "without blind prejudice hobbling your every step."

"It's hardly blind," Jane said.

"Isn't it?" Molly said, her blue eyes glinting like steel. "You haven't judged Hyde and his sons as Englishmen first and family second, or even third? You haven't looked at Edenham, a perfectly lovely man by anyone's reckoning, and judged him first an English duke and then I don't know what? But not as a man, Jane. You haven't judged him, considered him, as a man."

Of course she was correct, and Jane hadn't seen anything wrong with that, until Molly put it in those terms with that disapproving look in her eyes. Put that way, it did sound, if not precisely petty, then at least shortsighted. Perhaps even unfair. After all, her biggest fear had been that these English aristocrats would judge her, having not truly met her, as an ill-mannered, inferior American.

To be perfectly fair to Edenham, if only for the barest moment, he hadn't judged her that way at all. He had taken her at face value, very nearly literally. Still, it was better than what she had done to him.

Jane nodded slowly. "I'm still not going to marry him."

Molly smiled, a true smile this time, and said, "Just enjoy him, Jane. He probably doesn't want to marry you anymore, anyway. What man would, after all that? Now, go get him and make good use of him while you can. You aren't going to be in London forever, and the Season is almost over."

And with that final insult? Advice? Encouragement? Molly continued to make her way through the crowd, apologizing for the delay regarding breakfast, blaming the cook, the baker, the butler, the housekeeper, and anyone else she could think of. The problem, if Jane could call it that, and she thought she would, was that Molly made her way directly into the music room.

Jane knew what to expect next. She really was getting to be an old hand at these London town house games. She felt almost sophisticated.

❧

"For a sophisticated man, Edenham, you are muddying things up quite badly," Molly said, having marched into the music room and straight over to Edenham. "And you, Cranleigh," she said, whirling on her son. Both men leapt to their feet upon seeing her enter the room and now stood as abashed as two young boys who'd been found tormenting the stable kittens. "I expected far better of you. You simply must allow Edenham to get on with it! You can visit with him later, perhaps at his own wedding to your cousin?"

Edenham blinked and dipped his head down. Molly was fully a foot shorter than he and he did not want this conversation overheard, any more than it already was, that is.

"You approve my suit?" he asked.

"Your suit? Is that what you're calling it?" Molly said sharply, looking him over in apparent disgust. "A muddle, that's what it is. I arrange for you to meet the most beautiful, interesting, wholesome girl and you put your foot in it from the first word. Do you know how many letters I had to write to persuade my sister to agree to this trip for Jane? Can you have any concept of how poor Sally, once convinced that this visit to England would do Jane good, had to tirelessly persuade her husband to allow it?"

"Not cajole?" Cranleigh said.

Molly fixed him with a quelling look. Cranleigh instantly looked quelled. "You know better than anyone that the women of my family do not cajole, Cranleigh. If you are attempting to be humorous, this is *not* the moment for it."

"You did all this for me?" Edenham asked. "Or for her?"

"For her, obviously," Molly said. "But I have no objection to you at all, Edenham. You saw her and you recognized what a treasure she is. Well done, as far as it goes. You will make her a stellar husband. If you can convince her to accept you. I never saw such a tangle in my life. Why, Hyde managed it better in five minutes, and with a rebellion brewing, and he across an ocean, *and* my father not at all pleased with him, than you have done in two hours. Of course," Molly said musingly, "he did have the advantage of a sparkling uniform, perfectly tailored down to the last buttonhole."

Molly cast a critical eye over Edenham, from his head to his feet. Edenham shifted his weight and lifted his chin against the constraints of his cravat. There was nothing wrong with his tailoring, he was certain of it, but there was nothing that could quite compare to a military uniform, though in Jane's case, she might just choose to shoot at it . . . him.

She wasn't far from that now, actually.

He did have every advantage, and he wasn't using his advantages nearly as well as he ought. He was an experienced man, experienced in the ways of the world, and particularly in the ways of women. He'd been married three times, hadn't he? And that was just the tip of the feather.

"Knowing I have your endorsement," Edenham said, bowing slightly, "I shall proceed with more vigor. Thank you, Molly."

Edenham walked out of the door Molly had entered by, the entire room watching his exit.

"If he proceeds with any more vigor, you shall need to replace a few items of furniture," Cranleigh said.

"All to a good cause, Cranleigh," Molly said, smiling. "All to a good cause."

❧

"THERE you are," Jane said as Edenham approached her, a most determined, and one might even say cheerful, look in his eyes. "You show remarkable vigor, I must say."

"Thank you?" he said, his brows lifting comically.

"It didn't take Molly long to bludgeon you into seeking me out. You are having a time of it today, aren't you, *Hugh*." He didn't look shocked by the intimacy. She gave him credit for that. "First I use you outrageously, then my brothers beat you nearly senseless, and then the hostess forces you to reenter the fray. Perhaps you should have stayed home today. It would certainly have been more restful."

"But not more entertaining," he said. "And I wasn't nearly senseless."

"Fine," she said, smiling. "You kept your senses."

"And if that is how you use men outrageously, I am entirely at your disposal. Use me again. Please," he said.

Something had changed. He had changed, that was certain, but she didn't know why. Molly, certainly. She was pushing them together, that much was obvious. Molly wanted her to marry Edenham? Perhaps. Almost certainly.

But what did Jane want? She hadn't ever got her chance at what she wanted. Too much interference in her life, too many brothers and a slightly overbearing father, that was her trouble. She hadn't thought her adventure would look quite like this, and she looked Edenham up and down as she thought it, but why not? He wanted her. Everyone wanted her to want him. She did like him; in fact, she liked him more with every conversation they had. Why not? Edenham could be her London Adventure.

But she was not going to marry him.

She would . . . Ezekiel Biddle him.

That sounded like it might be fun. And with everyone in the room endeavoring to help her be alone with Edenham, her brothers would find themselves taken care of, at least for a time. She'd never had so much help in her life, and she'd likely never find herself in this position again.

She was going to do it. She was going to . . . let Edenham have a bit of cake.

"Why, Hugh," she said with a grin, "I would be quite willing to use you again."

Edenham's eyes widened, looking quite green, and then he smiled a most wicked and knowing smile. Another edge of her stomach flopped over.

Mercy.

Eighteen

ANTOINETTE, Lady Lanreath, knew exactly where Lord George Blakesley, the third son of the Duke of Hyde, was as she'd been watching him almost since she'd arrived. He had not been watching her, which was so very like him.

Antoinette, married to a friend of her father's, a man even older than her father, had always been a dutiful child who lived a dutiful life. She had married Lanreath, tolerated Lanreath, and buried Lanreath. She had not borne a child by Lanreath, or anyone else, just to be perfectly clear, and so her marriage had resulted in nothing. Nothing beyond making her a well-to-do widow who could do whatever she pleased.

As being dutiful was surely a part of her nature by now, if only by sheer repetition, she did not have any idea what pleased her.

But she did know that Lord George Blakesley did something to her. What she did to him, if anything, she had no idea.

She'd met George after her marriage, during her first Season in Town. It was at the theater, she'd been mildly bored by the play, and then she'd been introduced to George. The play had ceased to enter her thoughts from that moment on. Her own husband had nearly ceased to enter her thoughts from that moment on, not that he'd been aware of it, of course. *He* being her husband. Or George. Both of them, certainly. She was then and continued to be now most, *most* careful about revealing anything that could possibly embarrass either herself or her family. That Bernadette had been formed in a completely different mold was perfectly obvious.

As careful as she'd always been, George Blakesley might not even be aware that she remembered him from that first night to now. George was either completely unmoved by her or he was also a very careful sort.

Today she was going to find out which.

He was in the yellow salon, standing by the hearth, the golden yellow walls of the room doing marvelous things to his dark blond hair. Like all the Blakesley men, he was blond and blue-eyed. His shade of blond, quite unlike his elder brother Iveston, whose marriage they honored today, was dark honey in color. George's eyes were the blue of winter, a white-washed, pale gray blue that had sent a shiver into her loins upon her first introduction and which continued to reverberate even now. His lips were full, his lids slightly hooded, and his nose hawkish. He looked utterly arrogant. Lanreath had looked like a spoilt mushroom, and had occasionally behaved like one as well.

The yellow salon was not deserted, but neither was it a crush, which did suit her purposes. She did not want anyone to overhear what she was to say to George, yet neither did she want it to appear as if she had urgently sought him out.

Dutiful and proper to the last, even when attempting to see if a man was available for an almost entirely proper something or other. Seduction? She didn't know if she had it in her. She had just recently decided that she might, if the proper man made himself available, want to remarry. She was tired of spending her time alone, living out her life on the public stage she had found herself upon. Had she always been so careful, so cautious?

Probably. She was the eldest and had tried very hard to make things easier on her three younger sisters: Bernadette, Camille, and Delphine. She thought she'd made an adequate job of it. Bernadette hadn't been at all then what she was now, and for that change she blamed, although perhaps *blame* was too strong a word and judged Bernie too harshly . . . *careful*. She was being careful again. Antoinette shook her head mildly, yes, *mildly*, and finished her thought. Paignton was to blame. *Blame*, there, she'd said it, even if only to herself. What had he done to Bernie? Aside from introducing her to lechery and recklessness, that is. He'd done something to her, something dark and destructive, and Antoinette had given considerable thought to her own welfare in the light of Bernadette's transformation. Would she, if she dallied, become like Bernie?

It seemed more than possible, though it probably depended upon the man.

Certainly George Blakesley would do no such thing to her, particularly as she wanted him for a husband, possibly, and not a lover, probably.

She was still very undecided, obviously. She was, however, trying very purposefully not to be so very *careful*.

She approached him casually, a very mild expression painted on her face, all the while her heart hammering and her spine shivering. He stood alone, which she decided was destiny, and watched her approach. His brows lowered and his lips pursed. He did not look pleased. Perhaps he was only hungry. Breakfast was being scandalously delayed.

"Lord George," she said as he was bowing to her, his bow most thorough, "how well you look." He did look well, even if he also looked hungry. When a man was as compelling as George Blakesley, hunger was no obstacle. "I'm so glad I found you alone."

He scowled. Perhaps that had been too forward? No matter. She wasn't going to turn tail now.

"Were you looking for me, Lady Lanreath?" he asked, his voice low.

"I was," she said calmly, meeting his gaze. "I don't know if this matter is of any concern to you. Indeed, I don't know if it's a *matter* at all, but I did think I should tell someone in the family and as I have more of an acquaintance with you than with anyone else . . ." She allowed her voice to trail away. She really didn't know why she thought this would work. It wasn't at all direct, and it might seem pointlessly minor, but it was the only even slightly logical reason she could give him for seeking him out. No matter what she wished of herself, she was no Bernadette, though she did not wish to be that at all.

"Yes, Lady Lanreath?" he said, taking a half step toward her. "Is there some problem? I would assist you, if I could."

Not at all bad. He at least seemed eager to help her, in a lady in distress sort of fashion, which was perfectly lovely of him. It was a start.

"You are kindness itself, Lord George," she said, smiling up at him. "It was actually more of a service to you and your family that I sought you out. I happened to overhear Lady Louisa and Lady Amelia in conversation with Miss Elliot, and from that brief snatch of conversation I do believe that there is some form of wager in place that pertains to Miss Elliot . . . and the Duke of Edenham." The look on his face grew by turns stony and then hot, rather like a volcano about to erupt. She took a breath and hurried on, determined to be bold for once. "As Miss Elliot is a stranger to our country, and as she is also a beloved cousin, I did think you should be informed of . . . that . . . well, there might be a chance that she is . . . in some danger of . . . being compromised."

George looked over her head to scour the rest of the room. She chanced a look around as well. Jane Elliot's brother, the elder one, stood not fifteen away, deeply embroiled in a conversation with Edenham's sister, Lady Richard. Lord Dutton was sitting on one of the sofas, his chin on his chest, snoring drunkenly. And before breakfast, too! Whatever had happened to that man? Some woman, almost certainly. Antoinette thought she knew the woman, too. Mrs. Warren, who had recently become Lady Staverton. She would have felt far more compassion for Dutton if he had managed his disappointment in some more pleasing and discreet way, one that did not involve public snoring.

George looked back to her and she swiftly met his gaze. "I am flattered that you have come to me with this, Lady Lanreath. As Lady Richard is conversing with Jedidiah Elliot, it shows profound sensitivity that you chose not to interrupt them."

And it would have accomplished very little in the way of talking to George, but wasn't it perfect that he didn't realize her motive? Or was it? She didn't actually want him completely in the dark about her interest in him. That was the whole point!

Oh, bother. Men were such idiots.

"Thank you, Lord George," she said. "I also must confess that, because of our prior warm relationship, I felt so much more at ease in discussing this with you. I knew you would know just how to manage things."

There. That should let him see her true feelings.

He looked into her eyes, his hooded gaze intense. Everything about George Blakesley was intense. It was quite exhilarating.

"Lady Lanreath, I shall attempt to do so now. Thank you. If you will excuse me?" he said, and then he bowed and walked away from her.

Antoinette watched him leave the room by the doorway

to the red reception room. Well, that hadn't gone quite as well as she had hoped, but perhaps it was a start.

❧

KATHERINE, Lady Richard had hoped for a more enthusiastic start in her conversation with Jedidiah Elliot. Rather typical for her, really. She always hoped for much and received very far below her hopes. Small wonder she rarely left Edenham House. What would have been the point? At least the children didn't disappoint her.

William and Sarah, Hugh's two small ones, were the center of her life. They were not her children, yet they were the center of her life. Pathetic, really, but at least she had them. Or would, until Edenham married again.

He would marry again. He always did. No reason for him not to, really. He was a loving man, a man who loved family and children and women, which was not as common as one might have thought.

Katherine sighed under her breath and watched Jedidiah speak. He was a man of few words, and those words spoken with care, but he was clearly passionate about his ship and the sea. He was going on about it now, something about how much sail she could carry, and his eyes were lit like beacon fires.

If she did manage to get him into her bed, she really must make certain she did not conceive a child. That would be highly awkward. She wasn't even certain Edenham would forgive her.

Jedidiah would likely make lovely children.

Katherine jerked her attention back to what he was saying, banishing all thoughts of children from her mind. Not, however, banishing Jedidiah from them. She simply would have to be more direct. There was nothing for it. He didn't seem to understand that, by talking to him for so long, in such privacy, that she was nearly shouting her intentions into his very handsome face. Americans apparently didn't hear shouts in this particular language, the language of propriety and decorum.

Well, then, she'd made up her mind, chosen her man, and she'd just be out with it.

Right, then.

The next time he stopped for breath . . .

Something about the size of the fish off of Newfoundland . . . and then . . .

"It does sound fascinating," she said, "and I'm sure you'll be back to sea quite soon, and eager for that day, as I can quite clearly understand, but before the tide turns, Captain Elliot," she said, drawing her words out, looking down at the fan in her hands, turning it over and over not at all gracefully, "I was wondering if you'd like to spend an hour or two in my bed?"

There! She'd done it!

Silence greeted her question, which was a bit disappointing considering how hard she'd worked at it all.

She dared to look up at his face, and, quite unexpectedly, Jedidiah Elliot did not have any expression on his face at all, not even mild curiosity. Certainly nothing so enthusiastic as interest.

In fact, out of that barren face, void of all emotion, he said, "I beg your pardon?"

❦

"I beg your pardon, Lady Paignton," Joel said. "I don't believe I heard you."

Bernadette, having spent the better part of half an hour in the Hyde back garden, which was quite nice as gardens went but as she was not interested in horticulture, particularly when it was starting to mist and her shoes were not at all designed to scramble over a slippery stone walk, was entirely certain that Joel Elliot had heard her. She was, after all, leaning against his arm and whispering into his ear.

It was utterly absurd to think that such a young man could already be deaf.

No, it was not that. Could it be that he was refusing her? But, why?

"Would you like me to repeat it, or would you rather I show you?" she purred.

Joel jumped slightly and moved away from her on the walk. The hedge was thick. The walk was narrow. Where was he going to go?

"Lady Paignton, I begin to wonder if there has been some misunderstanding between us," Joel said. His back was stiff, his shoulders rigid. He was not smiling. Not very fun-loving, these Americans.

"I don't see how," she said, rubbing against him. "Is it that you've never taken a lover before, Captain Elliot? Have I shamed you somehow? I can assure you that I would not take it at all amiss to be your first. We all must have a first, after all. Some are endured and some are enjoyed. I would make very certain that you enjoyed yourself completely."

Now he looked annoyed, even outraged. Perhaps there was something wrong with her dress? She'd never had so much trouble before in getting a man to unbutton and deliver the goods. Bernadette couldn't help glancing down at her dress; it looked perfectly fine to her, the muslin unsullied and petal thin. What more did the man want?

"Is this a jest?" he asked, scowling down at her. He was even handsome when he scowled. Perhaps he was one of those men who grimaced and groaned whilst coupling; done well, with the right degree of fervor, it could be very entertaining. "Baiting the rough American?" he said.

"Not at all," she said, studying him. Oh, this was taking far too long and becoming needlessly complicated. "Whyever should you think that? I find you a most attractive man. I had hoped you found me at least mildly appealing. I am unencumbered. You are as well." She shrugged and looked at him, one eyebrow raised. "Can we not enjoy

each other, at least until breakfast is called, and perhaps, if
we mutually desire, even after? Wouldn't that be a pleasant
way to spend a few empty moments?"

"*Moments*?" Joel said in a hushed voice.

A hushed voice; did that mean he was still outraged or
perhaps only trying to be discreet? It was so difficult to
read these Americans. What did they do to entertain themselves on that continent? One assumed they did, actually,
have time for entertainment. One did hear so many tales
of their endless labors and ceaseless strivings. Perhaps that
was the problem. Joel Elliot simply might not know how to
pass a few minutes in a highly pleasurable yet essentially
meaningless pastime. Poor boy. There was so much she
could teach him.

"You would lift your skirts to fill a few empty moments?"
Joel said.

Bernadette smiled and said, "You could lift them. That
might be fun. Won't you give it a try? I do think you'll like
it. Everyone does."

Joel's expression changed again. The sun was low
against the sky and the sky heavy with cloud. It was not
the most ideal of situations, but should certainly serve for
a quick assignation of the most casual sort. Why, if he had
his wits about him, they could tussle together for five minutes, getting all the necessary bits done, and then be back
inside well in time for the first course.

"Everyone likes what, Lady Paignton?" Joel asked. His
voice sounded carefully bland. *Carefully* . . . that was the
bit that alerted her. "Lifting your skirts for a quick tumble
or just coupling in general? I find I'm confused about
which. You can understand that, can't you?"

The deportment of a pig, that much was more than clear.
Here she'd made the simplest, most pleasant of offers, and
this was his response?

"Captain Elliot," Bernadette said, refusing to run
screaming into the house. She never screamed, not unless

it would add to the moment. "I seem to have offended you. I do apologize."

He did not look appeased. Well, what was to be done? She'd behaved beautifully and he'd mangled the entire thing. Odd behavior, even for an American.

❧

"CAPTAIN Elliot," Katherine said, refusing to back down. She'd come this far, made her offer, and she was not going to ruin it all now by sobbing. Not unless she thought it might help. It didn't look likely. "I fear I have shocked you. Shall I apologize?"

By the look on Jedidiah's face, an apology was not going to be enough.

"I'm afraid I don't know the protocol, Lady Richard," Jedidiah said, looking quite grim, which did not hamper his attractiveness in the least. She did think he was her best choice for a quick assignation. Weren't seamen supposed to be rather more willing than not to indulge in sultry liaisons with women all over the earth? What was wrong with her that even a man like Jedidiah, a sailor and an *American*, found her wanting? "You seem to have more experience at this than I. Why don't you do what seems best to you?"

That was most assuredly an insult. How could he have failed to understand the high compliment she was paying him? Did he think she lifted her skirts for anyone?

Actually, he might have done. What did he know of her? Nothing. It was partly for that reason that she had chosen him. He was a stranger, and would remain so, even . . . after.

Coupling with Richard had been quite nice. He had been clean and pleasant, saying all the correct things, but more importantly, not saying anything to give offense. That had been very important to her, and it still was, but why had it been *the* important thing? Richard had said everything beautifully, and he had behaved abysmally. He had dressed well and ridden well and looked entirely proper upon any occasion, and he been a vain, thoughtless, selfish man.

But the coupling had not been a problem. She'd liked that well enough. Oh, it was not anything to inspire a sonnet, but it had been . . . fine. Simply fine. He had been very *clean*. That made a good bit of difference, in everything.

Jedidiah looked very clean, his blue eyes and light hair adding to the impression. Richard's hair had been brown, his eyes brown; nothing at all remarkable, but pleasant enough. Jedidiah did not look pleasant. Ever. He looked something else entirely. What, she wasn't quite certain, but it was not pleasant. Clean, though. She did like that.

"Captain Elliot," she said, taking a step nearer to him. He might have wanted to back away from her, but he was in between the window and a corner of the room. She'd caught him nicely, if she did say so. For someone so new to this, it could have gone a lot worse. "I have done what seems best to me. I am a widow, of which you may or may not be aware, and I . . . find you to be a very fine-looking man. I had hoped you might find me . . ."

How to say it? That she expected him to find her beautiful? A most awkward thing to say. However did Sophia manage it? This luring men into seductions was most difficult.

"Willing?" Jedidiah supplied.

A definite insult. This truly was not going at all well.

Nineteen

IT was going well. Of course, nothing had actually happened yet, but he was with her and seemed eager enough to. . . .whatever it was that he wanted to do. What Jane wanted was to be kissed, and even, if conditions were right, to be fondled. Everything that had already happened to her, only more so. This was her perfect opportunity, and Edenham was her perfect man . . . no, no, that's not at all what she meant. What she meant was that Edenham was the perfect man for *this*.

Because she would never see him again.

Because he seemed eager to do it.

Because he also gave every appearance of being very, very good at it.

That one kiss had been quite remarkable. Nothing at all like Nathaniel Talbott's cool lips pressed tightly against her own. What would it be like without light and sound distracting her? All those eyes watching them; she had lost herself in his kiss, but not to the point of forgetting. Only to the point of not truly caring.

There was power in a kiss like that.

But where to do it? A house full of guests, every candle lit, every room occupied. Her brothers about somewhere.

Perhaps Edenham didn't even realize what she wanted of him. It was more than likely. She had been rather abrupt with him, more than once, too. Men did like a certain level of warmth from a woman, there was no secret about that. On the other hand, he kept coming back, didn't he? That bespoke a certain level of interest, a very high level.

Jane nearly preened. She didn't want Edenham, but since everyone else thought he was the most handsome, the most desirable man of the Town, it wasn't *entirely* unpleasant to be hotly pursued by him.

"I don't suppose you want to tell me about Ezekiel Biddle," Edenham said as they walked casually, or as casually as they could with everyone staring at them, across the room toward the door to the stair hall. "A woman throws a man's name about like that, it inspires more than a little curiosity."

Good. Although Ezekiel Biddle, with his very average looks, if one discounted his crooked nose, was no Duke of Edenham. And she wasn't referring to his title. No, Edenham was easily the most handsome man she had ever seen. In that, women of both England and America were in firm agreement. He was tall, fully as tall as President Washington had been, his hair was a pleasing shade of dark brown, his eyes were a tantalizing color, both green and brown at once, and his features were most pleasingly arranged. His nose was not crooked. Not even after Jed taking a fist to the face once or twice. That had been a good bit of luck. For him, certainly, not for her. She didn't care what happened to his nose. She was leaving the country, after all. She'd never see his face again, no, nor any other part of him.

She could see Ezekiel Biddle any time she wanted.

The thought did nothing to cheer her. It never had.

"Mentioning him distresses you?" Edenham said,

leaning slightly to look into her face as they passed into the stair hall. The stair hall was not deserted. She had hardly expected it to be, but what were they to do here?

"No, not at all," she said.

"He did not break your heart?"

Jane smiled. "Of course not. I protect my heart very well, which is no secret to Mr. Biddle," she said.

"Ah, you beat him," Edenham said, nodding, a smile teasing his mouth. His bruised, cut mouth. Her heart skipped a beat, perhaps two. "Did you use a cudgel or did your brothers do your beating for you?"

"I can take care of myself," she said, "and that doesn't necessarily mean . . . what you are implying."

"And what is that?"

"Sometimes, Hugh, a woman is not interested in . . . avoiding a man's attentions," she said, looking up at him, her smile bright. "Sometimes, in taking care of herself, she welcomes them."

Edenham grinned. "Why, Libby, are American women truly that free?"

This was it. Her chance, if she dared take it. Looking at Edenham, it was very difficult to think of any reason to avoid him. It. Her chance.

"Why not find out?" she said.

It was the most daring thing she had ever said. She was grinning from ear to ear. She couldn't help herself. She felt positively inspired. Inspired to do what, she was too demure to list, even to herself.

"A challenge? I accept," he said without a moment's hesitation. "To defeat the memory of Ezekiel Biddle, I accept."

Jane laughed. "Poor Mr. Biddle. I do think he would be much alarmed by your fascination with him. He is a simple man, who simply happened to . . ." She shrugged. It was suggestive, she was almost certain. Certainly Ezekiel had more currency as a mysterious suitor than what he had been, a groper.

"Whatever he happened to do," Edenham said, "I must and shall do better. Now, where shall this challenge be taken up? I do think I know a place. Are you willing, Libby?"

She could refuse him. She had that power and she wasn't afraid to use it. But why refuse him now? She could just as easily refuse him later, after she had enjoyed herself for a bit. How was a woman supposed to gain any experience at these things if she went about refusing men out of hand, before they had actually done anything remotely interesting?

"I do think that Ezekiel must be challenged. He shall grow so very arrogant in his talents if he is not," she said. Poor Ezekiel. She was using him dreadfully.

"And we both know how you dislike arrogance in a man," he said, indicating by a wave of his arm that she should follow him across the stair hall to a small door on the far side, leaving the doorways to both the blue and red reception rooms behind them. She followed, intrigued.

"Where are we going?" she asked. "You seem to know this house very well."

"I do," he said. "In fact, most of the guests here today know this floor very well. Hyde hosts an *assemblie* every year, this circuit of rooms visited by one and all."

They had passed through a small doorway from the stair hall into an antechamber done up in shades of cream and ivory and some very discreet gilding. It was a smallish room by Hyde House standards, but it had three windows so it was quite impressive if only in that. But they did not stay in the antechamber. Edenham, taking her by the hand, which he did with such easy confidence that she couldn't be alarmed, and certainly it was nothing like the tentative touch of her hand that Reliance Jones had proffered, led her into a larger room. A bedroom, to be precise. The room was nearly covered in gold leaf, the bed was colossal in size and appointments, the bed curtains lush, and a thick carpet covered nearly the entire floor.

Edenham, still holding her hand, looked at her with a very boyish and slightly mischievous smile, and said, "I hardly know where to begin, but no matter where I begin it, this is the perfect place to start and end it, isn't it, Libby?"

"A bedroom?" she said, pulling her hand out of his.

Well, actually, that was what she intended to do, but he held her fast. Reliance Jones had certainly not been so bold. She yanked her hand back again. Edenham smiled and pulled her to him. Her feet skidded across the carpet. It was most shocking.

"This is the state bed. It's rumored that George I slept in it."

"Didn't he have his own bed?" Jane said, pushing against his chest with her free hand. Edenham had the other one tucked behind him, the result being that she was hugging him. By force, though, not by choice. An important distinction.

"Sometimes, you use whatever bed you can find," Edenham said, his half smile fading from his mouth as he lowered his lips to hers.

It was not at all what she had expected. For one, she had lost all control of the situation, which was most, most distressing. For another, he was behaving entirely more aggressively than he had done previously, which did put quite a different spin on everything, didn't it? And finally, she was thrown far beyond curiosity or adventure or even a sort of intellectual excitement.

Far beyond.

Her intellect was not even remotely involved. No, this was . . . keelhauling and nothing less. She was being pulled under, her breath stopped in her lungs, her heart slamming against her ribs in a desperate attempt to survive, her mind spinning as sensations rushed through her.

Some would have called it a kiss. It was far too simple and too innocent a word for what Edenham was doing to her.

His mouth moved over hers, open and wet, licking her, biting her lower lip, nibbling . . . and then his tongue swept in, a blaze of passion, rolling, searching, plumbing her depths.

Shocking. Completely.

And worse? She responded instantly, opening to him, mirroring his kiss, doing to him what he did to her.

It seemed . . . appropriate, though she could not think why.

Her hand against his chest no longer pushed, but pulled him to her, her hand a fist in his coat. Her hand that was in his, tugged behind his back, pressed hard against him, pushing him nearer and nearer again.

He was so very large. It should have been impossible for her to force his body to move in any direction, but she did it. He moved closer, his knee pressing between her legs, the muslin of her skirts tightening against her thighs. She lifted herself onto her toes, her free hand sliding up his chest to wrap itself around his neck.

Mindless movement. She did not intend to do any of it, indeed, was barely aware of doing anything at all. She only wanted more. To be closer. To get more of what he was doing. To dive deeper. To submerge herself in him.

"Breathe, Libby," he whispered, lifting his mouth from hers. "Breathe into me."

Oh. Right. She'd been holding her breath. Silly. But breathe into him? Could she? Would she not drown?

"I've got you. Trust me," he said, his mouth moving down her throat, across her jaw, and then he captured her mouth again.

Trust him? No, that was absurd. She could not trust him. She knew that better than anything else she knew. He was *not* to be trusted. He was English. He was a duke. He was . . . kissing her.

Well, it might be all right to trust him with kissing her. It certainly felt all right. All the rest, though . . . she would not trust him on that.

She felt immeasurably better and threw herself into kissing him, breathing deeply of him, her mouth and his joined, open and wet, seeking and finding.

She dove in. Without reserve. And he had spoken truly. He did have her.

His hand released hers, yet she still held him to her. His hands, now free, moved over her body. He wrapped one long arm around her waist and held her firmly against him, but no more firmly than she held him against her. His other hand, his fingertips, traced the line of her jaw, her neck, trailing down and down until he brushed, just barely, against the rigid tip of her nipple.

A fondle. Was it? It was so delicate. Nothing at all like Ezekiel's clumsy, heavy-handed grope at the top of her breast.

He touched her there again, his fingertip moving up, and then down, and then up again.

Oh, definitely a fondle. As delicate yet as precise as a hummingbird. She shivered and moaned into his mouth, wrapping her arms about him tighter, pushing her breasts and her aching nipples against his chest, the pressure answering a need she had not known she had. She wanted him to lift her off her feet as he had done before. She wanted him to carry her away, to carry all her rules of deportment and class and nation to the edge of this cliff she was on and drop them into the deep blue sea.

She wanted freedom.

He pulled back from her, set her back down upon her heels, his large hands on her hips, and ended the kiss.

That was not the freedom she had been hoping for.

"Now tell me about Ezekiel Biddle," Edenham said, his eyes glowing quite green. He did not look at all happy. Odd, for she felt very happy, nearly euphoric, a bubbling swirl spinning inside her like a whirlpool. She wanted to laugh out loud, to throw her arms around his neck again and kiss the lobe of his ear.

In fact, she did just that. All of it.

Edenham grabbed her around the waist, held her to him for an instant, and she could feel that he was happy *somewhere* down below the hem of his waistcoat, and then he unwrapped her arms from around his neck and set her down again.

"I don't want to talk about him," she said, grinning. "I'm happy. Aren't you happy?"

"You made him up, didn't you? Pure invention."

"Oh, no. He exists," she said, still grinning, still bubbling. "Do you know you have very pretty ears? Has anyone ever told you that?"

Edenham rubbed his ear where she'd kissed him, looking at her a bit cautiously. She'd bite him there next time, just a nibble. She could hardly wait.

"No, no one has," he said. "Now, Jane, about Ezekiel Biddle . . ."

"Oh, he's miles away," she said, coming closer to him, touching a button on his waistcoat. He backed up a step. She took a matching step nearer. "You're not in pain are you? Did my brothers hurt you awfully?"

If she said it with a certain cheerful lilt . . . well, she just couldn't help it. She was happy. And he looked so confused and wary. And his bruised face and cut lip called to her in a most humiliating way. She just wouldn't confess it to him; there was no reason she should, after all. Was there any reason for him to know every thought in her head? Naturally not.

"I'm fine," he said.

"You look very fine," she said, grinning, taking another step nearer. Edenham scowled and backed up again. "What's wrong? Are you suddenly shy?"

"I am not," he snapped out, his dark brows drawn together in a dignified scowl.

"Well, then. Why don't you kiss me again?" He didn't say anything. He didn't do anything either. There was only one thing left for her to do. So she did it. "Nathaniel Talbott certainly would never have stopped at one innocent kiss."

"Nathaniel Talbott?" he said very abruptly and not at all quietly. "What happened to Ezekiel Biddle?"

"Your grace," she said sweetly, smiling up at him, "I certainly think you must have the wrong impression of me entirely. I am not some unsophisticated rustic, sitting alone at the hearth, doing needlework."

"No, you're running through the streets of New York catching men in your hem like burrs!" he said, looking very, very unhappy. She was so glad.

"Why are you surprised? You did say I was very beautiful. What did you expect?"

"Nothing," he growled. "I don't know what I expected. Certainly . . . nothing," he said again, running a hand through his hair.

It was a most lovely gesture. He had lovely hands and lovely hair. Could she induce him to do it again?

Very likely.

"Don't you want to kiss me again?" she asked. "Don't you want to . . . touch me?" His eyes lifted to hers at the last question and a certain speculative gleam arose in his eyes. She shouldn't have hesitated. It had given him some idea or other. "Who knows how long my brothers may be kept occupied."

She meant it not so much as a threat but as a spur to action. He certainly had taken a drubbing at their hands. He was clearly overmatched, not that she thought any less of him for that. Her brothers were known ruffians, of the most gentile sort, naturally.

"You're not concerned that there's a bed in this room?" he asked, taking a step nearer.

She couldn't help it. She backed up a step, just a gentle sliding of her foot. The look in his eyes did not look at all cordial.

"No, not at all," she said. "I trust you."

"Do you? Why, Libby?" He took another step nearer. She held her ground . . . for all of five seconds, and then she backed up a half step.

"Why, what could happen?" she said. "Nothing that we both won't enjoy."

"True," Edenham said, smiling fractionally. His smile didn't look at all cordial either. "And now that I know that no matter what I do to you, your brothers won't force marriage upon me, I should say that we may have reached the perfect understanding."

"What?" she squeaked. Oh, yes, *squeaked*. There was no denying it. The problem was, she forgot to back up again. In the next instant, the next long step, Edenham had her.

"As you are a woman of such vast experience, I can let my guard down completely, can't I?" he said, sweeping her up into his arms and then, without any ceremony whatsoever, tossing her upon that great, high, curtained bed.

Jane sat up immediately from her undignified sprawl and sputtered, "Keep your guard up! Keep it up!"

She moved frantically to the edge of the bed, and did anyone truly need a bed as large as this? Only a king would think so. Before she got there, Edenham, who, now that they were in bed together, really should be referred to as Hugh, the intimacy they shared being much more than implied, anyway, Hugh grabbed her around the waist and pulled her quite neatly and without any fuss at all back to the center of the bed. The mattress sagged slightly, the result being that Jane and Hugh were enveloped in the bed rather like a pair of eggs in a nest.

"Oh, it's up," Hugh said, leaning over her, his excessively large hand fully encompassing her from her waist to her ribs, his thumb pressed against the underside of her breast. "Now, how many other of your many admirers has had you in his bed? Your list appears quite comprehensive."

"This is not *your* bed," she said, her hands and forearms a shield between them. He didn't seem to notice that she'd made a shield, likely because his leg was thrown over her thigh. "And I don't have a list!"

"Any bed will do," Hugh said. "Haven't I just proved that? But I do appreciate your precision about these things, Libby. So few women take the time to be precise. Now, whose bed? Take your time, dear. I'm in no hurry."

And so saying, he began to tickle her, right on her ribs. He held her down, the brute, his leg trapping hers, his body leaning over her. She kept her arms over her chest, buried her face between his shoulder and the bed, and laughed until she begged for mercy. Hugh laughed right along with her.

"Quarter!" she shrieked over her laughter.

"Quarter given," he said, his hand stilling and lying on her side.

When she'd caught her breath, they lay like that, side by side, grinning at each other. It was the most unusual experience of her life. They were lying in a bed, side by side, fully clothed . . . and she had never felt more at ease. He was an odd sort of duke, wasn't he?

"Tell me about your children," she said, making no move to leave the bed.

Hugh braced himself up on one elbow, his hand to his head, and took a deep breath. My, he was handsome. She felt light-headed just looking at him. Jane lay on her back and stared up at the bed coverings above her, her hands folded just under her breasts.

"William and Sarah," he said. "William's the elder, and the heir. His mother died when he was less than a week old."

"Her name?" she asked softly.

"Maria," he answered just as softly. "William has her eyes. The blue of heather."

"I'm sorry," she whispered. "How old is William?"

"Five in July. Sarah will be three come September. I named her for my sister who died long ago, a riding accident when she was only a child. I wish I hadn't now," he said softly, lying back on the bed, his hands behind his head. "I can hardly bear to allow her near horses."

"That's understandable," she said. "Loss is always difficult. Especially the loss of . . . oh, that's nonsense. Losing anyone is difficult; child, spouse, sibling, friend. Even an enemy, I suppose. Whom to toil against then?"

Hugh looked at her with a slight turning of his head. "I'm not your enemy, Libby. You know that, don't you? Jane Liberty Elliot. 'Tis a fine name to wear proudly. I like that you do."

She did not answer, for what was there to say? Her enemy? No, he was hardly that. Not anymore. Had he ever been? He could not have been, could he? It didn't seem possible. What was there to hate about this man, this man who had loved and lost three wives, a young sister, an infant child? He was just a man. A lovely, funny, gentle man of the most remarkable looks on three continents.

"Thank you," she said. "I've never had anyone call me Libby before. I think I like it." She turned to look at him, propping her head on her hand. "You've never had a wife named Libby, have you?"

Hugh chuckled. "No, a Maria, an Elizabeth, an Ophelia. Ophelia and the baby died within minutes of each other. I named him Richard." Needless to say, the laughter had bled out of his voice. "I never thought to have three wives. I never thought that . . ." His voice trailed off and sadness had him by the throat.

Jane did not let anything take her by the throat, nor anyone else, if she could help it. "Hugh, life is full of *I never thought that* moments, yet when is life is ever predictable? We delude ourselves by believing otherwise. Why, look at me. I never thought that I'd be sharing a bed with an English duke, yet here I am. But no one must find out, you understand. My reputation back home would be in tatters, ripped in such a way that I could never repair it."

"A woman who shares a bed with a man she is not married to will face that problem," he said, his mood lightening noticeably.

"Oh, that's the least of it," she said, smiling. "It's your being a duke that would ruin me. How could I live it down? New Yorkers are very sensitive about such breaches, I assure you."

"I rest assured," he said, studying her face. She turned from him and stared at the canopy again. It was easier to breathe that way.

What was she doing? Lying in bed next to a man, and in the middle of her cousin's wedding party? Having an adventure was one thing, but this was madness. She'd been reared with more care than that.

"Well," she said, scooting to the edge of the bed and sitting up, "I can't think how I got here, but—"

"You were thrown," Edenham said mildly, his weight resting upon one elbow as he looked at her. "I take full responsibility."

"As well you should," she said, looking back at him. He made quite a picture, his hair tumbled over his forehead, his eyes gleaming quite seductively. Did he do it on purpose, or was that his natural look when in bed with a woman?

Mercy, he was not in bed with her! Not in that way.

"But, as I was saying," she said, reaching her toes for the floor; it was quite a high bed. Hugh stopped her words by touching her hand. She couldn't, from that instant on, remember what she'd been trying to say.

"Stay, Liberty," he breathed. "Stay just a moment more . . . 'When in the Course of human events, it becomes necessary . . .'"

And, with the first line of the Declaration of Independence still warm on his lips, he kissed her gently on the mouth. He lifted his lips from hers almost immediately and whispered, "It does become necessary. Very necessary."

Her head fell back upon the bed, his mouth following her down, kissing her tenderly, an entreaty to stay, to lose herself, to fall into him and lose herself forever. She could feel it, feel the call of him, feel the pure male pull of him, and it shattered her.

Shattered her will.

Shattered her memory.

Shattered her identity.

No, not that. She was Jane Liberty Elliot. She was not going to lose herself in any man, and never this one.

She pulled back, turning her head, and quoted in a breathless voice, "'. . . requires that they should declare the causes which impel them to the separation.' The separation," she repeated, pushing against his chest.

He let her go and simply stared into her eyes for a long moment.

"Declare your causes, Libby, and I shall declare mine. 'We hold these truths to be self-evident, that all men are created equal.' All men, Libby, even dukes."

"You'd quote the Declaration to me?" she said. "How do you dare?"

"'Tis a document well known throughout the world. Of course I know it."

"But do you believe it?" she said, her heart pounding against her ribs.

"'. . . that they are endowed by their Creator with certain unalienable Rights, that among these are Life, Liberty, and the pursuit of Happiness,'" he said. "Am I not to be granted Liberty simply because I am a duke?"

"Hugh, I—" And then he kissed her, his hands holding her face up to his, his mouth, his silent mouth, more convincing than any words.

She felt lost, foundering, awash in swelling passion and foggy confusion. One hand left her face and moved down her throat, caressing her, touching her with gentle fire. He cupped her breast, his thumb kneading her nipple. She groaned into his mouth while her breast lifted itself into his hand, urgently seeking more of his touch, more of everything he offered.

Without knowing how it had happened, he was over her, pinning her to the lush fabric of the bed coverings, his leg between hers. His hands were on her breasts and her back arched into his hands, her nipples throbbing and demanding. His thigh pressed into the heat spiraling out of her, welcome friction, doubly welcome weight pressing her down, down, taking her far out of herself.

His hips ground against her, a slow swirling motion, and she answered in kind. A violent thrust upward, meeting his weight, supporting him. They ground together, her breath frantic and erratic, her breasts hot and heavy under his hands.

There wasn't enough. Not enough. Everything that was happening to her, it was more than anything she'd ever dreamed of, but it still wasn't enough.

Hugh, inexplicably, stopped. Her hands were around his shoulders, pressing him to her, gasping for breath, demanding more, demanding that he not stop, that he never stop until it was enough. Silently, all without words, but she knew he understood what she wanted.

He lifted his head and turned away from her, removing her hands and gathering them to her chest. She panted, a ragged sound, and moaned a weak sound of distress.

What was wrong with her? She'd never made a sound like that before in her life.

Gradually, her breathing slowing, Jane looked at Hugh, and then followed his gaze. On the far wall of the bedchamber there was a door, a very unimpressive door, but in this open doorway stood Sophia Dalby. Sophia was leaning against the doorframe, her arms crossed, and her smile quite clearly grim.

Jane, as was to be expected, swallowed heavily and closed her eyes in pure mortification. Hugh slithered off of her, straightened his coat, and offered his hand to her. She took it and slid off the bed, her hands going instantly to her hair. It was a complete disaster, and indeed, it could have been nothing else.

Edenham, not behaving at all as embarrassed as he should have been and as she certainly was, said to Sophia, " 'Give me Liberty or give me death'?"

"Darling," Sophia said blandly, "I do think it entirely possible."

Twenty

"THE thing is," Sophia continued, coming into the room, "I do not believe you shall be given a choice. I assume one is as good as the other?"

"Now, Sophia," Edenham said, "you know you're overstating it."

"Jane? Am I overstating it?" Sophia asked.

"No, not really," Jane said a bit breathlessly.

Edenham smiled indulgently. Women were so apt to make too much of a thing, getting entirely too emotionally charged about what was a simple and straightforward situation. Of course, he'd never known Sophia to behave in anything approaching an emotional manner, and even Jane, as young and unsophisticated as she was, was more determined and forthright than emotional.

Bother it, now things were getting complicated, needlessly so, he was certain. Or nearly certain.

"The girl's ruined, fully and completely," Edenham said bluntly. Upon hearing Jane's gasp, he did consider that he could have phrased it more delicately. But blast it, certainly the girl knew she was ruined! Even in America, she'd be ruined. "And entirely pleasantly, I hope," he said by way of a salve. Jane didn't look salved. She looked murderous. Blast and bother all women! He was just trying to marry the girl! Couldn't he get any help, or at least praise, at all for it? He was doing the best he could with the weapons at his disposal with an entirely unreasonable, one might even say illogical family. "I only mean that now, certainly, they will consent to our marriage."

"You complete and utter ass!" Jane hissed, snatching her hand from his and hitting him quite forcefully on the shoulder. "You utter . . . *duke*! 'Tis *I* who won't consent. 'Tis *I* whom you must convince! And you have not. And you shall not. Thank you," she said, unpinning her hair so that it fell in a long tumble down her back, long dark waves of glossy hair. He felt himself harden again just looking at her. With her pins in her mouth, she ran her hands through her hair a few hurried times, swept it up with a twist or two of her hands, and jabbed pins into the entire mess. Except that it wasn't a mess. It looked lovely. He'd never seen a woman manage her hair that quickly, and certainly never by herself. All she used for a mirror was the dim reflection of herself in the window glass. Most spectacular feat, he was forced to admit. "Thank you for a lovely adventure. I shall remember it always. Now leave me alone!" And with those words, she walked out the door into the passageway to the stair hall without a backward glance.

Not at all what he had expected, to put it mildly.

"Shall it be by the sword or a simple hanging, your grace? I do think the Americans are rather fond of hangings," Sophia said, checking her own hair in the window. There wasn't a thing wrong with her hair.

"I begin to think it possible that I've mishandled this from the start," Edenham said.

"How clever of you, darling," Sophia said, turning to face him, her hands clasped together around her closed fan.

She was not smiling at him. Sophia always smiled at him. They had a most cordial relationship and found many of the same things, and by things he meant people and the situations they found themselves in, amusing. "Now, shall I tell you how to get what you want, assuming you still want the lovely Miss Elliot?"

"I do," he said, trying not to sound like an abashed schoolboy facing a stern master. He did not succeed in the slightest degree.

"Darling, I've known you for many years and I find you to be an exceedingly pleasant and charming man, but I must know, Edenham, what is it about this girl that compels you so? She is a beautiful woman, but beauty alone is not enough."

Beauty alone not enough? But how absurd. Of course it was enough. It was always enough. His wives had all been lovely women, each in her particular way, as well as being from the right family and having enjoyed a proper upbringing. What else was there to it? Oh, naturally, some warmth of feeling, that special connection that one did not achieve with just anyone, but one could achieve it very regularly with the right sort of woman. Jane Elliot, American, was Hyde's niece. She was a beauty of the first water. She was, clearly, the right sort of woman. That she was American and not English was, most obviously, a hurdle to his desires, but it was surmountable, surely.

Although he had been more sure of that two hours ago. Things had not gone a bit well, not even close to plan. Cranleigh had tried to tell him something, something about Jane and her beauty and that being an American complicated the thing more than he wanted to admit . . . fine then, true, but there was an attraction between them, that had been more than adequately proved, even to the stubborn Miss Elliot, and she had been ruined, which was always enough to see the deed done, and there was an end to it.

Except that there wasn't an end to it, not yet.

What a confounded lot of trouble just to get a wife!

"Since when has beauty been not enough?" he said stiffly, straightening his shirt underneath his waistcoat.

"Since you first saw Jane Elliot," Sophia said, coming over to stand near him. She fussed with his cravat a bit, patted it, and put a hand to his cheek. "Darling Edenham, you don't know a thing about Americans, do you?"

"I am so weary of everyone telling me that!" he snapped, turning away from her touch to cross the room and then recross it, his strides long and frustrated.

"Then kindly take heed and it need not be repeated," she said, watching him pace.

"You're an American and you're no different than I!" he said, turning sharply to face her.

"I? An American?" Sophia said, her black brows raised in mild astonishment. "I am no more American than you are, darling. That lovely American document you were quoting so recently, did you not also commit to memory this line? 'He has excited domestic insurrections amongst us, and has endeavoured to bring on the inhabitants of our frontiers, the merciless Indian Savages whose known rule of warfare, is an undistinguished destruction of all ages, sexes and conditions.' No, Edenham, I am not an American. Jane knows this if you do not, which is another proof, if you require more, that she sees the world very differently from you. As I said, beauty is not enough."

Edenham felt himself deflate, the spark of hope and determination extinguished by a flood of words. Words. Why should words stop his heart? Why should he not have this woman, as he had had each of his wives, simply because he wanted her and she was flattered by his interest?

Did being a duke mean nothing anymore?

And that was when he knew.

His being a duke meant nothing, less than nothing to Jane.

Edenham looked at Sophia and said quietly, "She is beautiful, and no matter what you or she may wish, beauty is important to a man. My heart lifts when I look at her."

"And other parts as well, I should think," Sophia said, the smallest trace of a smile touching one corner of her mouth.

"Yes, I'd be a fool to deny that," he said. "Yet my soul lifts when I'm with her. She is not afraid of me, Sophia. Neither is she in awe. And she, unlike every one of my wives, does not hunger to be a duchess. Has there ever been a woman like that? Not in my life. Except," he added, smiling, "she is, in many ways, very like you, which surely must have something to do with the continent which birthed you both. Small wonder that I want to marry her. That I still intend to marry her."

Sophia smiled fully and let her gaze drift to the thick carpet between them. "If she'll have you."

"Will she? Do you know a way, Sophia?"

He stood with his heart, with his future in his hands. He had asked her help before and, not waiting, had proceeded without it. Pride had walked with him all his life, rooted in his very name. Edenham. The Duke of Edenham. Jane did not want Edenham, but she might be tempted to say yes to Hugh Austen.

"I may," Sophia said. And then she smiled.

❧

JANE smiled as she made her way from the stair hall back into the blue reception room. The guests were highly agitated, and she didn't think it was because her dress was wrinkled. No, it was near on seven and the wedding breakfast, due to be served at one, was still in the kitchens. Hunger did very predictable things to people, none of them pleasant.

"I trust you are well, Miss Elliot?" Mr. George Prestwick said after his very brief bow. He'd nearly bumped into her after what looked to have been almost hopping across the room to greet her. She didn't know Mr. Prestwick well at all, having met him only once, but he hadn't struck her as the jumpy sort. Quite the opposite, in fact.

Jane resisted the urge to check the condition of her hair, and instead smiled the brighter. "I am most well, though I confess to being curious about the state of our meal. You don't think the kitchen caught fire, do you?"

It was perfectly obvious it hadn't and it wasn't at all the thing to comment on the tardiness of the meal, but they were family, highly extended, and she would say anything to draw attention away from the strange arrangement of wrinkles on her muslin dress. No dress looked as hers did from sitting in a well-constructed chair, or even an over-flowing hay wagon on a sultry September evening.

She'd lain in bed with a man!

The words rang in her mind like a bell, and not a sweet-sounding bell either. A huge, gonging, awful bell. How could she have done it! What was wrong with her that she should *do* such a thing, with a stranger, no less!

No, that was absurd. It would have been just as bad if she'd done it with Ezekiel or Reliance, though they certainly would never have been so bold as to ask. As to that, Edenham hadn't asked, had he? No, he'd simply dragged her into a bedchamber and thrown her upon a bed!

It was without precedent. In her life, anyway. He likely did it on a weekly basis, just a bit of fun, tossing girls on beds, kissing them into delirium, pressing his hips against theirs . . . his leg moving and rubbing against the most delicate and demanding spot on her body . . .

"Are you certain you are well?" Mr. Prestwick asked quite seriously. "Perhaps you would like something to drink?"

Jane jerked out of her . . . no, no, no. Not reverie. Her

catalogue of outrage. Her list, *ha*, of offenses against her person. Her most private and untouched person. Untouched until now. Until today. Until Hugh.

"Yes, that would be lovely," she said as pleasantly as possible, considering. She did sound the slightest bit sharp to her own ears, but George Prestwick did not react adversely in any way. Stout fellow. Quite a nice man, really. Jane would bet hard currency that George Prestwick didn't throw nice girls into bed.

George did something with his head and a footman appeared with a tray of Madeira. Jane took a glass, raised it to George convivially, and then swallowed it down in four gulps.

George, dear George, brother of the bride, blanched as white as fresh linen.

"You've just come from Edenham, then?" George asked.

Was it that obvious? Of course it was. Wrinkles were wrinkles, and who else had picked her up and kissed her in the middle of a crowded room? No one but Edenham. Certainly it took no great intellect to determine who could drive a girl to slug down a glass of wine like a sailor chugging grog.

"I have, as a matter of fact," she said cordially, looking about for a place to put her empty glass. George did something with his head again, how did he do that?, and another footman appeared with another tray of Madeira. She put down her empty glass and hoisted a full one. "Why do you ask?" Without waiting for his answer, because truly she didn't care what he said, she resolved to sip her Madeira. She, very calmly and very smoothly, swallowed it down without taking a breath. Better, wasn't it?

"It is only that I was concerned about you, Miss Elliot," George said, his dark brown eyes looking at her earnestly.

Quite a good-looking man, was George Prestwick. He had black hair and eyes so brown as to be nearly black, finely drawn features, and a lithe form that reminded her a bit of a panther. Of course, he didn't have any bruises on his face, but that was easily remedied, wasn't it?

"Ha," she said softly, shaking her head, looking again for a place to put her empty glass.

She watched carefully this time and could make out that George did something very subtle involving the angle of his chin and a single eyebrow. The footman, the same one this time, reappeared with his tray. She rid herself of her empty glass and reached for a full one. George took a glass as well, though he did not look at all eager to drink from it. Ah, well. His loss.

"Miss Elliot," he said, "I don't know if you're aware, indeed I should be much surprised if you were, but Edenham spoke with Sophia Dalby and that has, at least lately, resulted in certain highly unlikely marriages being made at what some would say is an alarming speed. My own sister to Iveston for one."

"Oh, I've been made aware, Mr. Prestwick," she said, waving her glass in the general direction of his face. "What you may not know is that *I* have spoken to Sophia Dalby. I shall not be wed. Not to Edenham. Not to anyone here."

She said it with some pride, a great deal of certainty, and not a little annoyance.

"I see," he said, looking down at her, his brow furrowed in concern.

Clearly, he was concerned. He didn't want her to marry the most handsome duke in England, did he? Of course he didn't. He couldn't marry Edenham himself, obviously, and his only sister was just this day married to an heir apparent, which would simply have to do, wouldn't it? That die had been cast. If Penelope had wanted Edenham, she should have put her back into it, that's all.

"You are confident that Lady Dalby will . . . take your part in this?" Mr. Prestwick asked.

"Why shouldn't she? I asked for her help and she was

very glad to give it," Jane said, sounding just the slightest bit soggy to her own ears. She looked at her glass. It was empty. She tucked her chin down and raised both eyebrows. No footman appeared. Stupid English footmen. "I take it that no one else thought to talk to Sophia directly when they found they'd been . . . targeted?"

"I don't think so, no," Mr. Prestwick said, a smile starting to replace his frown. Good. He was no longer concerned. But she did wish he'd do that dip, lift motion with his face that resulted in a brimming glass of Madeira.

"How silly of them," she said. "When trouble comes, one must face it, Mr. Prestwick! One must bring one's cannons round and blow the matches! One must *act*, Mr. Prestwick!"

"I completely agree," he said. "What happened after you acted, Miss Elliot? Did the Duke of Edenham simply . . . sink?"

"He foundered, Mr. Prestwick, make no mistake of it," she said, pressing her glass against his chest for emphasis. Rot it, she'd meant to point to his chest. She did hope she hadn't got wine on his shirtfront. Where was the deuced footman?

Oh, there he was. She set her glass down with barely a clink and reached for another. George Prestwick raised his sable brows, yet kept his mouth closed. Good man. One didn't need a man who didn't enjoy the benefits of a lovely Madeira at a wedding. Ruined the mood completely. How nice for Penelope that she had a brother who knew how to enjoy himself, and was clever enough to allow others to enjoy themselves.

Not at all like her brothers, naturally. Her brothers, now that she considered it, were complete rotters. Sailing the globe, having adventures, leaving her at home with *Ezekiel* and his heavy hands. If a girl was going to be left home, leave her with some handsome bloke, some man who knew what he was about. Someone not unlike Edenham.

Oh, not Edenham *himself.* No, no, no. He was not at *all* the sort of man a woman wanted. He'd been married too many times and had all those children. Why his nursery must be enormous! How else to fit in the ten or twelve Williams and Sarahs and Ophelias he had stashed in there, hiding under beds and behind the drapery. Simply too many, too much, too handsome, too charming, too willing . . . oh, yes, too exceedingly willing. Why, a woman wanted a man she had to fight for! A man who went down swinging. A man who showed the slightest hesitation to . . . what did they call it here? . . . get leg-shackled, that was it. A man who ran to the altar, what was that to a woman? He was clearly marriage-mad, marry anything that moved, wouldn't he? Put him next to a black swan and he'd run to the parson with his coat on fire. No, it was all wrong. A man should only be eager because the woman inspired eagerness.

Desperation would be even better. Yes, a desperate man was precisely the sort of man she wanted to marry. He should be *desperate* to have her, but only her, not skipping to the church because he had a habit of marrying.

"I don't think I've ever heard it phrased in that particular way before," George Prestwick said.

"I beg your pardon?" she said, holding her glass to her breasts. It felt suspiciously light. She looked down. It was empty again. Oddly small glasses for a wedding. She would have thought Aunt Molly would have been more generous to her guests on such a special day as this. Yet another difference between their countries. In America, at least the guests were kept well watered! Where was that footman . . .

"I don't think anyone has ever before described the Duke of Edenham as having the habit of marrying," Mr. Prestwick said. "It might be quite apt."

Oh, mercy. But of course she hadn't meant to say any of that *out loud*, but now that she had, well? It was all true, wasn't it? She'd stand by her words. She had a right to her opinion, didn't she? She was the equal of any man here. *We hold these truths to be self-evident, that all men are created equal . . .* Just so.

"The evidence seems quite compelling to me," she said. "But I wouldn't think of presuming to speak for you, Mr. Prestwick. No, you must form your own conclusions. But the evidence, Mr. Prestwick! The evidence!"

"Quite so," he said, smiling. "Three wives and two children. He might well be a man out of control."

Two children? Oh. That wasn't so many, was it? The cooper they used most frequently had fifteen, but of course, he was much older than Edenham, had a head start, in a manner of speaking.

"How old is he, do you think, Mr. Prestwick?" she said, her voice hushed as she leaned toward him. Mr. Prestwick took her glass from her hand and passed it to a footman. Oh, *now* he came round. Typical. "He must be *horribly* old, yet he does seem to be wearing it well, wouldn't you say?"

"I'm afraid I don't know, Miss Elliot," George answered her. "He's reached his majority, that much I vouch."

"Oh, don't be coy, Mr. Prestwick," she said, leaning back from him. "I shan't think less of him to find that he's well above forty or even fifty. A man matures. It is nothing of which to be ashamed. I know a man who's been married five times and he's not yet sixty! Edenham is well on his way. Quite enthusiastically, too, wouldn't you agree?"

"Happily, Miss Elliot," he said, waving the footman away. Wave him forward, man, forward! But no, off he went. Jane sighed and gave Mr. Prestwick a most reproachful look. "You do seem to have enjoyed meeting the duke. And he you, naturally. Did you get on well? Find common ground between you?"

Jane stood as straight as a stick and said solemnly, "I always enjoy meeting new people, Mr. Prestwick. I am very, very cordial. Which cannot be said of everyone, if you take my meaning."

"I'm not sure I do, Miss Elliot," he said, a very worried look skittering over his brow. Dear man, to be so concerned. How nice that he was in the family now, although by a very thin thread stretched over a very great distance. "Was the Duke of Edenham not cordial to you? He gave every appearance of it."

"Ha!" she said, nodding vigorously, which gave her a most unappealing fuzzy feeling between her ears. "Ha, again I say, Mr. Prestwick. The *appearance* of cordiality is not the same as a true and proper attitude of *pure* cordiality. *I* have been cordial. Edenham has been . . ."

"Yes?"

"Familiar," she whispered. "Not at all the same. I trust you comprehend the difference?"

"Most assuredly, Miss Elliot," Mr. Prestwick answered. "I confess to being quite astounded. I can assure you that he does not have that reputation here, and certainly no history of excessive familiarity with lovely young women. Perhaps you inspired some sharp emotion within him?"

"Are you suggesting that *I* am responsible for his shoddy behavior, Mr. Prestwick?" she said a bit loudly. Yes, well, she'd been hideously insulted, hadn't she? This man was in her family? Thank Providence that an ocean separated them. "I had thought better of you, Mr. Prestwick. I *had* thought you exceptionally cordial. Now I cannot but wonder if you are to be ranked in the same class as Edenham. And by class, of course I mean, *rank*."

He looked confused. Preposterous. Her meaning was entirely clear.

"I am sorry if I have offended you, Miss Elliot. It was the farthest thing from my intention."

"Intentions are slippery things, Mr. Prestwick," she said dolefully. "In this country the Proclamation of Intention is very often used to smother a host of offenses. I speak, of course, of A Proposal of Marriage, which if done poorly, and even you must admit that it was done most poorly, is the most thinly veiled of insults. I trust you take my meaning."

By the puzzled look on his face, it appeared he did not.

"There are many women who would welcome a proposal of marriage from the Duke of Edenham, no matter how it was delivered. I think you might not realize how very desirable it is to have gathered a duke to your breast, loosely speaking," he said.

"To my breast, Mr. Prestwick?" she said, her voice booming with all the gentleness of a musket shot. "To my *breast*? I think you must apologize, sir, or I shall call you out. I'll permit no man to talk about my breasts, no matter how desirable they are."

The room was very crowded and many people had listened to the exchange between Miss Elliot and Mr. Prestwick; this last statement settled silence over the room like a shroud.

"Miss Elliot," Prestwick said, his voice quite low as his eyes scanned the room, "I apologize most ardently. I meant no disrespect to either your character or your person. I misspoke and beg your indulgence."

"My indulgence is given," she said with queenlike dignity, if she did say so herself. "I do think the wine has affected you, Mr. Prestwick. A steady hand, there, if you please. I distinctly dislike being offended, particularly in regards to my . . ." She waved one of her hands in front of her breasts, nodding at him conspiratorially. He hadn't meant any harm, she was certain. Mr. Prestwick was quite cordial as a general rule. "Now, about the insult I've been dealt by Edenham. I do think you have missed my point, sir. He has pronounced, has he not? He has proclaimed. He has decided. Ha!" she burst out, shaking her head at him. It made her dizzy. She stopped immediately. "He has not *proposed*. He has not . . ." What was the word she was looking for? She couldn't think of it, but she knew he'd bungled it badly.

"Pursued?" Prestwick offered.

"Suffered," Jane said grimly. "A man must suffer. It is in their suffering that they are made great." She gave Mr. Prestwick a most dire stare. And then she smiled and said brightly, "I heard a sermon on that once. It made a profound impression upon me."

"I can see that it has," Prestwick said, smiling. He was a smiling sort of man, was Mr. George Prestwick. She liked that about him. It reminded her of Joel.

"Something to do with fire and dross and gold," she said. "Most moving, most illuminating. I do think Edenham should be put to the torch, metaphorically, of course. Although . . ." Her face grew gleefully grim just thinking about it. Not at all the face one wore to a wedding celebration. She righted herself almost immediately, hoping that Aunt Molly hadn't seen her.

Where was Aunt Molly? Wasn't she a good deal responsible for Edenham plopping her down on that bed? Who'd arranged for the bed to be in that room, anyway, if not Molly? Oh, yes, a fine turn at playing Machiavelli. No wonder her mother had insisted she bring a small and tidy firearm with her to London. As it was in her bedchamber, it had done her no good at all against Edenham. Perhaps she could lure him upstairs to her room? Given his penchant for bedchambers it didn't seem at all a difficult thing to accomplish.

"You do not think he suffered at the hands of your brothers, Miss Elliot?" George asked, his black eyes glittering with good humor. As they were laughing at Edenham she found his humor quite well developed.

Jane made a dismissive motion with her hands, and it should be noted that no matter what she did with her hands or her face, no footman appeared with a tray of wine, which did stink of collusion, did it not? "A touch, Mr. Prestwick, the laying on of hands in a nearly spiritual sense, wouldn't you say? What were they supposed to do? Allow that man to put his hands on me with impunity? Never, Mr. Prestwick. We Elliots hold ourselves to a higher value than that. One may not, even if he be a duke, behave with impunity toward an Elliot. I am an Elliot, Mr. Prestwick. I shall not be—"

"Undersold?" George said.

"Mr. Prestwick, this is not the marketplace and I am not a loaf to be carted home from the ovens," she said sternly. "You seem to be of a mind with that duke. Could that be possible?"

"I hardly think so, Miss Elliot," George said cheerfully. "I am merely the son of a viscount. Edenham is a duke. We could scarcely share one mind."

Jane shook her head at Mr. Prestwick in woeful disappointment. "All men are created equal, Mr. Prestwick. Believe it, for it is true. You must not make light of yourself. Nor, equally, more of Edenham. He is hardly worth it."

"Miss Elliot," he said softly, "I can see that you have formed a firm opinion of the Duke of Edenham in a matter of hours. I should think he has done the same of you. You two do seem to have found a connection of sorts, a sympathy of hearts, perhaps?"

"Hardly that, Mr. Prestwick," she said.

How utterly absurd. She only knew Edenham well enough to dislike him thoroughly, though if he could be made to suffer she was certain she would like him far better. It was a problem, seeing to his suffering, though she did have such energy for it. What could she accomplish if she only put some small effort into it?

Arrogant, power blind fool, to try and force her into marriage by way of ruination. She was no woman to be forced to anything! She was an Elliot. She could not be forced.

Damned silly way to get a woman anyway. Couldn't he

simply put forth the effort to win her? Oh, she didn't want him, but as he wanted her, by his own words, couldn't he work for her?

Suffering. The man was shy on suffering. Not of the heartrending sort, for clearly he'd endured enough of that, but of the man-making, backbreaking, sweating blood sort.

The simple, healthy sort of suffering.

Jane smiled just thinking about it.

Twenty-one

It was the worst luck that Louisa was standing not fifteen feet away from her mother-in-law Molly, a woman who had not quite warmed to her, which was the usual way of things, wasn't it, when Blakes, his brother George at his elbow, accosted her with a cold gleam in his blue eyes and a very sharkish quality about his movements. Blakes was often sharkish. It made dealing with him a bit of a tussle. It made being married to him deliciously unpredictable. Now did not look to be one of the delicious times.

"What are you trying to do to Jane?" Blakes said under his breath, taking her by the arm and pulling her across the blue reception room into the music room. As she had been quite on the opposite side of the room, it made for quite a march.

"Nothing!" she said, which was *practically* true.

"You made some sort of wager with her," George Blakesley said.

"Nothing of the sort," Louisa said stiffly, giving George

a look of pure outrage that she was being so maligned. George was tall and rather severe-looking, quite an arrogant man given that he was merely a third son. As Blakes was a fourth son, his lack of arrogance was readily explained. Blakes, Lord Henry as the world called him, was not arrogant precisely, but he was sharp. As sharp as a blade or a shark's tooth. Far more chilling than being arrogant, not that George seemed to have discerned that. All that to explain why she was not at all intimidated by George and far more careful of Blakes. *Shark's tooth*: That did say it all. "I would never bet money with a relative," she said.

Blakes narrowed his eyes in that way he had when he'd caught her out. "Not money, then, but what? What have you done, Louisa?"

"Nothing. I am hardly a liar," she snapped, turning to walk away from him. Blakes grabbed her wrist until she turned back to him. If they weren't in a crowded room, for the music room was full of people, even if far fewer than the blue reception room, this wrist-grabbing argument might have led to interesting destinations. She could see that Blakes was thinking the same thing. She did love that about him, as well as everything else.

"We shall not waste time in listing all the things you deny being," he said. "Why is Jane pursuing Edenham?"

All thoughts of lovemaking fled. Louisa's mouth dropped open and she snatched her hand out of his grip. "Jane pursuing Edenham? If that isn't just like a man. Can't you see that he's nearly falling out of windows for her? Why, the man hasn't taken a straight step since he first saw her. Jane is moments away from running down Piccadilly to avoid the man!"

"An overstatement," Blakes said. "Kindly stick to the facts. You tricked her into pursuing him."

"Lady Lanreath overheard you discussing it with

Amelia," George said, apparently thinking he was the final nail in the coffin. Men. How could anyone communicate with them when they simply insisted on seeing things through their own distorted lens?

"If I tricked her into anything," Louisa said, "and I'm hardly admitting to that, it was only to give her a reason to give him a chance to pursue her, and that after he made a dribbling fool of himself over her first! Pursuing him, indeed."

"I won't have her tricked into marriage, Louisa," Blakes said, looking quite as calculating and cool as he normally did. She knew what lay beneath: a warm-blooded romantic. "She's my cousin and I won't see her used."

"If you won't see her used, I suggest you talk to Edenham," Louisa said sharply. Blakes wasn't the only one who could be sharp.

With that, she walked out of the music room and back into the blue reception room. Molly was standing near the doorway between the two rooms, caught Louisa's eye, and gave her a firm smile and crisp nod of approval.

Well. There was a surprise.

⤜⤏

"WHAT'S surprising about it?" Penelope asked, giving her husband a very assessing look.

"He is a duke," Iveston said, looking at her quite penetratingly. He did that often. She enjoyed it thoroughly, although less now than usually. She had the intense feeling that Iveston was going to say something excessively annoying. "I don't have to explain to you, of all people, how desirable that makes him."

Not to her of all people, because she'd been determined to marry a duke, Edenham in particular, and got Iveston instead. As Iveston was the heir apparent of the Duke of Hyde, she'd got what she wanted, ultimately, a point she was not at all shy about disclosing to him. What would have been the point? It was a worthy goal. She was not ashamed of it.

"Not every woman has the same goals, Iveston," she said, trying to be patient with him, but truly, did he think all women were cut from the same bolt? What did that make her? Just one scrap out of many in the bin?

"Edenham is highly desirable," Iveston repeated, as if repeating it one hundred times would make a difference. "She must want to marry him. It stands to reason. You certainly did."

Penelope smiled. It was not an attractive smile, and as it was her wedding day, she did think that Iveston should make more of an effort to encourage her to look as attractive as possible.

"You don't mention how desperately Edenham must want to marry Jane. She is a beautiful woman, unique to his experience, unattainable by every measure," Penelope said.

Iveston, that imbecile, laughed under his breath. "Unattainable? Come now, he's a duke, Pen, and can have his pick of women. Certainly, if he makes a serious offer, she'll jump at it."

"He's already offered for her, Iveston. How can you have forgotten that? She refused him soundly, and he has the bruises to prove it."

"*Jed* refused him, and small wonder, the way it was handled," Iveston said, shaking his head and looking out over the guests in the yellow drawing room. "As to that, I don't think Edenham meant a word of it. He was simply doing all he could to save Jane's reputation. Quite honorable of him, actually."

If they hadn't been at their wedding party, Penelope might have hit Iveston over the head with a serving tray. As it was, she did look around the room to calculate how many witnesses, and of what type, were present. Lord Dutton was snoring drunkenly on one of the sofas, but he was the only one who was. Everyone else was wide awake and beginning to stare at them.

"After kissing her soundly in the middle of a crowded room," Penelope said crisply, "I hardly think being honorable crossed Edenham's mind!"

"He's a duke. Being honorable is always on his mind," Iveston said.

"Then why did he kiss Jane?" she snapped, her voice rising harshly on the final words. Was any woman ever made to endure such idiocy on her wedding day?

Iveston shrugged and said mildly, "She must have provoked him mercilessly. You women are quite accomplished at that precise thing."

"Iveston, you have inspired me," she said, looking him up and down. "I simply will not rest until I am pronounced *merciless*. I don't think it should take very long to accomplish it, do you?"

❧

JOEL Elliot looked down at Lady Paignton and could not help but notice that she was mercilessly laughing at him. Oh, not outright, but slyly, deep inside, the only evidence of it glimmering in her green eyes and slipping past the corners of her mouth.

Treating him like a rustic, was she? Not for long. New York was a bustling city boasting the busiest port in America; he knew how to lift a skirt in his fist and what to do after that. In fact, why not do just that? He would do her the supreme honor of taking her at her word.

"I'm not offended, Lady Paignton," he said, taking a single backward step, the gravel crunching under his feet, crossing his arms over his chest to look her up and down. "I'm only taking your measure, if you will. You may lift your skirts to any man, but I do not respond to every invitation from every woman who issues one. How would I get any work done with that going on all day and night? No, a man must be particular as his time is so much more valuable than a woman's, even one who offers him a quick respite from his toils. How much time do you have? Nearly infinite, I should hazard. I might be able to spare you fifteen minutes. I can assure you that it will be fifteen minutes you won't forget."

Bernadette looked at him first in surprise, then in what appeared to be only mild outrage, which did tell the tale of her exploits most clearly, and then finally in what he could only name brittle humor.

"Fifteen minutes, Captain Elliot? My, you Americans are given far more credit for determination and endurance when faced with an English opponent than I believe you deserve. How ever did you win your revolution? In fifteen minute . . . spurts?"

Lady Paignton gave as good as she got.

Joel found that an admirable quality in anyone, even an English aristocrat, and he smiled in spite of himself.

"It can be stretched out, as the need or inclination requires," he said.

"Stretched out, can it?" she said, looking him up and down, her face displaying an overt eroticism that he found nearly irresistible, which was certainly no secret to her. "Upon whose need, Captain? Whose inclination? I fear it is upon such *points* that wars are begun."

"If I give you fifteen minutes, you can determine that for yourself."

"If I give *you* fifteen minutes, you shall beg to have far longer than that, which I can assure you, you will not forget."

Joel took a step nearer and looked down into her almond-shaped moss green eyes. "Is that a challenge?"

∽

"CAPTAIN Elliot," Lady Richard said, her hazel brown eyes looking at him quite cautiously, "I do feel that I must have put a foot wrong."

"By inviting me into your bed for an hour or two?" Jedidiah asked. "But why not longer, Lady Richard? Why not the whole night? Could it be that you do not think I would last the night? I assure you that my stamina is a match for yours. Or perhaps you think I could sustain your interest for merely an hour or two?"

She looked at him with all the vigor of a day old fawn, all wide eyes and trembling limbs. Everything about this woman bespoke gentility and fragility, and this is what pops out of her mouth? A fine bit of mummery. He had thought her the most exquisite woman he'd ever seen, her manner as gently wrought as her features. He felt like the rustic colonial she surely thought him.

"Captain Elliot, that is not at all—"

"Katherine," he breathed, taking her by the arm and pulling her a step closer to him, "please call me Jedidiah. As you have offered your body to me, it seems foolish not to share the intimacy of our names."

Her eyes widened and her mouth opened slightly. She looked ready to be kissed, and damned if he didn't want to be the man to do it.

"Ah," she squeaked, staring at his mouth.

"If I take an hour with you, Katherine," he said, his gaze skimming her face, "you will beg me to take you, and take you, and take you for a week."

"Ah!" she squeaked again, a bit more moanish this time.

"Or until the wind comes up and I'm away upon the sea," he said briskly, releasing her arm, but not stepping back from her. No, not quite able to do that.

She stared up into his face, her breath a shallow gasp

in her throat that he heard distinctly, and which pulled at something deep within him in a way that wasn't comfortable at all. She took a breath. She took another, a bit shaky, and then she smiled with all the innocent sweetness of a child.

"Is that a challenge, Jedidiah?" she said.

Twenty-two

"MOLLY," the Duke of Hyde said softly, "as it's past seven, I do think we must have the wedding breakfast now. Lady Melton is murmuring that she's feeling faint."

Molly snorted under her breath and said, "She's always finding a reason to faint. I can't think what she finds so entertaining about it."

"The last time I saw her fall into a faint, and a graceful one it was, she displayed the ankle of one leg and nearly half a calf on the other," Hyde said pleasantly. "I was entertained. Briefly, only briefly."

Molly looked up at him and laughed.

The Duke of Hyde was a tall, lean man of faded blond hair shot liberally with silver white, and pale blue eyes. He'd served as a general in the American colonies and whilst there he'd met Molly, a Boston girl born and bred, of a prosperous shipping family. Possessed of dark blond hair and gunmetal blue eyes, Molly's head came barely to Hyde's shoulder. They appeared to have nothing in common, including their temperaments, yet they shared the one commonality that was essential. They loved each other.

It was for this reason, this surprise of finding love with a Boston girl, of marrying her in the midst of a bloody political conflict, and bringing her home to England where she made his life as duke of some reputation far richer than it had been before, that Hyde had allowed Molly to encourage, by the most outlandish means imaginable, the marriages of three of their five sons. And now their American niece.

It was getting a bit sticky.

"She may not want to marry him, Molly," he said, when her laughter had run its course.

"Of course she does," Molly answered briskly. "Who wouldn't want to marry a handsome duke? I certainly did."

"You weren't marrying a duke. You were marrying me. And an uphill battle it was for me. Your family gave me the devil of a time. I despaired of ever achieving you, more than once."

Molly smiled up at him and patted his chest fondly. "A man is supposed to despair, that's the best purpose of any sort of courtship. A man without an uphill battle? Why, he'd stay sleeping on his cot in his tent, the battle raging on without him."

"You believe she's toying with him? Encouraging him to fight for her?"

"It is what she's doing, whether she knows it or not," Molly said, straightening her pearl necklace. "If he was nothing to her, if he meant nothing, if he aroused nothing, then she'd treat him . . . as nothing. It's not that she would ignore him, it's that she would do nothing to him. Whatever else she has done, or not done, she has engaged him. It's equally clear that she enjoys engaging him and wants to continue engaging him."

"It is equally clear that Edenham is still in the fight,"

Hyde said. "But marriage? Sally will not be pleased. Timothy less so."

"My mother was not pleased with you," Molly said. "I, however, am still pleased."

Hyde nodded slowly, convinced. "Our guests would be pleased if they could eat."

"Which goes directly back to my point, Hyde," she said pleasantly, "that not everyone is going to be pleased."

To that, he had no response but a smile.

⌘

JANE was still smiling, thinking of all the suffering she was going to require Edenham to endure, when two remarkable-looking men approached her. Actually, they approached Mr. Prestwick, but as she was standing with Mr. Prestwick, the effect was the same. Had she met them previously? She couldn't remember, certain things having gone a bit fuzzy, but as Mr. Prestwick was the thoughtful sort, he introduced them, again. Or not. She might remember later. Or not.

Really, there was something very disturbing about the quality of Aunt Molly's Madeira.

Lord Raithby was quite handsome; they all seemed to be quite handsome, didn't they? Likely something to do with the improved diet that was the direct result of being well-moneyed and spoilt from birth. Raithby's hair was dark brown, his eyes were dark blue, and his face was angular with a narrow chin. He had a scar near his eye.

She liked the look of that scar.

She truly was a most horrid girl and must get ahold of herself and her ruthless instincts immediately. Or at least soon. Or at least as soon as she could without undue fuss. Yes, that was it. There was no need to make a fuss about it, was there?

But she did like the look of that small scar. It gave Raithby a dangerous look. She was obviously the sort of girl who liked a dangerous look.

Which explained her unbecoming fascination with Lord Penrith. Handsome? Naturally. Dark blond hair that was arranged rather savagely, longish, and unruly. Green eyes that looked at her with all the subtlety of a wild cat. His voice was a rough purr, a throaty, velvety, smooth path to a most speedy seduction. Oh, there was no doubt about that. A more sensual man she had never met.

Did he know Lady Paignton? That seemed a most logical question. They had many points in common, those two.

Mr. Prestwick seemed only slightly alarmed by the arrival of his friends, or she assumed they were his friends. Although, if they were, why should he be alarmed? Jane drew her natural caution around her like a thick shawl.

It fell off.

"I do like the look of that scar, Lord Raithby," she said with a smile of pure female appreciation. "How did you come by it? Not by a woman's hand, I hope. Or perhaps I do hope. You probably deserved it. Did you?"

Raithby's blue eyes widened slightly. He glanced at Penrith. George Prestwick smiled and shook his head in what appeared to be amusement. Penrith grinned and looked at Jane.

"Oh, do tell me," Jane prompted. "I'm not from here, you know, and have missed what I'm certain is a wonderful story about your scar. You like it, don't you? You should. It's completely dashing."

"Completely," Penrith said. "Makes me wish I had one. Would you care to inflict a scar upon me, Miss Elliot? I would hold very still."

"A wound first, Lord Penrith," she said. "The scar follows."

"Ah, very true," Penrith said.

"And you would allow me to wound you? All for the dash of a carefully placed scar?"

"Miss Elliot, as you find scars alluring, I would indeed."

Jane burst out laughing. "Oh, that's absurd. I am only one woman, Lord Penrith. You should not remake yourself because of a whim of mine. I don't even live here."

"But perhaps you shall?" Penrith said, his eyes glittering with amusement.

She could have pretended ignorance, but why? It seemed suddenly too much effort would be required to do so. She was just a visitor and she would never see any of these people again. Why not say what she wished? Why not *do* what she wished?

Was there any greater adventure than that?

"Because of the Duke of Edenham's determination to marry me?" Jane asked in response. "Is that what you mean, Lord Penrith?" Without waiting for his response, but really, was it necessary, she said, "Did you not hear my brothers renounce him completely?"

"I did," Penrith said softly. "The thing is, Miss Elliot, I did not hear *you* renounce the duke. Certainly your wishes must count for something with your brothers? Or not? But perhaps it is that you would do nothing to distress them and since Edenham so clearly distresses them, you will be guided by their preferences."

That wasn't it at all, most obviously. Or not most obviously. Is that what this throng thought? That she was being managed by her brothers?

Oh, they did try. *Everyone* tried, even Penrith was now trying. Being managed was an exhausting bit of business to endure and, naturally, there was the equally exhausting business of then being required to outmaneuver them all. How much simpler it all would be if she only did what she wanted, no matter what anyone else wanted.

It was upon such thoughts that revolutions were begun.

As the world was awash in revolutions, who would notice the tiny one she would stage?

"Lord Penrith," she said, "you are an agitator, which in my country is a high compliment. Now," she continued, linking her arm in his, to his clear surprise, "I have not decided what to do about the duke. My thoughts lead me to one conclusion, yet my . . ." She wanted to say loins, but did think that might be a bit bold for them. She might be starting a revolution, but one didn't want to alienate potential allies at the first billow of gunpowder.

"Heart?" Mr. Prestwick offered.

"Very good, Mr. Prestwick," she said. "*Heart* will serve most admirably. The Duke of Edenham, his determination to wed me, was very much a surprise to me. An unwelcome surprise, to be sure, but one does find the man has some few compelling qualities."

His mouth, his eyes, his face, his hands, his very unlikely sense of decorum to name but a few. Which she would not name, clearly, for there was no point in telling one man what a woman found attractive about another man. Not unless . . .

Not unless . . . and Jane smiled so brilliantly that even Mr. Prestwick seemed struck dumb.

"Lord Penrith," she said, throwing her beauty all over the man like a riotous rainstorm, "would you walk with me about the room? I shall tell you all the reasons why I should prefer to remain in New York and you shall endeavor to convince me that England is a wondrous country and that I should be a fool not to want to live here. Can you do that, Lord Penrith?"

"Convince you or walk with you, Miss Elliot?" he asked, studying her with his cool green eyes, the tiniest of smiles pulling his lips upward in a cat's grin.

"Either. Both. I leave it up to you, Lord Penrith," she said.

"As it is being left up to me, I accept your challenge, Miss Elliot," Penrith said, and without a backward glance to either Prestwick or Raithby, Penrith walked off with Jane Elliot tucked against his side.

When they were a good fifteen feet away, Raithby said to Prestwick, "Ten pounds that Edenham marries her."

George Prestwick grinned and said, "And lose ten pounds? I think not."

"You're certain Edenham will get her," Raithby said.

"Not at all, Raithby," George said. "But I am certain that she will get him."

❦

"OF course she'll get him," Louisa said in a hushed voice. "If she wants him. I'm not entirely convinced that she does. He's made such a bungle of it. I'm very much surprised that a duke could be made to look so thoroughly ridiculous."

"I'm not," Amelia said. As her father was a duke and as her brother, whom she thought completely ridiculous, was the heir apparent, her sentiments were hardly surprising. "What I can't understand is why it's all taking so long. He's besotted, kissed her in full view of at least forty people, asked for her hand, been refused . . . and now, nothing! Nothing has happened. Shouldn't he be asking again? Seducing her somehow?"

"If she wants him, she could simply seduce *him*," Penelope said. "That hardly takes a minute of a woman's time. A very efficient way to get a man, I've always maintained."

The three women nodded. It was true. They'd each got their husbands by seducing them into it. Either Jane did not want to seduce Edenham, which on its surface was patently absurd as the man was as handsome as a Greek god, or she did not want to marry a duke, which was equally absurd. Who on earth would disdain that life of privilege, ease, and power?

She *was* an American. They might not have given that enough weight in their calculations.

"Blakes is being an absolute prig about the whole thing," Louisa said, toying with her fiery curls.

"Iveston is as well," Penelope said softly. "I do wish he would put some effort into appearing intelligent and insightful on our wedding day. One would think he would realize that on his own, but no, I am forced to point it out to him. He did not take it well, poor old thing."

They were sequestered in the antechamber of the gold bedchamber. No one would find them here, unless they were specifically being looked for. As they had each parted on slightly harsh words with their husbands, they were not likely to be looked for at present.

"What does Cranleigh say?" Louisa asked Amelia.

"Very little," Amelia said. "He knows the family better than anyone here and seems very concerned, though for Edenham and not for Jane. That does indicate something, though I'm not certain what."

"Something not very good for Edenham, I should think," Penelope said, patting her closed fan against her thigh. "Perhaps he believes that Jane will refuse him completely and permanently. That would devastate him for a week or two, wouldn't it?"

Amelia looked at Penelope a bit oddly. "Not longer? You don't think he would pine for her?"

"A duke? Pine?" Penelope snorted indelicately. After all, they were alone. There was no reason to be delicate now. "He could marry nearly anyone within the month, if he so chose."

"He hasn't chosen," Amelia said. "That's my entire point. He's been a widower for a year and this is the first woman he's shown any interest in."

"One year and four months, actually," Penelope corrected. "I've kept careful watch on Edenham, in a desperate panic that he would marry again before I'd found my way to him."

"And now he's found his way to Jane," Amelia said, "and botching it completely. I do wonder how a man can ever persuade himself to believe that he swoops in and carries the girl off when it is the girl doing every bit of the work."

"How utterly true," Penelope said.

"The only bit that redeems them is that they make it all so very much fun," Louisa said.

The three women smiled, their husbands almost forgiven for being such idiots on the subject of Jane and Edenham.

"You don't think that he's, well," Amelia said hesitantly, "had it beaten out of him, do you? I did think Edenham had more pluck than that."

"He has got all his previous wives quite easily," Louisa said, biting her lower lip. "I remember that very well. This is quite certainly more than he's accustomed to."

"I certainly thought better of him, if that's the case," Penelope said sternly, her sable brows furrowed in disapproval. "I did think Edenham showed such promise, and I hate to have my conclusions thrown into doubt."

"Don't we all," Louisa said musingly, tapping her fan against her mouth absently. "Cranleigh has no insight at all?" Louisa asked Amelia.

"None that he's sharing," Amelia said, which was stating it most clearly.

"I don't suppose there's anything we can do, anything further, to encourage Jane in Edenham's direction," Louisa mumbled, still tapping her fan, scowling at the floor, deeply in thought. "Or Edenham in hers, if he's lost the scent."

"Had it beaten out of him, you mean," Penelope said, thoroughly annoyed with dukes in general and Edenham in particular for not living up to her expectations of him.

"He did go to Sophia," Louisa said. "Certainly she should be able to manage him if Jane cannot."

It was at that precise moment that the Duke of Edenham opened the door between the antechamber and the gold bedchamber, a quite saucy smile upon his exquisitely handsome face. The women stood gaping, which was only to be expected.

"Ladies," he said, bowing, and then, grinning, he opened

the door to the music room and strolled through it, looking for all the world like a man prepared to conquer France, Russia, and Spain combined.

It was as they were still recovering from that shock, that they distinctly heard Sophia's voice coming from the direction of the gold bedchamber. Looking at each other, wide-eyed, they hurried over to the closed door of the gold bedchamber and, without a moment's pause or indeed a particle of shame, put their ears to the door and listened.

Twenty-three

QUINTON listened to the sounds of the people around him in the blue reception room in much the same manner as one listens to the surf: abstractly. He was a man given more to listening than to speaking, just as he was a man given more to solitude than crowds. As it was Hyde who had requested his presence, he had forgone his normal pursuits to honor Hyde.

The Earl of Quinton had the same triangular-shaped face as his son, Lord Raithby. He had the same blue eyes, the same set of the ears close to his well-shaped head, the same straight dark brown hair though just lightly threaded with silver, the same perfectly shaped nose. Quinton did not have a scar on the top of his left cheekbone. What Quinton did have was a small dimple in his chin. He had been born with the dimple. Raithby had acquired the scar.

As was his normal practice whilst in a crowd, Quinton stood with his back to the wall, studying the faces and mannerisms of everyone who passed before his gaze. It was thus that he observed the Marquis of Ruan approaching him casually. Actually, it was not so much that Ruan was approaching Quinton, but that Ruan was wandering through the crowd and found himself being directed toward Quinton. Ruan didn't seem to care where he wandered.

The earl did not know Ruan beyond the rumors of him, but he had not thought him a man to either wander or not care. He was therefore suspicious when Ruan stopped at his side without a word and turned to survey the room with him.

Quinton, as was his practice, waited for Ruan to speak. He had nothing at all to say to Ruan and so waiting was quite easy for him. Ruan, it became apparent, was not a man to be put off by uncomfortable silences, particularly as he didn't seem to find this silence uncomfortable. Quinton found himself slightly more disposed than usual to like the man on that fact alone.

The Marquis of Ruan was perhaps ten years younger than Quinton, although perhaps not quite that much. Ruan was possessed of rugged features and a few smallish scars scattered about his face. In all, he looked very much like a man who had seen his share of life and had not yet been tamed by it. Whether Quinton had been tamed by life he was not altogether sure; he rather suspected he had been and on some days he considered that very wise of him and on others he rode over his land, his dogs running at thc feet of his hunter, like a ghoul from hell.

Today, in London, was neither of those days.

"I've just had my ballocks handed to me on a plate by Sophia Dalby," Ruan said in a throaty murmur.

As a conversation starter, it was impressive. Quinton's attention was fully captured.

"That sounds not at all pleasant," Quinton said.

"It wasn't."

"I suppose you deserved it."

Ruan cut a glance at Quinton nearly without moving his head. "She'd say so. I don't have to agree with her, do I?"

"It will be easier for you if you do," Quinton said softly, his mouth tucking up into a brief smile.

"You know her." It was not a question. And so it became obvious why Ruan had *wandered* over to him.

"I do."

They said nothing after that. Ruan likely wanted to ask him all sorts of things about Sophia Dalby, the sort of things that every man who had not yet been tamed by life wanted to know about Sophia Dalby, but Quinton was not a man to offer up the details of a person's life as a form of entertainment, sordid or not. That Sophia's life had brushed often against the sordid made him more inclined to be tight-lipped, not less.

"Do you know why I sought you out, Quinton?" Ruan said after a few minutes of nearly companionable silence. Quinton didn't bother with a reply. "It is because I presumed you to be a man who would not eagerly discuss Sophia with me, or with anyone. I mean her only the best."

"And you are the best," Quinton said. It was not a question.

Ruan looked at him fully, his gaze unwavering and determined. The man's eyes were green, vividly green.

"No. I'm not. But I begin to wonder if she is," Ruan said.

It was a most unexpected reply. Quinton found himself wondering if he should be slightly impressed, or if Ruan was just cleverer than the usual sort who trailed after Sophia like a starving wolf.

"She's a remarkable woman," Quinton murmured, looking at Ruan. Ruan returned the look and said nothing. "What did you do to offend her?"

"I tried to help her."

Quinton smiled fractionally and looked at the floor beneath his feet. "You are too late to help her." Quinton lifted his gaze and looked at Ruan again. "You insulted her by suggesting she needed saving, am I correct?"

Ruan nodded, holding his gaze.

A footman approached carrying a tray of drinks. Ruan waved him off.

"I was in America," Quinton said. "I served with Hyde for a time in Boston, an aide of sorts back when I thought soldiering meant adventure. You knew that?"

"Hyde's youngest mentioned something about it to me today. Sophia's known Molly from the beginning, hasn't she? If Molly, then Hyde, then you?"

"No, not from the beginning," Quinton said quietly. "Sophia guards her beginning from everyone who knows her. I only know what I was there to see."

"And what did you see?"

Quinton lifted his head and looked at the ceiling for a moment. "Why do you want to dig into this woman's past, Ruan? She will hand you more than your ballocks on a plate if you disturb the image in the pond."

"I am riveted by the image, or was," Ruan said. "But having sensed that it is an image, I want to see what lies beneath. Will she be less fascinating to me? Impossible."

"You are not the first man to be beguiled," Quinton said.

"I know I am not," Ruan said. If he wanted to say he would be the last, he refrained. It did show some humility, or at least caution. "You are worried about her?"

"I have known her for many years," Quinton said. "I admire her."

"As do I."

"You want her in your bed. It is not the same."

"They are not mutually exclusive, Quinton. Have you never wanted her?"

"No, I haven't," Quinton answered, entirely truthfully.

"You hesitate not because you are afraid for her," Ruan said, studying Quinton's face, "but because you respect her."

Quinton smiled. "Sophia can take care of herself. She

does not need me to protect her. I will tell you what I can. Do with it what you will. Sophia will then do to you what she wills."

"I suspect I should be afraid," Ruan said. He did not smile.

"Perhaps when I finish, you will be," Quinton said. He also did not smile. "Did you know that Molly Hyde has a sister?"

"The mother of Jane Elliot and the Captains Elliot, yes."

"No, there was another, the oldest sister," Quinton said, his eyes unfocused as he looked across the room. "Betsy was her name. She was taken by the Abenakis. She did not return. It is not believed that she survived."

Quinton looked at Ruan, seeing understanding flicker behind his eyes.

"Yes," Quinton continued, "now you see why Molly Hyde has embraced Sophia. Sophia's mother, Elizabeth, was taken in the same year as Betsy. If Betsy had survived, had a child, Molly and Sally would have welcomed her back. They would do no less for Elizabeth's child, Sophia."

"But Sophia is Iroquois."

"Elizabeth was stolen by the Iroquois from the Abenakis, or rather, she encouraged Joseph, a Mohawk warrior, to fight for her. He did. He killed to have her, took her, married her by their custom . . ." Quinton shrugged. "This is what Hyde told me; I think Sally got it from Elizabeth when she first appeared in New York. Elizabeth left the Iroquois, taking Sophia with her. The brother, John, stayed with the Iroquois. They were children at the time, perhaps ten or so, I don't know the why of any of it. Only that when I met Elizabeth she was married to a man named Paxton and living in New York, Sophia a slender, dark-eyed child who watched all and said little."

Ruan's face was as hard as flint, his eyes burning with astonishment. "You knew her mother? You knew her as a child? What was she like?"

"Mother or daughter?" Quinton said on a grunt of air. He didn't wait for an answer. Strangely, talking about Sophia bled off some of his old wounds, the wounds of memory. "The mother was a beauty. Black-haired, black-eyed, just like Sophia. Her skin was exceptionally fair, her carriage queenly. She was composed, endlessly composed."

"Like mother, like daughter," Ruan said, his gaze contemplative.

Quinton smiled briefly. "More than you can imagine."

"What happened to her?"

"Their estate in New York was seized under the Act of Attainder. They were known Loyalists, you see, and so," Quinton paused, swallowed, "they were dragged out of their home and murdered. By the Patriots. By a mob calling themselves the Sons of Liberty."

"And Sophia?" Ruan asked sharply.

Quinton looked at him and said nothing.

"What happened to Sophia?" Ruan asked again.

"Just what you'd expect a mob of men to do to a beautiful young girl more Iroquois than English," Quinton said grimly, staring into the middle distance, not seeing the candlelight flickering against the blue silk damask on the walls, not seeing the twinkle of jewels or the white purity of women sheathed in muslin, seeing only torchlight in a black night, hearing only screams and anguished sobs. "I found her, bleeding, beaten, silent. One of the Patriots knelt beside her, trying to force water past her lips, his frayed coat laid upon her like a blanket. You may have met him. John Fredericks is his name. He's with her still."

"Fredericks? Her butler?"

To Ruan's look of astonishment, Quinton nodded and continued, "We took her to the Elliots' farm. I didn't know where else to go. They were the enemy, of course, but I knew I could trust them to take her in. The connection to Hyde, Molly and Sally still clinging to each other though their marriages should have dragged them apart, Sophia's very vulnerability . . . it all fit. I thought she would be cared for there."

"Why didn't they keep her?"

Quinton smiled without humor. "Clinton held New York. The Elliots were hardly safe themselves. Besides, Sophia insisted. She wanted to go home. She wanted to go home to England, to the family Elizabeth had told her of. God knows she had nowhere else to go. And so Sally Elliot got her to Boston and onto an Elliot ship bound for the Brittany coast. After that . . ." Quinton shook his head. "I don't know what happened after that. The war ended and when I came home, Sophia was the Countess Dalby."

"She was just a child," Ruan said softly.

"I'm not sure she was ever a child, not in the way you mean," Quinton said.

Ruan looked at him sharply, his green eyes slicing. "You told me far more than I expected, and far more easily. Why? This is not a tale you tell often. I would have heard of it if you had."

"It's a tale I've never told," Quinton said quietly, returning Ruan's look. "I told it now only because Sophia asked me to."

"What? When?"

"Not a half hour ago," Quinton said. "She came up to me and said, 'When Ruan asks you what you know, tell him.' And so I have. Why does she want you to know this, Lord Ruan? That is what I want to know."

Ruan lowered his eyes, his brow furrowed in thought. "As do I."

Twenty-four

It took Lord Ruan very little time, but some small effort to find Sophia within the rooms of Hyde House. She was not in the main reception rooms, nor in the stair hall, where she had so efficiently cut his ballocks off him for the insult of searching into her past. He could well understand the sentiment. He had no wish to have anyone, for good or ill intent, look too closely into his past either.

It had been a serious misstep. Anyone else might have decided to avoid anything remotely like it again, but having stomped into the tangled wood, his only recourse was to delve deeper in an effort to find the path that led the way out. Or that's how it seemed to him. Clearly Sophia understood him well enough to anticipate that was exactly what he would do.

She was a most wary and most bewildering adversary.

Adversary she surely was, at least in this dance they danced between them. He had never been so engaged, so intrigued by a woman like this before. He scarcely knew what he was doing, only that he was nearly compelled to keep doing it. He had to know her, to know more about her, to plumb her every thought and emotion, to learn the scent of her skin and memorize the taste of her in his mouth.

He knew without question that she would reject such knowing as the worst sort of assault, an invasion she would fight against, offering no quarter.

Was there ever such a woman?

The more she eluded him, the more determined he became to find her. The more determined he grew, the more she withdrew, laughing at him as he stumbled all over himself, lost in the dark wild wood that was Sophia.

He would not, could not think of what her life had been, of how she had been used so callously. Not now. Not just before he found her. If she saw pity or anguish or sorrow in his eyes, she would slice the heart from his ribs for the insult. He knew that now. And he now knew why.

She had survived. In three lands, this lone girl had fought for her survival and won.

He was hard-pressed not to stand in awe, but that would not do. She would not want that from him either. He could not think of anything that she would want from him at the moment, he had stumbled so thoroughly, but something would come to him. He was sure of it. He had to be.

He found her by the sound of her voice, the softly amused tremor of it coming through the closed door between the dressing room and the gold bedchamber. A man's voice retreating, the sound of a door opening, and then Ruan was through the door to the gold bedchamber, Sophia turning, a coiled black curl sweeping over one shoulder to catch in spider web strands across the white muslin of her gown, her long gold earrings gleaming in the red-tinged light of the setting sun.

She did not look even slightly surprised to see him. Nor did she look enraged. Of course, neither did she look delighted.

"Talked to Lord Quinton already, have you, Lord Ruan?" she asked softly. "Did you find yourself soundly entertained? When a man wants to find out more about a woman, let him drink deeply of that brew, I say. Perhaps he then shall choke upon the draught. But how did it all go down, darling? Smooth as buttered rum? Or have you been poisoned?"

"Did you want to poison me, Sophia? Did you think I would ever turn away from you?" he asked, closing the distance between them. She watched him come, her dark eyes shining with grim amusement.

"I had hoped for something of the sort, I simply must confess," she said.

"I don't believe you," he said. Not because he didn't, but because he wouldn't.

The light was very dim, the room sparkling in gilt glimmers, the bed behind her, the windows darkening and turning to black mirrors to her left. He came on. He couldn't stop. He knew then that he'd never be able to stop.

"How very like a man," she said, her smile erased, her eyes not leaving his. "I tell you what I think and what I want, and you don't believe me. What will it take to convince you, darling Ruan? A blade to the throat? I'm prepared. Are you?"

"Yes," he whispered, the distance between them erased, his coat brushing the tips of her breasts. She did not move away. Neither would he. "Do what you will, and so will I." Where was that blasted fan? Not clutched in her hands, so where was her blade?

His hands slipped around her waist, pulling her hips tightly against his own, the ridge of his arousal pressing into the softness of her belly. Her hands came up between them, her palms against his chest, yet she did not force him away.

He had not intended this. He had thought to charm her anger with clever words, to start the dance they always danced between them, the cut and thrust of spoken seduction luring her defenses down. He had not meant to touch her. He had not thought to cast words down like broken glass, both sparkling and useless.

Useless. Words were useless against her. She could talk him in circles, tying him up and leaving him for dead. No, not dead. Merely left.

No more words. Touch. He had to touch her. He wanted to *reach* her.

One hand rose higher upon her back whilst the other slipped down to her hip, forcing her against him, pulling her to him. She did not pull back. Her hands did not clench. Her fingers were relaxed, as was her face. She looked, dare he say it, nearly bored. She endured his touch, that was all. He was losing himself, losing every bit of dignity and restraint, and she was bored. She stared into his eyes . . . and felt nothing. Revealed nothing.

"You won't give me a thing, will you?" he murmured, staring at her mouth.

"Not *that* thing, no. Will you take it? It's been done before, as you know," she said. "I think you enjoy knowing that about me. Does it excite you, Ruan? Do you want to plunder now what's been plundered before?"

"What's before is before. I am now," he said, and then he lowered his head and softly, gently kissed her.

She allowed herself to be kissed. She even, blandly and without any enthusiasm, kissed him in return.

It was not at all what he had imagined his first kiss of Sophia Dalby to be. And he had imagined it, which was a boyish bit of infatuation and nothing less.

Fine, then. She would reject the boy. What would she do with the man?

He deepened the kiss, plunging into her mouth, tasting her, licking her, devouring her.

She submitted to him. Only that. His hips ground

against hers. She did not move against him, yet she did not resist him.

His hands came up, swiftly flying up her ribs to cup her breasts, to tease her nipples, poking at him through the thin muslin, to press and coddle and tempt a response from her. She was not blind to him. She wanted him, had wanted him, had been tempted by him, and would be again. He would flay her desire until she panted, until she ached, until . . .

Her body did nothing. She stood calmly and let him touch her, let him grind his cock against her, let him scour the inside of her mouth with his tongue, let him thumb her nipples until they were swollen buds. She let him touch her, but having her was out of his reach.

"Damn you," he breathed against her mouth.

"That's hardly heroic," she said placidly. "Didn't you want to play the hero? What part did you have in mind for me, Ruan? Not the damsel in need of rescuing? What were you going to rescue me with? Your mighty cock?"

"Upon the word, the deed," he bit out, and he pushed her down upon the high bed, her skirts flying up to her knees, her hands lying submissively next to her head, the ornamented gold pins she wore to bind up the coils of her black hair gleaming dully.

Her legs were covered in white stockings, pink silk ribbons tying them off at her knees, her bare white legs just barely visible above the ribbons. The sight was impossibly erotic. Her bosom lifted against the sheer muslin. Her dark eyes gleamed up at him, her black hair swirling over her shoulders, a shining shadow against the white of her dress and her skin. She wore lengths of gold chain around her throat, finely wrought, and they glittered against her neck, banded and tangled. Bound.

Without thought, without guilt, he lifted her skirts in one fist, lifted the muslin up in one hard motion to reveal her sex, black curling hair tucked against cloud white skin.

There was a worn leather band around her thigh, from it hung a narrow scabbard. Within the scabbard the hilt of a blade gleamed in warning against her skin.

She did not move.

She also did not reach for her blade, which he found dimly encouraging.

He moved for her, spreading one of her creamy thighs with his hand, the other still clenching the muslin as high as her breasts. She opened to him without resistance.

Without encouragement.

Without enthusiasm.

Without passion.

Without interest.

Ruan took a shallow breath. He unclenched his fist and laid it upon her chest, between the soft mounds of her bosoms. Her breathing did not hitch. She did not gasp. She did not even protest.

He lifted his hand from her chest. He let go of her thigh. He simply and completely released her.

She lifted herself up onto her elbows to stare into his eyes, her legs still splayed, and said calmly, "Will you not take what you can, Ruan? I can see you want to."

"I will not take. I want only what you will give me, Sophia," he said, forcing his breathing to calm, to force the wolf inside him back into its cage.

"Then you will get nothing," she said. "I do not give myself away."

"I will not pay for you."

"No? You will not rape me and you will not pay me. What's left, my lord? There is no other way to have Sophia. Did you not learn that from the tales you heard today?"

Tales? Was she implying they were not wholly true? No, they were. He could see the truth of them in her eyes.

"Are you not tired of being paid for?"

Sophia smiled and slid off the bed, her skirts falling to her ankles in a smooth fall of fragile muslin. "Does anyone grow tired of being paid? I certainly don't. Lord Ruan," she said, walking up to him and laying her hand against his cheek, "do you not seek passion? Do you not want to look into my eyes and see desire burning within me?"

He said nothing. He looked into her eyes, unable to turn away, and watched passion rise up in her. Suddenly, she was a woman who wanted a man. A woman who wanted him.

"I can give you everything you want. I can make your dreams come true. Won't you make mine come true, darling Ruan?"

It was lie. He knew it for a lie. Hadn't she just told him as much?

But when he looked at her, he couldn't quite believe it. This was just some way of hers, some devious way to show him what she truly felt. She *did* feel desire for him. Her behavior, her cold boredom on the bed, had been the lie. A punishment. *This* was true. This, now.

"Ah, Ruan, don't you want me?" she breathed, urging his face down to hers, her mouth opening.

She lifted herself up onto her toes and kissed him, a hungry kiss full of hot yearning. He could not stop himself from responding in kind. She was fire in his arms, twisting her arms around his neck, pulling him into her, wrapping a leg around his, moaning into his mouth.

"Can't we stop playing these games? I've waited weeks for you to come to me as you are now," she said breathlessly, her lips nipping at his jaw, his throat, rubbing her breasts against his chest. "Why did you make me wait? Why did you not give me *this*?"

"Sophia," he said, his hands moving up her back to hold her head, to take her mouth in a deep, penetrating kiss.

She moaned and put her hands on his hips, pulling him against her, squirming and grinding against the hard jut of his sex. Walking, stumbling, blind with passion, he backed her against the bed and fell with her onto it.

"Hurry," she said, panting, clutching at his clothes. "I

want to feel you against me, inside of me. Hurry, darling. I can't wait another moment for you."

Even as his hands fondled her, lifting her skirts once again, the small voice of reason whispered that it was wrong. This was all wrong. But he could not stop. He simply refused to listen.

Once again he saw the thatch of her black hair curled between her thighs. She moaned and bucked toward his hand and when he touched her there her eyes went wide and desperate, hungry. She was wet and hot for him, and she quivered against his touch.

"Kiss me!" she demanded, pulling at his shoulders.

He fell against her and she wrapped her legs around his waist, her mouth nipping at his lips, her breathing frenzied.

His hand slipped down to work his buttons, to free himself to enter her with one quick thrust. Her hand covered his, coldly and efficiently. Her passion tremors vanishing like mist in the sun. She let her legs drop and, with a darting movement, she had her blade pressed against his sac. It was a dagger, smooth and sleek, and it was not new. How many times had she held this blade against a man? How many times had she needed to? He froze, staring into her black, bottomless eyes. She lowered her gaze and with a shift of her legs, her feet were against his chest and she pushed him off of her. In the next instant she had rolled off the bed and was smiling at him.

"I should have disarmed you when I had the chance," he said with grudging respect.

She smiled coldly, the dagger held comfortably in her hand, and said, "You never had the chance." With the other hand, she pulled one of the gold pins in her hair free; it was a blade, small and gleaming.

He believed her. This woman would never be forced again.

"I am not free, Lord Ruan. I never was, not then and

not now. Unless you meet my price, I shall keep myself, to myself."

He had known it. But he had not wanted to know it. He had not wanted, and still did not want, her passion to be a deceit she practiced on man after man. He would be more than that to her. Perhaps he was already. Did she truly work so hard to humiliate every man who wanted her?

No, his crime wasn't that he wanted her, but that he had dared to pierce the armor of her secrecy. He had, by learning what he had about her past, become truly intimate with her. She was punishing him for that.

"Your body is your weapon," he said, searching her for signs of bridled passion, that she had felt something when he touched her. He saw none.

"My mind is my weapon," she countered, straightening her golden chains so that they fell cleanly across her throat. "My body is its sheath. The sheath serves its purpose, but it is the weapon which matters, isn't it? Oh, but as I am a woman and you are a man, the sheath will be all that matters to you. You have your own weapon, do you not, Ruan? You long to plunge into my sheath. It is what men do best, or so they would like to think."

"Not all I care about. Not all," he said. "What the body does cannot be separated from the mind, Sophia, or from the soul."

"A sermon? How interesting coming from the man who nearly raped me. What is your topic to be? Fornication? Or perhaps you will expound upon lust?"

"Perhaps mercy," he said, forcing himself to walk away from her, to cross the room to the doorway to the antechamber. "Even forgiveness."

"Would you shame me into showing you mercy? Must I forgive you, Lord Ruan?" she said, smiling at him as if nothing at all had happened between them, as if it were weeks ago and they were fencing with foils of flirtation, enjoying the sharp, bright wounds they pinked upon each other.

"I care about you, Sophia," he said softly. "I care."

"You care only about satisfying your lust upon me. I recognize the signs clearly enough. Can you possibly be in doubt about that, Lord Ruan? I supposed you to be a man of some experience."

"I am not like the others," he said, wondering if that were true. Wanting it to be true. "I do not want you for myself. I want you for yourself. I want to know you, Sophia."

"Lord Ruan, you don't know me," she said, her smile disappearing as quickly as it had come. "Having started on this path, have you not learned that one simple truth? My life has not been easy nor has it been simple. You insult me by looking for simple causes and by anticipating simple solutions."

"I never thought anything about you was either simple or easy."

"Except my virtue."

"No, not even that," he said, studying her face. She held his gaze without blinking, a hard-eyed warrior facing a foe. He had never wanted to be that to her. Hardly that. "You say that no one takes from you that which you have not freely given nor been paid for. When did that begin? Not on Staten Island for you did not give and they did not pay. I think Westlin did that to you. Westlin and Melverley and the others. I only wanted to right that wrong. Somehow."

"*Somehow*," she echoed, her voice lightly mocking. "Such a wistful word, Lord Ruan. I have no tolerance for wistfulness." She slid the golden blade back into her hair where it shone innocently; the dagger she slid back into the sheath on her thigh, lifting her skirts casually and gracefully to do so. "If you believe that I have forgotten Staten Island, that I have ever forgotten the faces, the hands, the feel of those men who took the virginity that Westlin so highly prized from me, you truly do not know me at all.

Which I think is just as well, don't you? Be content with Sophia Dalby as you first heard of her. Let your heroic tendencies fade, if it's at all possible," she said with mock sincerity.

"I wanted to know you, Sophia, to understand why you are the woman you are. That is all I've tried to do. And perhaps to save you just a little. I am a man. Some small, dying part of me wanted to be a very small sort of hero to you. It is a grievous flaw, I do agree with you. But my crime is that I looked into the shadows surrounding you, and for that there is no mercy and no forgiveness, is there?"

He walked out without waiting for her answer.

He walked into three gaping girls, the new brides of Hyde House.

Twenty-five

"LORD Penrith, do you have a sister?" Jane asked as they strolled the blue reception room, looking for Edenham, not that Jane expected Penrith to know she was looking for Edenham. Yet even if he did, what of it? She was going to do as she pleased for once. Perhaps forever. Wouldn't it be lovely if that became a firm habit?

"I do indeed, Miss Elliot," Penrith said. He truly did have the most astounding voice. It put one in mind of a velvet cat. "She's abroad at present."

"As am I," Jane said pleasantly. "I'm certain you must want her to have all sorts of marvelous adventures while she's exploring foreign shores. Don't you?"

Penrith looked quite uncomfortably pensive for a moment and then answered, "Well, not *all* sorts."

"You are thinking of men, Lord Penrith," Jane said, because that is precisely what she was thinking and what she therefore said. This was wonderful fun. Why hadn't she ever done this before now? "Brothers are always so terribly worried about men when they think of their sisters, but it's ridiculous, isn't it? Certainly not all men are troublesome and certainly even a brother must want his sister to be attractive to men, because doesn't a brother want to see his sister happy and well married? I don't suppose you can have any argument against that for your sister, can you? What is her name, by the way?"

Penrith looked positively stricken. Jane was nearly afraid he'd bolt across the room to find shelter in the safe company of Mr. Prestwick and Lord Raithby. Penrith rallied and stayed at her side, brave fellow.

"Her name is Charlotte. Charlotte Aubourn. She is just sixteen and far too young to be considering marriage or men or . . . happiness."

Jane looked at Penrith askance. "Lord Penrith, I am so sorry to disillusion you, but at sixteen your sister is already considering all of that, and in particular she is wondering if she is attractive to men. How could you have thought otherwise? Don't you look at sixteen-year-old girls and conclude if they are attractive or not? And are you somehow ignorant of the fact that these sixteen-year-old girls are aware of your presence and perusal? Dear Lord Penrith, you cannot possibly be that naïve."

From the look on Penrith's face it did indeed appear that he had never thought of that and, what's more, no one had ever, or at least not in a very long time, implied that he was naïve.

"Miss Elliot, you are frightening me," he said softly, looking at her almost comically. "It cannot be so different in America, can it? When a man takes a turn about the room with a beautiful woman, he does not care to discuss his sister, and who may or may not be escorting her about in some distant room in the same instant. It's most distracting."

"I do apologize, Lord Penrith," she said, grinning. "I have no wish to distract you. No, in fact, I want you to be at your most fully alert. I am a sister, Lord Penrith, and I have brothers who are very much like you, only perhaps not nearly so civilized, and I want to enjoy myself with a handsome man before they can stop me. Are you willing, Lord Penrith?"

Penrith stopped to stare down into her eyes. They were just inside the music room, which had filled up quite considerably since her last visit to this room, meaning there were no empty chairs, which was most disheartening as her feet were starting to hurt, when she saw Edenham loitering by the doorway into the antechamber, talking to her cousin Henry.

"I am not to be that man, am I?" he asked, looking not nearly as disappointed as she would have liked.

"I'm afraid not. You don't mind? I'm not going to be in London for very long and I do feel that I must direct my attention extremely precisely, in the interest of time only. I do find you exquisitely attractive. I want you to know that."

Penrith smiled, nearly laughed really, and said, "It has been my express wish since a small child to be found exquisitely attractive, Miss Elliot. Thank you."

"Oh, you're making fun, but I don't want you to feel slighted. You don't, do you?"

"Quite the reverse, Miss Elliot. Now what horrors do you plan to visit upon Edenham and how would you like me to help? It won't require that I get a torn face, will it? I should so hate to disrupt my exquisiteness for even a day."

"Not even for the dash of a smallish scar, Lord Penrith?" she said, laughing softly. "Don't disappoint me now. I did believe every word you said."

"You did not," he said, chuckling. "You did not and you do not, Miss Elliot. I must say you give every appearance of being incorruptible. I fear my reputation has been damaged irreparably."

"Lord Penrith, are you in the habit of corrupting innocent women after only five minutes of polite conversation?"

"I dare not answer."

"You dare not answer *truthfully*."

"Which is answer enough."

"Lord Penrith, I do begin to wonder about English Society. Is it even possible to corrupt a woman so quickly? I should never have thought so. Of course, perhaps English women are more malleable? More given to follow every suggestion put to them? Is that it, do you think? Is it not then that I am incorruptible, but that they are so very willing to be corrupted?"

"Miss Elliot," he said, looking at her most suggestively, which was so cordial of him, "I can find no answer to your questions that will not serve insult to everyone of my acquaintance, therefore, I will allow that you must and should form your own conclusions."

"But do I have enough information, my lord? Five minutes, can it be enough to form a valid conclusion? Must I not test you to a full ten, or even, risking all, attempt thirty? Can I withstand you, Lord Penrith? I begin to wonder. Should I dare it? Should I dare . . . you?"

Penrith smiled slowly, his eyes never leaving hers. "Miss Elliot, do not. I would not see a sister so ill used."

"Ah, you are afraid of my brothers? They are not here, my lord. You are quite safe."

"Miss Elliot, there is yet another man who would fight to keep you from me or from any other man and he stands not fifteen feet from you. I need not name him, I trust?"

"Oh, Lord Penrith, you are a hopeful sort, aren't you? Did you not see the gentleman you allude to, a certain duke, whom I shall not trouble myself to name, refuse to fight at all? You are a brother; what would you think of a man who refused to fight for your sister?"

"Miss Elliot," he said, offering her his arm, which she took, and leading her across the music room to the corner where the harp was positioned, "I would ask myself *why* he did not fight. Men fight, as you have surely noticed, for any reason at all. It is when they don't fight when they clearly should that the matter must be looked into. Have you? Looked into it, I mean?"

She had not.

"Lord Penrith, you do not think you are putting too much thought into what is a most simple situation?"

"You think he was afraid to fight back?"

Jane shrugged. It was obvious, was it not?

"If he was afraid, of what was he afraid, Miss Elliot?"

"Of being hurt, Lord Penrith. Isn't that the reason men do not fight?"

"But he *was* hurt, Miss Elliot, and that is not the reason men do not fight. They do not fight when they fear to lose more by fighting than what they hope to gain by fighting."

What?

"Really, Lord Penrith, I have seen men fight before, many times, in fact. I do think you are being very optimistic and even aggressively overreaching in your rather poetic description of men and their various fights. I understand your prejudice about it, being a man you can hardly avoid it, but I certainly don't see that there is anything beyond a man and his defense of his honor in his fighting. As to not lifting a hand when set upon, what honor in that?"

Penrith smiled at her, and it was a thrilling sight. The man was sensual to an alarming and entirely delightful degree. "Miss Elliot," he said, lifting his gaze from her to look across the room; she followed his gaze. He was looking at Edenham, who did look quite as handsome as ever, his bruise visible even from where she stood. A rumble of something or other twisted under her ribs. Hunger, most definitely. When would they eat? "I do believe that the gentleman in question was simply trying to avoid angering your family further, as well as considering their safety."

"It is not possible that they could have been angered further, Lord Penrith, and as to endangering their safety, what can you possibly mean?"

"That he would have injured them, perhaps seriously,

by fighting back," Penrith said. "How could he win your regard if he had damaged your brothers?"

Well, what was she to say to that? She couldn't think of a thing as she was far too busy laughing, and not at all quietly either.

❧

"Now he's got her laughing," Henry Blakesley said in an annoyed rumble of expelled breath. "I don't suppose you made her laugh."

Edenham looked at Jane and Penrith and couldn't stop the scowl from knitting his brow. "Not like that. I mostly make her angry."

"Anger's not bad. You can make it work for you, if you're quick on your feet. Are you?"

"Quick enough. I did kiss her straight off," Edenham said, scowling at Lord Henry now.

"Look, are you going to marry this girl or not? She's my cousin; I've not laid eyes upon her until two days ago, but I do feel responsible for her welfare and her happiness. Family, you know," Henry Blakesley said curtly, looking not at all excited about feeling responsible for a woman he did not know. Well, but who would?

"She doesn't want to marry me."

"I heard," Henry said sarcastically. "What have you done about it?"

"Talked to Sophia, for one. Nearly seduced Jane for another," Edenham said, eyeing Henry. Family was family, after all. He only wanted to marry Jane, not find himself on a dueling field for her.

Henry's mood lightened immediately. "That's that, then. If Sophia is helping you, you'll be married to Jane nearly as soon as you wish it. Just hurry it along, will you? The wedding *breakfast* shan't be served until you've tucked dear Jane under your arm and carted her to the archbishop himself. As it's nearing eight, I do want my breakfast."

"And I want Jane. Sophia has an idea as to how I may manage for her to jump into my arms."

"Well, don't tarry with me then, Edenham. Off you go, claim the girl, do what needs doing, and promise me now that your wedding breakfast will take place before midnight."

To which Edenham could only laugh.

❧

WHAT was *he* laughing about? Here she was, chatting it up with the lovely Lord Penrith, who was the most overwhelmingly seductive man she'd ever met, even if his seductive techniques didn't work at all on her, and Edenham had the time and the lack of fortitude to ignore what should have been a most alarming situation? Was any more proof needed that the man was . . . well, she wouldn't go quite so far as to name him a coward, but only because she'd only just met him. Jane was entirely certain that once she got to know him better, she'd know he was as cowardly as the worst coward she'd ever met.

As to that, she wasn't sure she had met any cowards. How could one tell? It wasn't very often in the normal course of life that cowardice became extremely obvious. Not like here, now, with him.

Coward.

"What are we doing hiding behind the harp, Lord Penrith?" she said. "I do think it would be considered more proper if we mingled."

"Were we hiding?" he said, his mouth tipped up in that now familiar cat smile of his. It was becoming most annoying. Lord Penrith smiled entirely too much, part of his seductive technique, no doubt.

"Do you care to walk about the room with me or not?" she said crisply, giving him her most forceful stare and not ruining it by smiling insipidly.

Penrith wisely kept his mouth closed, though still

smiling, and offered her his arm. She led him in a most meandering manner to where Edenham stood with her cousin. Entirely appropriate, that. One cousin to another. Not that she particularly cared about what was appropriate, not with Penrith on her arm and Edenham's bruised mouth staring her in the face.

"How well you look, Jane," Henry said after a lengthy silence in which Jane stared at Edenham and then looked at Penrith to make a point. "Are you enjoying yourself?"

"It's been a very entertaining day, Henry," she said. "However, it hasn't been at all as you predicted. I've found everyone to be utterly delightful, but of course some more than others." She leaned against Penrith for just a moment to underline her point. Penrith cleared his throat and smiled. Of course he smiled. The man seemed to have no other talent.

"I do believe that says more about you, Miss Elliot, than anything about the other guests today," Edenham said mildly. "She is, you will find, Penrith, a most exceptionally easy woman to please. She tolerates nearly anything with good humor and is nearly impossible to offend. Her brothers, while displaying the inherent differences between men and women, are also most affable. Why, when they should have been insisting that I marry Miss Elliot, they were most determinedly insisting that I would not." Edenham smiled at Penrith and lowered his voice, as if that helped anything. "As I know Miss Elliot prizes honesty and direct discourse in all things, I may say to you that you should enjoy yourself however you please. There will be no marriage penalty to face. You are entirely free to enjoy Miss Elliot as you see fit."

Jane gasped.

Henry coughed again and looked up at the ceiling.

Penrith was likely still smiling. She didn't bother to look. She simply could not look away from Edenham and his loathsome speechifying.

"I do begin to wonder," Edenham continued, crossing his arms over his chest and rocking back on his heels, "if the American situation, handled differently, could not have yielded a more favorable outcome. These Americans seem so very willing to turn the other cheek, to deny their own best interests in deference to their, it must be admitted, *betters*."

Jane's hand connected with Edenham's cheek in a resounding crack. She had held nothing back. His lip began to bleed again.

She could not possibly have been more overjoyed.

In fact, she was so delighted by the outcome, she did it again.

Another crack echoed through the room as her hand connected with his face. Naturally, everyone stopped talking to stare in their direction. She hardly cared.

"Why, Miss Elliot," Edenham said, licking the blood from his lip. Her stomach flopped around under her ribs. She ignored it. "I begin to think you want to kiss me again. They do have strange, violent notions of bed play, Penrith," Edenham said conversationally, staring down at Jane with a strange look in his green eyes, "do be warned. It's not unpleasant, but it is a bit unruly, even slightly barbaric. Not unlike the people themselves."

"I am not unruly!" she snapped. When Henry raised his golden brows, she added, "And you know nothing about my bed play!"

Upon which Penrith looked hard at her, his smile obliterated.

"You know there has been no bed play!" she yelled at Edenham.

Edenham looked over her head at the occupants of the silent room, bowed crisply, and said, "I misspoke. There has been no bed play betwixt Miss Elliot and myself."

"What? Now you make it sound as though there has been . . . *that* . . . with others and myself!"

"But Miss Elliot, I can't speak for everyone," he said

with false charm, most assuredly. "It must be enough that I speak only for myself. An act of gallantry, if you will."

"I will *not*! Gallantry? As if you're lying on my behalf, for my benefit? I won't have it, Hugh. I won't! You are implying . . . the words you're using . . . kindly just tell the truth!"

"The truth, Libby? Are you certain that's what you want of me?"

Actually, no.

"She calls you Hugh?" Henry said, a dark scowl transforming his face. "Why is that, Edenham?"

"She was most insistent upon it," Edenham said. "It seemed a small concession, considering."

"Considering *what*?" Henry said, and then, rubbing his hands through his blond hair, he muttered, "Damn me, if I'm not going to have to get the pistols out."

"No, no, Lord Henry," Edenham said pleasantly. "That isn't at all how it's done with dear Miss Elliot. Her brothers have made that vividly clear, haven't they? You are not required to defend your cousin's honor, or perhaps a better word would be *virtue*, if her brothers have relinquished the duty. What else but to follow their dictates on the matter? They are her countrymen, after all, and Americans quite obviously practice different rituals. As to that, Miss Elliot has made her position plain more than once. She will not marry me. She will, however, kiss me. As I have tired of the practice, carry on, Lord Penrith. She's all yours."

"You're . . . giving me away? I am not yours to give!" she said, her voice rising. "And my virtue does not need defending!" Jane barked, reviewing his list of insults. "But if it did, I would defend it myself!"

Edenham rubbed his face where she'd slapped him, touching his fingertips to his mouth to check for blood. It had oozed to a stop, which was such a shame.

"Most enthusiastically, no doubt," Edenham said, "when it occurs to you to do so."

"And I only kissed you," she went on, ignoring him completely, because he was acting utterly reprehensible, which was not at all a surprise, "as a response to your kissing *me*! The entire party saw that, Edenham, so you shan't put that upon my shoulders. It's a very odd thing, I must say, for a man of your mature years and blatant experience to try and lay your debauched and sordid behavior at my innocent feet."

"My *years*?" Edenham said a bit sharply. It was lovely to see him rising to a well-deserved rage. Perhaps he'd have a small stroke.

"Innocent *feet*," Henry interjected softly, "and all the other bits innocent as well, I trust?"

No one bothered to answer Henry. Really, what part did he have in this?

"You *are* very old," Jane said primly. "I can't think how you could even try to deny that. Did you think it was a secret?"

Penrith began to shuffle away. Jane grabbed his arm and looped her hand through it, holding him to the spot. Were all Englishmen cowards?

Edenham stared at her for a moment and then smiled politely. She braced herself.

"And you are a very accomplished kisser, for a woman who feels it necessary to proclaim her innocence nearly upon the quarter hour," he said.

"I can see it shocks you that I am so very quick to defend myself, a trait you do not share, obviously," she said sweetly, smiling at him in return. "As to your heartfelt compliment, and the clear depth of emotion you felt upon my kiss, I can only say, without false modesty, that I am a very quick study." She smiled brightly. Edenham narrowed his eyes. "Particularly when my tutor has so many years of learning to his credit. I am a novice. I stand respectfully in awe of your so very eager tutelage. Tell me, your grace, do you teach all the girls who catch your eye?"

"Yes," he said crisply, "I like to start when they're young, their teeth having just come in. I do think they learn more effortlessly how to please a man at that tender age, before defiance and recalcitrance become imbedded in their natures. But I don't have to explain that to you, do I, Libby?"

Whatever he meant by that, and she wasn't at all sure, she was certain that it was an insult of the worst sort. He was simply that sort of man.

"If you think to insult me by describing me as defiant, you are far off the mark," she said, taking a step nearer to him, dragging Penrith with her, the useless puppy. "I shall defy any man who seeks to drag me under his thumb."

"Or under him in his bed," Edenham said.

Henry looked positively ill, quite red about the ears. Penrith was a lump at her side, useless.

"Which you would have no way of knowing?" Henry prompted, looking at Edenham with something like sorrow.

Jane looked at Edenham, her eyes wide. Edenham returned her look with a smug smile on his arrogant face. That was not a good sign, was it?

"Is this one of those moments where I simply tell the truth, Libby?" he said.

"Please do," she snapped. "Please, tell my cousin that you *did* have to drag me into bed. I'm certain he will believe every word of it. Your reputation, built upon your character, both as old as you are which is very old indeed, must certainly have proclaimed to the world before now the sort of habits you have perfected."

"Perfected?" Edenham shot back, taking a step nearer to her, which brought them very close indeed. "I would be flattered but for the fact that, as it is my habit, I *know* I do it very well. Wouldn't you agree? Oh, but you needn't bother. I could see that I did."

Jane smiled, reluctantly impressed. He wasn't a bad salon battler.

"I'm surprised you cared enough to look. A man like you certainly doesn't care what happens, as long as his needs are met."

"What *precisely* was he looking at?" Henry asked Jane, looking truly aggrieved.

"You had your *needs* met?" Penrith asked Edenham, looking truly curious.

"Of course I looked," Edenham said to her, ignoring everyone else in the room, as she was doing. He did have that odd effect on her. She did become so absorbed by his presence, which was not a good thing, though she couldn't seem to think why it was a bad thing. "You captured me by a look. I can't *not* look. I begin to believe that I am destined to look at you for as long as I live, even if I find myself dragging you into the closest bed to do it."

Her heart, yes, her recalcitrant heart tingled quite alarmingly at his words. She even found herself, more shocking yet, grinning at him like . . . well, like a woman in love.

It was most embarrassing.

"The closest bed?" Henry asked. "That would be the gold bedchamber? I can't think the duchess knows about that."

"Nor Jane's brothers," Edenham said breezily, still smiling down at her. "I do think they should know all about that, don't you, Libby?"

Absolutely not.

Twenty-six

BERNADETTE, Lady Paignton, eyed Joel Elliot like the intoxicating cordial he was. He didn't appear to mind it at all.

The sun had deserted the garden, which was most convenient timing. Bernadette had lifted her skirts before whilst out in nature and at a party of Society's uppermost, but never before at a party whilst out in nature during daylight hours. If she were going to break the party nature boundary, she'd prefer to do it at deepest twilight, where she might expect a bit more privacy. Bit by bit, all her boundaries were being chipped away, which was the duty of boundaries, wasn't it? To fall at the slightest push? Or even a determined push?

Joel Elliot looked to be the *slightest* sort, which was so very pleasant of him.

"A challenge, Captain Elliot?" she said. "But of course it is. Can you manage it, I wonder?"

"'Tis only a bit of muslin, Lady Paignton," he replied, his fingertip brushing her skin just above her bodice. "I can manage that well enough."

"Can you?" she whispered, looking up at him.

He was a truly amazing-looking man, all dark curled hair and laughing dark eyes, his smile infectious. He had the barest suggestion of a dimple in the center of his chin and long dimples bracketing his cheeks when he smiled. If life had swept her along in a different direction than it had, she might find herself laughing right along with him.

But it hadn't, and she wouldn't.

"Are you so very bored, Lady Paignton," he murmured, his head dipping down, his gaze on her mouth, "or am I so very irresistible?"

"Kiss me, and then I'll tell you which," she said, wrapping her arms around his neck and gently urging him to her.

His breath was sweet and soft, his shoulders immense beneath the thin weight of her arms. An inch from her mouth, his smile relaxing into something far less jovial, she closed her eyes and waited for sensation to sweep her away. Please God, let it sweep her away.

Nothing happened.

"Joel, you're needed. It's Jane."

Joel released her instantly. Bernadette turned and saw George Blakesley standing in the doorway to the garden, looking quite grim. But then, he normally looked grim in one degree or another.

Joel Elliot offered her his arm and escorted her back into the house. George didn't spare her a glance. Joel didn't either, not after his sister's name had been mentioned.

It was situations like this that reminded Bernadette how very fortunate she was not to be encumbered with a brother. Just think how many back garden interludes would have been foiled by an overanxious brother.

Poor Jane.

❧

SHE was going to do it! Katherine was going to lure Jedidiah Elliot into her bed and she was going to wring every lustful action out of him that she could, and certainly she must be able to inspire *some* sort of lustful action? She was a woman. He was a man who spent months at sea. Was there very much more to it than that?

Jedidiah was such a bold, forceful-looking man, his features neatly chiseled, his nose straight and narrow. Richard had possessed a rather lumpy nose. Nothing hideous, yet not quite lovely. But it was the look in Jedidiah's eyes, his storm blue eyes, that captured every unspoken fantasy and brought them into daylight. He was so utterly masculine. It was overwhelming, in the best possible way.

"Captain Elliot?" she prompted.

"Am I challenging you?" he repeated, looking quite stern. Her heart did a fluttery dance. "Why, Katherine, it was not a challenge at all. Merely an invitation. Do you accept?"

Yes!

She didn't say that, naturally. She wanted to appear far more sophisticated and world-weary than that. She was nearly certain that men preferred a mild level of ennui in their women, that giggling, gushing girls were for wedding nights and little else.

"I receive invitations often enough . . . Jedidiah," she said, being so bold as to say his given name. "Challenges, however, are far more intriguing. However, as in this case the result will be the same, then, yes, I will accept your invitation."

She'd done it! She'd arranged a brief affaire that would change her life forever. Of course, it did seem to her that women who regularly arranged for affaires did so with the expectation that it would *not* change their lives in any way at all.

This was a muddle. Now she wasn't certain what she wanted to happen, though she was still entirely certain that she wanted it to happen with Jedidiah Elliot.

"Now?" he said, taking a step nearer.

They were still in the yellow drawing room, still facing the window into the back garden, still talking together as the other occupants of the room changed like the flow in a tidal pool. She and Jedidiah were rocks in that pool, unmoving, unchanging. She allowed herself to believe that he wanted it that way, that he wanted them to remain alone and apart, for how else could it have happened? It had certainly never happened to her before, not in any gathering. Jedidiah was the sort of man who could hold back the tide if he wished it; oh, not actually, but he did give off that sort of resolute force. It was a singular experience to be standing next to him, the sole focus of his attention.

What would it be like to share his bed?

She quivered just thinking it.

"Now?" she said. "Now what?"

"Now," he said, taking another step.

He was truly standing too close. It was utterly inappropriate. Katherine backed up a step. Her heel skidded down the skirting board and her shoulder bumped against a small painting, sending it rocking.

"I want you *now*. I want to begin *now*. I want—"

"Jed," a voice broke into Jedidiah's list of wants.

Jedidiah turned from her, his eyes a smoky blue that made it difficult to breathe deeply. "Yes?"

"You're needed. It's Jane," Lord Iveston said.

Oh. Right. Lord Iveston. This was his wedding breakfast. Jane was Iveston's cousin, Jedidiah's sister.

Katherine's thoughts arrayed themselves woodenly and with a great deal of stubbornness in her mind. It helped when she looked toward Iveston and away from Jedidiah. The hard, crushing force of his expression as he looked at her one last time before striding across the room with Iveston at his side had been oceanic, like those great waves one heard about.

Poor Jane.

৵

LORD Ruan gave each of the women a hard, searching glance, looked once at the closed door behind him, and then strode through the antechamber and into the music room. The swell of noise as he pulled open the door washed over the women like a wave and then disappeared upon the closing of the door.

The moment he was gone, Louisa turned to Penelope and Amelia and said, "Did you hear anything?"

"Just mumbling," Penelope said. "His voice, her voice, but no words. I'm not even positive it was Ruan and Sophia talking, but it seems a logical supposition."

"I thought I heard her say *fornication,*" Amelia said. "It could have been *fabrication,* but—"

"*Fornication* makes more sense," Louisa said, finishing the thought.

"There's a bed in that room," Penelope said, her dark brows lifting meaningfully.

"As if a bed is necessary," Louisa scoffed.

"It does make it easier!" Penelope said.

"You were just married this morning, Penelope," Amelia said. "Have you forgotten that?"

Penelope snapped her mouth closed and crossed her arms over her chest.

"Do you think she needs . . . help?" Amelia said.

Louisa shook her head, puzzled. "It doesn't seem likely. Sophia Dalby can manage any man she chooses to. Certainly Ruan didn't look happy."

"He'd look happy if they'd been fornicating," Penelope said. When Amelia and Louisa looked at her, she added, "Everyone knows that, married or not."

"True," Louisa said. "Even a man as jaded as Ruan would likely still have a happy aspect if he'd just been fornicating. So, what were they doing in the gold bedchamber?"

"Talking, obviously," Penelope said. "We could hear that much."

"But what about? And Edenham had just left," Amelia said. "You don't suppose . . ." The three women looked at each other in various degrees of disbelief and disappointment.

"No, Edenham was for Jane!" Louisa said. "Sophia wouldn't snatch Edenham up now, not when he was so besotted by Jane."

"Perhaps she was jealous," Penelope said, then shook her head firmly. "No, that's not like her at all. Still, Edenham has had all day and he hasn't managed to get any sort of declaration from Jane yet. Men are so slow about these things."

"How very true. One would think they didn't want to marry," Amelia said.

"Oh, he's had declarations from Jane," Louisa said, "all in the negative. How long does it take to convince someone that the thing to do is marry? I had thought Edenham better than this. How did he ever acquire three wives with this sort of slipshod behavior?"

"He's a duke, Louisa," Penelope said. "There is hardly much more he needs to do than that."

"Jane is requiring very much more of him, that's certain," Amelia said.

"Good for Jane," Louisa said. "It will be only good for him. Dukes can be entirely too confident, can't they?"

"And difficult," Amelia said. As her father was a duke, she spoke with considerable authority.

"Jane shall manage him," Penelope said. "She seems the sort of girl who can deal very sharply with a difficult man."

It was upon those words that the door to the music room opened again and Lord Ruan once more strode through the antechamber. He nodded to them, but did nothing to recognize them beyond that.

Without ceremony, he opened the door to the gold bedchamber, leaned in, and said in a low voice, "Something's gone amiss with Edenham, Sophia. Jane needs you."

Sophia swept through the room like a dark mist, Ruan at her side. They seemed not at all angry with each other, yet gave no appearance of having recently fornicated. In fact, they seemed oddly united. It was all very confusing.

All but one bit. Jane had mismanaged Edenham and required Sophia's aid in righting things. As Louisa and Amelia and Penelope had each required Sophia's help in managing the right man to the altar, they had only one shared response.

Poor Jane.

Twenty-seven

THE Hyde House music room was not the smallest room on the first floor of Hyde House, but it was the smallest truly public room. Of course the antechamber, gold bedchamber, and dressing room were smaller, but they were not open to the public for Lord Iveston's wedding breakfast. Not formally, anyway. It was becoming clear that the gold bedchamber, and to a far lesser degree, the antechamber had been made use of. By Jane. By Edenham. By Jane and Edenham together.

Molly, the Duchess of Hyde, gave every appearance of being violently displeased.

That the music room, a quite lovely room just recently done up in aqua damask wallpaper, and with a new harp with the most elegantly applied gilding holding pride of place near one of the front windows, was becoming a mass of seething, if well-dressed, humanity, was also contributing to Molly's nervousness.

No one knew quite how it happened, but there was an

altercation in progress involving everyone in the Blakesley family, everyone in the Elliot family, and the Duke of Edenham and his heretofore very retiring sister. The Lords Penrith and Raithby, along with Mr. Prestwick, the brother of the bride, were standing with their well-tailored backs against the fireplace wall, looking on avidly and, in Penrith's case, a little sickly. It need not be overstated that anyone not in the above mentioned list who had been in the music room prior to the altercation could not be compelled to leave it now. Hardly that. No, in the place of a good, hearty breakfast a solidly entertaining brawl had been provided.

No one would have thought to complain.

"You are not going to marry Jane," Jed said stiffly, "no matter what happened, but what *did* happen?"

"I don't want to marry Jane," Edenham said calmly. "Having spent more time in her company, having shared a few intimacies with her, I find I've changed my mind about the whole thing."

Jane gritted her teeth and said as quietly as she could, "Don't listen to him, Jed. He's making it sound worse than it is simply because I've repeatedly explained to him that I don't want him."

Trust Edenham to turn everything on its head. She had just decided, by the barest particle, that he just might be slightly lovable, in a completely irritating manner, obviously, and he chose this moment to antagonize her brothers with what was an obvious bid to reclaim his negligible pride?

Edenham turned his gaze upon her and said softly, "Oh, you want me. We both know that. Why lie to your brothers? There's no point to it. I've tasted what I want of you, and now I'm relinquishing you. You get what you want. And I got what I want."

"I've got a nice brace of pistols," Henry said in an aside

to Jed that could be heard throughout the room, "but they want oiling."

"Pistols will not be necessary," Jane said. "Nothing has happened. Nothing will happen. Not even if he begged me."

Which, of course, he hadn't, but it would have been a nice touch. He really should have tried begging. She might have listened.

"You aren't listening, Libby dear," Edenham said, coming closer to lift her chin with his fingertips. "I am not the one who will be found begging."

Jed lunged forward and slapped Edenham's hand aside.

Lady Richard gasped out an outraged sound and reached out to lay a hand upon Jed's arm.

Jed instantly stilled.

So did Edenham.

"What have you done to my sister?" Edenham growled, pulling Lady Richard's hand away from Jed.

"Less than what you've done to mine," Jed said. "And with far more . . . provocation."

It had been clear he had been about to say something else, but no one could determine exactly what. The crowd, as discreetly as possible, which wasn't much, edged closer to the diverting wedding breakfast entertainment.

"Kay? What is he is saying?" Edenham asked.

"I have no idea," Lady Richard answered, looking at Jed beseechingly.

Well, that could only mean one thing. This was London, after all. They had all seen *that* look before.

"Who are you to question Jed?" Joel said, elbowing Jed aside. Jed did not seem to enjoy it. "You must answer for Jane. You *will* answer for Jane. You won't treat her as these London ladies beg to be treated. Not a bit of difference to a harbor whore, except a bit cleaner."

"*Joel!*" Jane said sharply, and loudly.

"Just whom have you treated as a whore in my home?" Lord Iveston asked Joel sternly.

"Not *my* sister," Edenham said. It was a challenge. Someone on the other side of the room, somewhere toward the windows, dropped a glass. He was instantly hushed by at least ten people.

"And I haven't been treated like a whore?" Jane said, pushing past Joel and Iveston to face Edenham. Jed made a disapproving sound. Jane snapped at him over her shoulder, "Oh, mercy, Jed. I've heard the word more than a time or two. Answer me, your grace. Haven't you treated me rather carelessly?"

Edenham swallowed a bit heavily, but then said, "I have treated you as you seemed to prefer. I would say that is the mark of a gentleman."

"In what country?" Joel asked sarcastically.

"In the only one that matters," Edenham said. "This one."

Jed reached back to hit him, but Henry caught his arm and held him fast.

The crowd breathed a heavy sigh of disappointment. After all, they had gone without eating for hour upon hour; was a little bloodletting not in order?

Jane was feeling most definitely outnumbered. She could manage Edenham on her own, usually, but having Jed and Joel tossed in, plus her male cousins . . . but where was Jos, the youngest Blakesley? She hadn't seen him since the wedding. In any regard, it was just too much for her. She could admit it. She was not experienced enough to handle six enraged men. How many women could?

It was at that perfect moment that Sophia Dalby entered the music room, Lord Ruan at her side, Louisa, Amelia, and Penelope rushing along behind her. Well, then. Things should get much more interesting from now on, as if they weren't already interesting enough.

Aunt Molly, most tellingly, had been silent throughout the altercation and looked nearly smug at Sophia's entrance.

Jane felt a violent impulse to practice extreme caution. Unfortunately, things became so hectic that the impulse was quickly lost. Oh, well.

"But Jane," Sophia said pleasantly, "are they *all* fighting over you? How charming."

"Not all," Edenham said. "There is some question about what Jane's brothers have been doing whilst waiting for breakfast. It seems they may have accosted some of the female guests. One of them being my sister."

At that comment, Jed reached back again, fist clenched. Henry and George between them held him in check. It was not done without a great deal of grunting and huffing. What a complete waste of time.

"Hugh, nothing of the sort happened," Katherine, Lady Richard said softly, looking at Jed, and then at Edenham, and then back at Jed.

She was lying, clearly. Jane thought it very wise of her.

"You are in no position to make accusations, *Hugh*," Jane said, a bit snidely and with a great deal of relish.

"Are you going to make accusations, Jane?" Jed said. "I should like to hear a recounting of what he did to offend you."

"But, darling," Sophia said before Jane could answer what was an impossible question. Bless Sophia Dalby. "Are you so very confident that Jane was offended? Were you, Miss Elliot? Did Edenham offend you?"

"I think the word is *annoy*, Lady Dalby. Perhaps *pester* and even *bedevil*. Yes, definitely *bedevil*."

"Which can so often be so pleasant, can it not?" Sophia asked, her dark eyes sparkling.

The truth was not an answer she could give with two brothers and four cousins staring at her.

"I'm afraid I can't say," Jane said. "I'm very young, you

see, and so inexperienced." She looked at Edenham as she said it, smirking unrepentantly.

Edenham's mouth turned up at one corner in response.

"Ah, from the lady's lips," Iveston said, "she is inexperienced. Shall we eat?"

"Iveston, it is not yet time for breakfast," Molly said from her spot near the pianoforte, her fan moving briskly. She said nothing more, which was highly irregular. Jane felt a prickle of suspicion, but it disappeared instantly when Edenham opened his mouth to speak.

"I suppose one may define inexperience differently, depending upon one's standards, even one's national rituals," Edenham said, smirking boldly at Jane. She returned the look. "By England's standards, which are of course my own, I would say Jane Elliot is far more experienced than an unmarried girl should be. I refuse to marry an experienced maiden, her maiden status being therefore in doubt."

Before Jed or Joel or Iveston or Henry or any of the other dozens of men in the room found it necessary to hit the Duke of Edenham, and certainly they all might have, Jane strode right up to Edenham and poked her finger against the third button of his waistcoat. "You know perfectly well the extent of my experience, you snake, as you have been my very *aged* tutor!" As Edenham was opening his mouth to speak, she poked him again, harder, and said, "And we both know that you want to marry me. Refuse me? You don't have the strength to refuse me. You are cream and I am the churn. You are powder and I am spark. You are—"

"Cream?" He interrupted what was a very fine romantic analogy on her part. "I don't care to be compared to cream. And I know you believe yourself plain, but you have more appeal than a butter churn, Jane. Really, I could never marry a woman who thinks so ill of herself. What would such an influence have upon my children?"

Jane laughed, catching her finger behind the button of his waistcoat and pulling him toward her. The button popped off. He was now missing three. "What influence? A wonderful one. I would dilute your outrageous and highly misinformed aristocratic arrogance, for one."

"And for another?" Edenham said, looking down at her quite arrogantly. It was most inexplicable, but she found it quite charming, even amusing.

"I could give them siblings. Your daughter will require many, many brothers, don't you think?" she said.

Edenham nodded and quirked a smile. "Never a bad idea. I don't know, though. You're very . . . American."

"The perfect compliment," she said. "Thank you."

"As amusing as this all is," Jed said, sounding not even slightly amused, "Jane is not going to marry you. Jane will have nothing further to do with you. Come, Jane. We'll stay on the ship. Aunt Molly, I apologize. This has no bearing on our feelings toward you and your family." Which, of course, made it sound precisely that: that he disliked and distrusted all of them, with the possible exception of American-born Molly.

Molly merely nodded her head in reply, which was entirely unlike her. Molly looked at Sophia. Sophia looked at Edenham, her inky brows raised expectantly.

Expectantly?

Edenham removed Jane's hand from his waistcoat and moved her to stand behind him. She moved back to his side. He moved her back behind him, and held her there.

"I shall marry her if I choose to do so," Edenham said quietly.

"If *I* choose to do so," Jane said from behind his shoulder, which was very tall and very broad and which she couldn't see around, "which I have not as yet, and likely never will," she added, more for her brothers than Edenham. She rather suspected Edenham wouldn't believe her.

She was right.

"You shall not," Jed said.

Jane knew that tone; it was his *master of the seas* voice.

She pulled at Edenham's hand, seeking release. He did not give it.

"I shall do what I wish with Jane. I will either marry her. Or not," Edenham said, which was the most insulting and provocative thing he could have said. Didn't he realize that?

"You will marry her if she wishes it," Joel said. Oh, no. That was Joel at his protective best. This conversation was not going well at all.

"No one can force me to do what I have chosen not to do, or can force me away from what I have chosen," Edenham said, gripping her hand more firmly, which might have been because she was yanking on it violently. From around Edenham's shoulder, Sophia caught her eye. And winked. Jane stopped yanking her hand for the merest moment. That's when it happened.

"No?" Jed said.

"No," Edenham replied.

Which was when Edenham finally released her hand, but only because Jed hit him and he needed it for other things.

It did not, quite surprisingly, go as it had gone before. This time, Edenham hit back. That was shocking enough, but when Edenham, after two or three punches, she did think she'd missed one, had Jed on his arse on the floor, well then, Joel jumped in and got in a good hit or two, but Edenham did return a sound two or three, and then Jed was back up and Henry was holding him back, mouthing something about fair play, which enraged Jed for obvious reasons—the British and fair play? Completely ironic. The direct result being that Jed punched Henry in the mouth. Which got Cranleigh involved, naturally, as he was a known brawler, and Jed took a solid blow to the ribs, which doubled him over briefly, but when he'd taken a full breath, was on Cranleigh snarling something about fair play and two on one, which was most apt, if she did say so, and Henry tried to back up but elbowed Joel in the kidney, so Joel turned around and dealt a blow to the side of Henry's jaw, which clearly enraged George, who pulled Henry aside to attack Joel from the rear, but Jed saw it and shoved Edenham back a few steps so that he could hit George, but was stopped by Iveston who almost calmly hit Jed twice, once to the face and again to the midsection.

It was at that moment that Jane took a breath and looked briefly around the room.

Sophia and Molly were grinning like well-fed cats.

Louisa, Amelia, and Penelope were watching the men, their husbands presumably, with an avid gleam of pure intoxication.

Katherine was looking at . . . Jed?

And Jane? Who was Jane watching?

Her brothers and her cousins, most definitely. But Edenham most specifically.

Mercy. She just might have to marry the man.

He was acquitting himself very well, wasn't he? His cravat had come unraveled, his hair was hanging over his forehead, his mouth was bleeding again, and he had a fresh bruise coming up on his left eye.

He looked as happy as a lamb in spring grass.

The fight continued, and seemed to be gaining. Lord Ruan, who had no true cause to fight, watched as Jed and Joel battled the five Englishmen swarming about them, shrugged, smiled, and landed a blow to Cranleigh's face in the general vicinity of his nose. It gushed blood promptly. No one seemed to notice or care.

The battle was now five to three, though nothing so simple as Americans versus British, not with Ruan fighting with Jed and Joel.

And then the battle turned again in a most surprising direction. George Prestwick moved through the crowd and turned George Blakesley around by the arm and hit him a good one to the gut.

"George! What are you doing?" Penelope shouted, looking very deeply annoyed.

"Have to, Pen," he said, his fists raised as he faced George Blakesley. "I feel responsible for Jane somehow."

He did? How sweet.

It was at that moment that George Blakesley hit George Prestwick in the face, a rounding blow that whipped George Prestwick's head around.

It was now five to four, though she didn't suppose anyone else was counting.

Edenham was locked with Jed, the two of them looking quite the worse for wear. The strange thing was, Edenham was smiling. Even stranger, so was Jed, albeit much more mildly.

"I didn't think you knew how to fight," Jed said, furiously blinking his left eye. It did look very red.

"Didn't you? That was stupid of you," Edenham said.

Jed responded by hitting Edenham in the gut. Only he missed. Edenham backed up quickly, nearly losing his footing, the harp base wobbling beneath his heel.

"Not the harp!" Molly shouted out, her hand to her throat.

One would have thought that a woman both a mother and an aunt would have been more concerned about her sons and nephews than a newly purchased gilded harp. One would have been wrong. As the mother of five sons, Molly saved her concern for defenseless harps.

"Jane will never have you," Jed said, stalking Edenham.

"You hope," Edenham said, lunging and catching a glancing blow to Jed's chin.

"I only want her to be happy," Jed said.

"As do I," Edenham said, dodging Jed's fist as it aimed for his head.

"You'll never convince her," Jed said, his shoulder bumping against the harp.

"And if I do?" Edenham said, pushing the harp down so that Jed's fist caught in the strings.

Someone cursed. Jane was certain it was Molly.

"Then welcome to the family," Jed said, reaching through the strings to grab Edenham's loose cravat to pull his face into the harp frame.

It was a direct hit.

Edenham, however, held Jed's hand to his chest and leaned back sharply. Jed's face hit the harp frame with a thud.

"Thank you," Edenham said, spitting out a wad of bloody saliva. "Not to worry, Molly. I'll buy you a new harp."

"You certainly shall," Molly said, rising to her feet. "Now, I do believe it is time to eat."

"Wait!" Jane said.

The entire room quieted, and that included the bleeding, contented men.

"Yes, Libby?" Edenham said, looking at her politely. His face was a ruin, bruised and bleeding, his clothing mussed and torn, his hair a tangle over one eye, and he was looking at her as calmly as if asking her the weather conditions.

"You seem very confident that you will convince me to accept you."

"I am confident. Now, shall we go in to dine?" He actually offered her his arm, the sot.

"What have you to offer, Hugh? I should like an accounting."

He straightened his waistcoat as best he could and lifted his chin above his wreck of a cravat.

"Very well," he said. "I have something you have neglected to consider, for all that you have no use for dukes. I have a seat in the House of Lords, Libby. Do you understand what that means?"

Actually, not really. A vapor of an impression, nothing more.

"It means that I may influence policy. Policies regarding, say, impressment?"

Jane's eyes widened. Even Jed looked intrigued.

"You would do something to stop the impressment of Americans onto British ships?" she said.

"I would certainly try," he said, oh so seriously.

"Well then," she said, walking over to him, tying up his cravat in the simplest of bows. "I suppose then I can't deny you. I'd be marrying you for the good of my countrymen. A simple act of patriotism on my part. It would be nearly treasonous for me to refuse you, wouldn't it?"

Edenham smiled, his eyes twinkling. "I thought you'd see it that way. Then we'll be married at the earliest convenience."

"Yes, which will be once you've met my father," she said, linking her arm through his, leading the grand and curious company out of the music room and into the blue reception room.

"He's coming here?"

"No, you'll have to go to him. He'll much appreciate the effort."

"I see," Edenham said solemnly. "I suppose we should take the children."

"Oh, definitely bring the children. I want them to get to know me before I become their mother. Besides, my father is extremely softhearted regarding small, lovely children. I take it your children are lovely?"

"Extremely," he said as they moved regally through the blue reception room, nodding pleasantly to any who had not been witness to the entertainment offered in the music room. There were not many, only the very old and the very drunk. "But it is your father who has a weakness for children? Not your mother?"

"Oh, no," Jane said. "Mother thinks all children are good for is bringing dirt into the house and making general mischief. As you've met Jed and Joel, you can understand why. My father sees children so rarely that he has quite idealized them, or so Mother has always alleged. She makes a strong point."

The red reception room was fully dressed to receive and pamper the wedding guests, the table laid out with heavy silver and Venetian glass, French porcelain, and English linen. If the footmen and the butler looked harried and frustrated, no one was willing to comment on it.

"If my children won't sway her, what reason will you give for wanting to marry me, Libby?"

Jane turned to face Edenham and laid her hand against his face. He had heavy bruising at his jaw and eye, green and purple and black mottling, his mouth was cut and swollen, his nose red.

He was the most handsome man she had ever seen.

"Because you're so very pretty, Hugh. I took one look, and that was that."

"I've never heard of such a thing, Libby. It sounds absurdly impulsive," he said, lifting her hand to his mouth and kissing it softly. "No one has ever called me *pretty* before."

"You'll get used to it," she said, pulling a dangling button from his waistcoat and tossing it into the air, catching it in her palm, grinning like the wildly in love woman she was.

"See to that, will you?" he said, smiling at her, torn mouth and all, as he made his way to his chair at the massive table.

It was then that, finally, the guests were allowed to sit and enjoy Lord and Lady Iveston's wedding breakfast. They relished every bite.

Twenty-eight

Three weeks later

EVERYONE was leaving. Oh, not literally everyone, but so very many. It was the end of another London Season. Town houses would be closed up and people would escape the heat and dirt of Town for their Country seats. The normal cycle of English life, for the aristocracy, that is. And Sophia was that, fulfilling her mother's whispered expectations. What Sophia wanted for herself, now, was something else entirely.

Jane and Edenham, his two lovely children, along with two female servants and two male servants, were sailing for New York today on the *Plain Jane*. The sun was bright, the water of the Pool of London sparkling silver and pewter, the ships rising tall against the wharves and smelling of tar and hemp. Sophia had come to see them off simply because she could not stay away.

The river called to her today.

It was a season for going.

Markham, her son, and John, her brother, along with his

three sons, had left from France for America over a week ago. Markham would be gone for a year at least, more likely two. John and his boys she might never see again. One never knew with John; the forests and fields between the Mohawk and the Ohio Rivers were not tamed. Markham would grow into a man there, which was why she had sent him, albeit without his knowledge. Caroline, her daughter, believed she was pregnant and was cozily nesting in her husband's estate.

The river called to her today.

One of the men she hunted had boarded a ship in New York bound for London. Perhaps he was here now. Perhaps the river was calling her to him. Perhaps, wherever he was, he thought himself safe.

Sophia smiled and looked up at the main mast of the *Plain Jane*, the gulls circling and crying shrilly against the sky. Life was not tamed. Only a fool, or a child, believed that he could ever be truly safe. Had she ever believed it?

No, she had not.

"Sophia?" Jane said, walking toward her across the wide planks of the wharf, her straw hat tied on with a scarlet ribbon, her cloak of amber wool. "Sophia," Jane repeated when she was closer, her smile wide. "Hugh won't tell me a thing, but I know you will. What advice did you give him to win me over?"

"Beyond his pretty face, you mean?" Sophia said, smiling. "I did think that his beauty should have been enough to beat against your strongest prejudices, but you are far stronger than that, aren't you?"

"Of course, though I'm sure that was a complete surprise to Hugh."

"Perhaps not a complete surprise, but a welcome one, nonetheless. Now, darling, of course I shall reveal all," Sophia said, looking out at the river and the crowd of masts, like a forest upon the water. "I simply and most astutely told darling Edenham that, being a true American, you valued most what you fought for the hardest. All he had to do, poor darling, was find a means to induce you to fight for him."

Jane's eyes revealed her disbelief. "But I did no such thing! He is the one who fought for me! You were there. You witnessed it all."

"I did," Sophia said. "And you are therefore not able to deny to me that you fought for Edenham's respect, attention, and regard. That you insisted he comply with your standards of a courtship, even to this sailing to New York to gain your father's approval. That his children meet you and approve of you first, which is never done by the way, which they have and do. That he fight your brothers to prove his worth. That he love Jane Elliot, American, and not Jane, the marginally acceptable niece of the Duke of Hyde. Now, was that not a fight? It took you the better part of a day, but you won it. You won it, darling."

Jane's beautiful hazel eyes shone with unshed tears, and then she began to softly laugh.

"I did all that? I did, didn't I?" Jane said over her laughter. "What an adventure it was, and still is."

Sophia took Jane's hand in her own and grew somber. "It is an adventure, Jane, but be certain you know where you are going. You will be a duchess, an English duchess. Your life will be here, just as his life is here. Your children will be part of the English aristocracy. There is no changing that once it is done."

"Yes," Jane said. "I know. I've thought of that. It is strange to consider."

"But consider it well. Your life will be *here*."

Jane searched Sophia's face, placing her hands around Sophia's. "Has it been so very difficult for you?"

Sophia pulled her hand free and smiled. "Nothing is very difficult for me, darling. I thought that was obvious." Her smile faded. "It is only that I want you to know what it all means."

"You were very young, Sophia," Jane said, still looking deeply into her eyes. "It was very different for you, I know, but your life has been so wonderful for so long now. According to Hugh you are nearly a legend."

"*Nearly* a legend," Sophia said smoothly, taking Jane's arm and linking it with hers, neatly redirecting her searching gaze. "Darling, either Edenham is being needlessly and insultingly modest on my behalf or I have my work in front of me."

Edenham came and collected her then. Jane hugged her warmly, kissing her cheek, and said, "I will never stop going home, because New York will always be my home." Jane took her hands in hers again, squeezing them encouragingly. "Come home, Sophia. My mother would love to see you again. She talks of you endlessly."

"Endlessly? *Your* mother?" Sophia said, feeling the burn of emotion in the back of her eyes.

Jane laughed and said, "Well, by that I mean two or three times a year, which for her is something of a record. I don't believe she mentions Jed more than once a year."

"I heard that!" Jed shouted from the deck. "Good-bye, Sophia!" he called out, his arm lifted. "Until next time."

"Until next time," she answered softly as Edenham and Jane climbed on board.

But there was not always a next time, was there? She knew that very well, indeed.

She did not wait to see them cast off. She simply walked away. Freddy, her butler, was waiting for her just a few feet away, his bushy brows lifted in question.

"A hard parting?" he asked.

"Too many partings lately," she said as he escorted her to her carriage at the end of the long wharf. "I'm turning sentimental, Freddy. It's appalling. I don't know how I shall go about in Society with sentiment dripping from my fingertips."

Freddy, or Fredericks, his proper name, was more than a butler. He was American, true, but he was more than that as well. Freddy had been with her from the start, or from one of her many starts. She trusted him, and she could say that of very few.

"He's still here," Freddy said softly.

"You have to credit him with stamina," Sophia answered. "He's like a wolf searching a herd to find the calf with the broken leg. Do I look broken to you, Freddy?"

Freddy looked askance at her, his blue eyes bright. "Or a wolf looking for his mate."

"I see we both agree that he's a wolf."

"I'm starting to feel guilty when you refuse to see him," Freddy said.

"I'm happy to report that I never feel guilty. For anything," Sophia said pleasantly. "Lord Ruan will eventually learn that there is no path to me, and then he will wander off and bedevil some other likely woman. Or an unlikely one, as to that."

The wharf was crowded, as was all of the Pool of London. The wharves were nearly a city unto themselves, the ships so crowded upon the Thames that the water was oftentimes assumed to be floating them, it being buried beneath wooden hulls. All the world came to London, all the ships of the world, carrying all the people of all the lands of the world.

And yet, though nearly buried, the river called to her today. Its call so softly insistent that it would never have occurred to her to ignore it. Something awaited her here. She did not choose to believe that it was simply Lord Ruan.

In that madness of people and noise and filth, the Marquis of Ruan stood in the shadowed and deep-set doorway of a mud-splattered inn with a crooked roof. The Red Bear. Sophia watched him watching her, his face half in shadow, his expression washed clean of emotion, his eyes trained on her face. It was a penance of sorts, and he was seeking absolution in her smile. What a pity for him that she did not deal in absolution.

He had touched her body. He had done it badly. He had ruined what could have been a fine and pleasant diversion for them both. He had pawed through her past, seeing what he could find, trying to see into her.

Her past was past. Dead. No one should dig up a corpse.

Upon that thought, the hard, quick thought of what lay forever behind her, a man's profile captured her. Not her attention, and not her eye. *Her*.

She paused. Freddy paused instantly at her side, looking at her face, following the direction of her gaze. The wharf was awash with people, which was to her advantage. She knew that face. It was burned in her mind like a fiery scar.

"Freddy," she said softly.

"I see him," he answered her. "It's him. The same."

She walked forward, casting a glance to Ruan. He caught her look like an embrace, and when she shifted her eyes to the man who had been a shadow in her heart for over twenty years, he followed her gaze like an arrow to the heart of a stag.

Why Ruan? Why did she seek out Ruan? Why had Ruan come to her in Hyde House that day, knowing that she was needed to help Jane over the final barrier to Edenham? Why had she trusted his judgment then, without question, without comment? Why did she now?

Pointless questions. She trusted him. An ally was an ally, whether you liked him or not.

The profile turned, three-quarter face now. There was no doubt. That face, the scarring upon his cheeks, the shape of his brow; he was older of course, as was she. His hair was heavily threaded with gray, his jaw and neck thickened with age, yet it was he.

He was standing on the edge of the wharf, near the shore, The Red Bear just beyond him and to the left, her carriage on the street and to the right. She could just see the rear wheels. Her escape. There was no point in attack without a way of escape. That lesson was old. She didn't need to even think it.

His clothing was filthy, old stains, sweat, and other things. His hair was lank. His hands dirty. He hadn't come to a good end, had he? A small, bare justice. He deserved a far richer justice, a more complete justice.

Sophia smiled and walked toward him, allowing the crowd to gently push her in his direction. Markham was in full possession of his title, and on a ship in the middle of the Atlantic; this could not touch him. Caro was married, Ashdon's property, under Ashdon's protection; she would be safe if this fell awry. Freddy was at her back; he would say whatever needed to be said, do what needed to be done.

Ruan was before her. What would Ruan do? She did not know. She only knew that, somehow, he was her ally. At least for now. Today.

There was never anything more than today. Today, always, had to be enough.

And there he was, right in front of her, the gulls above them crying eagerly over a dead fish floating beneath the wharf, its belly greenish white and already pecked open.

Not at all ironic, but beautifully poetic. Yes, poetic justice.

He turned slowly, presenting her with his back, his hands digging in his pockets.

Perfect. This was better, a better approach, and a better escape for her.

She pretended to lose her footing, tripped mildly, put her hands against him briefly. He turned his head at the contact and they looked into each other's eyes for the barest moment in time. There was no flare of recognition . . . had she expected that? That he would remember? Not really. Perhaps. She remembered him so well, but what was that? Of course she would. And she would remember this, too. This memory was to cherish. She did not care if he knew why. She knew why, and that was more than enough.

Her dagger punctured his spine, sliding between the bones, severing the cord. She pulled it out as quickly as it had gone in, the knife cleaning itself as it passed through his clothes. He cried out as he fell, or started to. Freddy turned him and spun him away, his fist in the man's throat, silencing him, "Stand back from her, you dog! Can't you tell a lady from a whore?"

She kept walking, Freddy at her back. She did not look to see what she had done, what he was doing, how quickly he was dying.

Ruan passed her without looking at her, a lord of England walking on the wharf, that's all he was. She heard a splash and knew Ruan had pushed him off the wharf, down to bleed with the dead fish. Could he still breathe enough to drown or was he dead already?

She did not care. He was finally dead. That was all that mattered to her.

The river called to her today. Now she knew why.

She was at her carriage when Ruan caught up with her. A casual meeting to curious eyes, nothing more. A lord and lady, a chance meeting, if any should question it.

She smiled into his eyes, so startling a shade of green as to seem unnatural. He bowed, his smile more polite than pleased.

"How delightful to see you again," she said, keeping his name from her lips, let them mark the crest upon the carriage door if they would know her name and house; she would not do their work for them.

"An unexpected pleasure," he said, showing the same restraint.

Freddy held the carriage door, his features schooled to that perfectly tutored stamp of deaf boredom that every servant wore.

"Unexpected, yet so very timely," she said. "I feel certain that I shall always remember stumbling upon you, upon this day, upon this hour."

She looked into his eyes, thanking him, trusting him. He heard her. In all the words she would not say, he heard her.

"I am honored, and flattered. I," he said slowly, "I apologize for offending you earlier. In my zeal, I stepped too deeply, looked back too far."

"When a hero hunts dragons, he must prepare to be scorched," she said with a brief smile. "Your zeal is forgiven."

Ruan smiled gently, his gaze touching her face. "A hero? Then may I impose upon you a bit further?" he asked.

Sophia laughed lightly. A woman who had just killed a man would not laugh and flirt, that is what would be concluded, if conclusions were ever drawn. "That reprieve bore instant fruit. A single boon, lord knight. I shall grant one wish. Use it wisely."

"I fear I will not," he said. "Wisdom is clearly beyond my grasp."

"But not discretion?" she asked.

"On that point you need not fear," he said, smiling. "'Tis only wisdom, particularly with women, most particularly with beautiful women, that I lack."

"How fortunate for you that beautiful women do not require wisdom in discreet men," she said. "Discretion is quite enough."

Still smiling, he leaned toward her, a flirtatious remark clearly longing to burst free, and said, "May I ask whom I helped you murder?"

She laughed and offered him her hand while she climbed

into the carriage. Once inside, Freddy having closed the door, she leaned toward Ruan and said softly, "That was justice, not murder, lord knight. I watched him kill my mother. She is now avenged. I could do no less for her."

Ruan's eyes met hers calmly. "A worthy deed for which I have no regret. The other, I do regret, because I stepped clumsily and shattered our accord."

She put her gloved hand on the door. There was a splattering of blood on the leather. "Lord knight?"

He looked at her, his eyes clear of guilt. There were starting to be cries of alarm along the wharf. The drunkard who had fallen into the river was now more than drunk; he was bleeding. He was dead. It would not be wise to tarry longer.

"Yes?"

"A gift for a gift," she said softly. "My husband knew about the satire. But he knew nothing about New York. That history was my gift to you."

Ruan's brilliant green eyes flared at the quiet meaning of that message, at the intimacy she had initiated between them, but before he could react beyond that, she called out, "Drive on!" and her carriage merged with the traffic of Wapping, Freddy entering from the other door as the wheels began to turn.

"That's done, and well done," Freddy said. "What next? Will you be *in* for him now?"

Ruan. She could not think of Ruan now. He slid into her thoughts like an encompassing mist, yet this moment must be reserved for reflecting upon the memory of her mother. That was right and proper.

Yes, even Lady Dalby could sometimes do what was right and proper.

Sophia looked out the carriage window, removing her gloves and tucking them in her reticule. She would burn them when they got home.

Home. Dalby House.

The masts of all the ships crowding together in the London Pool soared like a leafless forest above the rooftops of Wapping. Her thoughts dwelt on forests today, dark and thick and endless, the forests of her memory, while her eyes were captured by the river that was a highway to the world. In the curving, twisting streets that led to the many wharves, the span of a ship's hull could sometimes be seen, the sounds of voices from other lands blending harshly with the London rhythms of the east end.

But not the rhythms of the Iroquois and the Mohawk, not the rhythms of her childhood. Had England ever been her home? England had been her mother's home, but had it ever been hers?

Her mother had tried very hard to make it so. She was of England and the children of her body were of her place. The Iroquois way. In that one instance, the Iroquois way had eased her mother's heart.

Yet what would ease her heart?

The man who had killed her mother was dead, and dead by her hand, as was only fitting. That thread was finally snipped off, a heavy pack laid down, a low-burning fire put out. Her heart felt the release of a burden she had grown long accustomed to carrying.

She had attained her mother's dreams for her. She had come to England, come home, and become a countess. She had, with a great many exceptions, lived the life her mother had wanted for her. Her own children were English, fully planted in the soil of their country.

Was England her country?

Was she her mother's daughter or her father's daughter?

"Sophia?" Freddy asked, his voice betraying his confusion at her silence. "A good day's work today. I need to get off a pack of letters, let my friends know they need not keep watch for that one any longer."

When she only nodded, Freddy said, "Tea when we get home, with a good dollop of whisky to warm it up."

Home.

"Freddy," she said, looking at the masts in the distance, "I'm going home."

*E*nter the rich world of
historical romance
with Berkley Books.

Lynn Kurland

Patricia Potter

Betina Krahn

Jodi Thomas

Anne Gracie

Love is timeless.
penguin.com